I DARE YOU

SHANTEL TESSIER

I Dare You
Copyright © 2018 by Shantel Tessier
All rights reserved.

This book is a work of fiction. Names, characters, places, and
incidents either are products of the author's imagination or are
used fictitiously. Any resemblance to actual persons, living or dead,
events, or locales is entirely coincidental.

For more information about the author and her books, visit her
website- www.shanteltessierauthor.com.

Editor: Jenny Sims
Formatter: CP Smith
Cover Designer: Tracie Douglas with Dark Water Covers.

PLAYLIST

DIAMANTE – "Sleepwalking"
Like A Storm – "Love the Way You Hate Me"
Papa Roach – "Gravity"
Korn – "Coming Undone"
Onlap – "Everywhere I Go"
Sivik – "High – Remastered"
No Resolve – "Love Me to Death"
Nothing More – "Sex & Lies"
Divide the Day – "Fuck Away the Pain"
Starset – "Die for You"
Eminem, Rihanna – "Love the Way You Lie"
Chase Atlantic – "Triggered"
From Ashes to New – "An Ocean of its Own"
Egypt Central – "White Rabbit"
The Veer Union – "Bitter End"
Breathe Carolina – "Shots Fired"
Sick Puppies – "Here with You"
Skillet – "Feel Invincible"
Shinedown – "How Did You Love"
Ruelle – "Fear on Fire"
Too Close To Touch – "Sympathy"
Theory of A Deadman – "Angel"
Meg Myers – "Desire"
Blacklite District – "With Me Now"
Nothing More – "Go To War"
Valerie Broussard – "A Little Wicked"

PROLOGUE

COLE

Have you ever been to a funeral where the preacher stands before the friends and loved ones of the deceased and talks about how shitty the person was? How he fucked around on his wife? Or spent his family's life savings to feed his gambling addiction? How about during his bachelor party when he snorted coke off a hooker's ass?

Me neither.

Why is it that we're fucking saints the moment we die?

You hear the preacher say things like, *"Oh, John Smith was a lovely man who loved his wife and kids,"* when he should really be saying, *"John Smith was a worthless piece of shit who fucked the underage babysitter every chance he fucking got while his wife was busy working two jobs and raising his ungrateful children."*

And let's not forget that the deceased in that casket before you never even went to church. Let alone knew the preacher who speaks so highly of him. All he knows are the stories the blinded loved ones wrote down on a little card for him to share.

He's a fucking puppet.

Now, I haven't read the Bible word for word, but I know the Lord says if we confess our sins and ask for forgiveness, he will cleanse our souls, and we will be forgiven.

Poof. It's like magic.

Now that begs the question—what if you're not sorry? What if you don't care to be forgiven?

No amount of holy water could cleanse my soul, and I'm okay with that because when I sinned, I understood that I would one day have to pay. We're all going to die eventually. You can be one of those people who bury your head in the sand to avoid talking about it all you want, but it's life!

Live or die.

Heaven or hell.

Angel or devil.

It's black and white. There are no gray areas.

So tell me ... when you're lying in that casket in front of your friends and family, what are they going to think of you? Are they gonna believe that preacher who talks bullshit, or are they gonna know you didn't care if you were going to burn for eternity?

Now, I'm not a religious person. Obviously. But I do know this. When I am damned to hell, it'll be because I fucking earned it.

CHAPTER ONE
COLE

I look up at the dark, cloudy sky. It's officially a new year. January first. Some would consider it a chance for a new beginning, but I'm not like most people. The sun set hours ago, but I stayed out here in the heated pool, trying to clear my mind. But like always, it's a mess. Constantly reminding me of that day. A day that took so much from me ... as if I had it to give.

I didn't.

I stand at the bar in the kitchen next to my friends Eli and Landen. Maddox, our other friend, stands across from us.

"Go on. Take it," I taunt Maddox, looking down at the stopwatch on my phone.

He lets out a long breath and throws back the shot.

"Five," I count, and everyone in the room shouts and applauds him.

"Fuck, man." He gasps for air. He places his palms on the bar and bows his head. "You wouldn't think that would be that hard."

Eli laughs beside me. "You're such a fucking pussy."

"Let's see you do five shots of Crown."

Eli waves him off like it's nothing.

"In one minute," Maddox adds.

Eli rolls up his sleeves. "Line 'em up."

A raindrop falls on my face, and I roll over onto my stomach and dive to the bottom of the pool. I sit here and just enjoy the silence. Trying to forget. They always come back to me, though. Like ghosts. They haunt me, reminding me I failed them.

I let out a long breath and watch the bubbles float up to the surface. Closing my eyes, I fist my hands, feeling that tightness in my chest at the need for air. I hold out just a little longer.

Something hits my arm, and I open my eyes to see it's a diving ring. I place my feet on the bottom and shoot up, sucking in a deep breath when I hit the cold night air.

I see my best friend Deke standing by the lounge chair and table. The white umbrella from the table shields him from the rain.

"We're ready," he says, placing his hands in the pockets of his black jeans.

I swim over to the side of the pool and climb out. Grabbing the towel off the table, I wrap it around my hips. "Where are the guys?" I ask.

"Meeting us there."

I nod and run a hand through my spiked hair to knock the water out of it.

Deke looks over at the dark pool. "How is your shoulder?"

"Fine," I lie. It always hurts, but I've learned to live with the pain.

He nods as if he believes me. He doesn't. "Kellan doesn't like your plan."

"Then Kellan can sit out," I snap.

"That's what I told him. But you know him." He sighs. "He thinks people will look for *him*."

"That's the point." You kill a mouse and leave it in the open, then other rodents come out to feed on it. It's called bait. I go to step around him to head into the house, but his hand shoots out and lands on my wet chest, stopping me.

"You sure you're ready, Cole?" His eyes go to the scar on my shoulder. "I'm not doubting your plan. It's solid. But I want to make sure you can execute it."

I nod. "We've waited long enough."

AUSTIN

I sit in the back, staring out the window of the white Escalade SUV. It's decked out with all the amenities required by a rich person. Heated leather seats and steering wheel. TV screens in the dash and headrests. Oversized tires with some shiny chrome wheels. Blacked-out windows. A booming stereo system. The interior is a beige color and smells of leather. Things I've never had before. I never needed them.

He thinks they'll intimidate me. He's wrong.

It's been ten years since *he* saw me last. Four since I've spoken to him on the phone. I just need to get through the next four months and then I'm out after graduation. In two months, I'll be eighteen and won't have to live with either one of my parents.

Raylan slows down, veering onto the wide shoulder before turning down a private road. The trees lining the narrow drive look like claws as the branches nearly scrape the sides and top of the SUV.

"He's a good man," he says, breaking the silence.

He's got you fooled!

I snort, seeing nothing but what the headlights allow us to see. It's past eleven on a Saturday night and eerie out here in the middle of nowhere.

For as long as I can remember, my father has preferred to live in seclusion. No one comes this far out of town. That's why he picked this property after all. He had this house built for his wife when they got married. They chose to settle down in Collins, Oregon, a small, rich city on the coast, even though he was living in Vegas at the time he met her. She was a showgirl, and he had money. A match made in heaven.

"He's not home often," he adds, sliding his green eyes to mine in the rearview. *Well, that's a bonus!*

The trees part, and through the soft drizzle, I see a house fifty yards ahead, facing us. Three stories tall, it looks every bit like the small castles I used to read about in fairy tales. Green vines climb up the sides of the house like hands grabbing on for dear life. Last time

I was here, I used them to climb out from my second-story window. Its white stucco and black shutters make it look a tad on the evil side when lit up at night from the spotlights on the ground. It has twelve fireplaces, a six-car garage, and living quarters for the people he hires to do the jobs his wife is very capable of. A five-tier fountain sits in the middle of the circular drive. Large trees cover his twenty acres, hiding them away from anyone who happens to be nearby.

Raylan brings the SUV to a stop and gets out. I step out and shut my door, following him. The only sound is the wind whipping the trees around. Raindrops on my skin cause a chill to run up my spine.

"Come on," he calls out, already climbing the stairs.

I take them two at a time, passing the white columns and entering the house. I stand in the massive foyer looking over the black and white checkered floor and to the staircase to the left. It lacks anything resembling a home. And makes me think more of a museum with priceless artifacts. It smells the same. Like money. Crisp hundred-dollar bills. As if the walls and floors are made of them.

"Austin? Is that you?"

I hear the annoying voice and sigh. My father's wife, who is young enough to be my older sister, comes running into the foyer. Her bleach blond hair down and straight. Her makeup done as if she just finished getting ready for the day. Dressed in a pair of black slacks and a blouse to match, she looks as if she's spent her day at an office.

She doesn't work.

"Oh my gosh, you've gotten so big," she squeals, pulling me in for a hug. The smell of her expensive perfume almost makes me sneeze.

"Hello, Celeste," I say, giving her a half hug.

She pulls back but holds my arms and smiles. Her brown eyes soft. "Wow, haven't you grown up?"

"That's what kids do."

She smiles at Raylan. "Please put her things in her room." Then she takes my hand and starts dragging me out of the foyer and down the hall. We take a right into the elaborate kitchen. "Your father left these for you," she says, patting the kitchen island.

I walk over to them and pick them up. It's my school schedule, a set of keys, and a credit card. Along with a note.

I bought you a new car. Don't wreck it. And here is some money. The limit is thirty thousand.

That is my father. Always buying shit. He paid my mother off. Bought us a big fancy house that she let go to shit. Gave her a fancy car she sold for more money. He gives her more child support than we could ever need, but she uses it on drugs, alcohol, and her boyfriend. Anything to feed her addiction. Instead of me.

"He got me a car?" I question.

She claps her hands excitedly. "Want to go see it? It's in the garage. I helped him pick it out."

I shake my head, hoping she didn't have it custom painted bubble-gum pink to match her personality. "It's late. And I'm tired."

It didn't take very long to fly from California to this fucking town on the coast of Oregon, but she doesn't need to know that. I could use some sleep.

She nods, her smile falling. "Of course. Let me show you to your room," she says as if I don't remember where I stayed last time I was here.

I leave everything on the counter and follow her up the grand staircase, noticing the lack of pictures on the walls. My room is the first door on the left.

To my surprise, it doesn't look like a teenager threw up in it. It's large with a white sleigh bed and matching long dresser. It has big bay windows overlooking the forest in the back, and a TV mounted on the wall. It looks the same as it did when I was seven.

When she looks at me, I arch a brow, causing her to laugh nervously. "I don't know what the trend is these days. But I figured we could go shopping this week and you can pick out some things for your room."

"Thanks. Sounds good," I say, reaching out and picking up a dark gray scarf from the bed.

"I bought you these today," she says, holding up the other four in various colors. "It's up into the fifties now, but it can still get cold at night. I wasn't sure you had any since it stays pretty warm in California."

"Thank you," I say, dropping it onto the bed and rocking back on my Chucks. I just want her to leave. One thing about living with my mother was that I was always alone, and I liked it. I'll take silence over endless chatter any day.

"So I'll leave you alone to get settled in. I know it's late." She comes up to me and pulls me in for another hug. "I'm so glad to have you here, Austin." Then she pulls away and walks to the door to leave but comes to a stop. "Oh, Austin. Be ready to leave by ten in the morning."

I frown. "Where are we going?"

She smiles brightly. "Church." Then she shuts the door.

I fall onto my bed and close my eyes. My mother ships me to my dad's, and he has his young teeny-bopper wife babysit me. My life can't get any worse.

I pull my cell out of my back pocket to see if I have any messages. Nope. I have a feeling my friends have already forgotten about me. I didn't have many to begin with anyway. Digging into my purse, I pull out my journal. I've had it for as long as I can remember. It was like my therapy back when I needed someone to talk to but no one was there. The older I got, the less I wanted to talk to people. Kids my age don't wanna hear about my problems.

I sit up when I hear engines roaring and loud bass from outside. Making my way over to my window, I look out to see headlights over back in the trees. There's a dirt road that runs parallel to the house. I remember it from last time I stayed here. It used to lead up to the cemetery on top of the hill, a couple of hundred yards away, but now it dead ends down at the bottom of the hill. By the house.

A white SUV of some sort comes to a stop first, and the front two doors open. I can't make out the people—too far away and too dark out—but they're tall. The second car to pull up is a little black two door.

I quickly count five bodies and watch as they all make their way around to the back of the trunk. They pop it open, and one guy leans over, reaching down into it. He pulls out a man. He falls to the makeshift gravel road and tries to scurry away.

"What the …?" I trail off as two men grab him, picking him up. One at his feet, the other by his head, and they start to walk away with him.

The one man slams the trunk while another grabs a black duffel bag out of the SUV. And then they start to walk off. I duck to make sure they don't see me, which is stupid. They don't know I'm up here, and it's past eleven on a Saturday night.

Do they know my father lives here? Although trees cover most of this side of the house, you can still see it from where they are now. Do they just not care?

Going over to my suitcase, I yank out my black hoodie and slip it on before leaving my room. I quickly make my way down the staircase and to the back foyer.

I crack the back door open just enough to squeeze through, and then I crouch, going over to the far corner of the terrace. I peek over the railing and see the five figures walking. Two still carry the man, two others have flashlights in their hands, lighting their way, and the fifth trails behind them. Hands in his black jeans pockets, head down. None of them seem to be in a hurry.

"I didn't know …" the man they carry wails while some of the others laugh at him. "Please," he begs. "She never told me."

"Lying?" one asks with a snort. "Have some fucking balls to admit it, man."

"You're gonna kill me," he cries.

They don't respond to that statement.

With leaves and branches crunching under their weight, they walk farther and farther away from the house and up the hill toward the cemetery.

I squint and can barely make out their flashlights anymore. Where are they going? Do they really plan to kill him? Or just fuck with him? I can't not know.

Making up my mind, I stand, pulling my hoodie up and over my head, and take off after them.

I follow their lights, making sure to stay far enough behind them so I'm not seen. I only run into a couple of trees along the way. By the time we come to the top of the hill, I'm sweating and panting for breath. The cemetery finally comes into view, and I look back over my shoulder, but all I see is darkness. The house is no longer visible.

CHAPTER TWO

COLE

"Here she is," Deke says as he drops the man's legs.

Shane drops his arms, and Jeff lands face first in front of the pile of dirt. A grave he knows all too well.

"What?" he asks, doing the crab walk backward, but my legs stop him. I kick him forward. "Why are you doing this?" he cries.

"Because we believe in an eye for an eye," Bennett answers. "And I wanna see you fucking blind."

He places his hands up. "You guys are just kids …" My friends laugh at that.

"And you're just a sorry piece of shit." Deke spits on him.

My four friends circle him. Like sharks. I stay where I'm at, facing him and the cemetery. I take my hands out of my pockets and place them behind my back, watching him size us all up—weighing his odds. They're not in his favor. They never are when it comes to us. No one can get past the *GWS* unless we all agree to allow it. And walking away comes with a price.

That most can't afford.

"Just please … let me go." He swallows as the others shine their lights on him. "I won't tell anyone …"

Their laughter grows. I step up to him, and he looks up at me. His tear-streaked face makes me sick. "Every action has a consequence," I begin. "You can deny it all you want, but we all know why you're here. And we believe it's time for you to pay up."

"What about your consequences, Cole?" Jeff yells at me, and I stiffen. "Huh? You killed three of your best friends, and I don't remember you having to pay up!" he snaps.

I pay every day.

Deke takes a step toward Jeff, but I place my hand on his chest to stop him. "It's okay, Deke. Let the man speak. They're his last words, after all."

"You're not fucking God!" he shouts, pounding his fists into the wet ground. The earlier drizzle now falls steadier, soaking us all. I smile. *Find that fight, Jeff. You're gonna need it.* "You guys can't do this to people."

I look around the dark, abandoned cemetery where the dead are laid to rest and then forgotten.

You can't see the cliffs to the right, but you can hear the ocean hitting the jagged rocks below. *There's blood in that water.* "Who is here to stop us?" I ask simply.

"Cole!" He growls my name. I tilt my head to the side. "I knew your mother … She would be so ashamed of the man you've become."

A slow smile spreads across my face as the air around us thickens like fog. My friends take a step back from us, knowing that I'm gonna need a little more room.

"Goddammit …"

"You shouldn't take the Lord's name in vain," I muse.

"You shouldn't murder people," he snaps.

"I'm going to give you a chance," I tell him. "A chance to win your freedom." We both know that's a lie. He can't beat me. No one can.

His eyes dart from me to my four friends who still circle us. Their flashlights shining on him allow me to see. "Is this some sick joke?" he demands.

"Not at all," I say, reaching up behind me and grabbing the back of my black t-shirt. I rip it over my head and toss it to the ground away from us. Now shirtless, I'm ready for a fight. Then I remove my flashlight from the back pocket of my jeans and toss it as well. "I hope you don't faint at the sight of blood." I can already smell the copper, and my mouth starts to water. Fuck, it's been too long since I've had a good fight. I roll my shoulder, trying to release the tightness.

"You're just like your father," he shouts. "Fucking taking anything that you can get your hands on."

I hear something behind me. A faint sound of branches snapping. But I don't turn around. Not yet. "Get up and fight me," I order.

He shakes his head. "He doesn't want to play," Shane says with a chuckle.

"I'll let you have the first hit. More than fair." I can't help but smile.

I hear that sound again behind me, and it's closer. I take a quick look—on purpose—and he took the cheap shot I knew he would.

He jumps to his feet and lands a hit on the side of my face. I hit him back with a fist to his jaw. His head snaps to the side, and I pound my other fist into his nose. His hands come up to cover it as he stumbles back. I grit my teeth when my knuckles crack as I hit him in the mouth. His teeth rip my skin open like a knife to butter.

I love it!

He falls into Deke, and he holds him up while I hit him over and over. My fist connects with his stomach, face, and head. My skin continues to split. Blood runs down my fists, making them slippery. Deke gets tired of holding him up and pushes him toward me. I swing, hitting him one last time, and he falls back to the ground.

I stand over him, breathing heavy, and sweat covers my body as the rain comes to a stop. My hands are down to my sides, and I can feel the blood dripping off them like a faucet left on—mine mixed with his.

Jeff starts to cough.

"I dare you to get up," I growl.

"Is that … what this … is?" Jeff gasps for words. "Another dare?" He coughs. "You guys … and your sick … fucking pranks …"

"No!" I snap. "This is you paying for the life you took." My voice grows louder, and I clench my fists, wanting to hit him some more. My shoulder throbs, but I ignore it.

"When will you get what you deserve?" he whispers roughly. "Huh, Cole? What is your price …?"

I drop to my knees, straddling him. My balled fists rise and then come down on his already bloody face. I scream out of frustration when he just lies there and takes it. I want the sting of a punch. I want the feel of skin breaking. I need to feel it. Need the pain. I deserve it, after all. He was right. I killed my friends.

I fist his shirt and yank his limp head off the ground, my legs still straddling his hips. His eyes black and blue, face split and bloody. Lowering my face to his, I growl. "Give me what I deserve! Why don't you get your sorry ass up and hit me?" My voice rises. "Why don't you be a fucking man and fight me?"

He doesn't respond. His head falls back, and I shove him down, causing his head to hit the ground with a thud.

Deke slaps me on the back. "Go walk it off, Cole. We got it from here."

I stand and take a step back from them as they pick him up off the ground.

I fist my hands, loving the feel of the split knuckles. The wind picks up, and it makes the blood that covers my body shiver from the chill.

Fuck, I love a fight!

My father says I was born a fighter. He would say if a man can't use his hands, then what is he good for? The only difference is that my father pays to use someone else's hands.

A tree branch snaps behind us, and we all turn around to look. Four flashlights dance in the darkness. "Did you guys hear something?" Deke asks.

"I thought I did. But I don't see anything," Shane answers him.

"I'll go check it out," I say, walking away from them. "And hurry it up." I grab my light off the ground and shine it ahead of me, listening to them laughing behind me as they finish off the sick bastard who deserved every little thing he got tonight.

My tennis shoes crunch the ground, and I come to a stop to just listen. I shut my light off and stick it in my back pocket. I know this land like the back of my hand. And no one is ever out here. No one who is up to any good.

The Lowes estate is down at the bottom of the hill, but they're never home. And if for some reason they are, they're already in bed.

My hands hang by my sides, the blood slowly dripping off them and falling onto the leaves. My body craves more.

Slowly taking one step after another, I tune out the guys behind me as their voices grow quieter the farther away from them I get.

A sound to my right has me smiling. Whoever it is, is close. Very close. I stand and wait, not making a move. They're in the dark just like I am because I don't see any light. Then I hear it again. It could be an animal, but it doesn't sound like one. I hear two distinct sounds—a pair of shoes.

I take a step to the right, and I hear an intake of breath. *So close.*

Then they take off. Their shoes pound the ground, and I run after them. I run into a small frame, wrap my arms around it, and tackle it to the ground. It makes a noise of annoyance and two hands slap at my face unable to make contact. I grab them and pin them down to their sides and then straddle them to pin them down underneath me.

I yank my flashlight out of my back pocket and turn it on, shining it down onto the intruder.

Dark green eyes look up at me, framed by long dark lashes. Soft pink lips are parted, and she has a small diamond stud piercing in her button nose. Dark brown hair covers half her face, and she growls, "Get off me."

She blinks several times, the light blinding her, but I don't move it. It keeps her from seeing me.

"Get off me," she demands this time, panting.

I tilt my head to the side, just watching her squirm under me. I've never seen her before, and I know every woman in this town. I know every woman within thirty miles. But not her. Not this face. She starts fighting harder, but I hold her easily. She wears a black hoodie, and it's up, covering the top of her head and side of her face. I reach down and yank it back, causing her to twist her neck.

"Don't touch me!" Her voice snaps.

"Cole?" I hear Deke call out.

"Over here," I answer, not taking my eyes from her.

"You sorry son of a …"

"What did you find?" he asks as he comes up next to me. He shines his light on her, and she turns her face from him, closing her eyes. Six earrings run up her ear in various colors. "Oh, a toy. Where did she come from?"

"Not sure."

"Are there more?" he asks.

"Fuck you," she spits out while her body nervously shakes under my weight.

How much did she see? Does she know I almost beat a guy to death? She should be afraid of me. My demons like the rage. Feed off it. And I've never been one to starve.

Deke laughs. "I like when they have a dirty mouth."

She arches her back and delicate neck, letting out a scream of frustration that rings out in the dark night.

"No one can hear you out here," I tell her, my free hand coming up and wrapping around her throat but not choking her. The blood on my hand covers her sun-kissed skin as if I'm painting a picture on her body. She swallows hard against it. "There's no one to come save you."

She whimpers.

"I love it when they scream. Go ahead, sweetheart," Deke says softly. "Scream for me," he says, kneeling next to us. He wraps her long dark hair around his bloody fist, and he jerks her head to the side to face him.

She bares her perfect teeth, sucking in a breath, but she doesn't cry out from his force. Both of our lights stay on her face, and she squints, trying to see.

In the distance, I hear an engine roar as Shane, Kellan, and Bennett leave. "What were you doing out here all alone?" he asks her.

"Watching you murder someone," she snaps.

He throws his head back, laughing at her honesty. "Like to watch, do you?" he asks.

Her hips buck under me, but I keep her down. I'm well over twice her size, so she isn't going anywhere. She can wear herself out all she wants.

"What a coincidence. So do I," he tells her with a dark laugh.

She stiffens, and he looks at me. "Go ahead, Cole. Give me a show. I earned it. We gave her one, after all."

"Don't," she whispers as her lips part, and she sucks in a ragged breath.

I smile down at her even if she can't see me. My hand loosens around her slender neck, and I run my fingers down her skin and along her collarbone, pulling down her oversized hoodie in the process. The blood trail I leave behind makes my cock harden inside my jeans. I can feel her pulse race, and I like it. The fear in her green eyes. The sound of her ragged breathing and shaking of her body.

"You know how much I love to perform," I tell him.

"Please." Her body trembles with the plea while my fingers run over her shoulder, pushing her black bra strap off and watching it disappear into the sleeve of her hoodie.

Deke slaps me on the back. "She's begging you already, Cole. Fuck! That's some kind of record, right?" He whistles.

The wind picks up and tosses her hair around her face, causing it to stick to the blood along her neck and chest. "Red is your color," I tell her.

"Orange is gonna be yours," she growls, lifting her chin.

I smile at her words.

Deke just laughs it off. "She may have recorded it," he says, getting serious.

I sigh as if that thought is disappointing. "That would be very stupid of you."

I drop my flashlight beside her head. Letting go of her, I sit up, and just like I knew she would, she yanks her arms out from underneath me and lifts them to my chest, trying to shove me off her. I don't budge. Then she runs her nails down my skin. I feel it break at her force, and I refrain from moaning at the pain.

I wrap my hands around her wrists and push them above her head, holding them against the wet ground. Then I scoot my body up to her chest and sit down on her. "Check her pockets," I order Deke.

She screams out as she tries to fight me. Her hips buck, and she kicks her legs out, but Deke pulls a cell out of her back pocket. "It's locked."

"What's the passcode?" I demand.

She clamps her mouth shut, and her eyes narrow. I like the fight in her. Most women would already be sobbing. I lean down and give her a threatening smile even though she still can't see me. Lowering my voice, I say, "Either you give me the passcode, or I take it from you. What's it gonna be, sweetheart?" A part of me wants her to make me take it. I love it when someone forces my hand—making the decision for me.

"I didn't …"

"That's not the only thing we're gonna take," Deke says, cutting her off, and then I hear him undoing her pants behind me.

"No!" she cries out. Her hands fisting as I hold them down above her head. "It's retina … it's a retina scanner," she says in a rush.

"Fucking technology," he growls. "What happened to the good ole days where you just flipped the phone open, and it fucking worked?"

He holds it up to her, my flashlight lies on the ground next to us, shining on her face. It must open because he pulls it back and starts to go through it. He grunts.

"What is it?" I ask.

"No videos or pictures of it. But there is something interesting."

"I tried to tell you. I didn't record it," she says, panting. My weight on her chest makes it hard for her to breathe.

"What did you find?" I ask, ignoring her.

There's a long pause before he finally says, "Austin Lowes."

My brows shoot up. "As in Bruce Lowes?"

Silence.

I chuckle. "Well, well, well, I didn't know he had a daughter." She looks around our age. Seventeen, eighteen at the oldest.

She clamps her mouth shut. *Interesting.* She doesn't want to acknowledge the bastard either. Good for her. He's a sorry piece of shit.

"We don't have time for this," Deke growls, his patience wearing thin since he isn't going to get to play with her. He stands and pulls out the gun tucked in the back of his jeans. "Let's just kill her."

She narrows her eyes up at the darkness. My eyes trace the blood on her wrists, neck, and chest. She's too beautiful to kill. Too precious to destroy. Yet. He's afraid she'll talk, go to the police, but I'm not. She fears us. Thinks we'll hurt her. *She's not wrong.*

"Put the gun away," I order.

"But …"

"Now."

He tucks it back into his pants. "Let's take her with us. I don't trust her not to call the police afterward."

"I'm not going anywhere with you," she snaps.

I almost smile at her bravery. "You'll do whatever the fuck we say," Deke replies flatly.

"She won't call them," I tell him. Placing both of her wrists in one of my hands, I run my free hand down the side of her face, smearing more of her flawless skin with blood. "Will you?"

She clamps her mouth shut.

He snorts. "You don't fucking know that."

"No one will believe her." I lick my lips. "She's covered in his blood. It's underneath her fingernails from where she scratched my chest. It's on her clothes. In her hair. As far as they're concerned, she will be an accessory to murder."

"You fucking bastard …"

I get a thought. "What did you guys do with the body?"

"Kellan got a call and had to leave; he rode with Bennett, so they all left. I told them we would take care of it."

"Perfect. Call my phone with hers."

"What? Cole, we don't have time …"

"Call my phone with hers, Deke," I snap.

He lets out a huff, but then moments later, I hear mine ringing in my pocket. They remain quiet, probably wondering what the fuck I'm thinking, but they'll find out soon.

I stand off her, and she tries to scramble away, but I grip her hoodie and yank her to her feet. Wrapping my hand around the back of her neck, I start shoving her forward. She twists in my grip, and my hand slips, allowing her to get a few steps ahead of me. I run after her and fist her hair, pulling her against me. She whimpers. I wrap my free hand around her thin waist and press my front into her back. Her soaked clothes feel cool on my warm skin. Leaning my head down, I whisper in her ear, "We're not done, sweetheart."

"Where are we going?" she demands, and I smile against her skin. I love that she keeps fighting even though it's not gonna do her any good.

I don't answer, and Deke doesn't say because he doesn't know what I have in mind.

I remove my hand from around her waist but continue to hold her by her hair. I walk her over to where I know they had the body, and Deke shines his flashlight down on the now dead man. She doesn't gasp like I expected her to, which tells me she saw quite a bit earlier. She expected him to be dead.

"Hold her," I demand, shoving her into his arms.

"Let me go, you son of a bitch!" she screams as her chest hits his.

I hear him grunt. "Fuck," he hisses. "She punched me."

Ignoring them, I reach down into the black bag we brought and yank the now clean knife out of it. "Pin her to the ground. Face down."

The darkness covers us, but I hear her grunts as she cusses him while he easily tackles her to the ground.

Grabbing my flashlight out of my back pocket, I shine it down on them. He straddles her ass, his hands wrapped around her wrists, pinning them to her lower back. Her head is to the side, facing me. Those plump lips have thinned, and her green eyes simmer with rage.

I kneel beside them and yank up the right sleeve of her hoodie. "What are you doing?" she asks in a rush.

"Insurance," I say simply, and then I drag the blade against her forearm.

She cries out in the cemetery as the skin gives and blood starts to pour from the wound. I take the knife and run it through the stream of blood. Then I turn to the body and stab him in the chest with it. "Now your DNA is in him with the murder weapon," I say simply, and I hear Deke chuckle as he realizes what I'm doing. "You go to the cops. They dig him up and investigate his murder, and you go down with us."

"Fucking …"

"And you called me. More proof that we were communicating the night of the murder. Around the time of death."

Her breathing is labored, and I shine the light down on her again to see the tears rolling down her face cutting through the blood like my knife just did her skin. But they're not tears of sadness. They're tears of anger. She looks so beautiful.

"Return her phone and let her go so we can bury this body," I tell Deke.

He releases her wrists and then stands over her. She scrambles to her hands and knees and starts to crawl away. He tosses her the phone. She stands up on shaky legs as she holds her arm where I cut it. We both shine our lights on her.

"Get the fuck out of here before I change my mind," I growl.

She turns and runs.

"We should have killed her."

"That wasn't part of the plan," I argue.

He fists his hands. "I don't fucking care about the plan. What I care about is not going to prison. We should at the very least have taken her with us."

"Did you want to take her home?" I arch a brow. "Keep her as a pet?" I shake my head. "She won't say anything."

"She will …"

"She won't. She's Bruce Lowes's daughter. We kill her, and they start looking for a missing girl." I shake my head. "Then that brings questions."

"They'd never find her body, and you know it," he adds.

"I wasn't worried about them finding her body." We're smarter than that.

"Then why not let me shoot her?" he growls. "Two birds with one stone," he says, gesturing down at Jeff's body.

"Not yet," I respond.

He runs a hand through his hair. "You want to fuck with her." It wasn't a question. He chuckles. "This will be fun."

I smile.

AUSTIN

I run in the darkness, almost tripping over my own feet and the tree branches. But I don't stop. I continue down the hill toward the house.

Lights come into view, and I run through the back door and slam it shut. I make my way up the stairs and into my room. I close the door and lock it. Then I make my way into the bathroom. I rip off my hoodie, shirt, and then yank down my jeans that are still undone. Standing in front of the mirror in just my black bra and matching thong, I pull my strap back up onto my shoulder and look at myself. Blood covers both shoulders, arms, neck, and my face. He was right; it's also in my hair from their hands fisting it. I look like I belong on an episode of *The Walking Dead*. Like a zombie attacked me. Bile rises up the back of my throat, but I swallow it down.

Turning on the sink, I place my forearm under it and run warm water over it. Grinding my teeth against the sting, I grab the soap and quickly wash it. Who knows what the hell was on that knife. Or who all they've used it on.

Blood trails down my arm and drips onto the white tiled floor. I walk into my room to grab one of the scarves Celeste gave me and turn back to the bathroom, trying not to get blood on the carpet. I wrap it around the wound and pull it tight with my teeth, making me whimper at the pain as I try to figure out what the hell I'm gonna do to get it to stop bleeding.

I once watched my mother sew her crackhead boyfriend's face up with a needle and thread. It made me want to puke at the time. I was nine.

I place my hands on the counter and bow my head while angry

tears run down my face. Breathing heavy, I try to calm my racing heart.

"Bastards," I hiss.

I pound my fists into the countertop. *Fucking bastards.*

Then I yank open the medicine cabinet and start digging around for anything I can use on my arm. It needs stitches but how the hell do I explain that to Celeste? How do I explain it to the hospital staff? I find butterfly Band-Aids and a small tube of superglue. *That'll have to do.* But I won't be able to use it until later. Once I know the bleeding has stopped.

"Fuck," I hiss through clenched teeth.

I fall to the ground and lean my back against the cabinet, holding my right arm to my chest. What am I gonna do? They know that I know their names, but they didn't seem concerned in the least. Especially Cole. He was adamant that I wouldn't go to the police. And I had every intention to until he set me up to be a part of their murdering cult! Now my hands are tied and stained with blood.

I didn't get a look at their faces. They kept their lights on me or off, so they could be anyone. Anywhere. And they know my name, so they know I live here.

My hands shake as I run them through my matted hair. The dead guy had said they were kids, but they didn't sound young. Will they go to school with me? That thought makes my stomach knot. They could fuck with me, if that's the case. More than they already have. I have to show them that I could run their little fucking boy group into the ground. I'm smarter than they are.

As for the dead guy? I can't save him. It's too late for him. I have to save myself.

The smell of the blood is strong, and I swallow the lump in my throat. Sitting up on my knees, I yank the hand towel off the countertop and turn on the sink, wetting it. Then I get down on my hands and knees and scrub. The blood comes off the white tile easily, but it's stuck in the grout between them. Those angry tears come faster.

I have to rinse the towel out twice, but finally, I'm able to scrub it all away. I close my eyes and place my hand over the scarf covering the cut. How long will it bleed for? How …

The sound of laughter has me jumping to my feet. I turn off the bathroom lights, then run into my bedroom. I turn those lights off as well, then go over to the windows and see their flashlights. One stands at the back of the car by the trunk, and the other gets into the passenger seat.

Cole is the one at the trunk. I can feel it. Probably putting his bag and evidence away. He shuts the trunk and then the light hangs down by his side. A shiver runs up my spine. Even though I can't see his eyes, I know he's watching me. I'm also very aware that I'm standing in front of my window with nothing but my bra and underwear on. I get a feeling he can still see me even though my room is dark.

His light shuts off, covering them in nothing but darkness, and then I hear his car door open and close. The headlights come on as the engine roars to life. And then it takes off, driving back down the way it came.

I run back into my bathroom, put on the same blood-stained clothes I was wearing, and then grab a new pair of jeans and t-shirt and leave my room. Making my way down to the kitchen, I go into the pantry and grab a trash bag. Then I rush to the garage.

Flipping on the light, I see the white Escalade SUV, a yellow Hummer, a white Jag, and red BMW in the six-car garage. I ignore them all and start opening the cabinets along the wall until I find what I'm looking for.

Then I turn the lights off and head out the back door, knowing what I need to do.

CHAPTER THREE

COLE

Standing in my shower, I take deep breaths as the water washes away any remains of the man who we killed earlier. And although I should be happy, I'm not.

He was right. I'm not God. I shouldn't get to choose who lives and who dies, but I do anyway. He deserved to die for his sins. As far as mine? I should have died. Everyone in this town feels that way. I wish I could answer the questions they are too afraid to ask me. Because they fear me. My rage. I've had it for as long as I can remember. But over time, it has just gotten worse, and I'm growing tired of holding it back. I found comfort in letting it free and allowing it to take over me. But then when it leaves me, I'm cold all over again. Nothing but emptiness.

I hang my head and let it hit the white tiled wall with a thud as the water runs over my head and back. I fist my cracked knuckles and enjoy the tightness in my joints. The pull of my broken skin. It's the only reminder that I'm still alive. The only way that I know what I did was right.

Jeff deserved to die!

We didn't have time to sit back and wait for it to happen. And pray that it was a slow and painful death. Although we did take his life too fast, if you ask me. I would have drawn it out longer if we had not been interrupted tonight.

Austin Lowes. She's gonna be a fucking problem. But once I

figure out what my options are with her, I plan to take care of her.

I turn off the water and open the glass door, picking my towel up off the floor and drying off. Wrapping it around my hips, I make my way into my room and grab a pair of sweatpants out of my closet. Noticing the clock on my nightstand, I see it's almost 3:00 a.m. Kellan, Bennett, and Shane all had places to go and women to fuck after our get-together in the cemetery. Deke and I, however, went back to the clubhouse afterward. We had some things to discuss regarding Jeff and what we wanted to do next. He never once questioned the fact that I hadn't wiped the blood off. He knew better than to ask.

Once dressed in my sweatpants, I grab my phone off my nightstand and see I have a message. I frown. The number is not saved as one of my contacts.

Opening it up, I notice it's a video. And I just received it a few minutes ago. I press play.

It's dark, so I squint to make out the image. I hear a match being lit followed by flames. The person holding the phone takes a step back from the burning object.

"Do you see that, Cole?" an unfamiliar voice asks over the sound of the crackling fire.

"What …?" I trail off as the person starts to circle the fire. But I still can't place where they are or what is burning because it's too dark and the fire is causing a glare.

It comes to a stop, and the camera spins around. My jaw tightens when I see it's Austin. She looks the same as she did a little over three hours ago when I let her run off. All I can see is two black straps on her shoulders. Her face and neck smeared with *his blood* from my hands.

She smiles, the light from her phone making her green eyes shine like stars. It makes her look like an evil angel with perfect teeth and a blood-stained face. "What evidence, Cole?"

Then it goes dead.

I grip the phone in my hand, clenching my teeth. What the fuck did I just watch? What was she burning?

How did she get my number …? *I had Deke call my cell from her*

26

phone. That's how she got it.

And *what evidence, Cole?* What did that mean? Fire?

Realization hits me, and my heart starts to pound in my chest. I go to the number and press call.

"Hello, Cole." She answers on the first ring as if she was expecting me to call. Her smooth voice is no longer high-pitched in fear or anger. She's collected herself. Almost seductive.

"You fucking bitch …"

She laughs softly, and it runs over me like lava, burning my skin. "You know when I got back to the house, I thought what could I do that would clear my name if you decided to set me up?"

My jaw clenches.

"It occurred to me that if there's no DNA to be found, then there's no way for you to pin me for a murder. Did you know that it takes just a little over two hours to burn a body?"

I laugh nervously. "Fire doesn't destroy everything, sweetheart."

"I know." I can hear the smile in her voice that lets me know she's ahead of me again. "That's why after it finished burning, I took a hammer and crushed what bones were left and then tossed the dust over the cliff into the ocean. Oh, and no worries, I also burned my clothes as well."

"Fuck …"

"I know how to cover my ass, Cole. I'm a Lowes, after all."

I stare ahead at my dark gray wall, trying to decide my next move, but she's not done.

"But it was fun watching you think you had it all figured out." *Click.*

"Goddammit!" I throw my phone across my room.

I'm not mad she destroyed the body. Fuck what she does to him. But as far as I know, she just recorded that conversation to prove that she was innocent all along. She could go to the police, and it would be her word against ours. The guys and I don't have a good reputation in this town to begin with. The only reason we're not in jail is because we have rich parents who bail us out of trouble. And it doesn't hurt that Kellan's uncle is the chief in another town not far from here.

"Think, Cole," I say, starting to pace my room. What can I do to get her to keep her mouth shut? What could I do to make her understand why the bastard had to die?

My door opens, and I spin around to see Lilly standing in my doorway, her pink princess nightgown on, her blond hair a curly mess, and her brown eyes tired. "Cole?" she asks softly. "Are you okay? I heard something." She brings her favorite bunny to her chest and hugs him tightly.

"Everything is fine," I say, walking over to her. "Go back to bed."

"Will you come with me?" she asks, holding out her right hand.

I sigh and bend down, picking her up. "Come on." I walk her across the hall back to her room and lie down with her. I kiss her on the cheek as she curls up into my side. Placing my hands behind my head, I stare up at her pink ceiling. *Austin Lowes, you just fucked up.*

AUSTIN

I strip out of my hoodie and t-shirt. Then remove my jeans. I reach down into the garbage bag and put on a new pair of jeans but refrain from putting the clean shirt on. I'm still covered in his blood. I really didn't think this through all that well, so I'm winging it. I've never had to burn evidence before.

I pull out my cell, and taking a deep breath, I press record. I show the dead man lying on the ground. It didn't take me long to dig his ass up. I left him in the grave because they didn't bury him very deep. Mistake on their part. I take the matches out and light one. Then toss it onto him. I start to circle the body making sure not to trip over the gas can. Once I show it all, I turn it to face me and smile. Fuck you, Cole! *"What evidence, Cole?"*

Then I stop the video and put my phone away. I place my clothes in the fire and sit down. I'm shivering from the cold, but the fire heats my body. It's gonna take a while for him to burn completely. I grip the hammer and pound it into the wet ground just to waste time. When I'm ready, I'll take the dirt to smother the fire, make my way back to the house, and send the video. And he'll call me. He's a cocky son of a bitch who won't be able to stop himself. He'll wanna talk to me. Feel me out. And I'll be calm and collected and ready to show him that he shouldn't have fucked with me.

My head snaps up, and I look around the darkness. Ever have that feeling someone is watching you? Making the hair on the back of your neck stand up. That's how I feel right now.

"Hello?" I call out.

All I hear is the wind howling through the tall trees. I roll my eyes and go back to pounding the hammer into the ground.

You're paranoid, Austin. Lighting a dead man on fire will do that to you.

I groan, standing outside the church while Celeste fixes the red cardigan that I wore over my black dress for service this morning. Not gonna lie, listening to the preacher speak about how Cain killed Abel didn't set well with me when I only watched a guy get murdered hours ago and then burned his body to save my own ass. But living with two druggies, there's not much that you don't see. And you learn really quick that you do what you have to in order to survive. They don't call it a dog-eat-dog world for nothing.

I laid in bed early this morning before the sun rose, contemplating on going to the police, but then thought better of it. There's five of them. I'm sure one would cut a deal and get off free while the others took the fall. That would leave me in deep shit because someone would come after me. And I've watched enough shows on TV to know that I would get in trouble for tampering with evidence. I didn't save my ass just to go down with them.

"Were you up late, honey? You look awful." Celeste's brown eyes look me over slowly, taking in my hair. I washed it before I went to bed after I burned the guy, then I fell asleep with it wet. All I did this morning was run a brush through it. I didn't even put much makeup on. Bare minimum was gonna have to do.

"Thanks," I mumble.

She frowns. "I'm sorry, I just meant that you didn't look well. Are you sick?"

I wave her off her lame apology. I know I look like shit. "I knew what you meant. And no, I'm fine."

She nods. "Did you like the service? Pastor Fritz is so nice."

I'm sure he is. "Yeah," I say, looking away from her. I almost played the sick card this morning. And now I know I could have pulled it off.

"I spoke to your father earlier, and he said that he won't be home until next week."

I nod. *No surprise there.* "Where is he?"

"Trying to close a deal in Vancouver," she says excitedly. She's so proud of him it's sickening. "He wants to have a family dinner when he returns."

I go to open my mouth to say *no thanks* when the hairs on the back of my neck stand, and then I hear *his* voice.

"Hello, Celeste."

She looks over my shoulder, and a bright smile lights up her face. "Hello, Cole."

My stomach drops at her confirmation.

"Have you met my stepdaughter?" She looks back at me and starts fluffing my hair. I push her hands away. *Is she trying to set me up with a madman?*

"I haven't," he says and then chuckles.

She grips my shoulders and spins me around so fast I almost trip over my black pumps.

"This is Austin. Austin, this is Cole Reynolds. He's a senior with you this year."

I look up at the man who had me pinned to the ground just hours ago. The same man sliced my arm open with a knife, trying to pin me for murder. And my mouth goes dry because he's smiling down at me. Perfectly full lips pulled back to showcase a set of pearly whites. A straight nose and high cheekbones along with a square jaw. A pair of sunglasses shields his eyes, but I can feel them running over my body just like his hands did last night.

"It's nice to meet you," he says, reaching out and grabbing my right hand. He leans over and gently kisses my knuckles.

I yank my hand away, and he chuckles.

"Austin!" Celeste snaps. "I'm sorry, she's not quite herself today," she adds when I just stand there.

"It's quite all right." He continues to smile down at me, and I swallow nervously. *What is he doing here?* He's probably here to teach me a lesson that no one fucks with Cole. I may not know him, but I learned enough last night.

"How is Lilly?" she asks him.

He turns his attention to her, dismissing me at the mention of this Lilly. "She's doing well. Thanks for asking."

"Great. You'll have to bring her over, and we can all go swimming. I know how much she loves the water. Like you."

He laughs and nods. "Absolutely." Then I feel his eyes back on me. "How does that sound, *Austin*?"

The way he says my name sounds like he wants to drown me. I don't answer.

He throws me another sinister smile as if he knows how much being here is affecting me. "Well, we should get going," Celeste says.

"Actually, I was wondering if Austin would like to go to lunch. A bunch of us seniors are meeting up ..."

"No," I say, but Celeste speaks at the same time.

"That would be great." She leans down, kisses my cheek, and then looks at Cole. "You crazy kids have fun." Then she walks off, leaving me standing with a murderer.

The smile he's had this entire time drops off his face like he just removed a mask. His defined jaw sharpens, and his chest bows out— ready for a fight.

I take a nervous step back. "How did you find me?" I ask, and I hate that my voice shakes. Any courage I had last night now long gone.

He doesn't answer. Instead, he grips my forearm, the same one that he cut last night, and I know it was on purpose. I hiss in a breath as he turns and guides me down the stairs of the church and along the narrow walkway to the parked cars.

"I'm not going anywhere with you," I snap.

"You don't have a choice," he growls. "Now get in the fucking car." He yanks me to a stop and then shoves me through the driver's side of the black two-door car. Then he's falling into the driver's seat, pushing me across the center console.

I scramble into the passenger seat awkwardly and quickly push down my dress to cover my thighs.

Before I can even reach for the door handle, he has the car in reverse and then squeals out of the parking lot.

I sit with my back plastered to his seat, my eyes on him as he races down the highway. His hand fisted on the clutch as he shifts gears. His dark blue t-shirt showcasing his toned forearms.

"What do you want, Cole?" He doesn't answer. I see we are headed back the direction of my house, and I have a feeling he plans to place me in the grave he and Deke had dug for the guy who I burned. "I'm not going to tell the cops," I say, letting out a long breath. I open my mouth to speak, but something warm gets my attention.

I yank up the sleeve of my red cardigan and hiss in a breath when I see blood running down my arm. His hand grabbing my forearm must have pulled my cut open.

"Fuck!" He hisses, noticing it, and demands, "You didn't get that stitched up?"

I narrow my eyes on him. "Who the hell was going to *stitch it up*?"

He lets out a long breath and nods to the center console. "I've got a towel in there. Get it out and apply pressure to it."

"Like you care if I bleed to death," I snap.

"I don't. But I don't want that shit on my seats."

"Bastard," I mumble and open the console. When it pops up, I freeze as I stare down into it. There's a black handgun and a knife along with a small black hand towel, a roll of duct tape, and a pair of handcuffs. Everything a serial killer needs.

He takes a quick look down and growls. He yanks out the hand towel, tosses it to me, and then slams the console closed, placing his right forearm over it.

I sit back in my seat and stare straight ahead, applying pressure to my forearm with the towel. "Where are we going?" I ask roughly. The car is too small for us to be this close together. All of a sudden, I realize I know nothing about this man, and whatever plan he had last night, I fucked it up. On purpose.

He doesn't answer. Instead, he reaches over and presses a knob on his dash, and "Coming Undone" by Korn fills the speakers. He turns it up to drown out my heavy breathing as we fly down the highway.

The clouds have opened up, and the rain has started to fall. We passed a sign thirty minutes ago that said Marita fifty miles.

He still hasn't spoken or even looked my way. I've sat completely still, hoping he would forget I'm in the car.

"Has it stopped bleeding?"

No such luck. "Yes." Comes my clipped answer.

When he turns on his blinker and pulls off the highway, my heart starts to pound in my chest because I don't know what he plans to do with me. But now that I know there's a gun in the center console, I'll do whatever I can to get to it. Even though I have no idea how to use one.

He slows down and pulls into a parking garage. I look around, noticing how deserted it is on this rainy Sunday afternoon.

We spiral up and up until we're on the fifth floor. He pulls into a parking spot, the tires squealing at the sudden turn, and then he brings the car to a quick stop. The seat belt locks on my shoulder.

I look around, expecting his friends to circle us. My muscles tighten, ready to defend myself.

But nothing happens. He shuts the car off, and we just sit in silence. I swallow the lump in my throat. My hands shake, ready to reach for the door handle and run.

"Don't," he says calmly as if he knows what I'm thinking.

My head snaps to look over at him, but he stares straight ahead. "I'm not going to hurt you." I snort, and he turns his head to look at me. "Not today, anyway," he adds, and that nervousness bubbles up again.

He smiles at me, a soft one, and I fist my hands in my lap because I know he can feel my fear. Men like him feed off it. I reach out and yank his glasses off his face. It's raining, for Christ's sake; he doesn't need them.

A set of baby blue eyes stare into mine.

He reaches out, and I jump in surprise. I expect him to laugh, but he doesn't. Instead, his eyes drop to my cardigan as he takes a lock of my hair between his fingers. He twists the strands around it. "Red really is your color," he says softly, and then his eyes are back on mine.

Warmth spreads down my back as he threads his fingers through my hair. I whimper, half scared to shit. The other half turned on.

What is wrong with me?

He leans into me, stopping his face just inches from mine. I let out a long breath, trying to stop my racing heart. "Cole …" I whisper his name.

He smiles at me. "Don't be afraid, Austin. If I wanted you dead, I would have killed you last night. And I sure as hell wouldn't do it while Celeste knows you're with me."

I close my eyes and whimper, trying not to show my fear, but it's leaking from my pores. His car reeks of it.

"Look at me," he orders, and I open my eyes. He's still in my face, his hand still gripping my hair. "Although I did imagine sneaking into your room and making you pay for what you did. But thought better of it."

I swallow. "What do you want from me?"

He tilts his head to the side as if to think about his answer. "For you to understand." He pulls away from me, and I suck in a long breath. Sitting back in his seat, he looks straight ahead over the concrete barrier that comes up to the hood of the car. "See that man?" He points out at the building across from the parking garage.

I have to squint, but I see a man standing in his office. The glass windows showcasing everything. His hands in his hair. His suit jacket on his floor and white button up untucked. His suspenders hanging from his waist. "What about him?"

"That is Jeff's brother."

"Jeff?" I look at Cole.

"The guy we killed last night," he answers without any remorse.

"Oh," I say, looking back at the older man. And my breathing picks up. This is just another way for him to pull me in. Get me involved. "I don't wanna know …"

"This man killed his wife." He ignores me. "He beat her repeatedly. All the time. But he was smart about it. As smart as a bastard like him can be. He never touched her arms, legs, or face. He only touched where he knew she could cover up." He runs a hand through his dark hair. "One day, she had had enough and went to tell the one person she thought she could trust. His brother, Jeff." I look over at him. He stares straight ahead at the man. "She begged him to help her. Her husband kept her close because she had no family. Well, she had someone, but …" He trails off. "Anyway, so she turned to his family and asked for some money to leave her abusive husband. He told her to give him a few days." His hand grips the steering wheel. "But he went to his brother and told him what his wife had asked him to do. So when he got home, he beat her. He beat her, not caring where the bruises showed up because he knew she wasn't gonna survive this time." My throat tightens. "Then after he beat her to within an inch of her life, he took a knife and slit her throat." He speaks with no emotion, and tears sting my eyes. "He didn't even give her a proper burial. He carried her to the old cemetery, dug a hole, and dropped her in it."

I reach out and touch his arm. "I'm sorry …"

He yanks back from me, and his eyes meet mine. They have fire in them, and his breath has picked up.

I lower my eyes to my lap. "Who was she to you?"

"She was Eli's older sister."

"Eli?" I ask, looking up at him through my lashes.

"My best friend," he says, his eyes back on the man who runs around aimlessly in his office.

I don't remember that name from last night at the cemetery. "Why not kill him?" I ask.

"He doesn't deserve death yet." His eyes meet mine. "Death is no different than anything else. It too must be earned."

I look over at the man, and he has his cell in his hand. He keeps putting it to his ear and then pulls it away. Repeating the motion. "What do you think he's doing?"

"He's trying to contact Jeff."

I look over at Cole, and a soft smile covers his face. "They are business partners. And without Jeff, he'll lose everything. Jeff was the mastermind behind their shit show."

I look back at the guy who stands in his office. He reminds me of watching a hamster in his cage as he runs on his wheel, getting nowhere. He just keeps circling around, that phone still in his hand. "So you go around killing people who kill others?" I ask.

He snorts. "No. Jeff was … an exception."

I run a hand through my hair, trying to understand what is going on and how I feel about it. "You still killed someone …"

"It wasn't like he was innocent," he snaps.

I narrow my eyes on him. "You cut my arm."

He places his hand in my hair again, but instead of leaning into me, he yanks me across the center console. I gasp at the feel of his nails digging into my scalp. "I'll do whatever I have to do, sweetheart. And I watched the video. You're not as innocent as you claim to be."

"I've never killed anyone," I snap.

He chuckles, and his free hand comes up to my throat. "But you want to."

My heart starts to pound. "You don't know me …"

"You're a Lowes, after all. Remember? Everyone in our town knows what kind of man your father is. Including you."

I clamp my mouth shut because I know how terrible he can be. And I can't count how many times I've wished him dead.

He leans in, his nose running along my jawline like he did last night. I shudder. "We are all the same, Austin. Some of us just choose not to pretend."

CHAPTER FOUR

COLE

I pull away from her, and my eyes fall to her lips. Bringing her here was a mistake. Having her in my car alone with me was a mistake. But I made them anyway. I'm known for fuckups. No one expects much from me. Well, no one except Lilly. But she isn't hard to please.

I run my thumb over her bottom lip, wondering what it would feel like between my teeth. Or wrapped around my cock. Either one would do at the moment. She licks her lips, letting me know what she is thinking, and that's enough for now.

I sit back in my seat and throw the car in reverse. Pulling out of the parking spot, I don't look back once at the bastard who is gonna pay for killing my best friend's sister.

We're ten minutes from Collins when she finally speaks to me. "What did Jeff mean by *another one of your dares*?"

My jaw tightens. She heard more than I would have liked. I don't answer. Instead, I pull my cell out of my pocket and call Deke's older sister. She answers on the third ring. "Hey. I need a favor," I say, refusing to look over at Austin.

"Well, hello to you to, Cole," she says with sarcasm.

"Can you help me or not, Shelby?" I snap.

She sighs heavily. "Is it illegal?"

I don't answer, and a silence falls between us. I sit with my cell to my ear, waiting for a response. She knows she's not gonna get any info. After a minute, she finally answers. "Sure."

"I'll be there in fifteen."

"I don't want any trouble, Cole," she says softly. "You know I can't …"

"I know. It's not like that," I say and then hang up before she can say any more.

I chance a glance over at Austin, and she's already staring at me. "We're going to go see Shelby."

"Is she your girlfriend?" she asks softly.

I almost laugh. Deke would kill me if I tried anything with his sister. Plus, she's not my type. She wants commitment. Stability. Love. I have none of those things to give. Not to mention, I'm a senior in high school, and she is six years older than the guys and me. But I don't respond to Austin either. Because a part of me likes that she is curious. *Why would she care if I'm already taken?*

I don't have time to process that thought, though, because a phone rings, breaking the silence of the car.

Austin looks down at her cell in her hand, lets out a long sigh, and then places it to her ear. "Hey, Mom." There's a pause. "No, I haven't seen him." She bows her head and rubs her temple with her free hand. "I don't know …" she growls. "What do you want me to do?" she snaps. "You're the one who shipped me off like a Christmas present that you wanted to return." Her voice grows inside my car. "If you want to speak to him, then you call him." I glance over at her, and she stares straight ahead, but I can see her eyes start to glisten from unshed tears. "I'm not sending you money, Mom." Her hand fists in her lap. "Is that why you sent me here?" she demands. "To send you his money?" She gives a dark laugh. "You call him and ask him to send you money for you and your piece of shit boyfriend," she snaps. "I'm not gonna do it." She pulls the phone from her ear, shuts it off, and tosses it into my back seat.

The silence fills the car once again. I shift uncomfortably. "Do you wanna …?"

"No!" she interrupts me.

I'm not sure how long she has been in town, and I never stopped to question why she was here in the first place. I didn't even know that Bruce Lowes had a daughter. And today, standing outside the church, Celeste said she is a senior this year. I stayed up trying to decide what to do with her. How to corner her so she can't run from me. Then I remembered that Celeste never misses church on Sunday mornings. So I sat in my car in the parking lot until I watched them walk out of the church. Then I made my move.

"Where did you move here from?" I ask.

She reaches up and quickly wipes away a tear from her cheek. "What does it matter?"

"It doesn't. Just making small talk."

"I prefer when I thought you were trying to kill me over small talk," she snaps.

I smile. Yeah, there's something about Austin Lowes that I like. *A lot.*

AUSTIN

My hands fist in my lap. My throat is tight and heart pounding. I'm so angry with my mother.

I haven't always been the best daughter. I caused trouble. I got expelled from school for stupid shit. She had to talk the cops into not taking me to jail for smoking pot. She was just saving her own ass since she was the one who supplied me with it. But she made a big scene. *"That was the final straw,"* she said.

We walk in the house and she slams the front door behind me. "What the fuck were you thinking?" she demands.

I ignore her and keep walking toward my room. Wanting to get away from her.

"Hey!" Phillip, her boyfriend, steps out of their room and into the hallway in front of me. "Your mother asked you a question." His dark brown eyes stare down at me.

I ignore him and go to step around him. He reaches up, grabbing my backpack, and yanks me backward. I trip over my feet and fall on my ass. Before I can recover, he pulls me to my feet and throws me into the wall, causing my books to dig into my back. Then his hand comes up, and he slaps me across the face.

I slap him back. It's not the first time he's put his hands on me. But I prefer this kind over the soft and gentle kind he attempts when my mother isn't around.

"You ungrateful bitch!" he yells in my face. "Without us, you would have nothing."

"You would have nothing if not for me!" I scream. "I don't see you working for anything. My father gave my mother and me all this. What the fuck do you give us?"

He hits me again. So hard that it knocks me to my knees. I taste blood and get up, running to my room. I slam my door and lock it.

I lean up against it as angry tears sting my eyes. I can still hear them in the hallway. "Send that bitch to her dad's," he snarls.

"He never wanted her before. Why the hell would he want her now? She is nothing but trouble," she growls.

"We have to do something. I can't take her in this place with us any longer," he tells her.

There's a long pause. Then she says, "I'll call Celeste. That stupid bitch will want her."

The first tear falls down my cheek. I run over to my window, yank it up, and jump through it, wanting to get the fuck out of here.

Three weeks later, I was on a plane to Oregon.

My life wasn't a good one. And honestly, I wasn't all that surprised when my mother dropped me like a bad habit for her boyfriend. But I still thought she would fight for me. Want me. But she didn't; all she needed was him. She stood by and let him hit me. Touch me.

But now it's clear they have a hidden agenda. She wants me to get access to his money and send it to her. Fuck no! If she wants his money, she can call and ask for it. She's never been shy about asking before.

Cole slows the car down, and I realize we are pulling into a driveway. And I'm instantly on alert once I realize it's not my father's. "Where are we?" I ask as panic bubbles up my throat.

"Shelby's," he answers and shuts the car off, getting out.

I follow him up to the front door. He enters without even knocking. "Shelby?" he calls out.

"In here," a woman's soft voice says.

I follow much slower as I'm taking in my surroundings. The house is nothing like my father's. It's much smaller, homier. Smells of coconut.

We round a corner and walk into a kitchen. A beautiful blond sits at the table. She looks up at him, smiling warmly, her crystal blue eyes soft. She stands and walks right to him. He hugs her, and it makes me think they have something going on.

"This is Austin." He gestures to me without looking my way. "She needs stitches."

My eyes widen. *That's why we're here? Stitches?*

Her eyes widen as well. "Oh, my, what happened?" she asks, concern in her words.

"He took a knife to my forearm," I say, lifting my chin.

"He what?" Her wide eyes snap to his. "Cole …?"

"Just stitch her up so we can go. I need to get home," he snaps.

She closes her mouth and then walks over to me. "May I see it?"

I remove my red cardigan and lift my right hand in the air to show her my forearm. It's covered in blood from when he broke it open earlier. She gasps. "Cole Reynolds. Why the hell would you do this to her?" she demands.

We both look at him, and he's glaring at us, lips thinned. When she realizes he's not gonna answer, she looks back at me. "I tried to superglue it."

She sighs heavily. "That won't do on a cut like this."

His phone rings, and he pulls it out of his back pocket. A soft smile appears on his face and then he walks out, answering it to where we can't hear him.

"You poor thing. Come on. I have everything we need in my spare bedroom."

I follow her and sit down on the end of the bed like she instructs. "Do you do this for him often?" I ask. She frowns, walking into the adjoining bathroom. "Stitch people up?" I clarify.

She laughs softly, coming out with a wet washcloth to clean the blood off. "For others, no. For them, yes." I tilt my head to the side. "They tend to get into trouble a lot."

"They?"

"Great White Sharks."

"I don't understand what you are talking about," I say, shaking my head.

"Do you not know them?"

"I don't know who *them* are. I just moved here and …"

"Oh." She nods in understanding, tossing the washcloth into a dirty clothes hamper in the corner. "The GWS, *Great White Sharks* is what everyone calls them. Cole, Deke, Shane, Bennett, and Kellan are all on the school swim team. They are sharks in and out of the water. Cole is their captain. All of them already have scholarships for college next fall."

"Do you go to school with them?" She seems older than us but how else would she know them?

She chuckles. "I'll take that as a compliment. But, no, I am Deke's older sister."

"I see." *The bastard who wanted to kill me last night.* Now here I am, and his sister is going to stitch me up. "But you have done this before?" It's not that I'm afraid she's not qualified; at this point, I'll take anyone's help.

"Yes. I'm a trauma nurse. I keep stuff here just in case the guys need something done."

"What kind of *something* do you mean?" I ask slowly.

She sets down a box next to me on the bed. "They dare one another to do stupid shit. Half the time, they end up in an emergency room. And I'm there to patch them up only to send them on their way to do it again"

"Dare one another?" *Is this one of your dares?* Jeff had asked Cole last night.

She opens the box to pull out a package. She rips it open and takes out a cold cloth that she rubs over my cut. I hiss in a breath through gritted teeth. Then a syringe and a vial of clear liquid. She sticks the end of the needle into it. "It's hard to explain. Even I don't know all the details. But they dare one another to do something stupid, and if they don't complete the dare, they have consequences. It's so juvenile, if you ask me. But then again, they are still boys." She smiles at me. "Okay. Now you're gonna feel a sting. I'm going to numb the area."

Thirty minutes and fifteen stitches later, I'm walking out of the spare bedroom with my arm stitched and wrapped. I hold my forearm in my hand as I look at all the pictures that cover her soft yellow hallway. I stop at a picture of Cole. Seven other boys stand around him in front of an indoor pool. All of them in white sweatpants and matching jackets unzipped. Like they just finished a swim meet.

Shelby walks up behind me. "Which one is your brother?" I ask just because I want to know which guy wants me dead.

"This is Deke." She points at the one to the right of Cole. He has soft blue eyes and a pretty smile. Of course, the bastard is good looking. Hell, they're all pretty decent looking. "Then it goes Kellan, Bennett, and Shane." She points at the others to the right of Cole.

"Who are these guys?" I point at the three on his left side.

She sighs. "That is Maddox, Landen, and Eli."

"Eli?" I ask. He's the one who had the sister. The reason they killed Jeff. What was her name? Did Cole ever mention it?

"Yeah. He, Maddox, and Landen all passed away last year."

"What?" I ask, turning to face her. When Cole spoke of him earlier, he didn't mention that he was dead.

"They were in a car wreck. The only one who survived was Cole."

"Cole was with them?" What Jeff was saying makes sense now. *What about your consequences, Cole? You killed three of your best friends ...*

She nods. "Cole has always been a troubled soul. And then ... well ... He hasn't been himself since. He had a rough life growing up. Losing his mother at such a young age. And Lilly …"

That's who Celeste had asked about. "Lilly? Is that his girlfriend?" I keep asking this question because I'm curious for any personal information about him. And what's more personal than loving someone?

"No." She smiles down at me. "Lilly is his little sister. He raises her."

My brows pull together. "What about their dad?"

She goes to open her mouth, but Cole clears his throat from behind us. I spin around to see him glaring at me. His eyes briefly go to the picture on the wall of all his friends, then they are back on mine. "Let's go." He turns and walks out without a backward glance.

"Thank you," I tell her, and she surprises me by pulling me in for a hug.

"Anytime. Come back in a week and I'll remove them."

CHAPTER FIVE

COLE

Austin stayed silent in the car, but I could hear her mind working: The questions she had were ones I would never answer. Some things are just better left the way they are.

I dropped her off at her father's without a goodbye or a see you around. She got out, and I sped off, heading home.

As soon as I step into my father's house, I hear Lilly's voice. "Cole?"

"In here," I tell her, entering the kitchen. My father stands at the breakfast bar with a glass of his favorite scotch in his hand. It's not even five yet.

"Where have you been?" he demands.

Just then, Lilly runs in, carrying her stuffed bunny, Hippo, in her hands. "Hey, princess," I say, and she jumps into my arms. "How was ballet today?"

"Ms. Talon taught me how to twirl."

"That's awesome," I say, hugging her.

My father clears his throat. "Lilly, give Cole and me a moment."

I kiss her soft cheek. "I'll be right there." I set her down and then turn to my father.

"I spoke to Bruce Lowes this morning."

I fucking hate that guy! Knowing that he has a daughter makes me hate him even more. She's already causing problems for me. "And?"

"And his daughter is in town. Moved in with him." He eyes me skeptically.

"I don't see how this requires a conversation between us." I avoid my father at all costs. He's not any better than Bruce Lowes. They're best friends, after all.

He sets his glass down. "She's trouble. Stay away from her."

That piques my interest. But I'm not surprised, considering she burned a body and crushed the bones with a hammer. I like her creativity. It's sexy. "How so?"

"Guess her mother is some crack whore. The mom's boyfriend abuses her." He rolls his eyes. "He said the mother wants her to stay until she graduates. But he plans on sending her back the moment she fucks up."

"And you're telling me this why?"

"Because I'm giving you a warning. Lord knows you don't need anyone helping you and your friends get into trouble." Then he picks up his drink. "Oh, and quit fucking his wife."

I smile at that statement.

He grunts. "He knew that your car was over there one night last week. All night. He has help, for Christ's sake. You think you'd be a little more discreet." Then he walks out of the kitchen.

My smile widens. Pulling my cell out, I send a quick text to Celeste. I wanna know everything there is about Austin Lowes.

Up for swimming?

She sends a text back immediately. ***Absolutely. Bring that little princess on over.***

"Cole. Watch me," Lilly calls out from the side of the pool.

I stand in the shallow end, looking up at her. "Watching."

She puts her feet together, bends her knees, and leans over at the waist, her hands out in front of her before she falls into the pool face first, doing her version of a dive.

She comes up sucking in a long breath. I reach out and grab her even though she can swim. "That was awesome, Lil," I say with a big smile. Celeste claps from her raft in the deep end.

"I've been practicing," she says, smiling up at me. Her blond hair sticks to her face and neck because I forgot to braid it. Now it'll take me forever to get her tangles out.

"So how was lunch with Austin today?" Celeste asks from behind me.

I refrain from smiling. "It went well. She didn't say much."

She sighs. "Yeah, I asked her how it went, and she didn't respond. Just went up to her room and said she was tired."

That's because she spent last night watching us kill a guy and then she burned the body. I lick my lips and say, "I hate to be forward, but I didn't even know Bruce had a daughter."

She frowns. "You've met her before. I remembered that earlier this afternoon after I introduced you two."

"What? When?" She must be mistaken.

She sits up on her raft and uses her hands to paddle over to me. "You guys must have been around nine. Maybe ten. I don't know. Bruce and I have been married for ten years now, and she's seventeen. So seven." She laughs. "I was off on the math."

My frown deepens. "I don't remember."

"I don't think she does either." She sighs. "She came to stay with us for a few weeks during the summer. We had just gotten married. Her mother had been admitted to the hospital for an overdose."

"Then why did she go back?" Lilly throws some diving rings into the water and watches them sink as she puts her goggles on.

"Her mom went to rehab. Got better. Bruce bought them a house, sent her money ..."

He sounds like my father. Just wants to throw money at it. Bruce doesn't care about Austin any more than my father cares about Lilly. At least he knows I have a scholarship. He knows I have plans. He just doesn't know that I plan on taking Lilly with me when I go to college. It'll be hard, but I'll make it work. And he won't fight me. He's never wanted her.

"So why now?" I watch Lilly dive in and kick her little feet to make it to the bottom to grab a ring. Then she pushes off the bottom and shoots up. I help her to the side of the pool where she will get out to repeat the process again.

Celeste sighs. "She got expelled from school. Caught with drugs." She shakes her head. "Her mother called me, demanding I take her. That she was just too much to handle anymore."

Lilly jumps in, getting two rings that were close to one another this time.

"Bruce said no, that we didn't have time for her, but I have nothing but time." Her eyes fall to the water, and she runs her hand through it slowly. "He's always away. And I don't think Austin was safe. I think she just needs a different environment. Different friends." She looks up at me and smiles. "You could help her."

I chuckle. I'm not a good influence, by any means, and Celeste knows that. This entire town knows that I do what I want, when I want. No one tells me I can't do something. And when I find myself in trouble, my father bails me out because he hates it when I make him look bad. "You know that's not true, Celeste," I finally say as Lilly jumps in again, splashing me.

She drops her head. "We both know that you're the lesser of two evils," she whispers, and my chest tightens at her words.

Yeah, I try to beat the kind of men who she married. Like my father. Right now, I can only do so much. But one day, they will all pay. I will release all that anger bottled up inside me, and it will fucking rain blood on this town.

AUSTIN

I wake up with a headache and a throbbing forearm. Shelby couldn't give me any pain meds, but she said that it shouldn't hurt once the numbing shot wore off. It's not painful, just a dull ache.

Getting out of bed, I walk over to my closet and put on a white long-sleeve shirt to cover my stitches. It hangs off my right shoulder, letting whoever sees me know that I didn't take the time to put a bra on. Then I yank on a pair of yoga pants before walking out of my room in search of Celeste.

I make my way down the staircase. "Celeste?" I call out when I walk into the kitchen. "Oh, I'm sorry," I say to a woman who stands in front of the open fridge.

"You're fine, dear. Can I get you something?" she asks, placing strawberries on a silver platter.

"I'm looking for Celeste."

She nods. "They are out in the pool. I was just about to take them some fresh fruit. Would you like something?"

"No, thank you," I say and then walk out of the kitchen and then down the hall. *They?* I hope my father isn't back home. I want to avoid him as much as possible. I know he didn't want me here. As much as I hate my mother, she was right. My father's never wanted me, and he won't now. I'm here because of Celeste. And although she drives me nuts, I must admit she's pretty awesome. But you'll never hear me say that out loud.

I push open the back doors and step out onto the porch. I hear splashes coming from the right and make my way over to the edge of the terrace. I stop short when I see Celeste in the pool floating on her bright blue raft over by the rock slide in the deep end, and Cole is also in the pool with a little blonde on his hip.

"Austin!" Celeste spots me and waves. I wave back slowly. "Did you have a good nap?" she asks, and Cole looks over at me. He lets go of the little girl, and she swims over to the steps.

"Yeah," I say, walking around the pool and plopping down on a lounge chair. I look anywhere but at Cole. What is he doing here? Is he trying to fuck with me? Is he feeling Celeste out to see if I said anything to her? I wouldn't do that. She would tell my father, and who knows what he would do with me. He'd probably try to help Cole pin it on me so my ass would go to jail. Out of his life.

"You should come swimming with us." She lies back on her raft. Her purple string bikini reveals more than lingerie would. Letting the world know that my father paid for most of her body.

I think about saying yes but stop myself. "Not today." I just got stitches. I'll have to get those removed before she can see my arm. Plus, I don't think the chlorine would feel very good on it.

The little girl gets out of the pool and makes her way over to me. "Hi," she says with a big smile on her face.

"Hello."

"My name is Lilly. I'm six. Wanna watch me dive?"

This is his sister? They look nothing alike. She has blond hair where he has brown. She has brown eyes to his blue. "I'd love to," I say with a smile of my own.

"Cole, can I dive in the deep end? Please?" she begs, jumping up and down.

I take a chance to look at him, and he's staring right at me. My hair is still up in a messy bun from when I slept and pieces fall out down my back and shoulders. His eyes drop to my exposed shoulder and then down my chest. They slowly run down my body to my legs, and I feel them tighten at the look in his eyes.

The man who tried to pin me for murder is now at my father's house with his little sister, swimming with my stepmother.

He's up to something. And I need to get ahead of his game. I'm not some stupid little girl who he can play.

"Please, Cole? Just once," she asks, standing by my lounge chair. Water runs off her bright yellow one-piece and onto the concrete.

"Yeah. One time," he tells her, running his hand through his wet hair, making it stand straight up, and she squeals with excitement. He swims over to the deep end, passing Celeste on her raft. He comes to a stop and looks up at her. She prepares herself for her dive, takes a deep breath, and falls in head first. He reaches under the water and grabs her, pulling her up and then helps her to the side. She climbs out and comes running back over to me.

"Did you like it?" she asks with that excitement still on her face. I envy it. I wish life was that simple.

"I give it a ten." I hold up all my fingers, and she bounces up and down. "Perfect."

She lunges for me, wrapping her arms around me for a tight hug and soaking my shirt and legs. The water feels good. Not too cold but not warm either. She pulls away. "I can dive for rings." Her face falls all of a sudden. "I can only grab one at a time, though."

I refrain from laughing at how adorable she is. "I'd love to watch you dive for rings."

She bounces over to the edge of the pool and tosses five rings in the shallow end. "Cole?" she yells at him. "Cole?"

I look at him to see why he is ignoring her, but when my eyes meet his, he's staring down at my chest. His jaw tight and eyes glaring with anger.

I look down to see what he is staring at. "Geez," I mutter to myself. She soaked my white shirt, and I don't have a bra on.

I hunch over and pull it away from my chest. Standing up, I go to walk away, but Lilly stops me. "You're not gonna watch me?" She pouts.

Shit!

I reach over and grab a blue towel off the back of a lounge chair and drape it over my shoulders. "Of course, I am," I tell her, sitting back down and plastering a smile on my face.

I ignore Cole, but I can still feel his gaze on me for a few more seconds before he turns to her and helps her out with diving for her rings.

We spend another hour out in the pool when Cole finally announces that they have to get going. At first, Lilly tried to beg him for another five minutes, but he didn't budge. He's better than I would have been because the moment she pushed that bottom lip out, I would have caved. Then she threw a fit. He glared at her, but she didn't care. She just wanted to swim.

"She can stay out here with me," Celeste tells him.

"I don't think …"

"Please?" Lilly begs, interrupting him. She hugs his shoulders while they still stand in the pool.

"Lilly …"

"Let her swim a little longer, Cole. It'll be dark shortly. She can stay the night. We can have a girls' night. You kids go have some fun." She looks at me, and my brows rise. What is her deal with

Cole? Does she not know how much he hates me? That he wants me in jail? Or worse, dead?

"Please? Please?" Lilly begs. "I wanna stay. I wanna swim. And have a girls' night." She splashes the water around them with her hands.

"Fine," he says with a heavy sigh. "Just tonight, though. Okay?"

"Thank you." She hugs his neck, and he pats her back.

"Yay." Celeste claps her hands excitedly. And it makes me wonder why she and my father never had a child of their own. I've never thought about it. And sure as hell never asked. Then she looks at me. "Austin, we have a ten o'clock appointment at the salon in the morning."

"For what?"

"I figured you'd want to get you hair done." She shrugs. "Something new for school. And it gives us time together."

"Thanks." I'm not really into spending time at a salon, but I'll give her this. Celeste has been more of a mom in the past twenty-four hours than my mother has in the past seventeen years.

She claps excitedly as Cole hands her Lilly. She bounces on her raft, straddling Celeste's legs.

Cole goes under the water and then his head pops up in the shallow end. He stands, and I watch with complete fascination as he climbs the stairs to exit. Water drips off his lean body. Shelby had mentioned that he was the captain of the swim team, and I didn't understand what that meant until just now. His black swim trunks hang low on his narrow hips. He turns to face me, and my mouth starts to water at the defined V that dips into his shorts and his chiseled abs. Thoughts of him pinning me down to the ground last night come back, reminding me of how strong he was. You can still see the faint marks my nails left when I clawed at his chest.

He isn't overly muscular; he's lean. But what he does have is chiseled, and my legs threaten to buckle. *Good thing I'm sitting down.*

"You have my towel," he speaks, making me jump.

"Oh, sorry," I say in a rush and yank it from my shoulders and toss it to him.

I look up at him through my lashes when he just stands there in front of me, and now, he's the one looking down at me like he wants to push me up against the wall. Or down onto the lounge chair.

That's when I remember why I had his towel in the first place. My shirt is still wet. And my nipples are hard from the wind making me cold. "Excuse me," I say as I jump up. Turning around, I take off into the house.

CHAPTER SIX

COLE

Fuck!

That's the second time since she's walked out here in the past hour that she has got me hard. I fist my hands down by my sides. I don't have time for her. To be some teenage boy obsessed with a set of tits and ass. Especially Bruce Lowes's daughter.

"Cole?"

At the sound of Celeste's voice, I wrap the towel around my hips and turn to face her in the pool. Lilly's still on her lap. "Yeah?"

She sighs heavily, her eyes dropping to my hard cock, letting me know she knows what I'm thinking. "Keep an eye on her."

"I can't—"

"Cole," she interrupts my refusal. "You owe me."

Running a hand through my wet hair, I growl. "Pick something else."

She gives me a kind smile, but we both know it's fake. "I'm picking her. And that's not gonna change."

Fuck!

I turn around and walk into the house, water still dripping from my hair and board shorts. I take the stairs two at a time, knowing where her room is. I watched her stand at her window after Deke and I finished with Jeff.

I don't knock. I barge right into her room, and she squeals, jumping back from her dresser, a shirt in her hands but not on. She holds it up to cover her naked chest. And I wonder if her nipples are still hard. "What the hell, Cole …?"

"Get dressed, we're leaving in ten."

Her eyes narrow on me. "I'm not going anywhere with you," she snaps.

I smile. I gotta say, I do love how challenging she is. The fight. The constant back and forth. She actually thinks she has a chance to stand up against me. Austin Lowes doesn't have a choice. Her mother doesn't want her, her father is just itching to send her back, and her stepmother just threw her to the sharks. I'm all she has, which sucks for her because I destroy everything I touch. And as much as I don't want her around, I look forward to ripping her to shreds.

I shut the door, and she swallows nervously as her eyes go to it, then shoot back to mine. I advance on her with slow and confident strides as if I'm about to attack my prey. My hard cock reminds me that I could throw her on her bed and take her right now, and no one would stop me. But even I have limits.

"What are you doing in here?" Her voice shakes with fear.

I reach up and cup her soft face. She still has on the makeup from church this morning. Her dark green eyes lined with black. Her lashes long and thick, and her plump lips stained with a light pink. Her eyes widen, but she doesn't pull away from me. I lean down, my lips inches from hers. "Do I need to remind you again?" Her chest rising and falling fast with each breath. My free hand itches to yank the shirt she's using to shield her chest from me. To get a better look at her tits without the wet fabric she wore outside. To touch them. To suck on them. "That you don't have a choice."

She lifts her chin, and her green eyes simmer with rage. I like it. "You're not my boss, Cole. You can't tell me what to do."

I let my hand on her face trail down over her delicate neck, where her pulse races, to her bare shoulder. Her body shudders. My fingers continue downward over her bare arm and bent elbow, and then I stop on the bandage covering her stitches. My eyes meet hers. "We both know that I can." I take a step back before I go too far. "Now get dressed. We have somewhere to be."

Her narrowed eyes stay on mine. Almost as if she's challenging me. Her chin lifts, and nostrils flare. "Cole—"

"This is not up for discussion," I snap, interrupting her. "I will drag you to my car by your hair, if need be."

She lets out a growl, and I take that as her acceptance.

She sits next to me in my car as I drive down the curvy road, heading farther away from town.

I take the steep hills at a fast pace, speeding more than I normally would to keep her on her toes. I can taste her fear—smell it—and it's intoxicating.

She places her hands out in front of her on the dash, and I chuckle. Her head snaps to the side to look at me. "You're trying to scare me on purpose."

"We both know you're already scared of me." She doesn't comment.

I make my way down the last hill, and the road curves to the right. I take it, the rear end fishtailing, and I hear the intake of her breath.

"Where are we?" she asks, looking out her window.

"Does it matter?" I ask, and she rolls her eyes but doesn't respond.

I come to a stop at a stoplight and make a left turn and remove my seat belt.

"What are you doing?" she asks, looking over at me.

I throw her a smile, and her eyes narrow on me. She hates when I ignore her questions. *Too bad.* She'll find out soon enough.

We arrive at the warehouse and pull up to the curb. I look over at her. "Do you know how to drive a stick shift?"

"What?" she snaps. "Why would that matter, Cole?"

"Yes or no."

"Yes!" She crosses her arms over her chest, and my eyes fall to it. The memory of seeing her tits still fresh in my mind. They had looked round, perky, and so fucking perfect. *I need out of this car.*

I nod my head and then turn around, reaching for my black bag and hoodie. "Keep your phone on you," I tell her. "As soon as I call you, answer."

"Cole …"

I get out and slam my door shut before I hear her say anything else. My phone vibrates in my pocket, and I pull it out, expecting it to be her, but **Bennett** flashes across my screen.

"Hello?" I answer it, throwing my bag over the metal gate.

"Hey, man. Thought we were on for tonight."

I place my hands on the gate and climb it before jumping over it, landing on my feet. "I am."

"What?" He pauses, and I look up at the sky. The sun almost done setting. "Well, what time?"

"Now." I pick up my bag.

"Cole, how the fuck are you doing it right now? I'm with Deke and Shane. I spoke to Kellan earlier, and he said he hasn't spoken to you all day."

"I've got it covered. Disable the alarm system now and then head to the clubhouse. I'll meet you in an hour." I hang up, placing my phone back in my pocket.

I pull my hood up and over my head and throw the bag over my shoulder. I run around to the back. The dim light buzzing above my head, I keep my eyes down, staring at the ground, knowing where all the cameras are. I helped place them, after all. Then walk up to the back door. Seconds later, my phone vibrates, and I check it.

Deke: You've got two minutes.

Grabbing the tools of out my pocket, I place them in the lock and twist them. A pop sounds seconds later.

Walking in, I smile at the car that sits before me. A bright fucking red Ferrari 250 GTO. *My favorite color.* Only thirty-nine were produced, and I'm about to make this one mine. A few other cars are in the warehouse, but I ignore them. They're not why I'm here.

I grab the key off the hook that hangs on the wall and then jump into the car, throwing my bag in the passenger seat. I take out my phone and call Austin.

"Cole, what the hell are you doing?"

"Turn the car around," I order her.

"What? I don't have time for this. What are you—"

"Turn the fucking car around, Austin," I snap, interrupting her. She's right; we don't have time for this.

I sit in the silent, dark warehouse and can hear the engine of my car outside in the street as she pulls forward and turns around to face the right direction now. "Follow me," I tell her.

"Follow you?" she asks, her voice rising in panic. "You're not coming back?"

"Nope," I say and hit the door opener on the visor. "Don't lose me, Austin. You stay on my ass. Do you understand me?"

Silence.

"Fucking answer me, Austin!"

"Yeah." I finally hear her answer in her small voice.

"Let's go." I hang up, start the car, and take off.

AUSTIN

I hang up the phone and toss it into the passenger seat. *You stay on my ass!* What the hell does that mean?

My hands shake, and my knees bounce as I sit in his driver's seat, waiting for I don't know what to happen. I don't know where we are or what he has planned.

I hear an engine, and then a red car pulls out of a driveway to the gate I had watched him jump just minutes before.

He turns onto the road and takes off. I shove the car into gear and follow him.

He's gone before I can even figure out how to shift his car. It's been a long time since I've driven a standard. And I didn't wanna tell him, but I suck at it. My ex, Martin, had yelled at me for hours when he tried to teach me. I let off the clutch, and it jumps.

Shit!

I get it into second. And then third. I make it to fourth a lot better and press on the gas. He's long gone. I can't even see the taillights ahead of me. But I remembered what direction we came from. I hope that was the same one he took out of this town. It's officially dark, and the town is quiet. We must be on the outskirts because I haven't seen another car or person since we pulled in.

I hear sirens behind me, and I start to panic. What the hell was he doing? Does he want me to get caught? Is that his plan? Another game he wants me to lose? Well, I'd much rather it be robbery than murder, if I had to choose.

I see a tire repair shop at the end of the road with their garage open. I pull into it and get out quickly, pulling their bay door shut and lean up against it. Thankful it was open. I yank my ponytail out and run a hand through my hair. Frustrated and pissed that he has done this to me. Again!

Then I hear my phone ringing in the car. I run back to it and jump in, answering it when I see *shark* light up my screen.

"Hello?" My voice shakes with nervousness.

"Where the fuck did you go?" he demands.

"I could be asking you the same question," I snap.

He growls. "Where are you?"

"Hiding in a garage."

"Goddammit."

"Maybe if you had given me a heads-up, I would have had some time to prepare to help you steal a fucking car," I yell. My hand squeezing the phone a little too hard.

"Calm down," he snaps. "Take a deep breath." He lowers his voice.

My throat tightens as my heart pounds.

"I'll send someone to come get you," he says calmly.

"What?" *Come get me?* "Who?"

"Deke ..."

"Are you crazy?" My voice squeaks. "He wanted to shoot me!" I all but yell. "I'll drive myself."

"I'm not coming back to get you," he says matter-of-factly.

Translation—I'm on my own. If I get caught and arrested, I'll take the fall. But I'd rather take my chances with the cops than with Deke. Or any of those other guys who were with Cole the other night.

I fucking hate him!

"Where am I going?" I ask, running a hand through my hair. My nerves shot.

"I'll send you the address," he says. "And Austin …?"

I hang up. I don't have time to talk to him. I'm wanted by the police at the moment. I have got to get myself out of here.

The sad part is that this isn't the first time I've run from the cops.

I get out, yank up the bay doors, and look both ways but find no cop cars in sight. I get back into his car and take off, leaving black marks on the floor of the garage.

I hear my phone go off and take a quick look down at it and notice that he has me going back to Collins, so I toss the phone. I'll make my way there, then once I'm in town, I'll look at the exact address.

My shoulders start to relax once I hit the curves, climbing the mountains, the city lights behind me, and finally able to drive his car better.

Anger starts to set in. Just what the hell did he think he was doing? Was this just another situation he wanted me to be involved in that could possibly get me in trouble?

I laugh at myself. Of course, it is. The guy is hell-bent on getting my ass thrown in jail.

I take the curves just as fast as he did earlier. Not worried if I fall off the cliffs to my right. At least that wouldn't end in jail. Just death.

I take the next curve and then it dips down to a steep hill. I reach the top and see lights. "Shit!" I hiss when I see three cop cars. They must have tried to follow Cole, but he lost them. One is sitting on the right side, its ass almost falling off the cliff. The second, parked in the oncoming lane, faces me since the road is only two lanes. And the third is driving straight for me.

He comes to a quick stop on his side, and I have a moment of panic. Do I stop? Just pretend like I was speeding? Or do I gun it and try to outrun them? Maybe they don't know I'm involved in whatever Cole did.

I get my answer when the cop who is stopped on the cliff gets out and throws something in the road. A spike strip. *Fuck!* They know I'm involved. Even if I stop, they'll question me. Then I'll have four other guys on my ass for turning Cole in.

I gun it. I get right up to the spikes and swerve to the left. The driver's side of the car barely misses the cop car that sits there, but it doesn't miss the side of the mountain, and it rips off the mirror.

I laugh. Cole will not be happy about that. I look in the rearview mirror to see them jumping in their cars, but they're never gonna catch me. They had all their eggs in one basket, hoping I'd hit those spikes. Too bad for them.

I pull into town and punch in the address that Cole gave me. He's called me four times, and I've ignored them all. Let him sweat it if I got caught and turned him in.

I pull down a gravel road and look around seeing nothing but darkness. I shut off my headlights, not wanting to bring attention to me and the car even though he has a loud exhaust on this thing. It's not easy to hide.

I squint as I drive two miles an hour, not wanting to hit a tree or a person, until I see lights up ahead.

I speed up. As I get closer, I see a metal barn-like structure. The door swings open and out walks Cole followed by four others.

Of course! This night just keeps getting better and better. I gun it, then pull the e-brake, bringing the rear end around to stop in front of them. Dust from the gravel flies and all but Cole lift their hands to wave it away.

I open the door and jump out, slamming it shut behind me. "What in the fuck was that, Cole?" I demand.

He stands there, his blue eyes narrowed on me. His legs wide and hands in the front pockets of his black jeans. He still wears his black hoodie, but the hood is back.

"What the fuck?" I look to my right to see Deke, staring down at me with wide eyes and mouth opened. "You let cemetery girl help you?" he asks in surprise.

The other three look back and forth between Cole and me, trying to figure out what the hell is going on and who the hell I am.

My chest rises and falls fast, my heart racing. "You almost got me arrested," I snap.

"You should have kept up," he says.

My eyes bug out. "Kept up? I didn't know you were going to steal a car," I snap. He just stares at me. That look of hatred on his face. He should be thanking me for not turning him in. "Take me home," I demand.

"Deke." He looks at him. "Give her a ride home."

What? "No!" I say, taking a step toward Cole. "You take me—"

"Gladly," Deke says, interrupting me and takes a step toward me. I shut my mouth and take three back. He stares down at me with a smile on his handsome face, but the light shining down on us from the side of the barn makes him look crooked. Or maybe it's the fact that I know just how truly twisted he is.

"I'll just take your car," I say with a smile, and he stops walking away. His back still toward me. Then I look down at it and smile. "I knocked off the mirror."

"You what?" he snaps, turning to face me.

I give him the biggest fuck you smile I can. "I ran into the cops, and they threw a spike strip out." His brows rise. "I was able to dodge it but hit the side of the mountain. It knocked off your mirror."

He fists his hands down by his sides while Deke laughs. The other three still stand around, not knowing what is happening.

"Who is this girl?" I think it's Kellan who asks softly. I can't remember who Shelby said was who.

"I'm Austin." I answer his question when neither Deke nor Cole makes a move to do so. "Austin Lowes."

All their heads snap to look at Cole. And Deke looks down at his feet, but I don't miss his jaw hardening. Cole stares at me for a long moment as silence falls around us. And I feel like I'm back in the cemetery with him and Deke. Like he's trying to think of his next move.

Is he gonna stab me this time? Let Deke shoot me?

Finally, he looks away from me and to Deke. "Take her home," he orders and then turns, giving us all his back. He walks into the barn, letting the door shut behind him.

"Let's go home, baby," Deke says, walking over to me.

"No …"

He grabs my upper arm and squeezes, making me cry out as his fingers dig into my skin. The other guys turn their backs on me and walk into the same door as Cole. Deke drags me across the gravel and over to the side of the building where a black Range Rover sits. He tosses me in the passenger seat and then climbs in. I press my body against the door.

He chuckles. "I'm not the one you should be afraid of, baby."

"What does that mean?" I demand, pissed off over what Cole put me through tonight.

"It means …" He starts his SUV. "That Cole is the only one who decides if you live or die. Not me."

CHAPTER SEVEN
COLE

I rip my hoodie off and then my black t-shirt. I toss them both to the floor and raise my fists in front of me. I start bouncing around and hit the punching bag that hangs from the rafter.

I hear the door open and then Kellan's voice. "Cole, what is going on?" he asks.

"I'm handling it," I say, hitting the bag again.

"That's not what it looked like from where we stood," Shane argues.

I snort.

"She's Bruce's daughter—"

"Yes. I know who she is!" I snap, interrupting Kellan. I drop my hands and turn to face them. "I'm well aware of whose daughter she is."

Kellan looks like he's seen a ghost, but Shane smiles. "She's perfect."

I let out a growl. "She's mine!"

He doesn't even try to hide his smile at my possessiveness. "No. I mean she's perfect for what we need."

Kellan shakes his head. "Absolutely not. I'm not gonna be responsible for her."

"Between the five us, she would be fine."

"Look at what happened tonight," Kellan snaps, arguing with Shane.

"Were you not paying attention?" Shane asks. "She managed to get away from the cops. And she didn't even have any help." He points at me. "Cole left her to fend for herself." He smiles as if he's proud of her. "And I must say, I'm impressed."

I, however, want to strangle her. She fucked up my M4. I just bought that car. And the cops saw her, which brings up another thought. Why were the cops there? We disabled the alarm, and no one was around for miles. That warehouse is there for a reason; no one is ever in that part of the town. Barnes is a little town full of elderly people who live in retirement homes. Who would have seen us to call the authorities on us?

"I say we bring her in. See how she does." Shane nods to himself. "Challenge her. She seems like the kind who wouldn't back down from a fight."

"And?" Kellan asks.

"And what?" Shane looks at him.

"When she gets us caught and we're all in jail, then what?"

"That won't happen."

"How can you promise that?" Kellan snaps.

Shane looks back at me. "Because she won't turn on someone she loves."

I look at Bennett, the only one who has kept his mouth shut this entire time. He meets my eyes, and my chest tightens at the look in them. "You know damn well that she would be the best piece no one ever saw coming," he says.

My phone vibrates in my pocket, and I pull it out to see it's a message.

Deke: The princess was dropped off. Unharmed. You're welcome.

I put my cell back in my pocket, close my eyes, and let out a long breath. "You guys know what this means, right?" I ask.

When silence falls over the room, I look them all in the eyes before I speak. "We gotta throw a party."

AUSTIN

Shark: Party tomorrow night at my house. Be there at ten.

Cole sent me that last night while I was in the bathtub. As soon as Deke dropped me off, I jumped in the bath to clean off. To wash the day away. I never responded, but I don't think he expected me to. He had summoned me, and he knew I'd show because well, what else do I have to do? And I wanna know what those boys are up to.

Three had looked at me like I was a disease. Cole looked like he wanted to kill me, and Deke looked amused.

First, they kill a guy, then they steal a car? Like what is their deal? Was the car one of their dares? Shelby had mentioned how they were always getting into trouble.

And she had called them *Great White Sharks*? *In and out of the water*. That's why I put his number under ***Shark***. I could use them on my side at school. It's the second semester of my senior year at a new place. And the town is a stuck-up, wealthy city. I'm sure all the students are little brats, so I could use someone on my side who others are afraid to cross. Or five someones. Even if I'm afraid of them too. Deke said that my fate was in Cole's hands. So he runs the pack. That was obvious, though. As long as I stay on his good side, I should be okay.

"You look so pretty."

I look over to the chair next to me that Lilly occupies. She had stayed the night with us. Then this morning Celeste had asked Cole if she could tag along with us to the salon to get her hair washed along with her nails painted. I found it odd that she asks Cole for permission and not their father, but I shrugged it off. Shelby had told me that Cole is the one who pretty much raises her.

"Thank you," I tell her with a smile. "You look very beautiful."

She holds up her hands, showing me her little fingers. "Cole's favorite color is pink."

"Then he is going to love your nails."

She nods. "That's why I picked this color."

Celeste comes up to us, placing her cell in her pocket. "Well, Lilly, I just spoke with Cole. I had to beg and promise to have you in bed by eight thirty, but he said you could spend one more night."

"Yay." She throws both of her hands above her head.

It's probably because he is throwing a party. Celeste looks at me. "Oh, wow, Austin. I love your hair."

I look at myself in the mirror. "Really? I figured it was different."

"It's beautiful." She grabs my shoulders and leans over to whisper in my ear. "He's gonna love it."

I frown. "I didn't do it for a *he.*"

She gives me a small smile and pats my shoulder. "Whatever you say, dear."

I look back at myself in the mirror and sigh. I guess it can't hurt to try to impress him. I mean, he's a boy, after all. All men think with their dicks. "Where are we going after we leave here?" I ask her.

"Wherever you want," she says simply.

I smile. "I need something to wear tonight. Something red."

She nods her head as a woman comes up behind her. "Celeste?"

She spins around and opens her arms. "Ellie."

"What are you up to?" her friend asks as she pulls away.

"I'm out with my stepdaughter." She turns and gestures toward me. "Ellie, this is Austin. Austin, meet my friend Ellie."

Her friends smile drops off her face as her eyes meet mine, and she looks back at Celeste. "Stepdaughter?" she asks quietly as if I can't hear.

Celeste nods and gives a soft smile. "Yes. She is spending the rest of her senior year with us."

"Oh," She turns back to face me. "It's nice to meet you." She nods and then dismisses me, turning back to whisper to Celeste. She places her arm in the crook of Ellie's, and they walk off.

I turn and smile at a confused Lilly. "How about an Icee? I saw a cookie place downstairs that had them."

She nods excitedly as her brown eyes light up. "I like the Coke ones."

"What? No way. Me too."

She giggles, and I laugh, ignoring Celeste and her friend who are no doubt talking about me and where in the hell I came from. No one in this town probably even knows Bruce Lowes had a daughter except for the people I met back when I was seven. And most of them are probably long gone by now.

It's ten thirty when I finally pull up to Cole's house. Deke had messaged me the address an hour ago. And I tried not to let it bug me that Cole gave him my number. Like the bastard was too busy to even message me himself.

The house is just as big as my father's house, but I'm not surprised. I park the bright red BMW my father bought me in the front and get out. The evening chill making me shudder. During the daytime, it gets up to mid-fifties, but it gets cold at night. Thankfully, that gives me a reason to wear long sleeves to cover my stitches.

I bought a thin deep red sweater that hangs off the shoulders with a black, tank top to wear underneath. I paired it with black skinny jeans and black high heels. And topped off the look with red lipstick. I hate to admit that I tried a little harder than I would have if not for Cole. And then that pissed me off. But of course, I didn't change. Instead, I hung out at my house for thirty more minutes, knowing I would be later than he stated.

I walk into the house, and "Fuck Away the Pain" by Divide the Day pounds through speakers that hang on the walls. Kids of all ages crowd the foyer and hallways. Some even look old enough for college. I scan the crowd for Deke or Cole, not knowing what they have planned for me. Once again, I'm suspicious about why I was even invited.

I make my way into the large open kitchen and find red Solo cups along with bottles covering the countertops. I pick up the Fireball, pour a small amount into a cup, and toss it back, needing some courage to face them once again. Then I do another one.

"Hi," a girl says, coming up to me.

"Hello," I say with a head nod. She's got bleach blond hair and big blue eyes with pouty lips and a small face. She looks like one of those Instagram girls who have millions of followers—absolutely flawless.

"I've never seen you before." She holds out her right hand. "I'm Becky."

"Austin," I say. "And I just moved here."

"Oh, how exciting," she says, grabbing a Solo cup and filling it with rum and Coke. "Are you going to Collins High?"

I nod. "Yep."

"I'm a senior. How about you?"

"Same," I say and pour myself another shot of Fireball.

"I wonder if we'll have any classes together."

I secretly hope we do because she seems nice enough. Swallowing another shot, I look around the massive kitchen and the bodies that fill it. "Who throws a party on a Monday night?" I ask myself more than her.

"Cole Reynolds." She rolls her eyes. "He and the Great White Sharks do whatever they want, whenever they want." Then she smiles. "But they do throw some awesome parties."

"Where are their parents?" I ask.

"Never around. They are all socialites in this town with big careers. Always busy and not enough time for their children."

"I see." They're like my father. Maybe that's why Cole takes care of Lilly so much.

"Where are you—"

"Austin?" a demanding male voice interrupts her.

We both turn to see one of the guys standing in the entryway to the kitchen. I can't tell you if it's Kellan or Shane, but his narrowed dark eyes are on mine. Everyone stares at him as he glares at me.

I arch a brow in question.

"Cole is looking for you," he snaps. "Let's go."

I turn my back to him and roll my eyes, but when they meet Becky, hers are round in surprise. "What?" I ask.

She just shakes her head. I grab the bottle of Fireball, ignoring my cup, and walk out after the warden who was sent to fetch the servant.

"Shane?"

"Kellan," he growls.

Okay then. I take a sip of the Fireball as we walk past kids in the hallway. He takes me up a flight of stairs. My heels sink into the rich beige carpet. He comes to a stop at a door, and I go to walk in, but he blocks me. I look up at him. "I don't want you here," he states.

I smile. Finally, someone who feels the same as me. "Well, that makes two of us."

His brown eyes drop to my chest and slowly run down over my legs, and when his eyes meet mine again, there's a challenge in them that I'm not sure how to take.

He reaches behind him and opens the door. We step into a dimly lit room. There's a couch to my left. A few chaise lounge chairs ahead of me, facing a TV that hangs on the wall. There's a basketball game playing, but the sound is off. "Gravity" by Papa Roach plays through the speakers but not loud enough to where you can't hear yourself think.

"Found her," Kellan calls out to the room.

Three heads turn toward me as the guys stand over by a pool table in the corner. Each one has a girl under their arm. None of them are Cole.

I lift the bottle to take another sip, enjoying the burn of the alcohol.

"About time." I hear his voice, and my skin breaks out in goosebumps.

I look to my right to see him sitting on another chaise lounge with his right hand propped behind his head and his legs crossed at the ankles. He's dressed in a pair of blue jeans, a white t-shirt, and a pair of Nikes. Simple yet still looking just as frightening as he did on the steps of the church. His blue eyes take me in as he looks me up and down twice. They linger on my chest, and I bite my bottom lip. When his eyes meet mine, he stands.

I take a step back. My heart picks up speed, still very well aware of what this guy is capable of.

"Girls, leave," he orders. They all whine in unison, but the guys pull away from them and push them out the door, shutting me inside with them.

"Why am I here?" I ask, wanting to get this over with.

He takes the bottle from my hand and brings it to his lips, taking a big gulp. His Adam's apple working as he swallows.

I cross my arms over my chest, trying to look unaffected. But I'm having trouble breathing.

"We've been thinking …" Cole says, rubbing his chin.

"We want you to be part of our group." Deke finishes his sentence.

I look among the five of them and start laughing nervously. "You're joking, right?"

"Not one bit," Deke says, shaking his head.

"No thanks," I say and turn to the door. I twist the handle and start to pull it open, but a hand slaps on the door over my head, holding it shut.

I jump back to look at Cole. He leans against it casually, getting comfortable and blocking my only exit. "It wasn't an offer, Austin."

My eyes narrow on him. "What makes you think I want anything to do with you guys?"

"Deke," Cole says, lifting the bottle to his lips again.

I spin around to see Deke step up to us, his phone in his hand facing Cole and me. A video plays, and it's of me driving Cole's car away from the warehouse after he stole the red car.

"How did you get that?" I demand.

Deke just chuckles, placing the phone in his pocket. "I don't kiss and tell, baby."

My eyes narrow on him calling me *baby*. I turn back to face Cole. "You're blackmailing me. Again."

He shrugs carelessly. "You can call it whatever you want."

"I'm calling it what it is," I snap. "You know damn well that I had no idea what you had planned."

He pushes off the door and leans down, his face inches from mine. I can smell the cinnamon on his lips and can't help the shudder that courses through me. "I dare you to prove it."

"You son of—"

"In order to join," Deke interrupts me. "You have to pass a test," he says, crossing his arms over his broad chest.

"I'm not interested."

"Initiation." He corrects himself.

"I don't want to be involved with whatever fucked-up shit you guys are in." *How many different ways do I have to say it?*

"Just let her go," Kellan says. But no one listens to him.

Deke continues. "You have to fuck one of us while we all watch."

My heart starts to pound at his words. And my eyes widen when he takes a step toward me.

This is a joke. It has to be.

He arches a brow in challenge when I just stand there staring at him. "You want me, baby? I'm ready." He licks his lips as his blue eyes settle on my legs. Then he reaches down to his jeans and unbuttons them.

He's serious! I immediately look at Cole.

His eyes hold their usual anger as they glare down at me, but a slow, devious smile spreads across his face, and the guys start laughing. "Well, there's your answer, man," one of them calls out from behind me.

My jaw tightens. "I don't want to—"

"Leave us," Cole orders, interrupting me. And like the trained sheep they are, they all walk out. I can still hear their laughter as they walk down the hall, the door slowly shutting behind them.

I plop down on one of the chairs, trying to slow my racing heart. "You can't force my hand, Cole. Not with this."

He walks over to where I sit. Reaching out, he runs his busted knuckles along my cheek. I swat his hand away, afraid of what will come out of my mouth if he touches me.

His hand grips my hair and yanks me to stand. I cry out as he shoves my back into the closed door, making it rattle from the force. He towers over me, pushing his body into mine. I'm panting while he holds me still. He dips his head to whisper in my ear. "Are you a virgin, Austin?"

"No," I growl. My hands come up to push him off me, but he grabs them and pins them above my head. I whimper, and my thighs tighten.

"That's a shame." He sighs, and his breath skims across my skin, making me shudder. "I like to take pretty, innocent things and destroy them."

"You're sick," I say, panting.

He chuckles but doesn't deny it. "But that doesn't make you want me any less. I saw the way you stared at me in the car. The way you licked your lips when I thought about kissing you. The way you whispered my name. How you stared at me when I got out of the pool. And let's not forget the way you allowed me to touch you last night. Tell me, were you disappointed when I didn't throw you on the bed and fuck you right then?" I moan. "I bet you're wet right now."

"Cole." I growl his name, not wanting him to see how right he is.

But he ignores me. "You wore red for me again, sweetheart. You wanted my attention. And you got it. Now what are you gonna do with it?"

CHAPTER EIGHT

COLE

My body presses hers into the door, and I stare down at her, silently daring her to tell me to go to hell. She needs to. I'm not good for her. I shouldn't be anywhere near her, let alone touching her or thinking about fucking her right here. Because the only thing on my mind right now is pushing her down to the floor, spreading her legs, and burying myself inside her all night. Fuck the guys. Fuck the party. And fuck the fact that she hates me. Hate sex is always the best.

I lower my head to her neck, loving the smell of cherries, and whisper, "What's it gonna be, sweetheart?"

Her breathing is ragged, her body is soft, and my cock is hard. I just need her to say the words. "You want me, just admit it."

She stiffens against me, my words finally getting to her. "Get off me, Cole." They weren't as forceful as she meant for them to be, letting me know she's struggling. That's good enough for me.

I smile and when I let go of her hands, she shoves me backward. I go willingly to allow her space. My eyes roam over her hair. She changed it—the dark brown softly fades to blond at the bottom. The best of both worlds. It looks great on her.

She straightens her red sweater, and I love that she wore it for me. "But you don't have a choice about joining us."

She stomps her foot. "Why does it matter so much to you?"

Because we need you. "You'll have fun."

"I'll get arrested. Possibly die."

I smile. She's not far off. "Just give it a try."

"Why do I feel like people don't just *give it a try*?"

I step into her once again, and she looks up at me through long, dark lashes. "Do I need to remind you that—"

"That I don't have a choice." She cuts me off.

"See. Was that so hard?"

She rolls her eyes, turns around, and yanks the door open. I grab her upper arm and pull her to a stop. Leaning down, I whisper into her ear. "Tonight, you belong to me." She gives me a side glare, and I give her a threatening smile. "Understood?"

"Understood," she agrees through gritted teeth.

I take her hand in mine, and we walk out together. We make our way down to the kitchen, passing the partygoers. Some call out my name, giving me a head nod, and others lift their drinks. I ignore them. They came to kiss my ass, and I'm not in the mood to indulge them. Instead, I'm trying to figure out how to get away from her. I shouldn't want her. Not like this. Not at all.

But this is part of it. The guys agreed on it. They said if we have her join, then we need to show her off. Or else we wouldn't have had the party. It's all a formality.

"Hey, Becky," she says to a blonde as we enter the kitchen.

The girl looks at me and then at Austin. "Hi," she says softly. Her eyes shoot back to mine.

I ignore her. Letting go of Austin's hand, I grab a red Solo cup and make her a drink without even bothering to ask what she likes. She'll drink whatever I give her.

Once I finish her drink, I make myself one. "Here," I say, handing it to her.

She takes it without even looking at me. Her eyes remain on the girl as they chat about pointless shit.

Deke stands over in the corner with a blond bimbo under his arm. Shane sits at the table playing poker with some guys. And Kellan stands over by the entrance with his tongue down some redhead's throat. I don't know where the hell Bennett went.

I walk around the breakfast bar and put my arm around Austin's shoulders. She doesn't even acknowledge me. But the girl, Becky, looks up at me wide-eyed and then back at Austin.

What the fuck is he doing? Is going through her mind at the moment. Because I never show any affection to women. I ignore them until I have them naked in my bed. Of course, Austin doesn't know that, so she wouldn't understand what I'm doing right now. But I'm letting everyone here know that she is mine! That way, when she starts doing her dares, no one will turn her in if they see her. I can't risk getting my ass burned because of her.

I take a sip of my mixed drink as "Love the Way You Hate Me" by Like A Storm plays through the speakers of the house, and I smile. *She's gonna hate me, all right. And I'm gonna love it.*

AUSTIN

I take a big gulp of my drink, and Becky's eyes bore into mine. I don't think she's blinked once in the past twenty minutes, which is impossible.

"Are you okay?" I finally ask her.

Her eyes shoot behind me, and I look over my shoulder to see Cole, looking down at his phone. Bastard!

"How do you know Cole?" she asks.

"Just met him." I reach out and take her drink from her hand. She doesn't argue. I take a gulp of it and hiss in a breath. Hers is strong. Just how I like them.

Her eyes widen. "Are you serious?"

I nod, taking another drink. I'm starting to feel lightheaded. "Why?"

"Just be careful," she warns.

I look back at him over my shoulder again, and he leans against the countertop. His arms over his chest as he looks over at who I think is Shane. His defined jaw is sharp, and his eyes narrowed. He always looks so angry. Dark. But that is what draws me to him. He's so mysterious. I wanna know what goes on in his mind.

I lift the drink and take another swallow but pull it away when I see it's empty. "I drank it all," I say, handing it back to her.

She laughs and pours herself another one.

"You know them well?"

She nods and hands me a new full drink. "Been going to school with them since kindergarten."

"Girlfriend?" I ask.

Her laughter grows. "No."

I nod. Figures. Guys like Cole don't settle down. They don't allow girls to get close enough to see who they really are.

I take another drink and lick my lips. They're starting to tingle. He pushes off the counter and turns to face Shane, giving me a profile view. His arms still crossed over his chest, he stands to his full height, and I watch the way his jeans hang on his narrow hips and remember what his body looked like when he got out of my father's pool. I bite my bottom lip before taking another drink.

"Girl, you've got it bad." Becky laughs.

I whip around to look at her. But even I can't deny it. "I'm treading water," I admit. Guys like Cole Reynolds are why smart girls turn stupid. It's embarrassing on so many levels but understandable.

I mean, I fucking hate the guy, and I still want him to take me to his room. That alone tells me how unbelievably stupid I am.

She takes a step toward me, closing the small space, and whispers, "These waters are infested with sharks. And you are bleeding." She looks over my shoulder at Cole, then back at me. "But there are worse ways to die."

I take another big gulp of her drink and thoughts of how he held me against the door upstairs make my thighs tighten. And that first night in the cemetery … or when we were in his car and he was telling me about Eli's older sister. My heart starts to beat faster when the words he said to me upstairs come back to me. *And let's not forget the way you allowed me to touch you last night. Tell me, were you disappointed when I didn't throw you on the bed and fuck you right then?*

My heart starts to pound faster at the thought of him doing just that.

I finally nod at Becky as she stares at me expectantly, unable to deny that. I'm bleeding all right. I take another gulp. "What do I do?" I ask her.

She gives me a big smile and takes the drink from my hand. "Take advantage of it while you can." Then she tosses it back.

CHAPTER NINE

COLE

"I understand why you're doing it, but are you sure you want to do it?" Shane asks me.

I nod. "Not a doubt in my mind."

"Okay." He turns, giving me his back, and walks out of the kitchen.

I move to the kitchen island to make my third drink when Kellan comes up to me. They're all going to come to me one by one. Well, except for Deke. He knows my mind is made up. And none of the others are gonna be able to change it. They should know that by now. "I think we should call it quits," he growls.

I arch a brow. "Why is that?"

He sighs heavily. "She's a liability. What if one of us gets in trouble because of her?"

I shake my head. "Won't happen. We'll let her take the fall before we go down with her."

"How can you guarantee that? She could roll over on us."

I slap his shoulder. "Don't worry, okay? I've got your back."

He stares at me as if he doesn't believe me, but I give him the drink I just made, and he downs it in a few gulps. His nerves showing.

I'm making myself a new drink since I just gave mine away when my side is bumped and two arms wrap around my waist. "What the …?" I look down to see Austin standing beside me with her eyes closed and a big smile on her face.

My first thought is to shove her off me. The second is to lean down and kiss her hair.

I do neither.

Instead, I stand staring down at her like she has two heads. "Austin?" I finally say. "What are you doing?"

She looks up at me, and her big green eyes look glazed over. *She's tipsy.* Great! I've only made her two drinks, and neither one were strong. For this very reason. I didn't wanna put up with a drunk girl. *She had a bottle of Fireball in her hand when she entered the game room.* Shit!

"I know you want to kiss me. Go ahead," she says softly.

I laugh nervously. She can't read me that easily. "You had your chance upstairs. You passed." *Good choice.*

She leans up on her tiptoes, her mouth next to my ear, and whispers. "I dare you."

My body stiffens. She doesn't understand what those words mean to me. How they give me a pass to do whatever the fuck I want. As if I needed that.

I turn in her arms, so I'm facing her, and slide my right hand into her hair. Her eyes close, and those perfect red lips release a moan. The soft sound goes straight to my cock. "You don't know what you're doing," I say against her lips.

Her eyes open and look up into mine, and her hands slip up the back of my shirt. I feel eyes on us in the packed kitchen, but I ignore them. She has all my attention. And this is what I wanted, right? For everyone to know that she belongs to me. A message so no other guy even attempts to take her from me.

Her nails drag down my back, and I imagine her doing that while I fuck her up in my room. Just her and me. "I know exactly what I'm doing," she purrs. "Now. I dare you to kiss me."

I smile because I'm gonna make her wait for it. I tilt her head back and run my lips along her jawline. And down her neck. She smells like heaven and sex all wrapped in one small package that I just wanna rip open.

A shiver runs through her body, and she moans, "Cole."

"You asked for it, Austin. Remember that." I nip at her neck, and her breath hitches. Her nails dig into my back, but only now, she's pulling me toward her. Needing me closer. I agree.

I let go of her hair, grab her thighs, and lift her off the floor. Spinning us around, I set her ass on the kitchen island. I hear the faint sound of bottles being knocked over, but neither one of us pays attention to them. Both of my hands return to fisting her hair. I yank her head back as she lets out a whimper, and then my lips are on hers. She opens for me, and I dive in. My lips on hers aggressively. My tongue in her mouth with determination, and she tastes like cinnamon.

So fucking good!

I growl into her mouth, and she moans into mine. Her hips grind into me, and I know she can feel how hard I am for her. 'Cause she pulls her lips from mine and pants. "Fuck me, Cole."

AUSTIN

My heart pounds in my chest, and I try to suck in a calming breath. I just asked him to fuck me.

I'm so dead. And so drunk.

But I want him. Why do I want him? He's done nothing but try to get me arrested. Blackmailed me. Over and over yet I just asked him to fuck me.

Is it the danger? The way he touches me? The way he speaks to me? I wasn't lying when I told him I'm not a virgin. But that doesn't mean I have a lot of experience either.

He pulls away from me, causing my legs to fall from around his waist. His blue eyes look me up and down, and then he turns, giving me his back, and walks out of the packed kitchen. Denying me.

Shame washes over me at what I just did. He wants me dead. Not for sex.

"Whoa," Becky says, fanning herself as she sidles up beside me. "That was intense."

I jump off the island and grab the bottle of Fireball. I take a gulp and then shove kids out of way who stare at me like I'm some kind of joke. I push a couple making out in the hall and make my way toward the back door.

I need some fresh air.

I stumble my way out to a gazebo. The night air hits my face, and I take another drink.

I plop down and look over the large backyard. An Olympic-size swimming pool sits to my left, and I wonder why Cole and Lilly were over at my father's house swimming today when he has his own. Looking at my right, I see tennis courts lit up and kids drinking from kegs.

"There you are," Becky says, coming out the back door.

I blow the hair out of my face. I just wanna be alone.

"Mind if I join you?"

"Not at all," I lie.

She plops down beside me. "Wanna hit?" She offers me a joint.

"Thanks," I say and put it to my lips. I take a long drag. The smoke fills my lungs, and I lean my head back, holding my breath. Then let it out. And hand it back to her.

"So you and Cole … I get it now."

"I hate him," I say without thought. My body doesn't understand that.

She laughs and takes a long drag from the joint and passes it back to me. "You guys weren't fooling anyone, honey."

I take a drag. "What do you mean you guys?"

"Cole doesn't kiss and tell. Well, he doesn't kiss and show either." I arch a brow. "He's a manwhore, don't get me wrong, but he is very discreet about who he takes to bed. I thought he was going to lay you down on the island and do you right then and there for all of us to watch." She chuckles.

"Me too," I say honestly.

"Not gonna lie. I wouldn't have looked away."

I throw my head back, laughing. "Well, you told me to take advantage of it while I can." I take another hit of the joint. "I intended to do just that."

"I didn't mean right then." She laughs. "But I'm sure everyone enjoyed the show."

"That wasn't a show. That was pathetic," I say, and she chuckles. I take another hit.

"Hey, girls," a man says as he enters the gazebo. He's got blond spiky hair and a set of soft brown eyes. His black long-sleeve t-shirt and dark faded jeans show off his large, muscular size.

"Hey, Bryan," Becky greets him.

He offers us a Solo cup. "I brought you girls a drink."

"No thanks," I say, holding up the joint between my fingers.

But Becky takes a drink and then passes it to me. "Vodka," she says.

"Okay, one drink." Vodka is my favorite. My mother's boyfriend always had it at the house, and when you're in the mood to get drunk, you drink what is available.

"Becky, Christopher is looking for you. Something about you owing him a shot for some bet you guys made." She rolls her eyes but jumps up and walks off with a wave of her hand, leaving me alone with the new stranger.

He takes her seat next to me. "Where's Cole?"

"Why the hell would I know?" I ask, wishing the weed would kick in. So I lean back against the wood, relaxing.

"Isn't he your boyfriend?"

"No," I say quickly.

"That's not what it looked like."

I let out a sigh. "Why does everyone care what we were doing minutes ago?"

"Because I thought you would want to start your year out right by being on the arm of the hottest guy in school."

I refrain from rolling my eyes. Cole may be a dick, but he doesn't say corny lines like that. *No. He just tries to blackmail you for murder.* "And who is that?" I indulge him.

"Me." He grabs the Solo cup from my hand and takes a drink of the vodka. He goes to hand it back to me but drops it.

I stand quickly, gasping as the cold liquid spills all over my lap.

"I'm so sorry," He jumps up. And then his hands are on me. I go to move backward, but my knees hit the bench.

"It's okay,'" I say, but he pushes into me, causing me to fall back down onto my ass. My head even with the zipper on his jeans.

He stands over me, and he leans in and sniffs my hair. "What the ...?"

"Bryan!"

His voice interrupts what I was about to say.

Bryan sighs heavily and turns around to face Cole but blocks me so I can't get up from the bench.

"Just what the fuck do you think you're doing?" Cole demands.

"What you didn't have the balls to do earlier," Bryan answers, crossing his arms over his chest.

Cole gives me a quick once-over before his narrowed eyes go back to Bryan as he storms across the backyard toward us.

I look away from him. I don't need him to save me. I reach up and shove Bryan out of my way. When I stand, Bryan turns to face me. "Let's go." He grabs my arm.

"I'm not ..."

"Let her go!" Cole growls at him and yanks him forward. Bryan pulls me in the process, and we all fall down the two stairs at the entrance to the gazebo.

I roll onto my back as I look up and see Cole punch Bryan in the face.

"Austin? Are you okay?" Becky asks as she runs over to me.

"Fine," I snap, getting up. She reaches up to pull the grass out of my hair, but I shake her off as I turn to face the guys.

The backyard starts to fill with people. Deke and Shane run out the back door.

Cole is straddling Bryan, punching him in the face. Bryan manages to block it and then land a punch to Cole's chin, knocking him off.

Bryan goes to hit him while he's down, but Cole lifts his right leg, kicking him in the stomach. Bryan stumbles back, and Cole jumps up in time to hit him in the face. Blood runs from Bryan's mouth, and then Cole hits him again. Bryan stumbles back. Before he can recover, Cole hits him again. When Bryan falls to the ground this time, he doesn't get back up.

People gather around the backyard with their phones out, recording the fight. Deke and Shane both just stand there, looking at their friend but waiting for I don't know what. They let him beat Jeff almost to death. Maybe they don't get in his way until the job is almost done. I shake my head as I walk past them toward the house. *It's time for me to go.*

I've already got my phone out of my pocket and ordering an Uber when Becky comes up beside me. "I'm going home," I tell her. "Wanna share an Uber?" I know she is just as drunk as I am. And she smoked too.

"Absolutely," she says.

I walk into the house just to be pulled back. I spin around to see who placed their hands on me and come face to face with Cole. His chest is heaving, and his forehead is covered in a thin layer of sweat. He has a cut on his upper lip.

"Where are you going?" he demands.

"Home." I spin around, giving him my back, but he yanks me back again.

I turn around and shove him backward. He doesn't budge. "Stop putting your hands on me, Cole," I yell.

"Austin …"

"You had your chance. You passed." I throw his same words back at him.

His jaw sharpens, but this time when I turn around, he doesn't try to stop me.

CHAPTER TEN
COLE

I pull up to Bruce Lowes's house in Austin's car that she left at my father's house last night.

Deke pulls up behind me in his Range Rover. "Dude, you know she's still gonna be pissed at you, right?"

"Yep."

He snorts. "What are you gonna do about it?"

"Nothing."

He jogs to catch up to me as I climb their front steps. "Seriously? We need her."

"She doesn't have to be happy with me to do what I say. She's hated me up until this point, and I've still managed to …"

"Blackmail her," he finishes.

I don't respond.

"Don't you think it would be easier to have her compliant?" he asks, and I turn to face him as we stand at the front door. He runs his hand through his disheveled hair. His blue eyes bloodshot from all the drinks we had last night. After she left, he and I locked ourselves in the game room and drank until we woke up this morning with pounding headaches. "I mean, she's already afraid of us. Especially me." He gives me a cruel smile. "But last night, that was a different side of her. A side you can work with. Fear is a good motivator but so is seduction." He shrugs. "And it's not like it would be hard for you to fuck her. She's hot."

My jaw clenches, and I turn to face the door. This conversation is over. I knock on the door, and Celeste answers in a yellow sundress and a smile on her face. "Hey, boys. Please, come in."

"Celeste." Deke greets her.

"Where's Lilly?" I ask, wanting to get the hell out of here.

She frowns. "She's in the media room with Austin. They are watching *Cinderella*."

My hands fist. I don't like Lilly getting close to Austin. Because she isn't gonna be here long. "Austin's car is in the driveway," I say and then toss her the keys. I hear them hit the tile because Celeste was not quick enough to catch them as I walk off. And me too big of a dick just to hand them to her.

I walk up the stairs and pass Austin's bedroom, continuing to the end of the hall, and open the door to the media room.

The only light comes from the big screen on the wall. I don't see them, but I hear Lilly's voice. "Do fairy tales exist?"

"Depends on what you consider a fairy tale," Austin tells her.

"What do you mean?"

I walk around the circular couch and stand in the shadows as they lie on the fluffy cushions. A bowl of popcorn sits between Austin's legs. Lilly's head on Austin's chest. They both look straight ahead at the big screen.

"Well, not all girls are princesses in need of a knight to save them," Austin tells her. "Some save themselves."

"Belle didn't have a prince. She had a beast."

Austin smiles. "She did."

"But in the end, he turned back into a prince. I liked him better as the beast," Lilly says.

Austin chuckles. "Me too. He was much more appealing. She didn't love him for his looks. She was in love with how he made her feel. Special."

"Has anyone ever made you feel special?" Lilly asks her.

Austin tilts her head to the side. "No."

"I'm sorry," Lilly says softly.

Austin just laughs it off. "You don't need a man to make you feel special, Lilly. You are already special. All on your own. Don't forget that."

Lilly sighs heavily, and they both stare straight ahead at the movie. "What about *Frozen*?" Lilly asks, unable to stay quiet.

"Easy. There was no love story between princess and prince. Only sister love. And it still had a fantastic ending. It also proved that love could be deceiving."

"What is deceiving?" Lilly draws out the word, sounding it out.

"It means he lied to her to get what he wanted."

She nods as if she understands.

Austin pops a piece of popcorn into her mouth. And I find myself backing out of the room to let them finish their movie. Deke's words run through my mind. *Fear is a good motivator but so is seduction.*

Deke and I stand in the kitchen with Celeste. They're talking about his sister, Shelby, when Lilly enters. "Where's Austin?" I ask her.

She smiles up at me, not catching my tone. I have a *don't fuck with me* attitude today that I can't hide even if I wanted to. "Upstairs in her room."

Before anyone can stop me, I make my way back up the stairs, and like last time, I don't stop to knock. I barge right on in. She sits on her bed but jumps up as I enter. "Jesus Christ, Cole. Don't you ever knock?"

I round the bed, and she takes a step back. We both stand there, staring at one another. My heart pounds in my chest, and my mind wanders to her and me. And what we could be doing if I wasn't so fucked up. If I didn't hate her father so much.

"What do you want, Cole?" she demands. Her face is free of makeup. Her hair down and over her shoulders. She wears a white t-shirt and cotton shorts. She looks like she just rolled out of bed, and I hate that it wasn't with me. "Cole …"

I take her face in my hands, and I press my lips to hers. Taking what I fucking want as I have always done.

She shoves me away as I knew she would. Now that she is no longer drunk, things are back to normal. That's why I didn't take her up on her offer last night. "What do you want from me?" she yells, her anger rising as easily as mine does.

"Isn't it obvious?"

"No," she snaps.

"Everything."

She lifts her right arm. "You want me to bleed for you? You want me to go to jail for you? You want me to fucking kill for you? Jesus, Cole."

"I want all of those things. And more," I say with a nod, and her eyes narrow on me like I'm playing some sick game. *She's not wrong.* "Don't you see, Austin? I'm that guy who wants to take everything from you. I want to destroy you. I want to hurt you."

"You already have," she says through gritted teeth.

I smile. She's referring to her stitches from where I cut her. I could make her bleed to death for me without a fucking knife. "You have no idea what I can do to you. You have no idea what I'm capable of. I could make you nothing." The thought of destroying her and putting her pieces back as crooked as mine is so fucking strong.

Her jaw sharpens, and then she slaps me.

My hands fist down by my sides at the sting on my face. I hate that I like it. *I've been raised to love a fight.* "I dare you to slap me again," I growl. Testing her.

I expect her to laugh. To call me fucked up but she doesn't. Instead, she does what I say. It was harder than the first, and I find myself pushing her backward, my fists hitting the wall on either side of her head, but she doesn't back down. Not her. She has so much fight in her that it makes her dark green eyes shine. And I love it.

"I'll hit you as many times as you want," she growls, breathing heavily.

"I wanna hit you back." I lie. I don't want to hurt her. Not in the way she thinks. I wanna break her from the inside.

She lifts her chin. "Go ahead. I can take a hit."

"I wanna punish you for burning Jeff's body. I wanna punish you for fucking up my car. And I wanna punish you for how much you make me want you," I tell her. My dick is still hard from that kiss we shared in my kitchen. The thought of fucking her is so strong that it's hard to think about anything else.

"Why?" she asks, her chest rising and falling fast with each breath.

"I told you, sweetheart. I like destroying pretty, innocent things."

Her eyes look up into mine. She searches as if she's trying to decipher my words, but they were honest. There was no hidden meaning.

"Why?" she asks again, and her voice wavers. That fear creeping back into her features.

"Because perfect things don't belong in a fucked-up world." It's that simple.

She swallows. "I'm not perfect."

I lean in, my lips almost touching hers, and her breath hitches. "You are to me." I've never said anything more true to a woman. She is just like me. The fight. The anger. The hate. I see the way she fists her hands when I force her to do something. I see how she rises to every challenge I throw at her. With no warning. And I love that she refuses to back down. Give up. She'll go head to head with me, and in her mind, she feels she has a chance to win. It turns me on so much. She was built for a man like me—a savage.

"Cole," she whispers.

I remove my right hand from the wall and cup her face. She whimpers, and it fuels my desire to make her mine. "I wanna watch tears roll down your beautiful face because I think you're gorgeous when you cry. I wanna see blood on your flawless skin because you look like a priceless work of art. And I wanna look down at you while you're on your knees because you want to please me." My thumb runs over her trembling bottom lip. "I wanna make you a beautiful, broken doll, Austin." Her eyes widen at my confession. "All mine to play with." I look at her parted lips while licking my own. "All mine to fuck." She moans. "All mine to destroy."

She just stares up at me. Her eyes searching mine. When they fall to my lips, I close the small space and kiss her. She doesn't pull away or push me back. Instead, she opens up for me, and I tilt her head, deepening the kiss, stealing her breath away.

I wanna take everything from her. And I know it won't take much to get it. I pull away, and she slowly opens her eyes. "I'll be here to pick you up at seven thirty on Thursday morning."

"What?" she asks, breathlessly.

"You ride with me to and from school," I tell her. "You may not be mine yet, but to everyone else, you already are." Then I walk out, not giving her a chance to argue.

"Ready to go?" I ask, entering the kitchen.

Lilly runs to me, and I pick her up. Deke stands from the table. When we walk outside, I say to him. "Post the video."

AUSTIN

A horn blares from outside my window, and I yank my shirt off the hanger.

Bastard! He can't even come into the house?

I grab my Chucks and put them on as I hop down the stairs. Celeste is waiting for me by the door. "Here is your lunch, sweetie."

"I'm gonna eat at school." They have Chick-fil-A, for Christ's sake. Last night, I looked up the school online, and I couldn't believe my eyes. It's definitely for the rich kids.

She shakes the bag, and the horn blares again. "Thanks," I say and then run out as she tries to kiss my cheeks.

I run down the stairs and fall into the passenger seat. Man, he didn't waste any time getting his precious mirror fixed.

He doesn't say anything, but he stomps on the gas as he shifts gears. I buckle up and sit back, staring straight ahead. I haven't got much sleep the past two nights because of what he had said to me while in my room. He wants my mind. He had the chance to fuck me, and he didn't take it. He wants me broken, and a fucked-up part of me liked the way it sounded.

No one has ever wanted me like that.

"Hi, Austin."

I spin around in my seat to see a cute little blonde sitting in a booster seat. "Lilly."

She smiles at me. "We're late."

"I'm so sorry." I didn't know that we were taking her to school too.

She laughs. "It was Cole's fault. He was busy arguing with Daddy—"

"Lilly," he snaps, interrupting her.

She picks up the headphones that sit in her lap and puts them over her head and starts pressing buttons on an iPhone.

I turn back around and pull down the visor. Pulling my red lipstick out of my bag, I line my lips and then press them together. I see Cole watching me out of the corner of my eyes. He wants to mind fuck me? I'm gonna return the favor. I'm stronger than he thinks. I'm smarter than he thinks.

"Cole?"

"What is it, Lil?" he asks, looking at her in the rearview.

"My phone died." She pouts. "You didn't charge it last night."

"I forgot," he tells her.

"I was listening to my song." She whines.

He sighs heavily.

"Please …" She begs.

He picks up his phone and scrolls through it while we sit at a stoplight. Moments later, he reaches over and turns up the knob on the dash, and Taylor Swift fills the inside of the car. I can't help it. I smile, and he glares over at me as Lilly starts to sing along to "Everything Has Changed."

And then the smile drops off my face. Because my life has officially become a Taylor Swift song.

Four times. That's how many times the song played on repeat before we get to her school. He pulls up to the drop-off line and gets out, pulling his seat forward.

"Bye, Austin," she says, grabbing her pink sparkly backpack and matching lunch box and getting out of the car.

"Bye, Lilly," I say with a wave.

He crouches between his open door and the car. Eye level with her. He helps her put her lunch box inside her backpack and then helps put it on her shoulders. He kisses her cheeks. "Have a great day, princess. Make sure to eat your yogurt," he says sternly, and she nods her head.

She hugs him, and he hugs her back. "I love you, Lil."

"Love you too, Cole," she tells him, and she runs around the front of the car and up the stairs. He stands and watches her until she's safely inside the building, then climbs back into the car. Even though teachers cover the walkway and entrance.

He puts the car in gear and takes off.

The guy acts like he knows nothing but evil, but I know the truth. To that little girl, he's a savior. She's so young, and he does so much for her. Shelby said he practically raises her. Lilly is six, so he would have been eleven, maybe twelve when she was born. I want to ask him how old he was when his mother died but think better of it. Cole isn't the kind of guy you ask questions. If he wants you to know something, he'll tell you.

I look over at him as he drives us to school. He has his left hand on the steering wheel and his right on the shifter. His glasses rest on top of his head and he wears a scowl on his face. Even angry, he looks gorgeous.

He pulls his hand away from the steering wheel to check the black watch on his wrist. Then he speeds up. He wears a pair of blue jeans, and his long-sleeve gray t-shirt shows off every ripple as he fists his hands. He's angrier than usual. And I wonder what he was fighting about with his dad.

I don't even think he realizes that Taylor's song continues to play. His mind is elsewhere as he speeds down the road.

We pull into the parking lot of the high school, and I let out a long breath. It looks more like a college campus. Multiple buildings scatter around acres of green grass and three stories tall. A huge football stadium is to right of the parking lot. We get out, but before I can take off, he grabs my hand.

We walk into a set of doors, and he pulls me through the busy halls, knowing exactly where we're going. I notice some kids that see him coming avoid eye contact with him. A few nod their heads in greeting. Others call out his name. He ignores all of them.

"We have second and fourth period together." He finally speaks to me.

"You know my schedule?"

"Yes."

I bet Celeste gave it to him.

"Hey, man," Deke says, coming up to join us. "Austin." He gives me a big smile that makes my skin crawl. *He's up to something.*

I just stare.

"We've got calculus together," he tells Cole.

"Yeah, I'm gonna walk Austin to class first."

I snort. "I don't need an escort."

They both ignore me. What the hell is up with him? Just two days ago, he wanted to break me, and today, he's treating me like I can't walk the halls of the school alone.

The bell rings, and I growl. "Crap." Not a good way to start your first day.

Cole grabs my hand, and we walk down the hall as kids scatter like roaches when the lights come on. He and Deke talk about their plans for tomorrow night. I ignore them. We come up to a door. He opens it and shoves me inside. I start to protest, but he spins me around and grips my hair before he leans down and kisses me. I gasp into his mouth, and he takes the opportunity to slide his tongue between my lips. I kiss him back without thought. His lips feel so soft even though his words are as sharp as a knife. He pulls away quickly and slaps my ass. "See you after class, sweetheart." Then he walks out.

I turn to face the classroom half dazed and half horrified. It's full.

"Hey, Austin," the blond headed guy who sits in the front row says.

"Huh?" I manage to say.

"How's it going, Austin?" the guy next to him says with a wave.

"Good to see you again, Austin," another says.

My eyes dart around the room as these guys I've never seen before greet me by my name.

"Austin?"

Finally, a voice I recognize. I look at the back to see Becky—my kind of girl. I walk back to her, ignoring those who say hi to me. I plop down in the empty seat next to her. "What the hell?"

"What?" she asks.

"How do these people know me?" I ask like she would freaking know.

She smiles softly and pulls her phone out of her bag. "The video."

"What video?" I ask in horror. Did Deke share the video of me driving Cole's car? Are the cops gonna show up here to arrest me?

She scrolls through her iPhone and then holds it up to me. It's of Cole and me at his house party Monday night. I walk up to him and wrap my arms around him. He looks down at me in surprise, and then I smile up at him like I'm his doting fucking girlfriend. You can hear every word I say to him. He spins around in my arms, and then he's whispering against my lips. All of a sudden, he picks me up and places me on the counter …

"He posted this?" I demand.

"Deke did," she answers, putting it away. "Cole doesn't do social media. But Deke"—she rolls her eyes—"is an attention whore."

I fist my hands. *Tonight, you're mine.* He wanted everyone to know I belong to him.

CHAPTER ELEVEN
COLE

When I walk into class and sit down, Deke sits next to me. He leans over his desk. "What's the plan?"

"With what?"

"Tomorrow night? How are we gonna play it?"

"Like we always do," I say simply.

"We're not gonna give her any special rules?"

I shake my head. "Nope. She's gonna play just like the rest of us."

He smiles. "This is gonna be so much fun."

The door opens, and a few students walk in. The last one is a blonde by the name of Natalia. She spots me right away and plops down in the free seat to my left. Deke grunts when he sees her.

"Hey, Cole," she says excitedly.

I don't acknowledge her.

Deke speaks to me. "I have a feeling she is gonna surprise us."

"Doubtful."

He snorts. "You don't give her enough credit." He sits back in his seat. "I see the way she looks at you."

"Oh, yeah? How's that?" I can't get the look of want she gave me out of my mind from my party or in her room. I should have taken her up on her offer. Next time she throws herself at me, I'm not gonna back down. She'll have me. And she'll realize what a mistake wanting me is.

"Like she wants to rip your heart out," he answers.

I smile.

"I wouldn't be surprised if your dare is that she wants you to jump off a cliff." Deke chuckles to himself. "Or stab yourself in the eyes."

"How was your winter break?" Natalia asks, not caring that she's interrupting our conversation.

"Hey, Nat!" Deke calls out, leaning forward in his seat to look past me to her. "His break was great. He's seeing someone so quit trying."

"Dick," she mumbles but sits back and doesn't say anything else to me.

I look over at Deke, and he winks. "You're welcome."

I chuckle.

An hour later, Deke and I are walking out of class. I was planning to get Austin at her classroom, but she's already standing in the hall, leaning up against a locker right outside the door. Her arms are crossed over her chest, and a look of rage flares in her green eyes. She looks like she wants me dead. And that thought makes my body heat rise.

"Guess she saw the video." Deke laughs.

She throws him a fuck you look, and then her eyes are back on mine. "You had him record that on purpose," she snaps.

"No." Not a lie. "That implies I was aware you were going to throw yourself at me." She gasps as I step into her, pressing my body into hers. Her eyes hold mine as she stares up at me, not pushing me away or backing down. "You have to admit the way you asked me to fuck you was sexy as fuck."

She sucks in a long breath, her chest rising in the process. "I didn't watch the whole thing."

I lower my face to her neck, and my hands go to her narrow hips. I can't keep my hands to myself anymore. "Well, then you need to watch it again."

"No thanks. I saw enough." She huffs, but her body physically melts into mine.

I kiss her neck, and her hands come up to my shirt, gripping it tightly like she wants to rip it off me. "You still want me to fuck you,

Austin?"

"Don't," she warns me breathlessly.

My lips trail up to her ear, and I nibble on it. She whimpers. "Because I still wanna break you, sweetheart. Like …"

"Cole!"

I let out a growl as I hear Kellan call out my name. I pull away from a panting Austin and look over at him. He stands with Deke and Shane.

"What?" I snap.

His dark narrowed eyes go to Austin, then back to mine. "I need to talk to you."

"Later," I say and grab her hand, yanking her away from the locker and pulling her down the hallway toward second period.

"What you did was not okay, Cole," she says as I shove her into a seat. I sit down next to her.

"Out of all the things I've done to you in the past week and that is the thing you are gonna harp on about?"

Her green eyes narrow. "This has to do with my reputation."

I snort and look away from her.

"I'm serious." She slams her delicate hand down on my desk. "You're trying to make the school think I'm a whore."

"Are you?"

Her eyes widen, and then she purses her lips. She sits back in her seat, folding her arms over her chest again. I lean over, whispering, "How many guys have you fucked, Austin?"

"Fuck you, Cole," she replies flatly.

I go to open my mouth, but the teacher gets our attention, so I sit back and watch her anger simmer. Thinking how explosive she is going to be when I finally give her what she wants.

AUSTIN

Sitting in the cafeteria with the guys, I'm still pissed at Cole. Every guy in the freaking school seems to know my name. And that I want to spread my legs for him. I guess Deke has like tens of thousands of followers. Becky did say he was an attention whore.

Cole sits to my left and Deke to my right. They've got me sandwiched in as if I'm going to get up and run toward the nearest exit. I wanted to sit with Becky, but I haven't seen her since first period, and I didn't get her number.

Kellan sits across from me, chewing his food like it's alive and about to walk off his plate at any given second. Bennett and Shane argue about which car is faster.

Cole slams his phone down onto the table, and I look over at him. "What's wrong?"

I roll my eyes at myself the moment the words are out of my mouth. Like he's gonna tell me. And like I really care. Not even sure why I asked. But he surprises me by answering. "Celeste isn't responding to my texts."

"Why are you messaging her?"

"Coach wants a meeting after school, and I need Celeste to go get Lilly since I'm having to stay late. I don't want them to put her on a bus without warning."

"I can do it." All the guys fall silent. Kellan even stops chewing his food, and his brown eyes glare at me. "What?" I ask, looking at Cole.

He stares down at me. His blue eyes search mine as if he's trying to decide if I would be a better option than putting her on a bus. "She likes me," I say as if that will make a difference. I don't have a lot of experience with children, but Lilly is six. She can tell me if something is wrong. She can tell me if she's hungry. She can go to the bathroom by herself. All I gotta do is drive her home.

Finally, he nods.

"Cole—"

"I'll call the office and let them know," he interrupts Kellan.

"Can you do that?" I ask, just realizing what he said. "Isn't that a parental thing? You're not really her dad, are you?" I ask, and he tenses.

"Cole is …"

"Kellan!" he interrupts him again. Then he looks at me. "After

99

lunch, I'll give you my car keys. They're in my locker." Everyone resumes their previous conversation, making me think I've missed something.

Then a thought hits me. "Uh …" I trail off, and he looks back down at me.

"What?" he barks.

I ignore his anger and lower my voice. "What about your gun?" I don't wanna get pulled over in his car and go to jail. Then again, maybe that is his plan.

"It's not in there," he answers.

I eye him skeptically. His eyes narrow on mine, angry that I don't take his word for it. "It's never in the car when Lilly is present."

"Oh."

He looks away from me, dismissing me once again.

CHAPTER TWELVE

COLE

I stand in the locker room after our meeting with Coach about our upcoming season. My phone beeps, and I pull it out of my pocket to find a text from Austin, and my heart starts to pound. I shouldn't have let her pick up Lilly. I don't want them getting close because I don't want to hurt Lilly when I push Austin away after I'm done with her. But Celeste wasn't answering, and Lilly and I haven't gone over the procedures for her to ride a bus yet. It's second semester of my senior year. Even last semester when I had after-school meetings or meets, I always had someone lined up when I couldn't make it. Either the nanny, Blanche, or Celeste helped me out.

I open it, thinking something is wrong, but it's a picture of Lilly sitting at a round red table eating a cup of ice cream. A big smile on her face and a text from Austin.

She said she had a great first day back, and she made a new friend. His name is George. I hope you don't mind. I took her for ice cream.

I smile. I'm glad she had a good day, but this George shit won't work.

"What the fuck are you doing, man?" Kellan asks from behind me.

I close out of the text and place my phone back in my pocket.

"Drop it," Deke warns.

"No! This shit is getting out of hand," he snaps. "He's in way over his head."

I whirl around on him. "You doubting me?"

"Yes."

I grind my teeth.

"You're not thinking clearly. I understand you wanna fuck her over, but this is too far. She is gonna burn you. And I'm not gonna go down 'cause you wanna get your dick wet."

I step into him, but Bennett grabs Kellan's shoulder and pulls him out of my reach. "Watch it," I warn.

"I'm gonna watch it all right. From the sidelines when she blows everything up in your face," he shouts. "You think she's any better than he is? You think she's not gonna find out that you're using her? That you want to fuck her dad over?" He shakes his head.

"I have it handled," I growl.

He snorts. "She's out with Lilly, for fuck's sake, Cole. When she takes everything you have, you'll only have yourself to blame."

I step into him and punch him in the face. His head snaps to the side, and he stumbles back, running into Bennett. I punch him again before he can recover, and then I'm yanked back.

"Calm down, Cole," Deke says as he holds me back.

My heart pounds in my chest as it rises and falls fast. I fist my hands, that feeling of split knuckles calming me. That familiar throb in my shoulder returns.

He rights himself and wipes the blood off his chin. "She needs to disappear."

"You stay the fuck away from her, Kellan!" I growl.

He shakes his head, letting out a chuckle. "You're already fucked up enough, Cole. You don't need some whore making you worse."

I go for Kellan, but Bennett grabs him, yanking him back. "Enough!" he demands. "Get the fuck out of here, Kellan." Then he shoves him toward the door.

Kellan throws his hands up and walks out backward, making sure he can see me the whole time. Letting me know that he no longer trusts me. I could say the same about him. He's keeping a very big secret from us. That only I know. What he doesn't know is that I plan on using it against him. Very soon.

Once the door closes, Deke releases me. I let out a long breath.

"Maybe we should reconsider," Shane says.

"No." Bennett beats me to it. "We stick with the plan." He looks at me.

I turn around and storm out, ready to get the fuck out of this school.

"Cole?" Deke calls out as I walk out the parking lot.

"I'm not in the mood, Deke," I tell him, coming to a stop by his Range Rover. He is taking me to Austin's house to get Lilly and my car.

He comes to a stop in front of me. "I just wanted you to know that I got your back."

"Thanks."

I walk into the Lowes house without even bothering to knock. I take the stairs two at a time to the second floor, but I don't find the girls in Austin's room.

"Austin?"

"In the kitchen," she calls out.

I make my way down the stairs slower and walk into the kitchen. Lilly is sitting on the counter, and Austin stands next to her with a tray of cookies in front of her.

"Hey, Cole," Lilly says, smiling brightly.

I walk over to her and kiss her hair. "How was school?"

"Good. I made a new friend. He's new. Just like Austin."

I look at Austin, and she is dipping a butter knife into a tub of pink icing—Lilly's favorite color. "That's great."

"Can he come over and swim with us?" she asks excitedly.

Hell no. "We'll talk about it later," I tell her.

"Here you go." Austin turns to face her and hands her a cookie that she just finished icing.

Lilly bites into it. "So good," she says with a nod. Then holds it up to me. "Try it, Cole."

I lean down and take a bite. Austin goes back to frosting another cookie, and I swallow. "You're right. Those are good." I pick her up and set her on her feet. "Go get your backpack. We're gonna leave soon."

She bounces out of the kitchen. Once she is gone, I position myself behind Austin, pressing my hips into her back. She stiffens against me. "Cole."

I reach up and pull her hair from her shoulder, wrapping it around my fist. I yank her head back, and she sucks in a breath. That anger I have for her rises because she's causing problems for me. Big ones. She was supposed to be a toy—something fun to use—but I haven't even got to play with her yet. Not how I imagine anyway.

I lean down to her ear. "Still mad at me, sweetheart?" I don't care how mad at me she is over the video. It got the job done. Everyone fucking knows she belongs to me. She surprised me with her actions. I knew she wanted me, but I didn't expect her to be so forward with an audience.

"Yes." She breathes.

"That was a weak answer." I chuckle. "But I like your fight, Austin. Your anger. It shows me that you haven't given up yet. And you're gonna need that."

She picks up the knife that sits next to the tub of icing. Her hand grips it like her life depends on it. She's not far off. "Are you gonna stab me?"

"It crossed my mind," she growls, but her ass pushes into my already hard dick. God, this woman drives me mad.

I smile. "You better make sure you kill me, sweetheart. Because you won't get a second chance."

"I'll only need one," she assures me.

I have no doubt.

I bring my free hand up and wrap it around her throat, and like always when I touch her, her pulse races. "I figured you for the type of girl to grab a gun over a knife."

"I'd go for whatever is in reach." She pants.

I let go of her neck and yank the knife from her hand and hold it up to her throat. She whimpers. "The thing about a knife is that you have to get up close and personal, sweetheart. And you have one chance to do the most damage." I run the knife down over her black shirt, between her breasts, and her chest rises and falls quickly with each breath. I wanna cut the annoying fabric off. "But we both know that you don't have a problem with letting me get close to you, do we?"

She shoves my hand away and spins around in my arms. My one hand still fists her hair. "You son of a …"

I cut her off, slamming my lips to hers. She tries to push me away, but I tighten my hand in her hair, and it causes her to cry out. I slide my tongue into her mouth and kiss her aggressively. Her legs buckle, and her hands grip my shirt just like they did in the hallway at school. I drop the knife, and it hits the floor with a clank. My now free hand goes underneath her shirt, and she doesn't try to stop me as I slide it up and cup her breast.

She whimpers.

"I guess you still want me to fuck you," I whisper against her lips.

"Why do you do this?" She pants.

"Do what, sweetheart?" I play dumb.

She groans. "Like you have to prove to yourself that I want you. When you don't want me."

I can't help it, I laugh. "Feel that?" I press my hard dick into her lower stomach. Her green eyes stare up into mine. "That's for you. You do that to me. Now tell me that I don't want you," I demand. I grab the top of her bra and yank it down, exposing her breast to my hand. I run my thumb over her nipple, and it hardens. I want my lips on it.

"You don't want me," she whispers hoarsely.

I remove my hand from her breast and out from underneath her shirt. I take a step back. "You're right. I don't."

Her eyes narrow on me as she fixes her shirt. "Got it," Lilly says, running in, and my eyes go to hers.

"Thank Austin for picking you up," I tell her because I refuse to say it. I didn't ask her to; she offered.

"Thank you, Austin," she says, walking over to her and hugs her hips.

Austin smiles down at her, our conversation no longer on her mind. "You're welcome, Lilly."

"Can she pick me up tomorrow?" she asks, looking at me.

I refrain from growling. This is why I didn't want Austin's help. "I'll be able to pick you up tomorrow," I tell her. She pouts, and her brown eyes look at the floor. "And Austin will be with me," I add, making her smile.

Fuck!

AUSTIN

Friday went as well as Thursday did. Cole showed up, and we dropped off Lilly. Then we went to school, and he walked me to first period. He kissed me in class and at lunch, and every time, I found myself leaning into him. And I have to remind myself that I still have stitches in my arm because of him.

We've just picked up Lilly, and I'm looking down at my phone, responding to a message I got from Becky. We finally exchanged numbers today. And she hasn't stopped texting me since third period.

I just happen to look up to see he missed the exit to my father's house. "Where are we going?" I ask, glancing at Lilly in the back seat. She has her headphones on as she watches videos on her phone.

"My house," he responds brusquely. He's been in a mood today, and I noticed the tension between him and Kellan at lunch. And I didn't miss the cut on Kellan's face either. Something is going on.

"Why aren't you taking me home?"

"We have plans."

My knees start to bounce. *We have plans.* And if there's one thing I've learned about Cole Reynolds, it's that I never like his plans. "Will you quit with the cryptic answers. Why didn't you take me home?"

He doesn't respond, and my anger for him grows like it always does. "Cole—"

"Later," he snaps, interrupting me before looking in his rearview mirror at Lilly. And I get it. He doesn't wanna say it with her in the car even if she has her headphones on. That makes me even more nervous.

"You'll already be asleep by the time I get home, okay?" he tells Lilly as we stand in the foyer of his father's house.

"Okay," she says, nodding her head.

"Be good for Blanche."

I'm not sure who the hell Blanche is, but if I had to guess, I would say a nanny.

"Always," she tells him, and then he hugs her. Before I can say anything, he's grabbing my hand and dragging me out of the house and back to his car.

"Now are you gonna tell me where we are going?" I ask.

"You'll find out soon enough."

I bite my bottom lip, wanting to demand he tell me what the hell we are doing, but I know fighting with him won't get me anywhere.

"Can you at least tell me how long we will be?"

"Why?"

"Really?" He can ask me questions, but I can't ask him any? When he doesn't say anything, I roll my eyes. "Becky is going to a party tonight and asked me to go."

"No," he says immediately.

"Excuse me?" I snap.

He looks in his side mirror and changes lanes. "No," he repeats as if I'm hard of hearing.

"You can't tell me what to do, Cole."

"Wanna bet?"

I grind my teeth in frustration. "I can go out if I want."

"Not without me and I'm not going out tonight," he says matter-of-factly.

"What the fuck, Cole? You're not my boyfriend," I grind out, tightening my hand on my phone. Even if he was, he still wouldn't have a say in what I do.

"The entire school thinks otherwise."

"That's because you told them that," I snap.

He glances over at me. "No. That was all you, sweetheart. And wanting my cock."

I suck in a breath through gritted teeth. I want to scream at him. Slam his head into his steering wheel and jump out of this moving car. Instead, I pick up my phone and text her.

Me: I'm down. Doing something right now. Will let you know when I'm done.

Then I lock my phone.

We sit in silence, and I stare out the passenger window, ignoring him as he flies down the highway.

Fifteen minutes later, he pulls off onto a dirt road, and I immediately know where we are. The barn. The same place he had me come to when he stole that car.

My back straightens when I see Deke's black Range Rover and a white Mercedes SUV parked on the side. He parks in front of them and then shuts the car off, getting out.

I take a deep breath and follow him inside.

It's one big open area. The ceiling comes to a high point with dark wooden rafters. There's a set of stairs to the right that leads up to what looks like a loft. A punching bag dangles from the ceiling. A dart board hangs on the wall to the right along with a shuffleboard and a pool table to the left. Three gaming chairs face a big screen TV. A small mini bar is over in the right corner.

It's a man cave.

It has to belong to one of their fathers. And they party here.

Deke is on his phone but nods his head at Cole when he sees us enter. Shane is sitting on a couch drinking a beer, and Bennett is sitting in a chair texting on his phone. I look around for Kellan but don't spot him anywhere.

I come to a stop and stand awkwardly, not really knowing what

I'm doing here with four guys. One wants to destroy me, and one wants me dead. Not sure how the other two feel at the moment.

My phone vibrates in my pocket, and I pull it out to see it's a text.

Becky: Okay. Sounds good.

I look up when I hear Deke finishing his call. He walks over to me, and I take a step back. He smiles. "Still afraid of me, baby?"

I pull my lip back in disgust and mumble, "Something like that."

Cole snaps his fingers at him. "Did you get it?"

Deke nods. "I sure did." He walks over to a table and picks up a black drawstring backpack. "Here you go, baby."

I roll my eyes, and Cole snatches the bag from his hands. "Is it all here?"

Deke snorts, offended by Cole's lack of trust. "Of course."

Cole grabs my arm and pulls me over to the table and hands me the bag. "Holy crap. This thing weighs a ton. What's in it? Bricks?" *Maybe I can use one to knock out Deke.*

Cole snatches it from me and holds it upside down, shaking it. Things start to hit the table with a thud. The first to fall out is a roll of duct tape. And then a small knife. Followed by a pair of handcuffs. A cell phone. Something that resembles a black box. The last thing is a driver's license. Serial killer starter kit.

I pick up the black box 'cause it looks the least threatening and take a step back from the table. "What is all this?" My voice shakes as the hairs on the back of my neck stand.

"It's all yours," Deke says with a wicked smile.

"Mine?" I ask wide-eyed. *Why would I need these?*

Cole picks up the handcuffs, and I take another step away from him at the sound of the metal clanking together. His eyes stay on mine, void of emotion.

"Remember that initiation we talked about?" Deke asks, wiggling his eyebrows.

My heart pounds in my chest, and my palms are sweaty. I tighten my grip on the black box.

Deke takes a step toward me. "I think it's time you give me that show, baby." He takes the handcuffs from Cole.

I grip the black box, and my eyes shoot to Cole, waiting for him to stop Deke. To tell me that this is another sick joke. But his eyes run up and down my body before meeting mine once again. This time, there's a coldness to them that I remember from outside the church, and my breathing picks up. Fear creeping up my spine.

I hear a door open behind me, and Deke reaches out for me. I spin around to run but hit a human wall. I squeal as my thumb presses a button on the black box. A buzzing noise has me jumping back. I then look down to see Kellan on the ground tensed up into a ball.

CHAPTER THIRTEEN
COLE

"Wwhhhhaaatt … thhheeeee … fffucckkk." Kellan growls as he lies on the floor of the clubhouse.

Deke stands beside me, bent at the waist laughing his ass off while Kellan shakes from the Taser Austin just zapped him with.

I just stand here thinking maybe this *was* a bad idea. If she doesn't get herself killed, she's gonna kill one of us.

"What was that?" she asks, spinning around to face Deke and me.

"You just tased his nuts," Deke tells her, still laughing.

"What?" She gasps wide-eyed. "Why would you give me a Taser?" she snaps.

"Get up, man. Walk it off," Bennett says, grabbing his hand.

Deke looks over at me. "I'm gonna keep her gun," he says, making a joke, and my jaw tightens.

Kellan still lies there, but he has stopped shaking. That's a plus.

"Why the fuck am I even here?" she demands, and no one answers her.

"Come on," Bennett says, offering his hand to Kellan.

He gets to his feet, his hands fisted down by his side. He's breathing heavy, and he glares at the back of her head. He grabs her shoulder and spins her around, then shoves her back against the wall. Her head hits it with a thud, and her eyes close for a brief second. "Bitch!" he shouts as his hand wraps around her throat.

I run over to him and yank him from her. She sucks in a deep breath the moment he releases her throat.

Deke grabs Kellan by the collar. "Whoa, man. It was my fault," he tells him.

"She fucking tased me!" he shouts, pointing at her.

I stand between them, blocking her. "Don't ever touch her again," I say, and I'm surprised how calm my voice is. Because I'm about to rip his fucking head off.

"Fuck you, Cole!" he shouts. "And your new fucking whore!"

I shove Deke out of the way and slam my fist into Kellan's nose. His head snaps back. "Ffffuuuucckk." Kellan's cupping his face, so his voice comes out muffled.

"Add that to the mark I gave you the other day."

"Cole," Deke growls in my face. His hands grip my shirt. "Go home," he tells me.

I shake my head. "No ..."

"Go home, Cole!" He shouts my name. I look over his shoulder at Kellan. Blood pours from his nose and onto his white button up. "Cole?" Deke snaps, giving me a little shake. My eyes finally meet his. "Take Austin home," he orders me. His blue eyes drill into mine.

He lets go of me, and I stand there, fisting my hands, breathing heavy. He walks away from me, and Kellan smiles. Blood runs down his nose and over his lips. "Have it under control, huh?"

I step toward him, but Deke slams the black drawstring backpack into my chest. Once again full of the items. "Go home," he repeats.

I spin around, and my eyes find Austin. She remains standing by the wall, and I can see her body physically shaking. And I realize it's time to go. I walk over to her and grab her hand, yanking her out of the clubhouse without another word.

She falls into the passenger seat, and I get in, start the car, and take off down the gravel road.

"Are you all right?" I ask her once we hit the pavement.

"Like you care." Her voice is rough, and I know it's from Kellan's hand around her throat.

My left hand grips the steering wheel. "I didn't know—"

"Just stop, Cole," she shouts, interrupting me. "Quit acting like you fucking care!" She fists her hands in her lap.

I shut my mouth because she's right. Asking if she's okay does imply I care. *And I don't.* Not one bit.

As I shift my car, my cracked knuckles remind me that I do. Or I wouldn't have just hit my friend over a girl. For the second time in as many days.

That thought makes my stomach tighten.

I pull into her driveway and come to a stop. She hasn't said one word in over fifteen minutes. She has been typing away on her phone. I've opened my mouth to ask her who it is a hundred times but managed not to. I have a feeling I know who it is anyway. She reaches for the door. "Austin …?"

She exits and slams it shut before I can say anything else. I sit back, running a hand through my hair in frustration. Then I put the car in gear and squeal my tires, circling the driveway to head home.

I walk into the silent house and make my way up to my room. As soon as the door shuts, my phone rings.

"Hello?"

"Hey, man," Deke greets me. "I just wanted to apologize. You know I was just fucking with her, right? I wasn't gonna touch her."

"Yeah," I say, letting out a long breath. I didn't stop him because I loved the look of fear in her eyes. The way she looked at me for help. I wanted her to know that she was on her own. See what she would do. If she'd fight.

"Kellan is gone," he says, getting my attention.

"Gone how?"

"Like threw his hands up in the air, said *fuck all of us,* and left."

"Good." Fuck him! He's been giving me shit, and I'm tired of it.

He starts to laugh. "You gotta admit that shit was funny."

I grunt. And his laughter fades. "We'll give things a week. See if it's died down."

"Sounds good," I say, and we hang up.

I remove my tennis shoes, shirt, and jeans. Then I walk over to my dresser and pull out my board shorts. I put them on, grab a towel, and head downstairs to the pool.

The night air is chilly, but the stars are out. I dive into the pool, and the chlorine burns the cuts on my knuckles. Coming up for air, I tread water.

When I'm all alone with my own thoughts is when the memories try to pull me under. And it's not just my friends; it's my mother too. God, I miss her so much. Every time I look at Lilly, I see her. I feel her. I think that's why my father hates her so much. But it's not Lilly's fault. She didn't ask to be born. To have a mother who died.

I dive under the water and push against the wall of the pool and swim. My shoulder screams. Four months of physical therapy helped it, but nothing numbs it. The cracked ribs and collapsed lung healed just fine, but the shoulder will always be a reminder that a mistake cost me three lives. Three best friends. I still have their numbers in my phone. Their last text messages. Sometimes when I'm alone, I read them as if they just sent them to me.

It makes my stomach knot and my chest tighten.

"Maddox!" I shout. "Maddox! Come on, man." I kneel over his bloody face as he lies in the middle of the street. I feel around his neck for any sign of life.

"Cole?" My name is called out from behind me.

I run over to Eli. He sits up in the ditch, coughing. Blood runs down his mouth, covering his shirt. "Hang on. Help is coming," I say, grabbing my shoulder.

"He's dead, isn't he?" he asks, looking over at Maddox. I can't answer. Can't make myself say the words.

"Where's Landen?" I ask instead. Looking around, I see the car upside down in the middle of the road ahead of us. Broken glass and beer cans litter the pavement. The front end is missing. The top crushed from the impact of the rolls. Eli starts to cough again, and blood pours out of his mouth. "Cole." He wheezes. "Please don't let me die."

My already tight chest constricts even more and I'm having problems catching my breath. "You're not gonna die," I promise him.

His big brown eyes meet mine. "Please ..."

I swim ten laps. My muscles are sore, and I'm breathing heavy. I think I've exhausted myself enough for bed. I have problems going to sleep at night. Most of the time, I end up crawling in bed with Lilly. She helps calm my demons.

I get out of the pool and grab my towel, wiping my face. "Deke?" I ask surprised when I pull it away. He comes walking over to me from the back porch. "What are you doing here?"

"I've been calling you."

"My phone is upstairs. What's up?"

"We have a problem."

I sigh. "What now?"

He holds up his phone, and I squint to look at the picture he's showing me. It's of a guy by the name of Nate Wax drinking from a keg. "I don't …" My eyes narrow on the picture when I look past him to see two girls standing in the background. Both laughing with drinks in their hands. It's of Austin and a blonde. "Becky," I growl.

"They're at a party." He nods his head.

"I told her she couldn't fucking go," I snap.

She doesn't understand how things work in this town. Guys see her at a party without me, and they'll wonder why I didn't go with her. They'll start to think maybe I dumped her. That she's available. Then they'll make their move. And that's just not gonna work with me. *She's mine.* Has been since I laid eyes on her. Even if she chooses not to acknowledge it.

"Well …" I look back at him. "Guess we're going to a party."

He smiles.

AUSTIN

"I'm so glad you could make it," Becky says, bumping her red Solo cup into mine.

"Me too." I tip the cup back and take a large gulp. It's my third one, and I've got a damn good buzz going. Some might even say I'm drunk.

As soon as Cole dropped me off at home, I changed my clothes, jumped in my car, and left. It's a Friday night, and I needed a fucking drink after what happened with the guys. I embarrassed myself and tased Kellan. And I started a fight. Even I know a girl who starts a fight between friends is never good.

If they didn't want me dead before, they do now.

I take another drink. My phone buzzes in my pocket, but I ignore it because I don't want to speak to anyone at the moment. It's probably Celeste. I didn't even tell her I was leaving. I'm not even sure she was at the house.

"I'm out," Becky announces as she stands from the couch in the living room at some rich kid's parents' house. "Let's do some shots." She smiles down at me. "I saw some bottles of vodka."

I stand, and the room sways a little. "You talked me into it."

We make our way through the people and into the kitchen. A guy who looks over twenty-one with his lip piercing and gauged ears stands behind the kitchen island. He reminds me of Martin, and I wonder if he ever thinks of me. He hasn't crossed my mind once until now.

The guy lines up five shot glasses and then starts pouring the vodka into them.

We clink our glasses together and then down them.

"Another," I say, not even feeling the burn.

Becky laughs, and we slam our glasses on the countertop.

She raises her phone, and I lean into her, pushing my lips out and throwing up the deuce. I have become the typical drunk teenage girl, and I'm not ashamed. She takes the picture, and then I see her starting to upload it to Instagram. "Don't upload that," I say, placing my hand on it and slamming it to the table. "That's all I need is for Cole to see it." She said he didn't do social media, but Deke does, and he has tons of friends. Someone is bound to inform Cole. I don't wanna have to hear about it.

"Okay." She smiles, and we both laugh.

"And why don't you want me to see it, sweetheart?"

My laughter dies off when I look across the counter and into a set of blue eyes. My throat instantly goes dry, and my stomach drops.

Cole stands before me, his hands on the island, spread out wide, and his eyes are staring down at me, void of emotion. "Hmm?"

I don't answer.

"Fancy seeing you here, baby. Hello, Becky."

I see Deke standing next to him, his eyes running over her chest, but mine go back to Cole. He pours a shot of vodka and then slowly pushes it across the countertop to me. "I dare you." A shiver runs through me at the challenge in his deep voice.

"Shit," I hear Becky whisper, and I lift my chin. He arches a brow.

He's not my dad. He's not even my boyfriend. I can do whatever I want whenever I want. I grab the cold shot glass and knock it back. I slam it on the countertop and shove it over to him. "Another," I demand.

Becky places her hand on mine. "Austin …"

"Another," I repeat, ignoring her.

He does as I say without taking his eyes off mine. But this time, he takes it instead of giving it to me.

"Thought you weren't coming out tonight?" And I slurred the last word. Becky laughs.

He is not amused. "That was the plan."

"And?" I ask, trying to act like I don't care he's standing in front of me. That he's here when I wanted to get away from him. How much can one person humiliate another? I think he is up to ten times. In six days.

"Plans change."

"Isn't that the truth?" I ask, yanking the bottle from his hand and pouring myself another shot. Then Becky. "To plans changing." We clink our glasses together.

He slams his hand down on the counter and leans over it. "Do not take that shot, Austin!" he shouts, getting everyone's attention.

My anger rises. Just two hours ago, his best friend had his hand around my throat. I wanna get drunk, and I wanna forget about this fucking week where I have completely lost all grasp of *my* life. "What are you going to do to me, Cole? Gonna hurt me?" I ask. A part of me wants him to. I want his hands fisted in my hair. Around my neck. I want him to make me weak in the knees like at his house party. Even if it was for show. I didn't realize how cold I was until he touched me. Now my body craves that burn.

His blue eyes narrow on me, and I notice he's changed his clothes since I was with him earlier. He had on a black t-shirt but now he has on a dark blue one that matches his eyes. I lick my lips, remembering what his chest looked like when he got out of my father's pool. *Just fuck me already!* At this point, I have no dignity left anyway.

"I dare you," I say and then toss back my shot.

He stands there, staring down at me like he wants to rip my head off. I've never seen such pretty blue eyes look so dark. All I can do is give him a lopsided smile, knowing I got to him. My lips went numb an hour ago. *Show me what you got, Cole.*

"Sleepwalking" by Diamante plays through the house, and I turn to face Becky, dismissing him when he just stands there. "Let's go dance."

She grabs my hand, but I don't even get a chance to step away from the countertop before I'm picked up and thrown over someone's shoulder.

I stare at an ass wrapped in blue denim as I hang upside down. "Cole!" I hit his muscular thighs with my fists. My head bouncing up and down. He slaps my ass. And I moan at the sting.

"That was just a warning," he growls.

I smile.

I hear people talking as he turns and walks down a hallway. Then he's opening a door. He steps in and places me on my feet. I stumble back, my heels clinking on the tile. He slams the door shut.

I spin around to see we're in a bathroom. "What …?"

His hand grips my hair, and he spins me back around. I pant as he shoves my hips into the counter. He stands behind me, staring at me in the mirror.

He lowers his lips to my ear. "I'm not gonna let you back out, sweetheart."

I moan, pushing my ass into him, and I can feel how hard he is.

He chuckles as his lips trail down my neck before his teeth sink into my skin. A shudder runs through me, and I rise on my tiptoes. "Cole." I swallow. "Please."

He starts kissing my neck again. "You're gonna hate me in the morning."

"I hate you now." I breathe.

He lets go of my hair and spins me around. His hands go to my hips, and he lifts me, setting me on the counter. Then his lips are on mine.

I grab the hem of his shirt. "Take it off," I mumble against his lips.

He pulls away, reaches up behind him, and yanks it up over his head. "Jesus," I whisper, placing my hands on his hard and chiseled abs. I didn't know a body could look like this.

My hands lower, and I yank at his belt and then his button. His hand is in my hair, and he's nipping at my lips as I pant. My mind screams this is a bad idea, but my body says nothing that looks like this good could be bad.

He grips the hem of my shirt and yanks it off, tossing it to the floor by his.

I pull his jeans down only to find he has a pair of black boxer briefs on. I go to remove them, but he yanks me off the counter. I stumble into him.

He chuckles at my lack of stability and patience. I don't care.

"Remove your heels," he orders, and I do as he asks without question. He undoes my jeans and yanks them down my legs. I kick them off. "Put your heels back on."

"What…?"

"Put them back on, Austin." He demands, kneeling and holding them out. One at a time, I slide them on. When he stands back to his full height, I realize why he wanted me to put them back on. Even though I'm still a few inches shorter than him with my heels.

He removes my thong next, and before I can stop him, he has my bra undone. The last time I stood naked in front of a man for the first time, I was terrified. My entire body shook. But I don't feel that way right now. And it has nothing to do with the alcohol in my system and everything to do with the way his blue eyes darken as he looks me up and down. They linger on my breasts, and he slowly licks his lips. They're not anything to show off, but they're not small either.

Then his hands are on me. He grips my sides and yanks me to him. His lips take over mine, and I moan into his mouth. My hand goes between our bodies, and I reach inside his boxers. My thighs tighten when I feel how big he is.

I pull away, panting. "Please."

"Please what?" he asks, kissing along my jawline. He lowers his lips to my neck, and he sucks on it hard. I arch my back, giving him better access and not caring if he leaves a hickey.

Goosebumps break out over my body, and I yank his boxers down his legs, shoving him backward. His back slams into the wall, and I drop to my knees before him. I'm not gonna allow him to take his time. To draw this out. I wanna fuck. And I'm gonna get what I what for a change.

"Goddamn." He hisses, throwing his head back into the wall with a thud.

I take his hard dick into my hand and run it up along the shaft. He's thick and long— he's going to feel amazing. I look up at him, watching his muscles clench with each ragged breath he takes. I almost smile at how gorgeous he is when he's all worked up. This is a side of Cole I haven't seen. And I like it.

He raises his hands and grips his dark hair. Those muscles rippling like waves.

He's equally evil as he is gorgeous.

"Fuck me, Cole."

He looks down at me, those blue eyes dark with lust. He lets go of his own hair to fist mine. I hiss in a breath as my scalp stings, but I didn't expect him to go easy on me.

"Open your mouth, sweetheart." He orders roughly, and I do as he says because I'm getting what I want. I'm gonna bring this bastard to his knees even if it means I have to stay on mine.

CHAPTER FOURTEEN

COLE

I open my mouth, but nothing comes out when she wraps her lips around my cock. She allows me to control her head as I pull her back and thrust my hips forward. I watch in complete fascination as I fuck her pretty mouth. I've been thinking of nothing but this for days, and here she is on her knees before me.

Yet it still isn't enough.

She can't scream if her mouth is full. She can't beg if she can't speak. I want her cries of pleasure—her begging me for more—more than I want her on her knees at this moment.

And I always get what I want.

I pull her head away, and she's panting. Tears have welled up in her green eyes. I yank her up by her hair, and she cries out.

I smile. That's more like it.

I know what she is doing. She's trying to play me at my own game. But that's not gonna happen. I'm better than she is.

"Cole …" She pants.

I spin her around with my hand still in her hair, and she hisses in a breath, then I shove her hips into the counter.

My free hand goes between her legs, and she spreads them more for me. I smile, sliding a finger easily into her.

"You're soaked, sweetheart." She moans, rocking her hips to get me to move faster. I remove my finger and grip her throat, pulling her back to my front.

She stares at me in the mirror. It's starting to fog up from our heavy breathing. "Fuck, you're beautiful," I say honestly. There's no denying that Austin Lowes is gorgeous. There isn't a single flaw on her skin. Well, except the stitches on her forearm. But even that makes me proud. Knowing I did that. I made her a little less perfect in someone else's eyes. To me, it's just a reminder of how strong she is. How much fight she has.

She swallows against my hand, and I lean down to whisper into her ear. "You're mine, sweetheart." Letting go of her throat, I replace my hand with my lips. I kiss her soft skin, and she tilts her head to the side for me. I feast on her neck like I'm starving. Nipping and sucking. The sounds she makes has me so hard it hurts.

I pull away to see two hickeys on her neck, and I smile.

She bends at the waist, lowering her head to the countertop, and her body starts to shake with need.

I slap her ass. She moans as she shifts on her feet. I slap it again, the sound bouncing off the bathroom walls. She pushes it into me. My hand goes back between her legs, and she's so wet, it's dripping down her thigh. "You like a little pain with your pleasure, Austin?" I ask. Her only response is the sound of her heavy breathing. "I like it rough too."

Not able to hold out any longer, I take my cock in my hand and push it into her. Not even bothering with a condom. I'm gonna fucking own Austin Lowes and I refuse to have anything between us.

She lifts her head up off the counter and screams out as I spread her wide to accommodate my size.

Fuck! She's tight!

She places her hands on the mirror in front of her, and I grip her hips as I pull back and slam into her again and again.

Her cries of pleasure have me smiling because I know everyone can hear her on the other side of this door. That's why Deke and I showed up here after all. It was to prove a point. I wasn't gonna leave until I fucking made it.

I pull her body back from the countertop and her hands fall from the fogged mirror. Leaning over, I press my chest to her back. I push her into the countertop, and my right hand reaches around her body to find her clit.

"Oh … God …" Her voice trails off and turns into a cry as I work her to orgasm.

"That's it, sweetheart. Come all over my cock," I growl before I bite her shoulder.

Her pussy tightens around me, and she screams out my name as she comes seconds later.

I pull my hand away and stand up to my full height. My hands grip her hair and I yank her head from the counter as I pick up my pace. Knowing what I need in order to get off.

I should pull out now. She got off, and that's all that matters. This part isn't about me. But as I look down at my slick cock moving in and out of her shaved pussy, I feel my breath pick up and my balls tighten. I can't stop now.

"Fuck!" I growl, slamming into her so hard that our knees hit the cabinets below the counter. She calls out my name, and it sounds like she's about to come again. I don't stop. I can't. At this point, I'm committed.

She's fucking mine!

Her eyes fall closed, and she cries out my name as she comes once again. I pull out just in time to come all over her perfectly round ass that has my handprint on it.

I pull up to her father's house in her car, and Deke rolls up beside me in his with Becky.

"Give me ten," I tell him as he rolls down his passenger window.

"Take your time." He smiles and then pulls her over the center console to kiss her.

I get Austin out of her car and carry her into the house. She passed out before I even hit the highway. Once up in her room, I lay her on the bed. I remove her heels, shirt, and jeans, and then cover her up with the blanket before walking out. I'm reaching for the front door when I hear Celeste.

"Cole?"

I turn around to face her. She comes down the hallway to stand in the foyer. Her blond hair down and a bit tangled, letting me know I woke her. A silk peach floor-length robe covers her with a matching sash wrapped around her waist, but I can tell she's naked underneath it. It leaves nothing to the imagination, and her nipples are hard.

She looks at the top of the stairs and then back at me. Her eyes slowly take in my wrinkled shirt and disheveled hair. The hickey on my neck. "Well, that didn't take long. Can't say I'm surprised, though. You always do get what you want."

My jaw tightens, but I don't acknowledge her statement.

She laughs softly, walks up to me, and places her right hand on my cheek. Then lifts on her tiptoes to kiss my lips. I don't kiss her back. "You don't have to rush off." She pulls away. "Come, I'll make us some coffee." She turns, walking away.

"I know you're fucking Kellan."

She comes to a stop and slowly spins around to face me. "I don't know …"

"I let him borrow my car last week while his was in the shop. He came to see you, didn't he?"

She runs a hand through her blond hair nervously. I was hoping she would have the balls to admit it. She's just like her pathetic husband.

"Spoke to my father the other day. He said that Bruce knows I'm fucking you." Her eyes widen. "That his trustworthy staff informed him my car was here all night." I look her over once and then say, "I've never fucked you, but I instantly knew who it was."

"Cole …"

"I didn't deny it."

"Jesus, Cole!" She hisses.

I shrug. "I don't care what he thinks I do."

"He's my husband," she snaps.

Now, she cares about her marriage. "See, I haven't told anyone that I know. Not even Kellan." I step to her and smile, loving that my father gave me this information. "Now, as long as I keep your secret, you owe me."

Her eyes narrow on me. "I'm not like her, Cole. You can't blackmail me."

"Is that so? You're fucking an underage *boy*." Kellan is the baby out of all of us. He doesn't turn eighteen until after graduation. "Do you wanna go to prison, Celeste? You see it all the time on the news. This town will rip you to pieces. Bruce will leave you, of course. He has money; he can find another woman. They're a dime a dozen to men like him." Her lips thin. "He's not gonna pay for the legal bills of a cheating wife." I take a quick look around his multi-million-dollar mansion. "That's why you stay with him, right? For what he can give you?" She opens her mouth to speak, but I continue. "You'd lose everything."

Her breath picks up as she stares at me with hatred.

"I'll let you think about it." I give her my back and walk toward the door. My hand touches the knob when she speaks again.

"What is it you want?" Her voice shakes with anger.

I spin around to face her. "I want you to get Kellan off Austin's back."

She sighs. "He's mad that I never told him about her."

"None of us knew about her," I snap.

"He wants her gone. Afraid her loyalty lies with him. That she'll tell Bruce about us. I tried to explain to him that she hates her dad. She wouldn't …"

"She'll never find out," I assure her. "I'll keep your secret if you do what I want."

She bites her bottom lip nervously. I'm not sure how she'll talk him into backing off, but she better fucking do it. "And I'll tell Bruce I haven't slept with you." Might as well clear my name. But he's not gonna like that I'm fucking his daughter any more than if it was his wife.

She finally nods. "Okay."

AUSTIN

125

I spent all day Saturday in bed nursing my hangover. Everything hurt. So bad. Plus, my body was sore on top of that due to Cole and me in the bathroom at the party.

I slept off and on, and by Sunday, I was back to myself, but I didn't venture from my room.

I didn't hear from Cole until Sunday night around nine. A text that said *I'll be there at 7:30 tomorrow.*

I ignored it, knowing he didn't care about a reply.

Monday morning came, and I was ready on time. Now that I know he takes Lilly to school, I don't wanna be late just to spite him.

And just like the other two times he took me to school, we didn't speak. Lilly sat in the back singing along with her headphones on, and I messed around on my phone. Running through social media pages of my friends back in California. Nothing seems to have changed, yet I still haven't heard from anyone. Big surprise.

I put it away as he pulls into the parking lot of the high school. I exit his car as Deke pulls in next to us. And my eyes widen when I see Becky get out of the passenger seat. "What?" I ask, eyeing her up and down.

She smiles and throws her arm over my shoulders. "Girl, I've got so much to tell you."

I laugh. "You can keep all your sex stories to yourself."

"Well, just FYI, yours seems to be public knowledge."

I stop walking. "What does that mean?"

She stops and turns toward me. "Everyone heard you and Cole in the bathroom. It's all everyone is talking about."

My mouth falls open. "How are they talking about it? It happened over the weekend."

She lifts her phone and shakes it. "I can show you ..."

"No!" I cut her off. Not wanting to know what they are saying. It was my fault. I did it. I dared him just like he wanted me to. Then I allowed him to carry me off to the bathroom and fuck me. I never even thought about stopping him.

I let out a long breath and then stomp my way into the school. I can hear Cole and Deke speaking behind me. I stop at my locker, grab what I need, and then continue to my class, ignoring him as he calls out my name in the busy hallway.

It's hard to avoid the looks guys give you when you know they are picturing you having sex. But I did it. I kept my nose down and eyes on my paper. Cole didn't come into the classroom and kiss me as he had last week, but I knew next period would be difficult. 'Cause we have it together.

An hour later, I walk in to our class and sit down. He walks in and takes the seat next to me. To my surprise, he doesn't say a word to me, and it makes me nervous.

I spend the entire hour biting an eraser off my pencil and bouncing my knees. He never once looks over at me. But kids keep looking back at us. The hickey I gave him on his neck is very visible. I, however, covered mine up with makeup the best I could.

After the bell rang, I ran out of class but was brought to a quick stop. "Don't," I say when he shoves my back against a locker.

He likes to corner me.

He glares down at me. "How long you gonna stay mad at me, sweetheart?"

"Stop calling me that," I snap.

"Would you prefer bitch?" I narrow my eyes on him. "Because that is how you're acting."

I reach up and slap him. The sound bounces off the busy hallway walls. Students come to a stop, and the loud chatter dies down to whispers. Everyone is looking over at us wide-eyed. I get the feeling people don't lay their hands on Cole unless they are prepared to get hit back.

A slow and devious smile spreads across his face before his head drops to my neck. His hands go to my hips, and he digs his fingers into my skin.

"Cole," I growl, trying to push him off me, but he doesn't budge.

His lips softly kiss up to my ear. "Pain turns me on, Austin." He presses his hips into mine and he's hard. And just like that, I melt like fucking butter.

Stay strong! You're mad at him.

"Want me to take you out to my car and fuck you?"

"Cole …" I say, but the bell cuts me off.

He pulls away, laughing, knowing exactly what he did to me. "Come on. I'm walking you to class."

I grind my teeth but am thankful for the interruption. Because I think I was going to tell him yes.

I look up to see Becky walking into the cafeteria. I call out her name and wave my hand. She comes bouncing over and plops down across from me. "You just love being the topic of the day," she says, shaking her head.

"What now?"

"Everyone is talking about how you slapped Cole." She wiggles her eyebrows. "They are saying he's whipped."

I throw my head back and laugh. If they only knew the truth. Cole comes to sit beside me, and Deke sits down next to Becky. "Traitor," I mumble, and she gives me a big smile before kissing him.

The one friend I have made is now sleeping with one of the enemies. This will not end well for me.

Kellan sits down to my right, and I stiffen. Even Cole squares his shoulders, but he doesn't look over at him.

Shane and Bennett join us, and all the guys talk about crap I can't keep up with.

Deke takes a second to shovel some food into his mouth between arguing with Shane when I look up at him. "Can I have Shelby's number?"

The table falls silent. His eyes meet mine, and they narrow. "Why do you want her number?"

"How do you even know her?" Kellan growls.

"She did my stitches. I need them out this week," I say.

"What stitches?" Shane asks.

Cole and Deke don't answer him. I frown. Have they not filled them in on what happened that night? I look over at Cole, and he's glaring at me. I glare back, not backing down from him.

"I'll take you today after school." Cole breaks the silence, and I don't even bother to argue as they resume their conversations.

A small victory, but a victory nonetheless.

"What about these stitches?" Kellan presses.

Cole looks down at his phone. "It doesn't concern you, Kellan," he says.

Becky makes an O face with her lips at Cole's tone. Deke shovels more food into his mouth, letting me know he isn't going to say a word about it. Shane and Bennett also let it go, knowing they aren't going to get any more info. Kellan slams his drink onto the table and then stands, walking away.

CHAPTER FIFTEEN

COLE

I already made the mistake of leaving her alone with Shelby once. I wasn't gonna make it again. I heard her talking to Austin about me last time we were here. So this time, I stand in the kitchen with them while they sit at the table as Shelby removes her stitches.

"It looks really good," Shelby tells her as she examines it. "And the scarring will be very minimal."

Austin smiles at her. "Thank you."

"Of course," Shelby says, waving off her gratitude and pulling her in for a hug.

"May I use your restroom?" Austin asks, standing.

She nods and shows her where it is.

I'm leaning up against the kitchen counter when Shelby reenters. Her smile drops off her face when her eyes meet mine. She comes to a stop in front of me with her arms crossed over her chest. "Why did you do that to her?"

I don't respond.

She sighs at my silence. "Why are you getting so close to her? I've seen the video Deke posted online. You're playing her. But the question is why?"

"What I do with her is none of your concern," I decide to say.

"Cole." She runs her hand through her hair. "You can't do this to people."

"I can do whatever I want."

She fists her hands down by her sides, clearly frustrated. I stare back at her unblinkingly, showing a sign of indifference. Shelby has too much heart. I don't have enough. "I saw the news. And that Jeff is missing." She changes the subject, her eyes searching mine for any indication I had something to do with his disappearance. She knows me better than that. I'm a wall. She gives me her back and lets out a nervous laugh. "This has to stop, Cole."

"Are you gonna stop me?"

She spins back around to face me. "This is serious! This is your life!"

I look away from her as guilt starts to eat at me. *A life I shouldn't be living.*

"Cole." She softens her voice. "It wasn't your fault."

I tense. No one talks to me about what happened that night I killed three friends. They know that's a line I never cross, but Shelby doesn't care about people's limits. "You can't right all the wrongs in the world. Eli would understand. It was an accident. It could have happened to any of us."

"We both know he deserved it," I growl, focusing on Jeff instead of my friends.

"Jesus." She hisses softly, realizing I just admitted to killing Jeff. "Who all knows?"

I clamp my mouth shut. She looks away from me.

"Was Deke involved?"

I stare at the back of her head, refusing to give in to the urge to look at the floor. I won't answer her question, but I also won't give her a reason to assume either.

My silence has her turning back to face me, and there are tears in her soft blue eyes. She reaches out for me, her hands gripping my shoulders, and her eyes meet mine. "I need him, Cole. You can't take him from me. Do you understand?"

My eyes search hers, a tear falls down her cheek. And my chest tightens at the thought of losing Deke. He and I are by far the closest. He, Eli, and I were inseparable. He was supposed to be with us that night. But plans changed, and he ended up not coming along. It probably saved his life.

"Thank you again …" Austin's voice trails off as she enters the kitchen.

Shelby lets go of me and turns her back to us quickly, rubbing the tears from her face.

Austin comes up to me and watches me closely, probably wondering what the hell is going on between us. But I give her a cold stare. I don't owe her an explanation.

"Anytime," Shelby says cheerfully. Her tears now gone. A smile on her face.

The silence in the car is as thick as fog, making it hard to breathe. To swallow. My hands fist the steering wheel and gear shift.

Austin sits beside me, and I can feel her anger toward me rolling off her shoulders. She's confused about what she saw between Shelby and me. Probably thinking I'm playing her—fucking her and others too. And I won't tell her otherwise. What I do is none of her business. Just like it's not Shelby's.

Her phone goes off, and she looks down at it. "Great," she mumbles.

"What?" I ask unable to help myself.

She types back a quick reply and then throws her phone back into her lap but stays silent.

"What, Austin?" I growl.

"That was Celeste," she answers.

"And?"

"My father is coming home tomorrow. He wants to have a family dinner."

And just like that, my tense body relaxes. I smile. "What time?"

Her head whips over to look at me. "Why?" she asks, eyeing me skeptically. "Have plans for me already?" she snaps, angry with me.

Ignoring her question, I grab her left hand and bring it to my lips to kiss her knuckles. "Because I'm gonna have dinner with my girlfriend and her dad."

She yanks her hand from my hold, and it reminds me of when I kissed it outside the church and how leery she was of me then. She knew I had ulterior motives. *I still do.*

"One, you're not my boyfriend. And two, why?"

"Do I have to have a reason?"

"Yes! I can see it all over your face. You just wanna piss him off," she says matter-of-factly.

"What's so wrong with that? Don't tell me you care if he gets mad? I already know you hate the man too."

"Yeah." She looks down at her hands in her lap. "But if he gets mad at me, he can ship me back."

I look over at her quickly surprised by her words. We don't share personal information because I don't talk about myself and because I don't care to know about her. Maybe I should … But then I remember what Celeste told me about how she didn't think she was safe and how I was a good influence for her. And my chest tightens. I'm a murderer. Evil. What could they do that would be worse than that? "Celeste wouldn't let him send you back," I tell her. She would fight for her to stay here. Because if it came down to it, I would force Celeste to make that happen. Like she said, I always get what I want. And too bad for Austin, she's it at the moment.

Plus, I still have some tricks up my sleeve. One that will get her father to do whatever I want. Including giving her to me.

She looks straight ahead and lets out a long breath. "I'll tell Celeste you're coming," she says and then picks up her phone again.

I look ahead as I drive her home, wondering just what has happened to her that she would rather stay here with the devil than go home to her mom and her mom's boyfriend. A part of me wants to know. The other just doesn't wanna acknowledge it.

Because I don't care. I don't.

AUSTIN

The next day was just like all the other days. Cole picked me up. We dropped off Lilly and then went to school. Once again, he didn't say anything to me, but he kissed me before class and made sure to put his hands on me. I didn't push him off.

His words and stares are so cold, but when he touches me, he's hot as fire. It doesn't make any sense. And he's starting to get in my head. The back and forth with our bickering. The way I like that he touches me. The way he is with Lilly. He thinks the world of that little girl. And every time I see him kiss her goodbye when we drop her off at school makes my chest hurt. I wanna ask why he seems to do everything for her but can't quite find the words. And I know he would ignore me. Cole is good at that, and it drives me crazy!

I haven't had many boyfriends. I only ever dated Martin, and he was nothing like Cole. So dark. So closed off. Something about him keeps me guessing. Makes me wonder what happened to him that has made him this way at such a young age.

Cole reaches over and grabs a fry off my plate, smearing it in ketchup as we sit in the cafeteria.

"We have a team meeting today," Deke tells him.

"I know. I got the message." Cole nods, looking down at his phone.

"Hey, we're going to the movies tonight. You guys wanna go?" Becky asks as she steals a fry from my plate. At this rate, I'm not gonna get any.

"Can't," I say through a mouthful of cheeseburger. "We're having dinner with my father and stepmom."

Deke is trying to pull her to him for a kiss, but she pushes him away. Shane and Bennett are too busy on their phones, but Kellan gets up, throws Cole a look of hatred, and then walks off. Cole ignores him completely.

"Meeting the parents, huh?" Becky smiles. "Things getting serious."

I choke on my cheeseburger, and Deke snorts.

"I knew her father long before I started fucking her," Cole replies flatly.

Becky gasps, and Deke chuckles like what he said was actually funny. I roll my eyes. He can be such a prick.

As we walk out of the cafeteria, I stop at his locker with him. "What's up with you and Kellan?" I ask.

He looks over at me for a quick second and then starts to dig in his locker. "Getting personal? Didn't think we did that."

I snort. "You seem to get really personal with me."

He shuts his locker and throws his arm over my shoulders as he walks me to my class. I notice the people who stare at us as they walk by, but I ignore them. "It's nothing to worry about," he says.

"I'm starting to feel like he's more of a threat to my life than Deke is," I say and give a nervous laugh. At least now Becky is keeping all his attention.

He stops walking and turns to face me. We stand in the middle of the hallway, and he stares down at my face with no emotion. He lifts his right hand and pushes a piece of hair behind my ear. Then his fingers continue downward and run over my hickey I have covered up. And fear creeps up my spine.

He's no better than the rest. Out of all five of them, he's the one who has done the most damage.

I take a step back from him, and his hand drops to his side as his blue eyes meet mine. "I'm no better." He says what I'm thinking.

I swallow nervously.

"I still wanna hurt you. I still wanna see you bleed. And I think of you bent over that countertop every second of the day." His hand reaches out and snakes around my waist, pulling me in. "The way you looked when you came … the way you cried out my name … it just made me want all those things even more. Don't think I've changed, Austin. Because I haven't. And I won't."

I tilt my head back to look up at him. My heart pounds in my chest. "Are you saying I should be afraid?"

He leans his head down and whispers into my ear, his hand still splayed across my back, holding me in place. "You should be terrified, sweetheart." My breath hitches. "Because I'm gonna get what I want."

"Which is?" I can't help but ask.

"Everything you have to give."

"You okay?" Becky asks as she shoves my arm.

"Huh?" I ask, looking over at her as we stand in the parking lot waiting for the guys to finish their meeting with their coach. Cole was able to get Blanche to pick Lilly up from school today, so I stayed with Becky to wait on the guys.

She frowns at me. Her white Gucci glasses cover her blue eyes. "I asked if you're okay."

"Yeah, I'm fine." I nod with a lie.

"I'm gonna go out on a limb here and say you're lying. Why?" She adjusts her backpack on her shoulder.

Mine sits on the ground by my feet while I lean against Cole's car. "I'm just … tired."

"Austin. I don't pry into Cole's and your relationship …"

"We're not together," I correct her.

She snorts. "But you know you can talk to me, right? I know I'm your only friend and all."

I shove her. "That's not true."

She arches her perfect brown brow. "Name another person."

I bite my bottom lip and let out a sigh. "Fine," I growl.

She throws me a winning smile. "See. Only friend."

"I'm about to replace you," I say jokingly.

She throws her head back and laughs. "Well, good luck with that. Most of the girls hate you because you're *dating* Cole and none of the boys would go near you because of him."

I roll my eyes. "He's ruining my life."

She stands tall, and the air around us changes. "That's what I'm talking about. I see how he keeps you secluded and the way he was with you at the party that night. Then yesterday at lunch you mentioned stitches, and he got pissed. It was like he was the reason you have them."

I run a hand through my hair. What would she do if she knew Deke wanted to shoot me just two weeks ago? "It's fine, Becky.

Really. Thanks for worrying about me, but I'll be fine."

She nods once as if she doesn't believe me. "What's up with you and Deke?" I change the subject.

"Oh, it's just sex," she says, waving me off.

I wish that's all it was between Cole and me.

I look over at the school and see Deke and Cole walk out of the gym, and my thighs instantly tighten. He wears a pair of black basketball shorts, and a white Under Armor shirt that clings to his lean body. And a pair of tennis shoes. He has a black duffle bag thrown over his right shoulder, and he's looking down at his phone, texting away as they walk toward us.

I hate how gorgeous he is. How my body wants him even though I know I shouldn't.

Deke reaches us first, and he picks Becky off her feet and kisses her. She giggles like a schoolgirl, and then he slaps her ass. Cole finally comes up to us and pops his trunk. He throws his bag in the back, picks mine up, and tosses it in there as well and then lifts his chin to Deke. "I'll call you later," he tells him and then gets in his car.

I fall into the passenger seat and buckle my seat belt. My hands fist in my lap as I think of what Becky said a minute ago. He's making me the laughing stock of school. If she sees how he treats me, then so does everyone else. It's just some game to him. "I'm driving myself tomorrow."

"No, you're not," he says, still staring down at his phone. I yank it out of his hand and throw it behind him. "Hey—"

"Why are we doing this, Cole?" I demand. "Huh? Why am I here?"

His defined jaw sharpens, showing me his annoyance.

Too bad.

"Why don't you just stop? Let me walk away? I haven't gone to the police about anything. And I'm not going to." I'm too far in. I know too much. They would hang my ass with them. And I refuse to let that happen.

"No," he growls. "You're not going anywhere."

I unbuckle my seat belt, shove open the door, and jump out. Deke and Becky have already left, so I start walking, not even caring about my bag being in his trunk.

"Austin!" I hear him yell my name and then his car door slam shut.

"I'm walking home, Cole." I shout, not bothering to look back at him.

"Why do you do this?" He yanks on my shoulder, spinning me around. "Why do you piss me off?"

"Me piss you off?" I hold up my right arm. "Look what you've done to me. You sliced my arm, and I had to get fifteen stitches. And let's not forget you almost got me arrested."

"Please." He rolls his eyes. "I knew what I was doing when I stole that car. You weren't going to get arrested."

"You may have, but I didn't! I'm not a criminal, Cole."

"That's not what I heard."

"What does that mean?" I snap.

"I heard you were doing drugs. Got in trouble with the police. That you were too much for your mother and her boyfriend, so they sent you to live with Bruce."

I wanna demand who told him that, but I already know. Celeste. No one else here knows anything about me.

"You're right," I say, and he frowns as if he wanted a fight. "I got in trouble. And was shipped here." I spread my arms out wide. "To my dad's because she wants me to send her his money." Not a total lie. "But I don't have to put up with you, Cole. You and your bullshit games."

I throw my hands up. "I'm done." My voice shakes. "You take whatever video you want of me and show the police, show the school." My throat tightens with emotion. "Show whoever the fuck you want. I'm done, Cole."

I turn my back to him and walk away. The first tear runs down my face and then another one. I'm not that girl who gets all emotional. But I cry when I get angry. And I'm so mad right now. At my mother. At my father. And at my life.

A hand fists in my hair, and I cry out when my back is pinned to a hard chest. "I'm not letting you walk away," Cole growls into my ear, making me shiver.

"You don't get to choose ..."

He spins me around, looking down at me and lifts his hand to my cheek. He runs his thumb through my tears. "Beautiful," he whispers.

"Please stop." I hate that I'm begging, but I've got nothing left. I'm treading water, but the water's too deep, and he's circling me. He smells the blood and is just waiting to strike. Waiting to pull me under into the darkness where he'll eat me alive. He's a shark, after all.

He smirks down at me. "You think no one wants you, Austin, but I do." Another tear runs down my face. "Why do you think I keep you so close? Why do you think I want everyone to know you belong to me?" I don't answer. "It's because I want you. And no matter how much you fight it, I know you like being mine."

"I don't belong to you," I say, fisting my hands.

He chuckles. "Are you wet right now, sweetheart?"

"Fuck you, Cole." My voice is breathless.

"That's exactly what I wanna do to you." His hand cups my face and tilts it back. I don't fight him. He lowers his lips to mine, and I open without thought.

This man has power over me. And it's scary. My body just reacts to him, no matter how hard I try to fight it.

His tongue slips between my lips, and my arms wrap around his neck. I taste my tears, and I know he can too. He presses his body into mine, and his hardness presses against my lower stomach. I moan.

Cole deepens the kiss, and it takes my breath away. When he bites my lip, I nip at his. Then he pulls away, panting. "Now. I'm gonna take you home. And I'm gonna fuck you."

CHAPTER SIXTEEN
COLE

I shift my car as I fly down the highway. My cock hard and needing her. I've tried to play it cool since Friday night in the bathroom at the party. I've tried to act like I did Austin Lowes a favor by fucking her, but I want her. And then when I saw her tears, I lost it. They turned me on so much. And the taste of them when I kissed her … They were amazing.

We pull up to the house, and we barge through the front door, my lips on hers. I grip her ass and start carrying her up the stairs.

"Celeste?" she asks against my lips.

I had spoken to her earlier when she messaged me that she couldn't pick up Lilly from school today. I had to get Blanche to do it. "At the airport …" *Kiss.* "Picking up Bruce …" *Kiss.* "We've got an hour …"

We enter her room, and I slam the door shut before I toss her onto the bed. She sits up immediately and removes her shirt and bra. I rip my shirt off as she goes for her jeans. She lifts her hips and kicks them off at the same time I toss mine to the side.

Then I crawl onto the bed and straddle her hips. My fingers run over her tattoo on her ribcage *even a white rose has a black shadow.*

"I'm not going to use protection," I tell her. She never did mention that last time, but we need to clear that up.

"I'm on the shot."

Perfect.

She looks up at me as her hands go to my chest, and she drags her nails down my bare skin. I hiss in a breath at the pain. It reminds me of that first night in the cemetery. It had turned me on then just as much as it does now.

I grab her hands and pin them above her head. She arches her back and lets out a moan. "What's wrong, Cole? Thought you liked a little pain with your pleasure?" She arches a brow in challenge.

I smile and let go of her wrists. "I do."

"Then ..." She does it again. This time a little slower and harder. Red marks cover my chest and abs, and my cock stands at attention. She looks at it, licking her lips. Then her eyes meet mine. "What are you waiting for, Cole?"

This woman tries my patience. Literally every day, I have to remind myself that this is a game I intend to win. At any cost. Otherwise, she will catch me at a weak moment, and lust makes a man weak. It can make the strongest man falter.

I wrap my hand around her throat and squeeze. She arches her back, and her pretty red lips part. I wish they were wrapped around my cock right now. This time isn't like the last. I'm not putting on a show for the ones who stand on the other side of the door. This is just for her and me.

"I love it when you challenge me, sweetheart." I lean down and whisper against her parted lips. She lifts her hips to meet mine, letting me know what she wants, but she's gonna have to wait. "It lets me remind you where I stand." I run my tongue along her upper lip while my free hand runs over her shaved pussy. She's wet. Not caring about foreplay at the moment, I push my hard cock inside her, and her eyes close. "Above you."

We sit at the table in the formal dining room. Celeste sits across from me, Austin to my left, and Bruce sits at the head of the table to my right. His right-hand man, Raylan, sits to the left. He doesn't speak. Never does. Not to me anyway. He's a pussy if you ask me.

It's going about as well as I thought it would—tense.

The only two people who have spoken since we've sat down are Celeste and Austin. And they're only speaking to one another.

I haven't touched my food. I didn't come here for dinner. Well, not the kind their cooks can make me. I came to see the look on Bruce's face when he saw me. It was priceless. Even now, he stares at me with his dark brown eyes narrowed, trying to figure out my angle. But he'll never guess. And the fact I was fucking his daughter only an hour ago upstairs makes it even better.

Celeste gets up. "I'm gonna do the dishes," she announces, and Bruce rolls his eyes. Probably because they have help who does that. But he allows it.

"I'll help you," Austin offers, all but running after her, not wanting to be anywhere near her father. The bastard hasn't even said one word to her, but I think she prefers it that way.

"Leave." He snaps his fingers at Raylan. He gets up and walks out of the room without a word.

"So," he starts the moment we're alone, "I'm a little confused. Which one are you fucking? My daughter or my wife?"

I wanna say *both* just to be a dick but refrain. Instead, I lean back in my seat, stretching out my legs. "Austin," I say her name. 'Cause she's not his daughter. He's not a dad to her in any way.

He narrows his eyes on me. "So you were screwing my wife before my daughter showed up?"

"I've never *screwed* Celeste."

He snorts.

"Why would I lie? I've got nothing to lose. But since you brought it up … My father told me that you think I spent the night here, but I assure you, I haven't. Not even since I started seeing Austin."

He arches a brow. "Trying to be a gentleman, Cole? That's so out of character for you. I still don't believe you haven't slept with my wife, though."

I lean forward, my forearms on the table. "Come on, Bruce. I'm offended. You know me better than that. If I wanted to fuck your wife, you would never know." He opens his mouth, but I continue. "But I have a proposition for you."

He can't mask his surprise at my words.

We don't work together. We're enemies.

All part of my plan.

"I'm listening."

"My dad also told me that Austin's mom wants her to live with you until graduation, and you want her out as soon as possible."

"She doesn't belong here." He fists his hands on the table.

"I don't disagree."

"I've already spoken to her mother. Today. I offered to send Austin back to California with twenty thousand. She said she could return."

I tilt my head to the side, choosing my words carefully. "I know how you can get rid of her and keep your money."

"How so?"

The bastard is so money hungry, he's already sold his soul once. And the devil is gonna be coming to collect soon. He just doesn't know I'm the one who will deliver him. "Give her to me. Let her stay here. I'll make sure she stays out of trouble."

He leans in, his eyes narrowing. "No." He stands from the table.

I knew he'd say no. That's why I came prepared. "What if I told you I have something you want?"

He comes to a stop. "What could you have that I would possibly want?"

I dig into my pocket and pull out the single key. I toss it onto the table.

He looks at it, and his eyes flare with anger. "You son of a bitch …"

"It's all yours. If she stays."

"It *is* mine! You stole it."

"I found it."

His fisted hands bang against the table, making our glasses rattle. "You fucking stole it!"

I smile up at him. "I dare you to prove it."

He snarls.

"Do we have a deal or not?"

"You planned this," he claims, eyes flaring with rage.

I knew I'd need insurance.

He looks at the key longingly. His eyes go from it to me, and he nods. "Done."

"How do I know you're not gonna fuck me over?" I ask, picking the key up and twirling the chain around my finger.

"Haven't you heard of honor among thieves?" he snarls.

I have. I also know how he operates. "She stays."

His eyes shoot to the direction of the kitchen and then back to me. "Until graduation. And then she's gone."

That's all I need.

"Why do you want her? She can't be that great of a fuck. Her mother sure as hell wasn't."

Sick bastard.

I stand from the table and ignore that statement. "Oh, and just a heads-up. My car will still be here in the morning."

Just then, Austin enters the dining room. "Let's go to the media room," I tell her. "I wanna watch a movie."

She frowns but nods.

"I'm leaving town tomorrow morning," her father scowls. "I'll be gone for two weeks." Then he walks off.

AUSTIN

"What was that about?" I ask as we enter the media room.

"Nothing," he says, closing the door behind us.

"Cole?"

"What?"

"Why do you blow off everything I ask?" I plop down onto the circular couch.

He walks past it and goes to the glass table that sits underneath the screen. Grabbing the remotes, he bends down, looking at the stacks of movies underneath it. "I don't know what you're talking about."

I shove off my shoes and lean back, crossing my arms over my chest. "Yes, you do," I argue.

He stays silent while he picks out a movie and pops *Gone in Sixty*

Seconds into the DVD player. He flips the lights off and comes to stand in front of me. I glare up at him as the movie begins.

Then being the bastard that he is, he reaches up and grabs his shirt and pulls it over his head, tossing it to the floor.

"What are you doing?" I ask, the room getting hotter by the second. I hate how my eyes run over the marks that my nails left just an hour ago when we were up in my room. The way he hissed in a breath as I drug my hands down his skin. I want to mark him just as much as he wants to claim me. It's very unhealthy.

He then reaches for the button on his jeans. "You."

"Cole." I look around as if we're not alone. But we are. "We could have done this in my bedroom." But my heart starts to pound at the thought of doing it in here while my dad and Celeste are downstairs.

"I wanna do you in here," he states.

His jeans hit the floor, and then he's crawling on top of me. I pull back, eyeing him nervously. "You're up to something." But my thighs are tight, and my pussy already wet.

He chuckles, gripping the hem of my shirt. "Don't trust me?"

"No."

He removes my shirt and tosses it to the floor with his. Then he pulls the straps of my bra down, exposing my breasts. My nipples are hard, and he licks his lips. "Good, because you shouldn't." Then he lowers his lips to my skin.

I arch my back and let out a long breath as he sucks on my nipple. Gently biting it. He releases with a popping sound and moves to the other side.

I reach up and grip his hair, pulling on it. He then trails kisses down my stomach. My breath starts coming faster as he kisses my hip bones before dipping between my legs. His tongue licks over my pussy, and I shudder. "Cole." I pant.

He positions himself between my legs and throws them over his shoulders. I arch my back when his tongue enters me. He fucks me with his mouth as hard as he does with his cock. I cry out and slap my hand over my mouth, not wanting anyone in the house to hear me even though I know they can't. This is a fifteen thousand square foot house. The odds of them standing on the other side of the door are slim.

That familiar feeling that I get every time he's had his hands on me starts to build and I arch my back as my eyes close. My thighs tighten around his head and I come with his name mumbled due to my hand still on my mouth.

He lowers my legs and he yanks my hand away. I suck in a raged breath as my body shakes.

He hovers over me as he licks his wet lips. "You taste amazing, sweetheart. Like me." Then his lips are on mine.

The following Sunday, I find myself back at the clubhouse. And once again, I didn't get much info about what the hell I'm doing here. But this time, they didn't give me anything I could use on any of them.

I stand, leaning up against the table to face the open room. Cole stands to my right talking to Deke while Shane and Bennett sit on the couch.

"Where's Kellan?" Shane asks what I'm thinking.

I've tried to steer clear of him at school, but for some reason, he continues to sit next to me at lunch. Thankfully, I don't have any classes with him, but I can't hide from him since he's friends with Cole. Even if their friendship seems to be on the rocks at the moment.

"He's coming," Deke assures him.

Cole turns to me. "I'm gonna go over the rules with you." I nod. Still not sure what we're doing here. "One, you have a month to complete your dare. But if you complete it sooner, then the next person goes the following week." So this is about the dares. I swallow, not wanting to do this. "Two, there has to be a consequence for each dare. If the dare is not completed, you must face the consequence by midnight on the last day. Three, there are no limits to the dares." No limits? That makes my stomach knot up. "Four, if your dare gets picked, you may choose to be present while the dare is being completed." I break out in a sweat and look at Deke. What if I get his, and he wants to go with me? I don't wanna be alone with him. He smiles and then gives me a wink like he knows what I'm thinking. "Last rule ... you get caught, you're on your own. Understand?"

"Yes," I say with a head nod, but on the inside, I am shaking.

The door opens, and Kellan walks in. His eyes are on mine while he walks over to the table. I take a step toward Cole, and he places his arm over my shoulders, and I let out a shaky breath. Although Cole is the reason I'm here, he makes me feel the safest. He's made it very clear that he won't tolerate Kellan touching me. I'm not so sure if he would stop Deke, though I'm hoping I don't have to find out.

"Here you go." Shane walks around, handing each of us a piece of paper and a pen. Then he goes back to sit down on the couch.

I remove myself from Cole's arm and turn to face the table. Bending over, my pen hovers over the paper.

What kind of dare could I possibly do? Shelby told me they have been doing these for a while, and they physically hurt themselves. I don't want to be responsible for someone getting hurt. That will just give them another reason to hate me.

Think! What all has Cole told me? Not much. I know they killed a guy. I know that the guy has a brother who beat his wife and then killed her ...

I get a thought. It's crazy and borderline illegal, but not enough to where I would spend the rest of my life in prison. Or end up dead.

I hear the guys behind me and know they are all done. They knew what tonight was so they already had their dares chosen before they walked in the door.

Even though I didn't want anything to do with this, I feel like now I have something to prove. I have to show them that I'm not afraid. I can hang with them.

I write down my dare and consequence and stick it in a bowl in the middle of the room. Then go sit on the couch next to Cole. I cross my legs, and he slides his hand between them, gripping my inner thigh. Kellan's eyes go to his hand and then to Cole's. He doesn't acknowledge him. But I tense.

Why does he hate me so much? Does he not understand that I don't want to be here?

Shane walks up to the bowl and draws a piece of paper out. His eyes go straight to mine. I swallow nervously.

He begins. "SURPRISE! I'll meet you in the sea. We'll swim together as we flee." He looks at Cole and then back down at the paper. "Consequence: you must dress like me for the day."

Kellan is the first one to speak. "What the fuck is this shit?'

Cole shifts his body on the couch and turns to me. "This isn't how it works, Austin."

"What?" I shrug. "You didn't say it couldn't be done like that." I didn't want to give the dare away because I don't want to be told I can't do it by someone. I had to make it to where no one would catch onto it. If they're making me do this, I'm all in. Too late to turn back now.

"It doesn't make any fucking sense," Kellan snaps.

"It's a riddle, idiot," Cole defends me. I almost smile.

"Absolutely not!" he snarls at Cole. "Draw again, Shane," he demands.

"No," Bennett says. "She's right. She isn't breaking any rules. And that is what he drew. We've never had anyone draw twice before, so we're not gonna start now."

CHAPTER SEVENTEEN

COLE

"This is bullshit!" Kellan barks, standing to his feet.

I slowly remove my hand from between her legs and stand, facing him. "You don't like it, you can pull out."

His eyes widen for a brief second before they land on Austin where she still sits on the couch. I don't agree with her dare, but that doesn't mean I'm not gonna back her. She doesn't know what we're doing. I've kept the rules as simple as possible for her. Not wanting her to know more than she needs to. She's a fucking chick. What did he think she was gonna have us do?

"Pull out?" Kellan growls at my words. "Want me to leave, Cole?"

Anyone can withdraw at any time. But to be thrown out, we all have to agree. I wish the fucker would just walk away. Kellan and I have always butted heads even though we've all been friends since we were little. I didn't hate him at first, but after Maddox, Landen, and Eli died, things changed between us. And the fact that he took my car to Bruce's house to fuck his wife isn't settling well with me. Why would he do it? Did he want me to get caught? If that's the case, why? And if so, would Celeste have said I was the one she fucked? Does he want me to rat him out? Me take the fall? I'm not sure, but I'm keeping my mouth shut until I find out.

"Cole—" Shane starts.

"No, let him make his decision," Deke interrupts him. He comes over to us and crosses his arms over his chest, ready to fight Kellan.

But I don't need his help, and he knows it. "I'm tired of you two fighting over fucking pussy."

"Hey," Austin says defensively.

"What is it, Kellan? You wanna fuck her too?" he asks, and she gasps. "You mad Cole found her first? Fuck, man, go stick your dick somewhere else. She's not worth it."

Austin shoots to her feet, eyes narrowed on Deke, but I shove her shoulder, making her sit back down. "Cole—"

"Is that the problem, Kellan?" I ask, interrupting her and taking a step toward him. His brown eyes meet mine. "You want her? Want me to share her with you? All you gotta do is ask. It wouldn't be the first time we've passed a girl around."

I know Celeste isn't the only bitch he's fucking at the moment. Just last week, he hooked up with Melanie, a girl on the volleyball team. Not like he has a reason to be faithful to Celeste. The bitch is married, after all.

His eyes go to Austin, and I hate how he looks over her like she is a piece of meat for him to eat. That would be the icing on the cake for him. To fuck Bruce's wife *and* daughter. And if he did sleep with her, that would piss off Celeste, and she would send her back without a second thought. I saw her eyes when she spoke of Kellan. She loves him. His eyes meet mine again.

I turn to Austin and grab her hand. I yank her up from the couch and slide my arm around her waist, pinning her back to my front. She tries to fight me, but I hold her in place. Her breath picks up in fear. "Cole, what are you …?"

"Did you listen to the video?" I ask him, cutting her off.

"What video?" she asks, and her voice shakes.

I bring my free hand up and wrap it around her throat and tilt her head back. It makes her arch her back, pushing her chest out. She whimpers, and her hands come up and grip my arm as if that's gonna stop me. Her pulse races, and she swallows nervously. His eyes go to her tits.

"Did you hear her scream my name inside that bathroom? Did you listen to her beg me for more?"

Her body trembles against mine.

"Everyone has heard that video," he snaps.

"I haven't," Deke chimes in.

Kellan looks at him and snorts. "You were fucking there. You were the one who recorded it."

He shrugs. "Doesn't mean I listened."

Kellan takes a step back, running a hand through his hair. "This is ridiculous," he says frustrated. Then his eyes meet mine. "I don't want your whore, Cole. I don't want her anywhere around me, let alone inside her pants. And I'm sure as hell not gonna let you push me out of the group because I don't like your little fuck-toy of the month." He grabs his jacket off the couch, turns around, and storms out the door.

I let go of Austin, and she takes three steps away from me, sucking in a deep breath. I turn to the guys, putting my back to her. "We need to vote his ass out."

Shane sighs heavily. "He's just going through a hard time."

"Bullshit!" Deke snaps. "He's always caused problems for us."

"Cole?" I hear Austin's voice behind me, but I ignore her. I'm busy at the moment.

Shane looks at Deke. "I can see where he's coming from. I'm still skeptical if she should even be here."

"She's not going anywhere," I growl.

"Cole?" she snaps. I still ignore her.

Bennett raises his hands. "This will blow over. Just let Kellan cool off."

"He's been this way for months now. He was like this before Austin ever came into the picture. He didn't even want to be involved with Jeff, and that makes me question his loyalty to the group," Deke growls.

"COLE!" she yells.

"He was just worried that we would get caught," Shane tells Deke.

I snort. "He just didn't wanna get his hands dirty." I hear the faint sound of a door opening and closing behind us.

"Cole?" Deke says.

"What?" I bark.

He looks over my shoulder. "Austin just left."

AUSTIN

As I come up to his car, I hear someone exiting the barn behind me. I know it's him. "Take me home!" I order, not even bothering to turn around and face him before I fall into the passenger seat and slam the door shut.

My body physically shakes with rage for what Cole just did.

He gets in and looks over at me, but I keep my eyes straight ahead. My hands ball into fists in my lap, and my heart pounds in my chest.

He offered me up to Kellan. To fucking Kellan of all people! I thought he had been protecting me from him these past two weeks, but I was so wrong.

And my mind can't seem to process that. I know Cole is a fucking savage. I have seen firsthand what he will do to get what he wants. But to just offer me up to any of them? Like I'm some toy they can just pass around? Is that why they wanted me to join so badly?

"Austin!" he growls my name, his irritation showing.

I turn and glare at him with hatred. I'm fucking panting; I'm breathing so heavily.

His narrowed blue eyes are on me like it's my fault. As if I should have said *yes, Kellan, if you want me, then go ahead and take me.*

"Austin ..."

I do what he once did to me, reach over and turn up the volume, blaring "Bitter End" by The Veer Union. Then I sit back in my seat, dismissing whatever the fuck he planned to say.

He allows it, putting the car into gear and throwing gravel as he takes off.

When he pulls up to my house, I'm out of the car before he can even bring it to a stop. I walk in, slam the front door, and run up to my room. The moment I shut it, it opens. I turn around to see him entering just as fast as I did. "Get the hell out, Cole," I say, pointing at the now closed door.

"No," he says simply.

"Get the fuck out!" I shout.

He takes a step toward me, and I throw up my hands, taking a step back. "Don't you dare come near me."

"Austin—"

"No, Cole!" I interrupt him. "What you did back there was completely unacceptable!"

"I—"

"You were out of line!" I shout, fisting my hands down by my sides. "You don't own me. And you can't just decide to offer me up to one of your *buddies*." I give him my back, planning on locking myself in my bathroom to get away from him.

He grabs my shoulder and yanks me back to face him. "I can do whatever I want."

My skin is boiling; I'm so mad. "No! You can't. This is my life!" I scream.

"Need a reminder?"

"No!" I jerk away from him. I wasn't expecting him to let me go, and I stumble backwards but manage not to fall. He smirks. "I don't need you to remind me that you are a man who doesn't care if he hurts a woman," I snap.

His eyes narrow on me. "Don't push me, Austin."

"Push you?" I ask and snort. Spreading my arms out wide, I say, "Do your worst, Cole." What else could this bastard do to me that he hasn't already?

"You don't mean that, sweetheart." He takes a step toward me; his eyes look me up and down, and he licks his lips.

"Not only did you offer me up to Kellan, but you have also humiliated me at school," I growl. "You recorded us …"

"You begged me for it. The video proved it."

My mouth falls open at his words. He knew he was coming to the party, and we were going to have sex. And he knew he was gonna have Deke record it.

I stand there speechless as he closes the small space between us. His right hand comes up, and he slides his fingers into my hair. I stare up at him at a complete loss while his eyes roam my face.

"You knew what you were doing, Austin. And I told you, you were going to hate me in the morning, but you didn't seem to care one bit."

"I didn't know you were going to record it," I say as angry tears start to sting my eyes. My body shakes, and my throat begins to close up.

He lowers his mouth to my ear. "It's not my fault you spread your legs for the devil, sweetheart. That's all on you."

"You set me up." I choke on the words.

He chuckles. "I did no such thing. You went to a party. You got drunk, and then you dared me." He pulls back, and his eyes stare into mine. I refuse to blink, to let the tears fall. I'm stronger than this. "You dared me to hurt you." He runs his busted knuckles over my cheek. He lowers his face where his lips almost touch mine. "And I did."

I swallow the lump in my throat, trying not to show him just how much. "You had no right …"

"Even if I hadn't had Deke record it, everyone there still heard you, sweetheart."

I swallow the knot in my throat and look away. I hate that he's right. It's my fault. I shouldn't have dared him. I shouldn't have played into his little fucking game. I've been pushing back just as much as he has, but I'm the one who seems to lose every time. He has help. He's got a team on his side. I have no one.

"And it's not like you didn't enjoy it."

I whimper at his words and whisper, "Go to hell, Cole."

His hand grips my hair, and he moves my head, forcing me to look up at him. His blue eyes search mine. They shine. He lowers his lips and smiles against mine. I don't dare move. "Sweetheart, I am hell."

I hate how right he is. "Please go." I swallow what pride I have left and beg him to leave.

He releases my hair, and his hand moves to cup my face. I try to swallow the knot in my throat. "I'll see you in the morning." He leans down, kisses my forehead, and then walks out. I throw myself onto my bed and scream into my pillow.

CHAPTER EIGHTEEN

COLE

I stand outside her door as I hear her muffled scream. She's breaking. Every day, I'm dragging her closer to the edge of no return. But in order to get her to fall, I'm gonna have to drag her. I won't be able to save myself, and we're both gonna hit fucking bottom.

Minutes later, I walk into my father's house and go straight up to Lilly's room. Her pink kitty lamp is on next to her bed, and she is sound asleep. I turn it off, and the only light comes from her nightlight.

Leaning down, I kiss her forehead and then walk out, leaving her door cracked open. I head to my bedroom, strip out of my clothes, and slide on my board shorts, then make my way down to the pool.

I dive in and the cold night air burns my skin when I come up for a breath.

Kellan is becoming a bigger problem every day that goes by. And I don't know what to do about it or what he has planned. He knows about our final dare. The one we have planned for graduation night. I wonder how much he has told Celeste about what we do. People in this town know we destroy shit. We've been daring each other to do stupid shit since we were little kids. But when I was sixteen, Eli dared me to steal my father's car and run it into the creek. I did it three hours later. I hated that car, and he fucking loved it. It was his *baby*. His beloved. Nothing mattered other than that car.

He never found out it was me. He was in a pissy mood for months, and I loved it.

The dares just snowballed from there. We got a system down, and it worked for us. Eight boys whose parents had money and could get away with anything. We did it all. Well, not murder. We just progressed to that recently.

I go back underwater and do a lap. Then another. I'm tired and exhausted when I finally get out. The time on my phone reads 1:05 a.m. I dry off, and thoughts of Austin enter my mind.

I need more from her.

I smile when I think of why I'm doing this to her. Because I can. It's that fucking simple. It's like she forgets she has no one. Except me.

The following morning, I pull up to her house, and she's already sitting on the front steps. Her backpack at her feet and phone in her hands. She stands when she sees my car and walks toward it. I find it odd but don't question it.

She wears a pair of holey jeans with her black Chucks and a simple black t-shirt. Her hair is down and in big curls. A pair of black sunglasses cover her green eyes, and red lipstick highlights her lips. She looks fucking delicious.

She gets in, not saying a word, and sits back in the seat. I take off, trying to ignore the erection in my pants. I can't think straight whenever she is around me. All I wanna do is bury myself in her.

After dropping Lilly off, we pull up to the school, and she still hasn't spoken a word. Not unusual for us, but it has me on alert. We walk inside and go to our lockers. She takes her time, and I watch her. She hasn't removed her sunglasses, nor has she smiled.

She's still pissed. And I find it sexy as fuck!

The bell rings, and I grab her hand, expecting her to pull away, but she doesn't. I walk her to class, and as we step inside her room, she turns to face me. And before I can do anything, she lifts on her tiptoes and kisses me. Which is unusual. I always initiate it.

She moans into my mouth, and I wrap my hands in her hair. She kisses me like she's desperate for me. Her body presses into mine, and I deepen the kiss. As if we are alone in my room and I'm about to rip her fucking clothes off.

Finally, she pulls away first, and I push her glasses up to her head. The smile she gives me is nothing short of wicked. I narrow my eyes on her.

She's up to something. The only other time she looked at me like that was when she sent me the video of Jeff's body burning.

She's like me, after all—has no limits.

"I'll see you next period," I say, and she turns, giving me her back. Not saying a word.

AUSTIN

I sit in first period in the back next to Becky. She is on her phone texting—Deke, I'm sure. For two people who are only having sex, they seem to be obsessed with one another. It's annoying. She was supposed to be my friend, but I only get her when he is at practice with the guys.

I have so many questions I want to ask her, but they are gonna have to wait. I decided last night after Cole left that I wasn't gonna let him get to me. Not anymore. I was gonna show all of them that I can do this. You don't see them crying or begging one another to stop doing something they don't like, so I'm not going to either.

I grab my bag, get up, and walk to the teacher's desk. "May I use the restroom?"

She raises her hand and waves me off without looking at me. I walk out of class and down the silent hallway. I pass Cole and Deke's calculus classroom and head straight to Cole's locker. I've watched him do his combination enough to know it by heart now.

Once it pops open, I reach up to the top shelf and grab his car keys and then slam it shut. I finish running down the hall and take a right, heading up the stairs to the second floor. I turn to the red box on the wall with a red handle. I then look up at the camera and pull it down.

Go big or go home!

The alarm sounds, and the lights start to flash. Doors bursts open, and students run out into the hallway. I stand on my tiptoes, looking for Shane. I see him exit the last classroom on the right. I make my way down the hall and to him. "Let's go," I yell over the sounding alarms.

"What are you doing, Austin?" he asks confused.

"We don't have time. Let's go." I grab his hand and drag him down the hall.

We make it down the stairs, and I see Cole out of the corner of my eye, but I don't stop. We barge out the double doors. "Where are we going?"

"You'll see soon enough." I tell him the same thing Cole has told me so many times. I press the unlock button on Cole's car, and it lights up.

"Whoa." Shane comes to a stop. "Why do you have Cole's car keys?" he demands.

"Because I'm gonna drive us."

He shakes his head. "Yes. This is your dare," I state, and he grinds his teeth, knowing he has to do it.

"Cole is gonna be pissed."

I smile. Fuckin' right, he will be. *All part of my plan.* "When is Cole not pissed?"

"We can't leave, Austin," he states.

"I didn't pull that fire alarm for nothing," I growl.

"You did that?" he asks wide-eyed. "Shit. You're gonna be in so much trouble."

I grab his arm and yank on it, finally getting him to move again. We get into the car, and I hold out my right hand. "Phone," I demand.

He digs it out of his pocket without question. I turn his off along with mine and shove them into the center console.

Then we're off.

I pull up to the same parking spot Cole brought me to three weeks ago and turn off his car.

"Why are we here, Austin?" Shane asks.

I let out a long breath, nervousness setting in. "Cole told me all about Jeff's brother," I say, and he stays quiet. "About how he beat his wife who was Eli's sister." I look over at him. "One of his best friends."

He looks away from me, his lips thinned. I look down at my hands knotted in my lap, letting out a long breath. I'm about to tell this guy too much about myself, but I want him to trust me, right? To have one more person on my side. "I know what it's like to have a man put his hands on you and not be able to stop it. To have no control." My chest tightens. "I don't believe in what you guys do or how you do it, but I do believe he deserves to suffer for hurting someone he was supposed to protect. Love." I clear my throat. "And I want to help."

I look over at him to find him staring at me with a blank expression. I bite my lip, nervously waiting for him to say no. That I'm screwing up plans they already have. Instead, he nods. "I'm guessing you have a plan?"

"I do." I smile at him.

CHAPTER NINETEEN
COLE

I sit in fourth period with only twenty minutes left when the door opens. Austin walks right in with a smile on her face and her head held high. I want to yank her back out the door and choke her.

"Where have you been?" I demand when she plops down next to me.

She doesn't answer.

I've been calling her for three hours. And then between classes, we realized that Shane was gone too. A call to his phone told me it was also off. And they were together. That's when I realized my car keys were gone. *Talk about pissed!*

"Mrs. Duncan, can you send Austin Lowes to the office please?" The office comes over the intercom.

"You heard her, Miss Lowes," the teacher tells her, and she stands.

I get up as well and follow her out. "What the hell did you do?" I demand, bringing her to a stop in the hall. "Austin?"

She just looks up at me. Her green eyes full of mischief.

"Where did you go?"

"To do Shane's dare."

I grind my teeth. "How did you get out of class?" She isn't eighteen yet. She can't sign herself out.

"I pulled the fire alarm," she explains.

"What?" I shout. *That was her?*

She doesn't even flinch at my tone. "I did it for the dare."

"What the hell were you thinking? They're gonna suspend you." Fuck! I told her dad I would keep her out of trouble. How the hell am I gonna get her out of this? The guys and I may do some really stupid, illegal shit, but it never involves the school. That jeopardizes our chance on the swim team. We're not that stupid.

"Get off my back, Cole," she snaps, her finger pressed into my chest. "You brought me into this," she shouts. "Don't blame me for something I didn't have any control over." She steps into me. "You should have taken what I did to Jeff as a warning. Instead, you took it as a challenge. But you know what, Cole? You underestimate me, and that's your fault. Not mine." Then she walks off down the quiet hall, heading to the office with a little too much hop in her step for someone who is about to get suspended.

And I can't help but smile. Austin Lowes is more of a shark than I thought.

AUSTIN

"I got suspended," I tell Celeste as I plop down on the couch in my father's house.

She stands in front of me, eyes narrowed and hands on her hips. Cole stands in the corner, glaring. He's still pissed off at me from earlier. After I walked out of the principal's office, he was waiting for me, looking every bit of the dick he is. We haven't spoken since, but he had to drive me home. I was hoping he would just drop me off and go, but no, he is obviously just as nosy as he is an asshole.

"Yes! The school called me!" she barks. Her eyes go to Cole. "You're supposed to be keeping her out of trouble."

I snort. "He's not my babysitter." If she only had a clue of what he's put me through, she'd see what I did was nothing.

"I had nothing to do with it," he chimes in, and my eyes narrow on him. He's the reason I did the damn dare in the first place!

"It's not a big deal. It's just three days," I tell her. I've been suspended for more.

"No big deal? Your father is gonna be pissed," she snaps.

"What's he gonna do, ground me?"

"He's sending you back to your mother's," Cole answers me.

"What?" I ask, looking back over at him.

"Cole—" Celeste starts.

But he continues. "He wanted to ship you back to your mother's the other day with twenty grand. Because, like your mother, he doesn't want you."

"Cole," she snaps.

How much does he know? "How do you know that?" I demand, standing from the couch. Then I look at her. "Jesus, how much have you told him about *my* life?"

She opens her mouth, but Cole speaks. "He told me at dinner the other night."

"What?" I snap. Why would he tell him that? Cole and Celeste are obviously close. But how close are he and my dad? As far as I know, he hates him as much as I do.

"I won't let that happen," Celeste assures me. "And I'm the only one the school contacts. So we just won't tell him." She bows her head and sighs.

I look back at Cole, and he looks at me with disgust. Like I'm some charity case he took on. As if I asked to be part of his little twisted group.

My eyes go back to Celeste. "I don't care. Let him send me back." That's what I want, right? It would get me away from Cole and his friends. It would get me out of all his twisted scams and blackmail. I look at Cole. "Not sure why you do."

"Austin?" Celeste starts, but I ignore her and pull my cell out of my back pocket.

I go to my contacts and find **Bruce**. Then hit call. Placing it to my ear, I tap my foot on the Persian rug, hoping he still has the same number. It has been four years since I've called him.

"Austin?" he growls in answer.

"I got suspended," I say without wasting a second.

Chuckling has me looking up, and I see Cole. He has his hand over his mouth trying to hide a smirk. His eyes meet mine, and he shakes his head like I've lost my mind.

"Austin!" Celeste snaps, taking a step toward me to yank my phone from my ear, but I place my hand up to stop her and take a step back.

"What?" he barks through the line. "What the hell did you do?"

"Pulled the fire alarm."

He lets out a growl of annoyance. "How long?"

"Three days."

Celeste throws her hands up and storms out of the room, and I look back at Cole. He is no longer laughing at me, but he does have a smirk on his face.

My father clears his throat. "Well …" He pauses. "Will it affect graduation?"

I frown but say, "No."

"Okay, then. Don't do it again," he snaps and then hangs up on me.

I place the phone in my back pocket, my eyes never leaving Cole's. "He's not sending me home." He arches a brow. "Just wanted to know if it would affect graduation." His smirk grows to a full smile, and my eyes narrow on him. *He wanted to ship you back to your mother's the other day with twenty grand.* "Did you have something to do with this?" I demand.

He reaches up and rubs his lips, his eyes on mine. "I have no clue what you're talking about."

I take a step toward him. "What did you do, Cole?"

"Insurance," he says simply.

It's the same thing he said to me before he sliced my arm open. "I know you've done something," I snap.

"I dare you to prove it."

I run a hand through my hair unable to play mind games right now. I can't take it anymore. "I need some air," I mutter. I shove open the door to the terrace and take off. I run because it feels good. I run because that's all I'm allowed to do. I feel like Eli's sister's husband. That hamster in the cage. Unable to do anything. Unable to go anywhere. I make it to the top of the hill, and the cemetery comes into view, but I don't stop. My lungs tighten as I try to suck in a breath. My side hurts, but it's something I did. It's my choice. *Fuck them!* And their rules for me. Screw …

I'm hit from behind and thrown to the ground. "What …?" I look up to see Cole on top of me. "What are you doing?"

"What are you doing?" he snaps.

"Trying to get away from you. Now get off." *God, he's relentless.*

I shove him, but he grabs me and pins my wrists down. I growl.

"You are so frustrating," he says, his blue eyes looking down at me, a smirk on his face. *He's enjoying this.*

Bastard!

"Fight me," he orders.

"Cole," I snap. Not in the mood for his shit.

"I dare you to fight me." My eyes narrow up at him, and he arches a brow. "Show me what you got, Austin."

I buck my hips, kick my feet, and try to yank my hands free of his iron grip, but nothing works. I arch my back and scream.

He lowers his head to my neck, and I can feel his heart racing against my chest. "Let it out, sweetheart," he whispers. "Just like you did that night I had you pinned. The night I decided you were going to be mine."

"Stop." I hate how he says *mine*. As if he really wants me to be his. No one has ever wanted me like he does, and that thought makes me a little nervous and excited.

He pulls away and looks down at me. "I'm gonna hold you here. Pinned to the ground. Helpless." My eyes narrow on him. "And you're gonna fight me until you have nothing left. Until you're weak. Worn out. Until you realize I'm stronger."

"Please," I growl the word. Unable to say it otherwise.

"No," he says simply.

"I hate you," I snap.

He frowns as if that hurt his feelings. "You hate yourself, Austin."

"No …"

"You hate that you're powerless. You hate that you have nowhere to go." He looks up at the cemetery and sighs. "I was once like this."

He looks back at me. "I once had no control too, Austin. But I picked myself up and fought. Now fucking fight me," he orders.

I try once again, kicking my feet and digging my heels into the ground to throw him off. Jerking on my hands but nothing works.

He lowers his head to my neck and laughs. He fucking laughs at how weak I am. "I can do this all day, sweetheart …"

I turn my head and sink my teeth into his neck.

His left hand releases mine, and he lets out a growl from the pain. I ball my fists, swinging. I hit him in the side of the head, and his body jerks back. I dig my heels into the ground and lift my hips, throwing him forward over my head. I roll out from underneath him. He recovers quickly and lunges for me. I stick out my leg, kicking him in the chest and knocking him back. I crawl on top of him and straddle his hips. I wrap my hands around his wrists, pinning them above his head. I'm panting. Heart racing.

He has a cut on the right cheek. His bottom lip is bleeding, and he's got a big smile on his face as he looks up at me. It's the first real smile I've ever seen from him. And even though I know how evil he can be, he looks absolutely gorgeous.

"You think you've got me?" The amusement in his voice lets me know he's indulging me.

I lick my lips. "I'm the one on top."

He chuckles softly. He pushes his arms out wide, and it forces me to release his wrists. Before I can plant them by his head and catch myself from falling, his hands are on my face, and he flips us over and pins me down.

"We need to work on your speed."

"We need to work on your attitude," I tell him.

"Oh, yeah?" he asks, arching a dark brow. That smile still on his face. It's so bright it's blinding. It almost makes me forget all the shit he's done to me. "Why do you say that?"

"'Cause I've known you for three weeks, and this is the first time I've ever seen you really smile."

It drops off his face like he didn't know it was there. And just like all the other times, he places that mask on that hides him from the world. *I knew he'd do that.* But I wanted him to know that I noticed it.

I wrap my arms around his neck and my legs around his hips. Letting him know his fuck you look doesn't intimidate me anymore.

I've got you, Cole Reynolds.

His hands are on the grass on either side of my head, holding himself up. "I'll fight you, Cole. I'll play this game even though I don't know what the hell I'm doing. But I dare you to smile for me. I dare you to show me something that nobody else sees."

CHAPTER TWENTY

COLE

I stand at the clubhouse with my arms crossed over my chest and wearing a scowl on my face. Her words from earlier in the cemetery gnaw at me. She fought. She showed me she has a little more in her. But then she had to go and ruin it by pointing out that I was smiling. That I, for once, was genuinely happy for a second. Nothing else mattered. It instantly pissed me off.

She's getting to me. *Not good.*

I shouldn't care. Actually, I should call the whole thing off. Call Bruce and tell him to send her ass back to her mom's. That would be the smart thing to do. She's clouding my head, and I need to think clearly. One fucking sentence was all it took to twist my mind. *I dare you to show me something that nobody else sees.*

What the fuck is that? What does she want to see? There's only me. The hate. The rage. The fuckups. I've got nothing else to show.

Shane walks in and sits down on the couch next to Austin. She is texting on her phone. We haven't spoken since that moment in the cemetery three hours ago. After she dared me, I got up and walked back to the house, leaving her lying on the ground. Then I got in my car and left. Shane sent a mass text an hour later that we all needed to meet. I sent her a text to *drive yourself.* She didn't respond, but I knew she read it.

"Where the fuck is Deke?" I snap. The time he is spending with Becky is really getting annoying.

"On his way," Kellan answers. I don't miss his eyes gliding over Austin. She avoids looking in his direction.

"Fuck! That man gets some pussy, and everything else goes to shit," I snap.

Just then, the door opens and in he walks. A smile on his face and licking his lips as if they were just between Becky's legs. "Let's get this over with." He rubs his hands together. "I've got plans."

Shane stands up and walks over to the table, not wasting another second. He places a laptop on it.

"Whose is this?" Bennett asks.

Shane smiles like a fucking idiot. "Jerrold's."

I stiffen. "What?"

He looks at me. "It was pretty awesome." He turns and looks at Austin who still sits on the couch. She's smiling as if proud of herself. "We walked in. And no one even questioned us …" I fist my hands. "She pushed her tits out and went into his office, asking about the bathroom. I've never seen a guy move so fast. He took her down to the lower level to show her the *nicest* restrooms they had." He rolls his eyes. "And I slipped inside and stole his laptop. Then on the way out, I pulled the fire alarm so it would take longer for him to notice it was missing …" He trails off. "Told you she'd be perfect," Shane says, looking over at Kellan. That smile still on his face. Those reservations he had last night about her, long gone.

"Seriously?" Deke asks surprised "But how did you …?"

"How did she even know who he was? Or where he was?" Kellan snaps, interrupting him. "How much have you fucking told her?"

I cross my arms over my chest.

He growls. "Cole …"

I look at her, and she throws me a smile. Like I just got caught in some big lie. "That night we killed Jeff. Remember when we heard something? It was her. She was there, and she watched us." I haven't told them because they never asked about where she came from or how I found her.

"Jesus!"

"I blackmailed her." I glare at Austin. "Had Deke call my cell with

168

hers. I took the knife and cut her arm."

"Stitches …" Shane whispers to himself, starting to put two and two together.

"Then I took the knife and stabbed Jeff with it. Told her if she went to the cops, they could link her to the body and she'd be a suspect."

Bennett looks amused. Shane runs his hand through his hair nervously. Kellan looks pissed, and Deke, he's texting on his phone. "She sent me a video later that night of her burning the body."

"What the fuck?" Kellan barks.

"Told me there was no evidence to pin her with. The following day, I took her to his work and explained why we killed him."

Deke smiles down at his phone but speaks to me. "Good one."

"Why the fuck didn't you tell us all this?" Kellan demands.

"I haven't told anyone," she snaps at him.

He turns to face her, and I bow my chest, ready for a fight. If he goes for her, I'm gonna take him down. "You need to leave," he snaps.

She stands from the couch, her green eyes full of rage. She gives him a sinister smile, like this was her plan all along, and then her eyes meet mine. "Gladly." She turns and heads toward the door.

"Don't you dare walk out that door!" I shout, and she stops. I look at the guys. "Everyone out except Austin and Shane."

"Cole …"

"Get the fuck out!"

They all look at one another for a long moment, and then their eyes go to her. She's got her chin lifted and a fuck you look in her eyes. One by one, they start to walk out, no one speaking.

Austin stays where she is at, and Shane comes to stand in front of me. "I didn't know what she had planned, man."

She rolls her eyes at him ratting her out. But all of them will do that. They owe her no loyalty.

"Why did you go to him?" I ask her.

She doesn't answer.

I turn to Shane again. He speaks without me having to ask twice. "She said she knew what it was like to have a man put his hands on her and not be able to stop it …"

My eyes shoot to her, and she is drilling holes into his head.

"Stop." I hold up my hand to cut off whatever else he was saying. I walk over to her. "Who has hit you?" I demand. *I can take a hit*, she had said, but I never gave much thought to it. Not until now.

Her hard eyes meet mine. "This isn't about me."

"Bullshit!" I snap.

"I just wanted to help Eli's sister."

"She's dead," I snarl.

"Yes, I fucking know that." Her voice grows louder.

I cup her cheek, softening my voice. "Who hit you?"

She flinches as if I slapped her and pulls away. "My life is none of your business."

My father said that her mother's boyfriend was abusing her, but at the time, I thought he meant her mom. *It was her.* "It was your mother's boyfriend, right?" Her jaw sharpens, and her eyes dart to Shane again. "Did she know he put his hands on you?" She looks away from me. "Did you tell anyone?" I demand.

She looks back at me. "Like I told people about you?" she snaps. "You blackmailed me. Twice."

"That is different."

"How? You offered me up to Kellan. You allowed Deke to undo my pants."

Shane's eyes widen, but I ignore him. "I'm talking about him hitting you." My eyes narrow on her. "Has he *touched* you before?"

She bites her bottom lip and looks down at her black Chucks. "Austin? This is serious."

She throws her head back laughing, but it's forced. "What are you gonna do, Cole?" Her green eyes meet mine again, and she spreads her arms out wide. "Gonna go to California and blackmail him? Kill him?"

"So he *has* touched you?" I ask through gritted teeth.

She runs a hand through her hair. "I'm not gonna discuss this."

"Yes, you are," I snap.

She crosses her arms over her chest. "Talking about it doesn't change it."

"Did he rape you?" I demand.

Shane shuffles from foot to foot.

"No," she answers, but that doesn't ease the tightness in my stomach. "Look." Her eyes meet mine. "I thought we weren't going to do this?"

I clench my fists. She's right, but Bruce is just waiting for the first opportunity to ship her back. I have a deal with him, but that doesn't mean he won't fuck me over at any given moment. "Just tell me what he did."

Her narrowed eyes go to Shane, and he looks away from her, feeling guilty for throwing her under the bus. "No, Cole!" she snaps, her anger taking over. "This conversation is over!" She turns her back to me and starts to walk toward the door.

"Austin!"

She spins around to face me, her long hair slapping her in the face while walking backward to the door. "I'll tell you what, Cole, when you feel like sharing your secrets with me, I'll share mine with you." And with that, she spins back around and walks out, slamming the door shut.

Shane and I stand in the silence, and I fist my hands down by my side. I shouldn't have made her drive herself here. Then she wouldn't have been able to leave.

I spin around and yank my shirt off, walking over to the punching bag. It's my go-to when I need to relieve some anger.

"I'm sorry, man," Shane says, clearing his throat.

"Don't repeat what you heard tonight," I say before I start pounding the bag, imagining it's her mother's boyfriend's face, until my shoulder is screaming from the pain.

Tuesday morning, I sit in fourth period as kids put their stuff in their bags. The bell getting ready to ring, and I look over at her empty seat next to me. I didn't get much sleep last night. I tossed and turned and imagined her as a kid—what her mom's boyfriend did to her—and it made me think of Lilly. How evil this world is and how many men would take advantage of a little girl who couldn't defend herself. Who has no one to protect them. It made me furious. Austin is a perfect example of that. I've been taking advantage of her ever since I laid eyes on her.

I got up and crawled in bed with Lilly. I held her close and kissed her hair. The thought of someone hurting her makes me sick, but nobody cares what happens to Austin.

While I laid there trying to figure out how I can protect Lilly from evil, my mind went back to Austin. I hate that she refused to tell me what her mother's piece of shit boyfriend has done. How old was she the first time he hit her? Touched her? Did her mother protect her?

I haven't heard from her, but the urge to pick up my phone and text her has been strong.

The bell rings, and I walk down the hallway, into the cafeteria, and sit down at our usual table.

Becky comes in with Deke on her arm, and they laugh like they've got nothing but jokes to tell. For the first time, I envy my best friend. He can turn it off like a switch. He can go from murderer to a fucking comedian in an instant. Not me. I hate the world. I hate myself. And I hate Austin.

No, you don't.

"What's wrong, Cole?" Becky asks me.

"Nothing," I growl.

Deke waves her off and chimes in. "He's just pissy 'cause Austin isn't here for him to hang all over."

Becky looks at me for a few seconds, her crystal blue eyes watching mine, and I look away. Noticing the white walls and students walking in, I hear them talking about their nonexistent lives. I feel her eyes on me, and I look back at her. Yep. Still staring. "Do you have something you want to say?" I snap.

"Do you and Austin have plans this weekend?" she asks, ignoring my anger.

"Why would *we* have plans?"

"Because you guys are dating," she says simply.

"Babe, I told you it's not like that," Deke says, shaking his head. Then he gets up to grab their lunches.

She leans forward, and I hold in a sigh. "I see it written all over your face."

"I don't know what you're talking about."

"I've gone to school with you my entire life, Cole." She lowers her voice. "I've seen you lose people you love." My fists clench. "And I've seen how you look at her. I've seen a change in you." I snort. "The other day, when she and I were standing outside the gym waiting for you guys to finish your meeting …" She looks down at the table. "I asked her how she was doing. If she was okay. I felt like something was wrong with her, but she blew me off and said she was just tired." Her eyes meet mine. That explains why Austin jumped out of the car and tried to walk home. Becky got to her. "She lied, of course. I could ask you if you're okay, and we both know you would lie too. But I know you better. Known you longer. I've watched you lately, and although I think you have hurt her, I also think you protect her."

"Becky …"

"I see how you pull her tighter when Kellan walks into a room. And some would just chalk that up to being possessive, but I think it's more than that."

"Like what?" I can't help but ask.

"Even the devil catches feelings, or he wouldn't go into rages. Even he knows how to love."

"Stop! I don't love her." What the fuck? *Has Deke warped her mind?*

"Maybe not love. But I see the way you kiss her in class and in the halls. How you touch her, not caring who is watching. And the look in your eyes when she isn't around and she consumes your thoughts. It's written all over your face. Like right now."

"And?" I ask, wondering what she sees. If she can read me that well.

"And you've always been the kind of guy who would burn this

town down if given a reason." She sits back in her seat, crossing her arms over her chest. She smiles at me. "And Austin is your reason."

AUSTIN

I lie on the couch, watching a rerun of Gilmore Girls, when I hear the front door open and shut and then Phillip's voice. "Where is your mother?"

"How the hell should I know?"

He walks over to me and knocks my feet off the couch and plops down next to me. He leans into me, grabbing my arm.

"Don't touch me," I snap, yanking out of his hold.

"Come on, Austin. You're gonna miss me. I know I'm gonna miss you."

I roll my eyes and stand, walking to my room because I know he's drunk. Just as I shut my door, it's shoved open and hits the interior wall. I spin around before he throws me onto the bed. "Get off me!" I shout.

"You know you want me, baby," he growls.

I lift my knee between us and aim right for his balls. He cries out when I make contact. "Get off me." I shove him, and he hits the floor with a thud.

"Little bitch," he growls.

"Honey?" I hear my mom call out to him, and the front door open and close. She enters my room seconds later. Her green eyes narrow on me and then they go to Phillip. "What happened?" She runs to him. "Did you do this to him?" she demands, helping him sit up.

I stand by my bed, my hands balled into fists and my body physically shaking.

"What did you do?" she yells at me as he gets up to his feet.

"I'm gonna teach you a lesson ..." He comes for me, and I grab the lamp off my nightstand and throw it, hitting him right in the face.

My mom cries out as he hits the floor once again. "Get the fuck out and don't come back!" she screams at me.

I grab my purse and phone, and jump out my window before it's too late for me to get away.

That was the day before they shipped me off to Oregon. That was the most aggressive he had ever gotten with me. I'm not sure how far he would have taken it, but I didn't wait to see.

I went out and partied all night. It wasn't hard to do since it was New Year's Eve. I went to a party, got wasted and smoked some weed. Then went home long enough the next afternoon to pack a couple of bags and take a cab to the airport. My mother didn't tell me bye, and she didn't call. Not until days later when she wanted to know if I had seen my father and could send her money.

They've been on my mind a lot since I walked out of the clubhouse last night. My conversation with Cole keeps playing in my mind, and it's driving me nuts. I can't understand for the life of me why he cares. Why he pretends. Why can't we just decide we hate one another but wanna fuck and leave it at that? I hate that he had Deke record us that first night, but I can't be mad for what he said. Everyone there knew what we were doing in that bathroom. And of course, I've done it multiple times with him since then. And let's not forget the fact that he touches me while at school. I kiss him. Fuck, the other day I moaned while in the hallway between classes. He hasn't forced me to do anything when it comes to sex. I've done all that on my own.

He's such a mystery. And that's what draws me to him.

To be honest, I'm comfortable with the violence. I've seen it all my life. My mother has dated her boyfriend for over fifteen years, but they never got married. It's all him. She would have done it in a heartbeat. He didn't wanna be tied to someone who had a kid. Another reason I think she always tried to get rid of me.

In a way, Cole is like me. We both do what it takes to survive. We're just fighting two completely different battles.

But Cole has taught me that I can turn that pain into power. That I have the ability to stick up for myself. Even if I fail every time I go up against him, he has a strange way of encouraging me. This is just another level of hell, and I feel like I'm doing better at it.

I lean my head back, soaking up the sun. Today is the first day of my three-day suspension, and I chose to do nothing but hang out in the pool. Celeste had a date with some girlfriends and asked me to join her, but I declined, wanting to spend it alone. Even though it is a cloudy day. It's Oregon, after all, and we're right on the ocean. Gloomy seems to be the norm. But I like it.

I've got a black bikini on that has silver hoops connecting the sides on the bottoms and straps for the top. It's gonna give me terrible tan lines, but I'm not really concerned 'cause I don't think I'll get much with the clouds. Plus, I'm already pretty tan.

I hear the back door open, and I sigh. "Did you bring me leftovers?" I ask Celeste as I place my hand down and run it through the water, turning around.

"I skipped lunch."

"Cole?" I ask when I see him standing by the pool. Wearing a pair of jeans and white t-shirt, he has his hands in his front pockets. "What are you doing here?" I ask, my eyes darting to the door to see if he came alone.

He walks over to the lounge chair and sits down. He bows his head and runs his hand through his dark hair. "Everything okay?" I ask, not expecting an answer.

He looks up at me. "I can't … I can't get you out of my mind," he admits softly.

"What?"

"What you told me at the clubhouse last night. I can't forget it."

I sigh. "Cole, please—"

"Just hear me out," he interrupts me.

I get off my raft and swim over to the edge, placing my forearms on the side. His blue eyes watch every move I make, and I can't decipher the look.

"I knew someone who was taken advantage of. She was strong, but I still saw it eat at her." He looks away from me. "I hated not being able to help her. To save her from the memories. And the betrayal." He swallows. "She was like you. Had no one." His eyes come back to mine, and I try to swallow the knot in my throat. "You know I would have never let Deke touch you, right?"

I look away from him because no, I didn't know that. That night in the cemetery and then again at the clubhouse—he never made a move to stop him.

"Kellan?" I can't help but ask.

"I was testing him."

"What does that mean?"

He runs a hand through his hair. "He wants you, Austin."

"Yeah, dead like the rest of you." I snort.

"No. He wants between your legs, sweetheart. Deke was baiting him. I had to follow through."

My eyes drop to my hands on the wet concrete, avoiding his gaze.

He sighs heavily, and I glance up at him. He's staring down at me. "Just know, I wouldn't let anyone touch you, Austin. No one but me." I've never seen his blue eyes so soft. And I hate that it makes me feel warm inside as if someone actually wants to protect me. It's crazy to think of Cole that way. Maybe this is just another one of his games.

"I want you to tell me—"

"I don't talk about it," I interrupt him.

His jaw sharpens. "Why not?"

I laugh like that was funny. "Because no one ever cared," I snap.

He gets up and walks over to me. Bending over, he grabs my hand and lifts it gently. I have no other choice but to climb out of the pool as he pulls me up. He cups my face and pulls my body flush to his, the water soaking his clothes instantly. "I care."

"Why?" I ask nervously. "You've hurt me. I'm not gonna tell you something just for you to play some sick game with me."

"It's not like that," he growls.

"Then what's it like, Cole? Because I'm getting a headache trying to figure it out," I snap.

He takes a step back, running his hand through his spiked hair. His white t-shirt and jeans cling to his body. "Just tell me one thing."

"What?" I ask, rubbing my temples. Not lying about getting a headache.

"Your mother sent you here to protect you, right? So he couldn't touch you?" His soft eyes meet mine, and I can't make myself hurt him. Not after what he told me about the friend he couldn't help. He didn't have to say her name, but I know he was talking about Eli's older sister.

"Yeah," I say.

"Austin." He grabs my arm and pulls me back into him. "You just lied to me." His eyes narrow on mine.

Teeth clenching, I argue. "No, I didn't—"

"Stop lying!" he interrupts me. "And tell me the truth, Austin!"

My anger rises that he can read me so well. And now that he knows, he's never gonna give up. Cole is relentless. He does whatever he needs to get what he wants. "The truth? The truth is that she thought I dressed too provocatively around him. She didn't like that I wore shorts in hundred-degree weather, and that he would stare at me when I walked through a room. She didn't like that my jeans weren't two sizes too big. She blamed me every time he touched me." Angry tears sting my eyes. "She blamed me when she found me cornered in the kitchen and his hand up my shirt," I scream, shoving him away. "She blamed me when she found him passed out drunk lying in my bed while I was out with my friends." He stares down at me, his blue eyes dark and jaw sharp. "Is that what you want?" I shout and shove him again. "You wanna know that no matter what I did to stop him, it was never enough for her?" I gasp for a breath. "She didn't care that I didn't come home. She didn't want me there anyway. That's just what she wanted my father to believe. She didn't care that I did drugs. She was the one who gave them to me. And she didn't fucking care one thing about me." The first tear falls down my cheek, and his blue eyes follow it.

He swallows. "Austin …"

"She didn't care, Cole." My voice cracks. "You were right. Is that what you want to hear?" I'm shaking, hating to admit that to him. "She chose him over me."

He steps into me and wraps his arms around my waist. I bury my head into his soaked chest and bite my bottom lip to hold in a sob. To keep my emotions in check.

His arms tighten around me. "I'm sorry." He breathes, kissing my hair.

The sincerity in his words makes me fail miserably. Fifteen years of silence rushes out like a dam breaking. And of all people to tell, I tell the one guy who can use it against me. He didn't deserve the truth, but a part of me wanted someone to care for so long. Someone to tell me she was in the wrong. And that I mattered.

CHAPTER TWENTY-ONE

COLE

She sobs into my shirt, and I just stand here, holding her. Not knowing what the fuck to do for her.

I'm at a loss for words. And I've never felt this way before. Just yesterday, I wanted to rip this girl to pieces. But what I didn't realize was that she is already ruined. She just hides it much better than I ever could.

I bend down and slide an arm under her legs and pick her up. I sit down on the lounge chair, and she curls up against my chest.

I look up at the cloudy sky, and my teeth clench. I don't like situations I can't control. And her mother and boyfriend back in California is something I can't do anything about. Same with Bruce. What if he decides to say fuck our deal and send her back? What the hell do I do then? I can't let her go. Not back to those worthless pieces of shit.

She calms her breathing and shifts in my lap, sitting up. I reach up and wipe the tears away from her face. And I feel guilty that I still find her gorgeous when she cries.

"You can go," she says, standing up and dismissing me.

I grab her arm and stand as well. Cupping her face, I stare down into her watery eyes. I hold her cheek, but she looks away from me, biting her bottom lip. You can see the shame written in her eyes. She hates that she made herself look so weak in front of me. That I got her to break so easily.

I love it. Finally something that I can use to get close to her. To make her trust me more. Need me more. No more of this back and forth shit. Even though I liked her fight, I like this more. Holding her. No one has ever needed me before other than Lilly. And that's a different kind of need.

But as her eyes come back up to mine, I realize that Becky was right. If she asked me to, I would burn this town to the ground for her. No matter who is standing in my way.

I press my lips to hers, needing her as much as she needs someone to protect her from her mother and the boyfriend.

And you.

I'm no better. I hurt her in other ways, and no matter how much I know it's wrong, I can't seem to stop.

She parts her soft lips and I kiss her gently, tasting her tears once again and they make me hard. I ignore my want to throw her to the lounge chair and rip off her bikini. Instead, I want to show her that I can be better. That I can be the one to save her. Even if it's a false sense of security. Because I'm not the one who saves. I destroy.

She pulls away from me first. My hands drop to my sides, and she wraps her arms around her waist as if she's protecting herself from me. Her instincts tell her I'm no good. That I would be no different from any other bastard who has hurt her. "Please go," she says, averting her eyes.

For once, I do as she asks.

Not gonna lie. Wednesday sucked not having her here at school with me. I like that I can kiss her and touch her whenever I want, but I haven't spoken to her. I still don't know what to say. I know better than anyone that words don't change the past or heal the scars any faster. And I've never been one for chitchat.

Thursday hasn't been any different. The day has gone by agonizingly slow. It feels like six in the evening, but it's only lunchtime.

Deke is cramming food in his mouth like usual. Becky is scrolling through her phone, and I'm just sitting here thinking about Austin. About how I could be taking advantage of her three-day suspension. I could be in bed with her right now. Naked. My hands in her hair, her lips on mine. And the thought makes me hard.

"Hey, Cole." Kaitlin Milton plops down beside me. Head cheerleader. Also a pain in my ass.

"Excuse me?" Becky says, placing her phone down.

Kaitlin ignores her. "I was wondering if you're free tonight," she asks, running her fingers down my arm.

"Excuse me!" Becky slaps her hands on the table and leans over it. "Just what the hell do you think you're doing?" she snaps.

Kaitlin throws her a hard look, tossing her red hair over her shoulder. "I wasn't talking to you, bitch."

"Oh, that's it …" She goes to crawl across the table, but Deke finally looks up from his food and grabs her arm, pulling her back to her seat.

"Not interested," I tell her, pulling away from her touch.

She looks back at me and giggles as if I just told a joke. "Come on, everyone knows that what's going on between you and that Ashley girl …"

"Austin!" Becky interrupts her.

"Whatever. Anyway, everyone knows it isn't serious." She rolls her brown eyes. "It's just a dare."

I stiffen, and Deke's eyes narrow on her. We don't make our dares public knowledge. If we wanted them to know what we did, we would spray-paint our names after we completed each one. They know we do them, but they think it's some little bullshit we do to pass the time.

"Austin is not a dare!" Becky snaps.

Kaitlin rolls her eyes. "That's not the word in the halls."

"What are they saying?" Deke asks before I can.

"That one of you guys dared Cole to seduce her." She smiles at me. "Of course, she fell for it. But you get an entire month to play with her, so you might as well take advantage of it, right? Use her all you can." She rubs her hand on my thigh.

I wrap my hand around her wrist and yank it off. Her smile never falters.

"Who said that?" Becky growls.

"Bryan."

Fucking Bryan!

"Well, it's a lie," she snaps.

"You, of all people, shouldn't believe everything you hear. Oh, by the way, congratulations on the baby," I add, looking away from her.

Becky throws her head back, laughing. "I thought you had gained some weight." She smirks, and Kaitlin throws her a heated look. Then she gets up and storms away.

AUSTIN

It was finally Friday and time for me to go back to school. I woke up an hour earlier, got ready, and drove myself to school. Cole had sent me a message last night that he had practice this afternoon and wanted to know if I could pick up Lilly after school. Of course, I told him yes.

I didn't see his car in the parking lot when I pulled up, so I figured he was running late getting Lilly to school. I walk into first period and see Becky in the back in our usual seats.

I plop down beside her and take a deep breath. "Did you know that Deke was the one who recorded Cole and me in the bathroom at the party?" I haven't spoken to her since all that shit went down at the clubhouse. One, because I haven't really had the time. And two, because she's so wrapped up in Deke, it's hard to get alone time with her, and I didn't wanna do this through text.

Her eyes widen. "What?"

I watch her features to see if I can tell if she's surprised or faking it. "Deke admitted to it. And I know you were standing there with us when Cole carried me away."

She shakes her head quickly. "I swear I had no idea. When you guys left the kitchen, I went outside."

"But you spent the night with him that night." When we got to school the next morning, she had ridden with him.

She nods. "He found me right before we left. Came up and asked me if what he had heard was true."

"Which was?"

"If David and I had broken up."

"David?"

She nods. "My ex. We were together for two years. He graduated last year, then dumped me over Christmas break. No surprise there." She rolls her eyes. "But no, I had no idea. I saw a video online, and I tried to show it to you that next morning, but you didn't want to see it."

"But you knew Deke had posted it."

She shakes her head quickly. "No. It wasn't on Deke's page. He must have sent it to someone else to post. I'm sorry, Austin."

I sit back in my seat. Of course not. Then I would know he was the one responsible. "It's fine." Nothing I can do about it now.

"But there is something that you need to know."

"What?" I ask with a sigh.

"Kaitlin sat down with us at lunch yesterday."

"Who is Kaitlin?" I have no idea who anyone is here. I stick to myself. I don't talk to any of the kids in my classes. Cole is always with me in the halls and lunch. Everyone stays clear of us.

"She's a fucking bitch. And she kept coming onto Cole." My fists clench in my lap at the thought of another girl throwing herself at him. I've never really thought about him and other girls, but she had told me that he's a manwhore. "But he totally blew her off." I relax a little. "I was about to crawl across the table and snap her neck. She's thrown herself at every Great White Shark." She shakes her head. "And believe me, they've all had their turns, but each one threw her back when they were done with her. That's what you do with used-up garbage."

I laugh.

"Anyway, she said that Bryan has started a rumor."

I frown. "What kind of rumor?"

"That you were a dare."

My heart starts to pound at those words. "What do you mean?" I never hear others at school talk about the guys and their dares. I don't know if they tell everyone about them or if they keep them secret, but I don't want others to think I do them too. People can't keep their mouths shut, and if that is the case, then I'll be caught in no time.

"Bryan is saying that one of the guys dared Cole to seduce you and that he has a month to …"

My eyes narrow on her. "A month to what?"

"Play with you. Were her words."

Second period, I walk in earlier than usual. I grabbed my books before first period so I wouldn't have to make the extra trip to my locker.

I'm pissed at Cole for what Bryan is saying. A part of me doesn't want to believe I'm a dare, but the other part says that is why he is so adamant about not leaving me alone.

I choose the chair in the back by the corner and sit down. The chairs to my right and in front of me are both occupied. I smile, knowing he won't be able to sit near me. It drops off the moment he walks in. Dressed in a pair of blue jeans and his black zip-up hoodie, he demands attention. His dark hair is looking freshly fucked, and I hate that my first thought is that Kaitlin did it. His blue eyes land on mine like he knows where I am, and he walks toward me.

"Get up," he orders the kid next to me. He grabs his books and scrambles away. "Hello, sweetheart," he says, sitting down.

I ignore him and look straight ahead.

He leans over his desk. "What's wrong?"

I turn to face him, and my eyes narrow. "A month, huh?"

His dark brows pull together as if he's confused. I don't elaborate. He can figure it out himself.

He goes to open his mouth, but the teacher gets our attention. She writes an assignment on the board before she excuses herself from the classroom. I pull out my pencil, a piece of paper, and the textbook. I start to read when the book is snatched off my desk. I look up to see Cole slamming it to the floor. All the kids turn around to look over at us as the sound bounces off the walls. I ignore them. His hard blue eyes are glaring at me.

He figured it out. Good for him.

"Mature," I snap, leaning down to grab it, but he kicks it out of the way. "Cole ..."

"You don't really believe that shit, do you?" he snaps.

"Why wouldn't I?" I demand. "It makes perfect sense all of a sudden. I don't know why I didn't think of it before."

He gives a rough laugh. "Maybe because it's not true."

I snort. "Like I believe you."

"Austin," he growls my name.

The kids are all still turned around facing us as we argue in the corner. Their eyes going back and forth between us. A few even have their phones out, and you can hear their fingers typing away.

"Cole," I challenge.

He leans over, his face inches from mine. "We haven't done a dare without you being present since I caught you that night in the cemetery."

I glare at him. "Bullshit."

He smiles, and it's wicked. "Do you not remember what just went down the other night at the clubhouse? They didn't even know how I knew you. Let alone dare me to fuck you, sweetheart." And with that, he sits back in his seat and opens his book.

I continue glaring, hating that he is right. I hadn't thought of that. They had no clue he had blackmailed me. Well, Deke did. But as far as I'm aware, one can't dare another without the others present. They have to draw for them.

I look at the guy sitting in front of Cole. His wide brown eyes are on me. "Will you hand me my book?" I ask. His eyes dart to Cole who still stares down at his. "Please," I growl. Cole had kicked it over under that boy's desk.

His eyes go back to mine, and then he spins around, facing forward, giving me his back. Ignoring me. All because he's afraid to help me out due to Cole. "Good grief," I growl as I shove out of my desk and go over to his. Bending down, I pick it up, and Cole slaps me on the ass.

I spin around to glare down at him, and he's giving me a smirk. "Bastard," I hiss.

CHAPTER TWENTY-TWO
COLE

Come lunchtime, she's still mad at me. And I love that she doesn't even try to hide it. It turns me on.

I sit across from her, next to Deke, and she seemed surprised. *I had a reason for it.*

"So how were your three days off school?" Deke asks her.

"Awesome. I didn't do shit," she says, dipping the fry into ketchup and smiling. Becky laughs.

Deke looks at me, and I give him a simple nod.

He smiles and dusts off his hands then grabs his phone. "Hey, girls. Smile." He holds up his phone, and like the girls they are, they lean into one another and smile as he snaps their picture. "Perfect," he says and then starts typing away on it.

"What are you doing, babe?" Becky asks him.

He waits until after he's done before he answers. "Just posted your guys' picture."

Her phone buzzes on the table.

"We're throwing you a party," I tell Austin.

She was picking up her drink but stops at my words. Her eyes narrow on me with suspicion, then dart to Deke. "Why?"

"Because you earned it," he says simply.

"What did I do to earn a party?" she asks slowly.

"Who the hell cares?" Becky asks excitedly.

The bell rings, and they get up to throw away their trash, and I turn to Deke. "Who did you invite?"

He smiles. "Everyone."

I walk out into the hall, and I find her and Becky by their locker. "I'll pick you up at ten," I tell her.

"It's tonight?"

I nod.

She blows a long breath out. "Where is it?"

"The beach," Becky answers, already checking her Facebook.

"It'll be cold." Austin frowns.

Becky just laughs and walks off to class. Austin looks up at me. "You're up to something."

I lean down and kiss her neck. "Aren't I always?"

"Cole," she whispers and pushes me away. I go willingly and look down at her. "Please don't embarrass me."

I frown. "What? Why would you think …?"

"You have a tendency to prove you're right, and I …" She looks away from me and lets out a long breath. "Never mind."

She turns to walk away, but I grab her arm and pull her to a stop. "What?"

"After the other day … what I told you …" She sighs heavily. "I get it," she says softly "You guys run this school. This town." Her eyes meet mine. "But you …" She pauses again, and I search her eyes, waiting to see angry tears, but instead, I see nothing but sadness. And I don't like it. I hate Bruce Lowes even more for allowing her mother and boyfriend to treat her the way they did. "That night in my bedroom, you told me that you could make me nothing. But what you didn't know is that I've always been nothing. But here"—she holds her hands out wide—"you're something, and no matter how hard I try to hide in the dark, you pull me into the spotlight. And that's not where I belong." With that, she walks off down the hall, holding her books to her chest.

I walk into fifth period and sit down next to Deke. "Are you friends with Austin on social media?"

He snorts. "She won't add me. I know she saw my request."

"Shit!" I hiss sitting back in my seat.

"Why?" he asks.

"I wanna see her page."

He laughs. "Well, I can make that happen. Hang on." He leans forward and grips Becky's shoulder. "Let me see your phone, babe."

"Why?" she asks.

He rolls his eyes. "It doesn't fucking matter why. Just give it to me," Deke orders.

She huffs but passes it back to him. He presses some buttons and then hands it to me.

"How do I look at pictures?" I ask.

She says she was nothing. Somehow, I don't believe that. Her mother and boyfriend probably just made her feel that way.

"Here you go. Just scroll to the side," he instructs me.

I come to a picture of her and a guy. He's about her height and tattoos come up from underneath his shirt and stop at his jawline. He's got big black gauges in his ears. His right arm is over her shoulders, and she's looking at him like she loves him. I've never seen that look on her face before.

"Who the hell is that?" Deke asks.

"I don't know," I growl.

"Oh, that's Martin," Becky says, looking down at it now.

"Who the hell is Martin?" Deke growls.

"Her ex," she answers.

I never thought that she may not be available. The thought never crossed my mind. Just like Celeste said, I always get what I want. Boyfriend be damned. But it's nice to know that I don't have to take her from him. Makes this easier for me.

"Were they serious?" Deke asks Becky.

"She doesn't talk about California much, so I don't think so. I just know they were together because of the pics she has of him on there."

Deke yanks the phone from my hands, and I lean over in my desk as he brings another picture up. It's of her standing in a living room. She wears a black leather mini-skirt and black fitted top. Another brunette her age stands to her left. A man behind her. He looks a lot older. He has a cigarette between his lips, and his eyes are right on her ass. I know exactly who it is. *Her mom's boyfriend.*

"Next," I order.

Deke moves on to another one of her, and it looks to be inside a club. There's neon lights, and she has her head thrown back, that guy with the tats has his head buried in her neck, his hands gripping her ass.

"Next," I growl.

This one is of her on the beach. She has her brown hair up and big glasses on her face. She is wearing a white bikini, and that guy is there with her again. But only this time he is holding her up. Her legs are wrapped around his waist, his arms around hers, and her head is bent down as she kisses him. You can see the tattoo on her side.

"Fuck, man. She has a tat? That's hot," Deke says with a nod. I glare at him.

Becky's phone vibrates in his hands, and he exits out of her pictures.

"Wait …" I reach for it, but he pulls it away.

"Hang on, I'll go back." He presses some more buttons then holds it up to me, but I don't know what I'm looking at. I don't this social media shit. "Look at this shit," he says.

"What?" I ask needing him to point it out to me.

"I posted that pic of the girls and tagged Becky. She then tagged Austin in it," Deke explains.

I still don't get it. "Meaning …?"

"Meaning that their friends see the post I made. And look who commented." He holds Becky's phone closer to my face.

Hey Austin. Looking better than ever. I sure miss hitting that ass.

My anger rises, and I fist my hands. "Who is that?" I demand.

"It's him," he answers. "The guy in the pictures with her."

I sit back in my seat. *I sure miss hitting that ass?* I'll be sure to tell her that tonight when I'm buried between those sweet legs.

"I deleted the comment," Deke announces, but I ignore him. "She needs to delete those pictures of him and her kissing now that she's with you, man." He hands Becky her phone back and growls. "Text

Austin and tell her to delete those pics of her ex off social media."

Becky lets out a sigh but starts to type away on her phone. It dings immediately with a response. "She said she will when Cole gets a social media page." Then she gives us her back, laughing at the thought of me ever doing that.

Deke looks at me. "You know what you gotta do."

I smile. She's calling my bluff. *Just wait and see, Austin.*

I've never wanted a woman to myself. Didn't wanna deal with the drama and bullshit. Looks like I don't do well with competition either.

I was already nothing.

Well, Austin Lowes, I'm about to make you something. *Completely fucking mine!* And the world is gonna know it.

AUSTIN

I pace inside my closet while Becky stands in front of me, staring at my clothes.

"I don't know what to wear," I tell her for the third time.

I called her in a panic. I may have lived in California, but the only time I went to the beach was to swim in the ocean. Not party on it.

"Do I wear boots?" I ask. "Like you can't wear heels unless you plan on carrying them. And then what's the point in that? I could wear tennis shoes but those aren't sexy for a party."

She laughs. "You can wear boots. The beach will be sandy and rocky but since it rains so much, it will be packed down somewhat." Looking down at her phone, she starts typing out a message. "Deke and Cole are on their way over."

"Both of them? Why?"

"I called Deke on my way here, and he said they would just come pick us up." She looks up from her phone. "And by the way, my parents think I'm staying with you tonight." Her eyebrows wiggle, and I laugh.

"Now let's get you dressed. The guys will be here soon."

Twenty minutes later, I'm in my bathroom just finishing up my lipstick when I hear my bedroom door open. "I don't know what time I'll be home. But I don't expect to be out too late," I holler, knowing it's Celeste.

"You're not coming home at all."

I spin around to see Cole leaning up against the doorframe to my bathroom. "What are you doing up here?" I ask.

He crosses his arms over his chest as his eyes scan over my black sweater and red skinny jeans with my black knee-high boots. When they meet mine, he pushes off the doorframe and walks toward me.

I take a step back, but the countertop stops me. He looks angry. His usual mask is in place, and his eyes are dark. His right hand slides into my hair, tilting my head back. "Cole …" His lips are on mine before I can say anything else.

I melt into him just like all the other times. My knees buckle when he deepens the kiss, demanding my breath. His tongue dances with mine, and I moan into his mouth. He presses his hips against mine, and I can feel he's already hard.

"Screw the party," I whisper when he pulls away.

He runs his hand through my hair. "As much as I'd like to do that, we can't let Deke down."

"Deke?"

Cole nods once. "He wanted to throw you this party."

"Now, I'm really nervous." I laugh.

"Don't be." He kisses my lips softly as if he can't get enough. Or it's all part of his game. At this point, I can't tell the difference anymore. And that's not good. "Don't tell Deke this, but he's harmless."

"I watched him help you kill someone," I remind him.

"Yeah." He smiles as if he's remembering that night fondly. "But he would never hurt you." I raise an eyebrow. He chuckles, that anger in his eyes fading a little. "If he didn't have me to beat his ass, Becky would do it. I didn't realize she was so feisty until yesterday at lunch."

I laugh. "Come on. Let's go. If we don't hurry, Becky and Deke may already be naked in the car."

"Pack a bag real quick."

I stop and turn back to face him. "That's not a good idea, Cole."

His eyes narrow, that anger returning so easily at my denial. "Pack. A. Bag." He orders this time.

I place my hand on my hips, refusing to back down to him. "I'm not staying at your father's house."

A smile spreads across his face. It's not friendly. "Who said we were staying at my father's house?"

"What the hell?" I ask as Deke pulls up to the beach. Cars are on the sand, well those who drive lifted trucks and Jeeps. There's a bonfire. Kegs line the shore, and white folding tables hold liquor bottles and Solo cups. Kids of all ages litter the sand. Some I recognize from school, but others I don't. "How did you pull this off?" I ask.

"Magic," Cole answers.

Deke scoffs. "Please. This isn't magic. This is all me, baby." I roll my eyes, but Becky laughs at him while we get out.

"Stay close to me," Cole orders.

"Where would I go?" I ask.

He grabs my hand and pulls me along with him. A Jeep missing its top and doors is parked on the sand, and it has speakers all inside it blasting out "Feel Invincible" by Skillet.

We make our way over to a white table, and Cole lets go of my hand to start making us drinks.

"Isn't this awesome?" Becky squeals, grabbing my arm.

I nod. "Deke outdid himself," I say, eyeing him. He sees me staring and winks at me. I narrow my eyes, and he laughs.

They're up to something. What the hell is it?

"Here," Cole says, turning back to face me and hands me a Solo cup. I take a sip and frown, looking up at him. "There's hardly any alcohol in this."

"There's enough."

"Where's yours?" I ask, noticing his hands are empty now.

"I'm fine," he says; his answer clipped.

I open my mouth to argue but shut it when I see Shane approach us. His eyes meet mine, and then he looks away quickly. I wanna throw my drink on him for ratting me out. But what did I expect? Once again, it was my fault to trust him. To trust any of them.

Deke and Cole walk over to Shane and turn their backs to us. I spin around and grab a bottle of vodka and pour it into my cup. "Want some more?" I ask, holding it up to Becky.

She shakes her head. "Deke made mine strong."

I set it down and take a drink. "Much better." Leaning up against the table, I look over at Cole. He has his hair spiked and looking like every bit a disheveled mess. He wears a pair of blue jeans, tennis shoes, and his black zip-up hoodie.

"He doesn't drink."

"What?" I ask, turning to look over at Becky.

"You had asked him where his drink was." She nods to Cole as he stands with his friends. His arms are crossed over his chest. Shane and Deke both drink from Solo cups. "Well, he does but only when he has parties at his house," she says, before taking a drink of hers. "If he goes to a party that isn't at his dad's, then he doesn't drink."

"He had a shot that one night we were at that party they showed up at."

She nods. "One shot. You won't see him have more than that."

That surprises me. "Why not?" I ask.

"The night Maddox, Landen, and Eli died, they had all been drinking at a party. Cole was driving them when he wrecked."

My brows shoot up. No one ever talks about what happened to his friends. It's like the ghost everyone can't see, but you know it's there. Jeff said he killed his friends, and Shelby told me it was a car wreck, but that's as much as I know.

"What happened?" I ask, looking to see that he and Shane are still talking to Deke, but now Bennett has joined them.

"The brakes went out, and the car rolled. They were all thrown out."

I take a sip. "Did Cole get in trouble?"

She shakes her head. "His dad has money. He'd just paid for the police academy's new training facility before the accident. He got a slap on the wrist." She lowers her voice. "It caused a lot of tension between him and Kellan."

I frown. "Why Kellan?"

"The other guys understood what happened was an accident and could have happened to any of them. They were all out of control, but Kellan blamed him. Still does. Maddox was Kellan's cousin."

"Oh," I say.

She nods quickly before taking another drink. "But I feel sorry for Cole." She looks over at him and sighs. "What happened was an accident. Hell, I've gone to parties and drove home drunk before. Not responsible, but I get it. He blames himself, and anyone who knows him can see it eats him alive. He and Eli were the closest, and he died in his arms."

"What?" I breathe.

"Lauren James, a sophomore, her dad is a paramedic, and she said that he told her when they pulled up to the scene, Cole was sitting in the ditch with Eli in his arms. Dead."

I look over at him and see he has turned and now faces our direction. His eyes are on the sand, hands now in the front pockets of his jeans, and he nods his head as Shane speaks to them. And I remember what he said to Jeff that night in the cemetery.

Give me what I deserve! Why don't you get your sorry ass up and hit me? Why don't you be a fucking man and fight me.

He wanted a fight. Needed it. I didn't understand then, but I do now. He lifts his head, and his eyes land on mine. I stare back without blinking, just taking in the color of his dark blue eyes. They're just like the sky—always clouded. And I can't imagine what he went through losing three friends and living with that guilt. It would destroy a weak person.

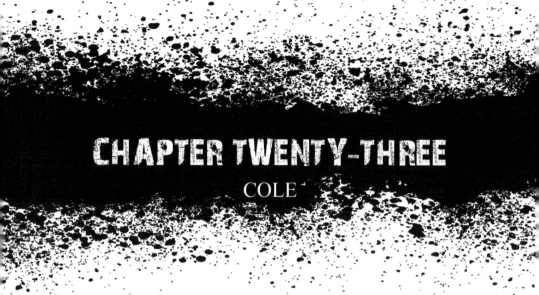

CHAPTER TWENTY-THREE
COLE

"Cole?"

I look away from Austin first to glare at Shane. "What?"

"Did you hear anything I just said?"

"Yes."

"Then what did I say?" he questions with an arch of his brow.

"That you didn't find much on the laptop."

Deke shakes his head. "I thought for sure we could use something on there."

"Well, there is some stuff. He's got accounts we can drain."

"He's still looking for him," Bennett chimes in.

I snort. "He won't give up because without Jeff, the business will plummet."

"Do you think he suspects us?" Shane asks.

I shake my head. "We made sure to cover our tracks. Why would he?"

He runs a hand through his hair. "Because we are the only ones who knew what he really did to Aimee."

"He has no proof that we knew," I argue.

"What if he found the cameras?" Shane continues.

"You're reaching," I growl, tired of talking about this shit.

"I'm trying to think of every angle so if something comes back to bite us in the ass, I can cover it," he snaps.

I turn and step up to him, my chest bumping his. "Drop it, Shane.

You're making a problem where there's not one."

His brown eyes narrow on mine. "No, you made a problem when you decided to continue what Eli had started."

"*We* all moved forward," Deke corrects him.

"I owed him that." My hands clench. "I …" A hand lands on my arm, and I jump back in surprise. Looking over, I see Austin standing beside me, her green eyes full of worry as they search mine. Her hand runs down my arm, and she unclenches my fist, then laces her fingers with mine.

"Hey, babe," Deke says, lightening the mood by pulling Becky in for a kiss.

"Everything okay?" Austin asks softly, still searching my eyes.

I put that mask over my face that I learned to do so long ago. Who knew it would become useful the older I got. "Fine." I release her hand and drape my arm over her shoulders, pulling her close to me.

"So …" She looks at Deke. "Why a party?"

He smiles at her warmly, and she eyes him skeptically. She doesn't trust him. I told her earlier at her house that he was harmless, and he is. As long as you stay out of his way. He never doubted me for a second when I told him what I wanted to do to Jeff. I've never questioned his loyalty and the need for revenge. He was best friends with Eli, too, along with Maddox and Landen. But with Austin—he would have killed her without thought that night in the cemetery had I not stopped him. He may fuck with her here and there now, but he would never put his hands on her because he knows she belongs to me. I decide her fate. If I told him to kill her, he would. If I told him to protect her with his life, he would. And I would do the same for him. That's what a brother does. They have your back. No matter what.

"Because you completed your first dare. And I'm not gonna lie; you impressed me. Just like I knew you would." He takes Becky's cup and places it in his empty one, tilting it to me. "He doubted your potential." Then he takes a drink. "I did not."

She scoffs. "I'm insulted."

Everyone laughs, including me. I lean down and kiss her hair, letting everyone out here know she's still mine. For those who are here and don't already know. "I was impressed. Pissed, but impressed nonetheless."

"Yeah, pulling that fire alarm was not the smartest move." Bennett laughs.

She shrugs awkwardly with my arm over her shoulders. "My only option was to do it during the day while he was at work."

"And you took my car. I'm keeping my keys on me at all times from now on."

"If you would let me drive myself, I wouldn't have had to take yours."

"Not gonna happen, sweetheart."

We've been out here on the beach for two hours now. The guys and I stand by the bonfire. People litter the beach—some stumbling and some already passed out up by the tree line. No one talks to me because they know unless they're my friends, I have nothing to say to them. Deke is a social butterfly online, but he, too, keeps to himself at school. Bennett and Shane are friends with everyone. Kellan stays to himself. He's only been this way for the past six months. I think some of that had to do with the wreck. The other, with Celeste.

I look over my shoulder to see Austin and Becky standing by one of the folding tables, and Austin's pouring herself another drink. It's her fourth. I've kept count. And I also know that she keeps adding alcohol to the ones I've made her.

"I thought Kellan would come out tonight," Shane says, getting my attention.

I knew he wouldn't show up. I bet my ass he's at Bruce's house fucking Celeste. Bruce is out of town, and Austin is here. That's what I would do, if I was him. "Maybe he didn't feel like getting his ass kicked tonight," I offer.

Shane sighs but doesn't say anything. He knows I'm not in the mood to be tested.

"I said stop!"

I spin around at the sound of Austin's voice. Their backs are to us as they face a guy. A guy who I fucking hate—Bryan!

"Go away, Bryan," Becky snaps, and then she shoves him.

The girls spin around and start to walk toward us, and I don't miss the way they link their arms together and stumble. *They're drunk.*

All four of us reach them before they can even take another step.

He and his friend Christopher laugh.

"What the fuck was that about?" Deke demands, looking down at Becky.

Before she can answer, Bryan and Christopher join us. "Hey, Austin?" he looks at her, and her green, glassy eyes are narrowed on him. "Bryan dared me to fuck you." He looks her up and down, smiling like the drunk he is. "Where do you want it …?"

My fist connecting with his face interrupts whatever he was about to say.

"Dude!" Bryan calls out, jumping back while Chris falls to the sand.

"You dared him to fuck her?" I shout at him.

He places his hands up in front of him and flinches. I wrap my hands around his wrists and yank him forward. Once his chest bumps mine, I head-butt him. He falls next to Christopher, and they both roll around moaning.

"Get your ass up," I order, already feeling that adrenaline that comes with a fight. My head pounds, and I clench and unclench my throbbing fist.

"Cole?" Austin calls from behind me. I spin around to face her. Those green eyes are now wide with fear. She looks at the guys on the ground for a second and then at me. "Let's just go."

"Not yet." I look at Shane. "Take the girls to Deke's SUV."

"No. Cole …" Bennett grabs Austin's arm and pulls her away as Becky clings to Deke. He shoves her off to Shane, and she fights him as he takes her to Deke's Range Rover.

Kids start to circle us, and I remove my black zip-up hoodie but leave my shirt on. Deke comes up beside me, and we turn around to look down at the bastards. "I'll take Christopher," he says.

"I got Bryan." At the mention of his name, Bryan gets up on his hands and knees, trying to crawl away. I grab his ankle and yank, flipping him onto his back. I stand over him, reminding myself that I can't kill him here with all the witnesses, and of course, they all have their phones out recording us.

"It was just a joke," Bryan says as blood runs down his face. He jumps to his feet, lifting his hands.

Deke is already on top of Christopher beating the hell out of him. I'm gonna take my time with Bryan. He deserves that.

"Fucking with what is mine is no joke," I tell him.

"Cole …" He growls my name as if his tone is gonna get me to back down. I've beat his ass before, so you would think the bastard would have learned his lesson.

I lift my fisted hands and smile at him. "I'm gonna kick your ass, Bryan." He swallows nervously. "I dare you to fight back."

AUSTIN

Becky and I sit in the back seat of Deke's Range Rover when we see the guys walking toward us. She opens the door and runs to him. I get out a little slower, knowing Cole and I aren't like her and Deke.

"Baby," she cries out, placing her hand on his face. He has a cut across his cheek, and his shirt is stretched out at the collar, but that's all.

"I'm fine," he assures her.

Cole's eyes meet mine, and I glare at him. He ignores me as he climbs into the driver's seat. I jump into the passenger side as Deke and Becky climb in behind us. They start panting as she crawls into his lap and straddles him while they make out.

I look straight ahead, trying to sober up. I drank too much. I added extra alcohol to every drink he made me plus took a few shots when he wasn't looking. Now I'm regretting it.

I look at Cole's hands as they grip the steering wheel. The skin broken and blood smeared on them. His black hoodie sits in his lap so I can see his toned forearms are also covered in blood.

"Did you kill him?" I can't help but ask.

"What do you care?" he replies; his answer clipped.

"Why are you mad at me?" I demand.

He takes a quick look over at me. His eyes run over me before they go back to the dark road.

"It's not my fault." His hands fist the wheel, tightening his bloody knuckles. "I didn't do anything …"

"I know," he snaps. "I didn't say you fucking did!"

"Then why the hell are you acting like it?"

Becky moans, and I don't dare look in the back seat afraid her jeans may be off.

"Just stop it," he snaps.

"No. I won't." I turn in my seat, the seat belt making it hard, but I yank on it, giving me some slack. "Why did you hit him?" He ignores me as he drives down the dark, two-lane road. "Because you needed the fight?"

"Don't," he growls.

"I may be a little drunk—"

"That's an understatement."

"But I saw you. You were pissed off before we ever got there. You were looking for a fight."

"Shut up, Austin."

"No, I wanna know why—"

"Because I'm not gonna let some punk-ass bitch speak to you like that," he shouts, interrupting me once again.

"Like you speak to me any better?" I snap. "I may not be a dare, but I am just a fucking game."

"What you are doesn't matter," he says simply.

I hear Becky gasp. "Cole …"

Her words are cut off, and I take a quick look to see Deke has his hand over her mouth and his lips by her ear. She still straddles him, but they're both clothed. He pulls his hands away, and her narrowed eyes go to Cole.

I look back at him as well. "If I don't fucking matter, then why didn't you just let him fuck me?"

He pulls the car over to the side of the road and slams on the brakes. My hand goes to the dash while my seat belt locks up.

He turns to face me. Those clouds rolling in his blue eyes. "If that's what you want, then go ahead." He shrugs carelessly. "Walk back to him and kiss his wounds, Austin. 'Cause I fucked him up good." Then he gets out, slamming the door behind him.

CHAPTER TWENTY-FOUR

COLE

I walk away from the SUV, not really knowing what I'm doing but needing a moment. Needing a fucking minute to think without her voice in my head. Her words choke me. She's still there. Ever since Monday night when I pinned her down in the cemetery and told her to fight me. Her words did more damage than her body could have ever done to me.

And what she told me about her mom and her boyfriend? Those words play over and over. Her words make me angry. Remembering those tears makes me hard.

It's no secret I love a fight. But to fight over a girl? Never happened before except when we threw her that party at my house. I fought Bryan because he put his hands on her. And then he went and dared his friend to fuck her.

I beat his ass. Just as Deke beat Christopher's. But everyone knows why Deke did what he did. He's falling for Becky. It's getting serious. He is completely fucking obsessed with her. I'm just fucking Austin 'cause I can. I'm just using her 'cause it's convenient and pisses her father off. I'm gonna make that motherfucker pay in every way I can think of. And Austin ups the ante. Mine to control. Mine to fuck. And mine to use.

You say that, but she is in your head.

I'm starting to care. Even I can't lie to myself about that. Because if I didn't, I would have already called Bruce and told him to fuck our deal. But I can't send her back. I won't send her back. She's mine. She belongs here with me.

I hear the door open to the Range Rover behind me, but I ignore it. The road starts to curve, and as I round it, I come to a stop once I realize where I'm at.

Skid marks cut through the double yellow lines and three, white wooden crosses stand over in the ditch. Each name written vertically—Maddox, Landen, and Eli.

And just like that, I'm pulled back to that night six months ago.

"Please ... Cole. Aimee needs you ..."

"She has you," I say, falling beside him in the ditch once again. They're dead. Maddox still lies in the street, and I found Landen over behind the car. They're both dead! I can't lose him too.

His hands grip my bloody shirt. "You have to help her. Save her." Tears roll down his face, and I can't hold mine back.

There's a knot in my throat, and I nod my head quickly.

"Promise ... me."

"I promise."

I stare at the three crosses, my breath caught in my throat. And my chest is tight. I imagine mine being next to his. Where it deserves to be. I couldn't save him. I couldn't save Aimee. And I sure as hell couldn't save my mother.

I'm fucking useless!

"Cole?"

I close my eyes when I hear her call my name.

Fuck! I fist my cracked knuckles. She's another reminder that I fuck up everything I touch. I once told her that I love to destroy pretty, innocent things. And that was the truth. To me, things are more beautiful broken. Anyone can love something that is pure and whole—perfect. But destroy something, then stand back and see how many people give it the time of day. Or how many will take the time to help it heal. No one will. I know from experience. I've seen it. I've lived it. I want to do that to her. I don't want anyone to want her when I'm finished with her. I wanna ruin Austin Lowes. More than she already is.

"What are you …?" Her voice trails off, and I feel her come to stand next to me. Her arm brushing mine.

I don't open my eyes. I don't dare look at her.

"Let's go," I manage to grind out and spin around, once again keeping my back to her. I make my way to the SUV and climb in. I look in the back seat and see Deke sitting up against the window with Becky's head in his lap. She's passed out asleep. His eyes go from mine to the windshield, and he swallows. He knows where we are. He helped me place those crosses there. The door opens, and Austin gets in without saying a word. I put the SUV in drive and pull back onto the road.

AUSTIN

If you had asked me three weeks ago what I thought of Cole Reynolds, I would have told you that I thought he was the devil himself! I hated him with every part of me.

If you asked me now, I would say that from what I have seen, he was dealt a shitty hand. His mother died. He raises his little sister. And he lost three best friends from a mistake he made.

I could feel his sadness when I stood beside him and stared at the three crosses. It took me a second for my drunk eyes to understand what I was looking at, but when it hit me, it took my breath away. He stood there and stared at the road like it was happening all over again. I felt his pain, and it was crippling.

I wanted to ask him about it. To know what happened. What he saw. Is that what made him so angry with the world? Did he try to save them and just not succeed? Becky said that the EMS found Cole sitting in the ditch with Eli in his arms. What were their last words? Did they get any? Did he die on impact? How did the other three die but Cole not? I'm sure that's a question he asks himself all the time. I know I would.

Cole gets my attention as he pulls up to a gated community. He presses a device on the visor, and the gate opens. He pulls in and passes house after house that looks bigger than my father's mansion. They set back off the two-lane road, hidden behind rows of trees. He slows down and pulls into a driveway.

"Just stop here," Deke says from the back seat.

Cole doesn't question him. He brings the SUV to a stop, and Deke speaks. "Just bring me the car tomorrow."

I turn around to watch him pull a sleeping Becky in his arms, and then he gets out and starts to walk down the long driveway with her in his arms.

Cole places his hand on my seat and looks back over his shoulder, ignoring the backup camera as he backs out. And then takes off down the street.

I bury my face in my hands and cover up a yawn. I'm tired. I'm drunk, and I'm so pissed at myself because a part of me feels like I shouldn't be mad at Cole. That was the second time he's taken up for me and beat someone's ass when they disrespected me. But another part of me wants to say *It's your fucking fault. You put me in those positions.*

But that wouldn't do us any good.

I lean my head back against the head rest and close my eyes. I feel his eyes on me, but I refuse to open them. He hasn't spoken to me, and I have so much to say to him that if I even open my mouth to try, I'll probably regret it. But then again. I've never been one to bite my tongue.

CHAPTER TWENTY-FIVE
COLE

We enter the clubhouse, and I walk past her over to the stairs. I take them two at a time and turn on the light once I hit the landing. A big wooden log bed sits in the middle of the area. And that's it. No TV, no dressers, no nightstands. There's a door to my right leading to the full bath.

She comes to the top of the stairs and looks around as I drop her bag. She hasn't spoken since we stood in the middle of the road, but I know she wants to.

And now that my anger has died down, I hate that I told her to go fuck Bryan. The words tasted like shit. The thought of him sleeping with her makes my stomach knot.

"Cole—"

"Stop," I interrupt her.

Her eyes narrow on me. I step to her. "Just stop talking," I say, placing my hand in her hair. Her heavy eyes close, and she lets out a sigh. She's drunk. And probably still pissed at me. Possibly tired. But I don't fucking care.

I want her!

I lean down and press my lips to hers. She opens without thought, tilting her head back. I push my hips into hers, and she moans in my mouth. I'm so hard for her all the fucking time. I's pathetic.

I reach for her sweater and pull it up over her head. "Can we take a shower?" she asks.

I'm about to say fuck a shower, but her eyes go to the blood on my hands, and I realize I just got it in her hair. "Sure." I don't want any part of Bryan on her. Even though I would love to paint her body red.

We walk into the bathroom, and she looks around as I start the shower. I remove my shirt and then kick off my tennis shoes. I'm removing my jeans and boxers when she comes up to me. I pause as she places her hands on my bare chest.

My heart starts to pound at the softness in her touch. No one has ever touched me like she does. Like it means something. As if she could save me from myself. I've always been the guy who got in and got out. The girls I brought home, didn't stay the night, and the older women I fucked, I left their house as soon as I was done. But I can't seem to leave her. I reach up and push her hair behind her ear, exposing all the piercings. I run my thumb over them.

She releases a long breath. "I don't wanna fight."

Her words surprise me. "I don't either," I say, and I'm just as surprised with myself that they are the truth. *I love a fight.* Doesn't matter if they are physical or mental. I love fucking with someone.

"Can we just forget about what happened?" she asks, biting on her bottom lip nervously.

I can't just forget that Bryan dared his friend to fuck her. What if someone else does that? What if someone else tries to take what belongs to me? Or worse? Forces her? I know I'm a sick bastard. I know that I prefer a fight over a civil conversation, but there are others in this city just like me. Some older and some younger. "Yeah," I tell her because I don't want to worry her. I'll continue to protect her no matter what the cost. Because I'm the only one who can destroy Austin Lowes.

Right.

She pulls away from me and goes to finish getting undressed. I turn and get into the shower, and she follows me. I stand under the sprayer, and she watches the blood run into the drain.

I grab her arm and pull her to me. "Don't think about it," I tell her.

She wraps her arms around my neck. "Then take my mind off it."

I capture her lips with mine and spin us around, her back hitting the wall. She gasps into my mouth at the coldness, and I deepen the kiss.

My right hand goes to her thigh, and I grip it in my hand and lift it up, wrapping it around my hip.

She pulls her lips away and tilts her head back. Her eyes are closed, and her wet lips are parted. I take my hard cock in my hands and slide it into her without wasting another second, and she whimpers. *Fuck, I love hearing that sound when I'm inside her.*

She's already wet for me. Just like I'm hard for her.

She opens her heavy eyes, and she moans as I begin to move in and out of her. Slowly teasing her.

I grab her other leg and pull it off the shower floor and push her more into the wall. She clings to me.

"Cole," she pants, and I pick up my pace. "Oh, God! Cole …"

I lower my head and capture her lips with mine again, knowing that she's mine. I get to have her. However I want, whenever I want.

I open my eyes to see Austin sleeping beside me. The sun shines through the one window up here and I roll over, picking my phone off the floor to check the time. It reads a quarter past nine.

Lying back down, I run a hand down my face. We didn't get much sleep. We didn't get back to the clubhouse until after two a.m. and then we spent almost an hour in the shower. And then another two awake in bed.

Like always, I couldn't get enough. She couldn't seem to either, and I'm not complaining.

"You okay?"

I look over to my left and find a set of dark green eyes on me. I smile at her, pushing her hair back from her face. I yank the covers back and grab her arm, yanking her up to straddle me. "I am now."

She throws her head back laughing, and I soak it in. I've never heard her laugh like that. I've only ever seen anger from her. Or sadness. I've never tried to make her laugh or smile.

I should make her do it more often.

She straddles me naked and beautiful. Her dark hair is down over her shoulder lying on my chest. It's finally dry from the shower we had hours ago, and the alcohol she consumed seems to have worn off.

Her eyes scan my chest, and her fingers graze my scar. She's never asked about it before. "What happened?"

"Broke my collarbone."

She tilts her head to the side. "How?"

My eyes look into hers while she stares at it. "Car wreck. Seat belt tightened and snapped it on impact."

Her hand freezes on the scar, and her eyes meet mine. She stares at me so intently that my pulse quickens.

"You lied."

My eyes narrow at the accusation in her voice. "Excuse me?"

"You lied," she repeats.

"About what?" I demand.

"You weren't driving."

I tense at her words. She searches my eyes and sighs heavily, her breath brushing her hair from my chest. "Who were you covering for?"

"Enough!"

"No, Cole. Why did you lie?" she demands. I grip her hips, my fingertips digging into her skin, and shove her off me. I stand, running a hand through my hair and walking toward the bathroom.

"You couldn't have been driving," she whispers. "It's your right shoulder. Not your left. You lied …"

I close my eyes. It took her two seconds to realize what no one else ever did. I was in a sling for months. My right arm was. Not my left. No one ever questioned it.

"Why would you lie, Cole?"

"Don't, Austin."

"No!" she shouts. "Fucking tell me why you would lie about something like that," she demands. "People think you killed three of your friends."

"I fucking know what they think!" I shout turning to face her.

"Who the hell do you think told them that?" I snap.

"Why?" She's on her knees in the middle of my bed. Her long dark hair over one shoulder, covering one of her breasts from me, and she's breathing heavy. Her eyes soft and my chest tightens.

"Get out!"

"It was Eli … That's why you …"

"I said get the fuck out, Austin," I snap, interrupting her.

"No."

I fist my hands, and her eyes drop to them.

"Becky said everyone was ejected. But you had your seat belt on …" She shakes her head confused. "I don't understand …"

I storm over to the bed and shove her onto her back, pinning her small wrists to the mattress. "You don't need to understand what I did, or why I did it. It's no one's Goddamn business, Austin."

She looks up at me, eyes soft. I'm fucking panting, and my heart races. I hate being exposed. So open. Guarded people are safe. But she keeps stabbing me. Making me bleed. Her eyes search my face, and I see tears in them. My jaw clenches.

"Cole," she whispers. "I'm sorry."

My chest tightens to the point I can't breathe.

"I'm sorry that no one sees you like I do. I'm sorry that no one understands your rage. Or your hate."

"Stop …" I choke on the word. She's twisting the knife. Cutting me more.

She wraps her legs around my hips. "I'm sorry that you lost three friends. And that you are left with a burden that is not yours to bear." Her tears spill out and down the sides of her face.

AUSTIN

He lied!

He let this town believe he killed three teenage boys who were all his friends when he wasn't at fault.

"Were you even drinking?" I ask.

I can feel his body physically shaking against mine. He's angry with me. Angry I figured out a secret.

"You don't know what you're talking about," he says instead. "You weren't there."

"I didn't have to be there to know that you weren't responsible for their deaths."

"Stop, Austin!" he yells in my face.

"Do the guys know?" I ask as another tear runs down the side of my face.

He doesn't answer.

"Becky also told me that Kellan blames you. Why didn't you tell him the truth?"

My heart breaks for him. Not only did he lose his friends, but he also took responsibility when it wasn't his.

He lets go of my wrists and crawls off me, forcing my legs apart. He sits on the side of the bed, his back toward me and bows his head.

I swallow and sit up. "I know that you felt you did the right thing, but Cole ..."

He jumps up and spins around to face me. My words cut off at the look on his face. I've never seen it so murderous. "Don't you dare sit there and pretend like you know why I did what I did," he snaps as he leans over and picks his jeans up off the floor. He yanks them up and buttons them. The he takes off down the stairs.

I sit here, waiting to hear the door open and close, but it doesn't come. I get off the bed and take the sheet with me, wrapping it around my shoulders. I walk down the stairs to find him standing in the middle of the room. His hands fisted in front of him as he punches the punching bag that hangs from the rafters.

"Tell me," I say softly. "Help me understand."

He ignores me. His breathing grows louder as he pounds away on it. His cuts from last night have already busted open from the force.

I drop my head to look at my hands knotted in the sheet, holding it in place. I lick my wet lips and taste my tears. "I was ten the first time my mom's boyfriend touched me." He stops at my words. Like I wanted him to. "At the time, I didn't understand what he was doing." I swallow the knot in my throat. "I was sitting on the couch. He sat down next to me and placed his hand on my inner thigh." I look up at him through my lashes. His back is toward me, and his head is down. "I didn't know what to do. It felt uncomfortable. Wrong. But he was telling me that I was pretty. No one had ever told me that before." The muscles in his back tighten. "Then his fingers started digging into my skin painfully. I told him he was hurting me. I tried to push him away, but his grip kept tightening. He said that I'd learn to love pain. It was a way he would show me that he cared about me." He slowly turns around to face me, and I look him in the eyes. Not backing down like I wanted to when we stood by the pool. "Loved me." He swallows, and his Adam's apple bobs.

"That's when my mother walked in. She saw us, and she ran over to me, grabbed my arm, and yanked me from the couch. She sent me to my room for the rest of the day." His chest rises and falls from breathing heavy. His jaw is sharp, and nostrils flared. "She said that he belonged to her. That my father had already left her because of me. She wouldn't let her bitch of a daughter take another one from her." A tear silently falls down my cheek, but it's for him, not for me. I came to terms with my life a long time ago.

"I might not understand why you did it, but I know what it's like to have a secret. You told me that you knew what it was like to be powerless. To have no control. We are the same, Cole. You blame yourself for losing your friends, and I blamed myself for a man wanting me. It took me years to realize he was the one in the wrong. And I had to figure that out on my own. I didn't have anyone to explain it to me. To help me." He releases a long breath, looking away from me. "So I'm gonna tell you what someone should have told me." His eyes come back to mine, and I walk over to him. I reach out to cup his face, and the sheet falls to the floor at my feet. Another tear runs down my face, and he gently wipes it away. "It wasn't your fault, Cole."

He lowers his forehead down to mine and closes his eyes. "We're not the same, Austin. Because unlike you, I wasn't innocent." He pulls away and stares down at me. "I knew what we were doing. We went to a party like we always did. Got drunk like we always did.

And then left. I took the blame because I should have been the one driving. In a matter of minutes, they were … just gone." His voice is rough as if he had been holding those words in for a long time. My tears start to fall faster.

"I'm sorry, Cole. I'm so sorry."

He wraps his harms around me and pulls me to him. "I'm sorry too, sweetheart." He kisses my hair.

CHAPTER TWENTY-SIX
COLE

I reach out and push a piece of hair behind her ear. Her eyes stare into mine, and I can see the fresh tears she hasn't allowed to fall yet. This is when she's the most gorgeous, when they make her green eyes look like they're swimming in a pool of water. A tear finally escapes, and I wipe it away.

But I hate why they're there. I hate that someone else can make her cry. I want to do that. I want to take from her.

I'm a fucking bastard.

Her mother and her fucking boyfriend will pay for what they have done to her. I'll make sure of it. Just as I did with Jeff.

Her hands go to my jeans, and she undoes them. I grab her wrists. "Austin."

"I need you, Cole," she whispers, pushing her hips into mine.

And warmth spreads through me at those words.

She needs me.

Releasing her wrists, I slide my hands into her hair and kiss her. Desperately. Because I need her too. We've both been ripped open and are bleeding. Something needs to cover the pain.

She kisses me back just as aggressively. My pants hit my ankles, and I step out of them. Then we're walking backwards. I fall onto the couch, my lips breaking from hers. She straddles me, her hand going between our bodies, and she grabs my hard dick. My head falls back to rest on the cushion, and I moan as she strokes me. Slow but firm. Teasing. I close my eyes and feel her lips on my neck. Sucking, licking, and biting.

"Fuck, Austin …" I trail off when she slides onto my hard cock. My breath instantly taken away.

My hands go to her narrow hips, and she begins to move. My fingers dig into her skin as our bodies slap. She sucks on my neck, and all I can do is sit here and pant as she rides me. Has her way with me.

She's incredible.

And all fucking mine.

My hands let go of her hips, and I slide them in her hair. Yanking her lips from my neck, I lift my head and slam them to mine. I kiss her with need. She pants in my mouth while her hips continue to work with mine.

Her pussy tightens around me, and she pulls her lips away, sucking in a long breath. I lean forward, pulling her hard nipple between my teeth. She cries out when I bite down on it, before sucking it gently.

"Cole." She whimpers my name, and I yank her head back, exposing her neck to me, and I do the same thing to her. I kiss, lick, bite, and suck every inch of her like it belongs to me. Because she does.

She needs me.

I need her.

We're like the devil is to sin. Without one, we wouldn't have the other.

I stand in the middle of the loft listening to the shower turn on when my cell rings. I pick up my phone to see *Deke* flash across my screen.

"Hello?" I ask, looking over at the bathroom door, hoping he doesn't have much to say. She said she needed a shower after she was done with me, and I wanna join her.

"Hey, man." He sighs. "Becky made me call you." I frown. "She won't stop bugging me. But she wants to know if you guys wanna go to lunch."

"I'm craving Italian," I hear her yell in the background.

"I tried to tell her you would say no. That it's not like that—"

"We can go," I interrupt him.

He's silent for a long second. "Come again?"

"We'll go. What time?" It's just another way for me to show her off. To prove to the world that she's mine.

Nothing else.

"Uh, an hour?" he asks slowly.

"Okay. See you then." I hang up.

Walking into the bathroom, I see her inside the shower. I open it up and enter. "We're going to lunch with Becky and Deke in an hour."

She stops shampooing her hair and looks at me. Her brows pull together. "Why?"

"Because Deke called and asked." I place my hands on her hips and press her back into the wall.

"Again. Why would he call and ask?"

I smirk. "Because Becky made him."

She laughs. "He's so whipped."

"You are correct. But he's been in love with her since sophomore year. So it's not like I didn't see that coming."

Her eyes widen. "What?"

I nod. "He never tried to get with her, though. Knew that she was the type of girl who deserved more than what he was willing to give."

She frowns. "But you just said he loved her. Why wouldn't he want to be with her? Doesn't make sense."

"He knew he'd break her heart. Too many options out there to stay with just one."

Her eyes narrow on mine. We haven't had the talk if I'm sleeping with other girls even though I think she suspects it. I don't know if she's afraid I'll say yes if she asks, or if she just doesn't care.

She slides out from between me and the wall, moving back under the spray to rinse out her shampoo. "So why now? Thought he would *play* with her since senior year is almost over?"

She uses the same word Bryan said I'm doing with her. "No. When he was ready to settle down with her last year, she was already in a serious relationship."

"David," she says. I nod. "She told me that Deke asked her if what he had heard was true about their breakup that night you guys showed up at the party." Leaning her head back, she runs her hands over her hair, making sure all the suds are gone. I watch the way her back arches and her tits push out and lick my lips. "So now what? He's changed his old ways?" She looks at me skeptically. "Because I watched him swallow a girl's tongue that night you threw a party at your house. That was just five days before they hooked up."

"What did you expect? Him to live his life pining for her?" I shake my head. "That's not how Deke works. Not how any guy with a set of balls works."

She rolls her eyes. "God forbid a man show a woman he actually has a heart."

I ignore that statement. "What about you?"

"What about me?" She pours some conditioner in her hand and runs it through her long dark hair.

"You and Martin."

Her hands freeze midway, and her eyes narrow on me. But she doesn't answer.

I take a step toward her. "I want you to delete any picture that you have of him off your social media page."

She tries to shove me away, but her hands are covered in conditioner, so they slide right off. "And I told you when you get a social media page, I'll do that." She gives me a big fuck you smile. Like she just asked me to give her the fucking moon. As if it's impossible.

"I do have one."

She throws her head back, laughing. "You're so full of shit."

I arch a brow. "Wanna bet."

Her laughter dies down, and her eyes search mine, looking for any indication that I'm pulling her chain. I'm not.

She shakes her head in acceptance. "You're such a dick."

"Did you love him?" The words are out of my mouth before I can even stop them. I try not to flinch at the question.

Her eyes narrow on me. "Why do you care, Cole?" she snaps, her patience of this conversation running short. I don't blame her. I'm not one to talk about pointless shit. But this is important.

Since I first laid eyes on Austin Lowes, I've wanted to control her. Own her. Hurt her. What more can a guy take from a woman than their love? Their soul?

She won't turn on someone she loves, was what Shane had said when we were all standing in the middle of the clubhouse the night I had Deke take her home after I stole her father's car. I didn't understand what he meant until now.

Now it makes perfect fucking sense!

I want Austin Lowes to fall in love with me.

AUSTIN

He's up to something.

Of course, he is. If Cole Reynolds is breathing, then he is up to no good. He doesn't understand how well I can read him. Or that I've been fed bullshit lines all my life. I'm not the girl who believes in fairy tales and happily ever afters.

"Yes," I say, playing along with his game.

His eyes narrow on me, but I ignore it. Instead, I go back to running conditioner through my hair. At this rate, the water is gonna be cold soon.

"How long were you guys together?" he asks.

"Almost four years." Not a total lie.

"You're seventeen," he argues as if I can't do the math.

"Yes. Thanks for the reminder," I say and turn around, giving him my back. I run the water over my face and tilt my head down to rinse out the conditioner. I could have stayed facing him but didn't feel like it.

Once done, I turn back around, and he stands there staring at me. His impatience evident in his narrowed eyes and sharp jaw. "We got together my freshman year. He was a senior."

"And?"

"And what?" I ask, not knowing what all he wants to know.

"What else?" he demands.

I place my hands on my hips and tilt my head. If he wants to know, then I'll tell him. Because it's just gonna piss him off anyway. And I love to piss this guy off. "At the time, I was fourteen, and he was seventeen. He asked me out, and I said yes. We dated for a few weeks, then I gave it up." His jaw sharpens. "After that, we were together. His uncle owned a tattoo and body piercing shop. After Martin graduated high school, he went to work with him."

His eyes go to my side, and he demands, "He gave you that tattoo?"

"Yep."

His eyes snap back up to mine, and I can see the rage behind them. He hates that another man marked me. Too bad. It's not like I let Martin write his name across my ass. "And then I had to move here. End of story."

"Do you still talk to him?" he asks, pressing.

I hate that the truth is no. That what I thought meant something was really nothing to Martin. He was there for me in a lot of ways. He never asked what went on in my house, but he knew. He kept me busy. Always wanted to hang out. He was a major pot head, and we spent most of our time high or drunk, but he still always made sure to come and get me to do things. He even taught me how to drive. He did the things that my mother and father should have shown me.

"Yes," I lie, looking down at the drain. Because I'm not gonna tell a man who wants to break me that a guy I thought I loved no longer speaks to me.

He grabs my chin and lifts my head to where I have to look up at him. "Delete the pictures, Austin. You're mine now. Not his." Then he lets go of me and steps out of the shower.

After the shower, I walk out to find Cole on his cell already dressed in a fresh pair of jeans and a clean black t-shirt. I'm not sure where they came from because I never saw him with a bag last night. I dig through my overnight bag and put on a new pair of jean shorts and t-shirt that says CALI across it in red letters. After I throw on my tennis shoes, I then dry my hair.

I didn't bring any makeup or a straightener, so I threw my hair up in a messy bun once dry and called it good. This'll have to do for lunch.

I'm coming down the stairs when I spot him sitting on the couch. He's got his legs crossed at the ankles and his head down staring at his phone as he types away.

He looks up at me and stands. We haven't spoken since he told me to delete those pictures and that I belonged to him now.

I really didn't have much to say on that matter. He thinks he's got me where he wants me. I'm not gonna say otherwise.

He takes my bag from my hand and opens the door for me. I mumble a thank you and fall into his passenger seat while he places my bag in the trunk. I look around for Deke's Range Rover but don't see where Cole parked it last night. He must have already come and got it.

"Where is your phone?" he asks.

"Why?"

He blows out a long breath, hating when I don't just answer his questions. "Because Celeste called me saying she's been trying to get a hold of you. But it goes straight to voicemail."

"It died last night while at the beach, and I forgot my charger."

"I'll plug it in," he says, opening his center console to grab his charger. I see his gun and knife in there before he shuts it.

I remove it from my back pocket and hand it to him. "What did she want?" I ask after he plugs it in.

"She wanted to know if you were going to be home tonight."

I nod my head. "Of course—"

"I told her no," he interrupts me.

"What?" I demand.

"You'll be with me."

I laugh like he's lost his mind. "And where will we be?"

He doesn't answer, just like always, and I fall back into my seat, crossing my arms over my chest.

I hate that he brings out every emotion in me. I hate how I told him secrets about me to get him to open up, but it didn't work. He didn't tell me anything that I hadn't already figured out about his friends dying. I stood there and told him things that no one else knows. And although he looked pissed, like he cared about what Phillip had done, he didn't give me what I really wanted. His story. His hate. His secrets. It's not fair.

Life isn't fair, my mother always says. But it's seemed pretty fucking fair to her if you ask me.

She fucked a man once and got knocked up. I was here nine months later. The only reason she had me was because she met a wealthy, good-looking man who only wanted a one-night stand. She saw me as her meal ticket. Even now that I'm living with him, my father still sends her monthly checks. But those will stop soon. I'll be eighteen and graduated. I don't know the law exactly, but I had a friend whose father stopped paying for her after she graduated high school last year.

Then what will my mother do? Will she beg me for money? Have me ask him? It won't happen. I won't get her a dime.

"Take it out on Me" by Thousand Foot Krutch starts to play through the speakers. I reach over and turn it up to try to drown out my own thoughts.

It doesn't.

I look over at him, and his left hand is on the steering wheel while his right is on the shifter. He wears his normal mask that hides his true thoughts and feelings from the world, but I see it. I thought it was anger, but after our talk earlier, I realize it's pain. He's hurting. He just refuses to let anyone see it. To see the real him.

He reaches out and turns off the radio. We sit in silence, and I wonder what he's thinking. If his mind is screaming as loud as mine is.

I look down at my hands knotted in my lap. "You know I would never tell anyone about what happened." He has to know by now that no matter what, he can trust me. He's blackmailed me to keep my mouth shut, but I would never tell a soul that he wasn't the one driving. He took that blame on his own for a reason, and I would never out him. No matter how much I disagree with it.

"Why did you take Jerrold's laptop?" he asks, ignoring my statement.

My brows rise, surprised by that question. "You know why," I say, not going back down that road. He doesn't want to share, then I won't either.

"I know why you are on our side when it comes to him. But I want to know why that dare? Why not something else?"

"It was the only dare I could think of," I answer honestly. "I tried to think of things that you had told me about, and I wanted to help Eli's sister. I thought maybe there was some info on there that you could use. You could get him arrested …"

His soft laugh interrupts me. "His ass isn't going to jail, sweetheart."

"Then what …?" My words trail off as I understand. "You're gonna kill him too?" I ask wide-eyed.

"Of course." He snorts.

Death too must be earned. He had said to me that day in his car as we watched Jerrold in his office. "You're gonna get caught," I say, fisting my hands.

"No, we won't."

"You didn't even do a good job with Jeff." I roll my eyes at his confidence.

He looks over at me for a quick second. "What are you talking about?"

"It took me twenty minutes to dig him up. It would take a full-grown man half that. You didn't bury him very deep. And you weren't very smart." He opens his mouth, but I continue. "You left him dressed in the clothes that had your blood on them. You should be thanking me that I burned his body." He shuts his mouth. "Plus, you buried him right next to where Eli's sister is. Very poetic. But anyone who would consider someone close to her as a suspect, would go there first."

I sit back in my seat and cross my arms over my chest as I look out the window, watching all the cars he passes.

"What would you have done?" he finally asks.

I turn back to look at him. He stares straight ahead. "Given the situation I was in, exactly what I did."

He nods his head once.

"And if I wouldn't have had the resources to set him on fire, I would have tied him to a couple of full dive tanks and dumped his body into the ocean." His brows lift in surprise. "Sharks and other fish would have smelled the blood. He would had been eaten to nothing in a matter of days." He nods to himself again. Slower this time. "But if I would have been part of it, I would have done it differently."

I've never killed someone but that doesn't mean it hasn't crossed my mind. The older I got, the more I despised Phillip. Every time he cornered me, I thought of killing him. Or at the very least chopping his hands off in a freak accident.

"Like what?"

"I know you're into the fight." He stiffens. "But if you didn't wanna get your hands dirty, you could have poisoned him and tossed his body into an abandoned well and thrown sulfuric acid down there with him to dissolve the body. It takes a little longer than lye, but it liquefies the bones and teeth as well as the soft tissue."

He whips his head over to look at me.

I give him a big smile. "I know how to cover my tracks." I say the same thing I told him the night he tried to blackmail me. The first time.

And for the first time in the three weeks I've known Cole Reynolds, he looks utterly impressed and speechless. It's awesome.

CHAPTER TWENTY-SEVEN
COLE

She's sick.

She's twisted.

She's fucking perfect.

I sit next to her in a booth as she speaks across the table to Becky, and all I can think about is what she said to me in the car. How she would kill someone. How she would cover her tracks. And how she saved our asses by burning Jeff's body. Had we been that sloppy? Had we not covered our tracks well enough? I would hate to think that Jerrold went to where he buried Aimee's body and thought to look next to her. That he would have found him and seen him covered in our blood. Would he have suspected us right off the bat? If Eli were still alive, then I would say yes without thought, but he's not.

But to suspect us? That's not possible. We were careful. Deke and I had picked him up outside his favorite bar that night. Threw him in my trunk and met the guys on the Lowes estate to carry him up to the cemetery. He had taken a cab to the bar, so we didn't need to mess with his car. As far as the police know, he got lost or mugged on his way home. Even this city has streets that you don't go down alone after the sun sets.

"Cole?" Deke snaps my name.

I look up at him. "What?"

"You okay?" he asks softly so the girls can't hear him. They're in their own world talking about some shit girls talk about.

I run a hand through my hair. "We'll be back," I say to Austin and Becky and slide out. Deke follows me without thought.

"What is it, man?" he asks when we walk outside.

I stop in front of my car and turn to face him on the sidewalk. "Do you think we covered our tracks well enough with Jeff?" I ask.

He snorts. "Don't let Shane get to you, man. All that shit he was saying last night didn't make any sense. He's just scared …"

"This has nothing to do with Shane."

He frowns. "Then what does it have to do with?"

"I was talking to Austin—"

"Austin?" he interrupts me. "What does she have to do with this? You think she's gonna go to the police?" he asks.

I shake my head and take a step back from him, running a hand through my hair again nervously. Then I start pacing the sidewalk.

"Cole."

I stop and look up at him.

He has a sly smile on his face. "She's getting to you."

"No, she's not," I say like he asked me a question.

He snorts and crosses his arms over his chest. "Becky was right."

My teeth clench. "No …"

"She said that it's more than you're letting on."

I roll my eyes. "Deke, come on."

He steps into me. "It's okay not to want to use her."

I shake my head. "She is nothing more than part of the game."

"You're not in the game," he says matter-of-factly. "You have your eyes on Austin a hundred percent of the time, and although I don't have a problem with it, it's blinding you."

"What the hell does that mean?" I growl.

"It means you're not seeing the big picture, Cole." He sighs heavily. "Kellan is up to something. That night at the clubhouse, I baited him to see what he would do, knowing you would test him. And you did. Even though he didn't fuck her right then and there, he still failed."

My body tenses at the thought of Kellan wanting her in any way. "I know!"

"He may want to fuck her, but he wants her gone more. And when he realizes what I've figured out." He smiles, and I wanna slap it off his face. "That she means more to you. He's gonna take you up on your offer to fuck her, and when you tell him no … He's gonna make a move." My hands fists. "Shane can't decide what side of the fence he wants to be on when it comes to her. And Bennett … is just, well, Bennett. In his own world. He's not a threat to her. Yet. But we both know that he would take her out without a thought if he felt she jeopardized—"

"I know all this," I snap, interrupting him.

He glares at me. "Then you need to decide what she means to you. Because I see it all fucking coming to a head. Not soon but eventually, and you're gonna have to pick a side. Save her. Or kill her before the others do."

"And you?" I demand. "Where does she stand with you?"

He uncrosses his arms and places them in his pockets. "She's my girlfriend's best friend and my brother's girl." He looks me in the eyes. "I do what you say. Whether that means protect her or kill her, so her blood isn't on your hands, is up to you." And with that, he turns and walks back into the restaurant.

AUSTIN

"So what are you guys doing tonight?" Becky asks me.

"Nothing—"

"We're going to a movie," Cole interrupts me as he slides in next to me.

"Really?" she asks excitedly.

I eye him skeptically.

He places his arm over my shoulders and pulls me to his side. I hate that my body instantly softens. "Really," he says, looking at her.

I'm about to open my mouth and say *no* when he continues. "We are taking Lilly to see the new Disney movie. She won't leave me alone about it." My heart melts a little bit at the mention of Lilly. "You guys wanna go?" he asks.

Becky looks at Deke. He shrugs. "If that's what you want—"

"Yes. We'll go," she interrupts him.

Deke looks at Cole and smiles. "I can drive if you want," he offers.

Lunch went well although I was tense for most of it. Cole is acting differently, and I can't figure it out. And Deke kept staring at me with a smirk on his face like he knew a secret. It put me on alert.

"What's wrong?" Cole asks while he drives me home.

"Nothing," I lie.

He looks over at me and snorts. "Your knees haven't stopped bouncing since we left the restaurant."

I slap my hands on my thighs to help tame them. "Why am I going to the movies with you?" I blurt out.

He frowns. "Why wouldn't you?"

"We don't do that." When his frown deepens, I add. "Date." This isn't even a real relationship. He told me I was his, and no one else will date me. I kinda have no other options.

"I promised Lilly yesterday I would take her to the movies tonight, and I figured you'd want to come. Is there a problem?"

I open my mouth but then close it. Not sure what to say. "No," I say when I come up with nothing. "I like spending time with Lilly."

He smiles. "But not with me."

Is he being playful?

I don't say anything to that because I'm not sure what I like at this moment. He's got my mind twisted. He's a killer. He's been nothing but a dick to me. But then I find out he has this heart that is so big he would rather the entire city hate him than soil his friend's reputation. Then, of course, Lilly. He thinks the world of her. Raises her. And then there's the sex. Fuck me! The sex. It's amazing. Sex with Martin was slow and soft. He was always high, and I was always on top while he played some slow blues music. Sex with Cole is crazy and animalistic. Makes me wanna play some hardcore metal and have his hand wrapped around my neck.

"Your phone is done charging," he says, unplugging and handing it to me. I go to reach for it, but he pulls it away. "Why do you have the retina scanner on it?"

"It came with the phone."

He comes to a stop at a red light and looks over at me. "The real reason, sweetheart."

"Just give it to me," I bark.

He places it in the side of his door. "When you can be truthful, I'll give it back."

"Cole," I growl.

"Austin." He smiles.

I don't like this new playful Cole. It's annoying. "You don't get to do this," I snap.

"Do what?"

"Not tell me anything but want me to tell you everything."

"So there is a reason you use the retina."

I sit back in my seat and the light turns green. He doesn't go. The car behind us honks its horn. I turn around to look as the guy swerves around us. "Cole. The light is green."

"I know," he says simply.

Another car honks its horn. "Well, why are we just sitting here?"

He yanks the emergency brake up and crosses his arms over his chest. "We're not moving until you tell me why you have a retina scanner on your phone."

Another car honks and flies by us. My teeth clench. "You are such a dick."

"Call me whatever you want, sweetheart. I always get what I want."

A car passes by, and the passenger sticks his right hand out flipping us off. Thankfully, Cole's windows are blacked out so no one can see us. Finally, the light turns red, and I just stare straight ahead. I remain silent as does he. I pray that he goes through the stoplight the moment it turns green again. But he stays put.

Fucking bastard.

I let out a long breath while cars pass us once again. "I walked into my bedroom one day and found Phillip going through my photos. Photos that I had taken of myself and sent to Martin. After that, I knew I needed to put a lock on it that he wouldn't be able to guess.

Retina scanner was the best bet."

He tosses my phone to me, and it hits the door. Then he releases the emergency brake and throws the car in gear and squeals the tires as he takes off, barely making it before the light turns red again.

I look over at him as he drives like a maniac now through traffic. Cutting cars off and tailgating. "What is your problem?" I demand.

He slams on the brakes at another red light. I can see his jaw tighten.

"Why do you make me tell you things and then get mad at me? If you don't want to know the answer, then don't make me tell you. It's not that hard of a concept," I snap.

He remains silent, and I look down to turn my phone on. It starts to ding instantly with notifications. I open my Facebook page and see I have over a hundred new friend requests, which is a surprise. But only one stands out. Cole Reynolds. His profile pic is of us. I'm sitting on the counter at his father's house, and he's standing between my legs, kissing me.

I ignore it and go to my pictures. I scroll through them, looking at the ones I have with Martin. Each one makes me angrier and angrier that I haven't heard from him.

I click on his page. His profile is still the same picture it has been for two years now. Him standing with his surfboard on the ocean. I scroll down through his posts and see that he is still addicted to the games. He likes to smoke weed, sit back, and play on his phone. I see he was tagged in a picture just a few days ago. The person doing the tagging is a girl. She has short brown hair and light brown eyes. His lips are on her cheek and her hand is on his chest. But there's no caption.

I swallow, hating the feeling that he is with someone else so fast. I'm not gonna say I thought we would get married, but he was a big part of my life. And then, boom. Nothing. It hurts.

It's not like Cole and I are anything important. Like I wanted this relationship with him.

I unfriend Martin, exit his page, and go back to mine, deleting every picture he was in.

Cole pulls up to my house, and I open the passenger door to get out. "Austin …" He grabs my upper arm.

I swing my head around to glare at him. "I didn't delete them for you." Then I yank my arm free and get out.

Sunday evening, I find myself back at the clubhouse with the guys to do another dare.

I sit on the couch with Cole to my left and Deke to my right. We haven't spoken much since yesterday afternoon. We went to see a movie last night, but the best thing about movies is that you can't talk during them. Then afterward I told him to take me home. He didn't argue even though earlier in the day he had told Celeste I would be staying the night with him. I think he knew I was pissed and didn't wanna to fight with me over it.

"So who's up?" I ask.

"Cole," Deke answers.

"Don't make your dare illegal," Cole warns me without looking my way. And I know it's for my sake, not his.

I ignore him.

Like last time, Shane passes out pieces of paper and pens. I write down a dare and put it in the bowl.

I peek over at Kellan standing by the table, and he's staring at me. I look away.

Cole gets up and goes over to the bowl. He draws out a piece of paper and silently reads it to himself at first. His jaw sharpens and nostrils flare. His eyes instantly go to Kellan who smiles back at Cole, then looks back at me.

"I dare you," Kellan says to Cole with a sinister smile on his face.

I swallow nervously.

CHAPTER TWENTY-EIGHT

COLE

My eyes go to Austin, and her face is white, eyes wide. She looks nervous. Looking back down at the paper, I read it out loud. "You must fuck Kaitlin. Consequence. If you do not complete your dare in one month, you must pull out of the group."

Deke snorts and mutters, "You can't be serious."

"Oh, I'm very serious," Kellan says, looking at Austin.

Her face has turned red, and I'm not sure if it's from anger or embarrassment.

Deke stands and looks at Kellan. "What the fuck, man?"

He shrugs carelessly. "Not sure what the problem is. We all know that he's just playing with Austin for the month, and he's fucked Kaitlin before. Not like she's a bad lay. We've all had a piece of that."

"You know why," he snaps.

Shane runs a hand through his hair nervously while Bennett looks at Kellan with a tight jaw. We all know what he's doing. But there's nothing we can do—rules are rules.

I smile. Kellan is just asking for me to fuck him over. He still doesn't know that I'm aware he's fucking Celeste. I know she hasn't said a word to him because he would have confronted me.

I could tell him. But what good would that do? It won't change anything now. Plus, I want him to continue fucking her. I need insurance. And I won't get it if he stops.

Kellan looks at me. That smirk still on his face. "You've got a month, Cole," he says, then looks to Austin and winks before he walks out.

Her eyes meet mine, and she looks absolutely pissed. And I find I like another side of her. One I've never seen before—jealousy.

Everyone but me, Austin, and Deke have left the clubhouse. She still sits on the couch. She hasn't said a word since I read my dare out loud over thirty minutes ago.

Deke sighs heavily as he approaches me. "What are you gonna do, man?" he asks, lowering his voice.

"What I have to do," I say simply.

He shakes his head. "I told you shit was gonna come to a head. And it's gonna happen within a month."

"It'll be fine."

He growls. "Kellan was out of line."

"He's playing the game." *Not very well*, I might add.

"Fuck the game," he snaps.

I slap his shoulder. "I've got it under control."

"You can't pull out of the group."

"I'm not going anywhere," I assure him.

"So you're gonna fuck Kaitlin?" He gives Austin a quick look over his shoulder. She is typing away on her cell. "You can't come back from that, Cole."

"Quit worrying so much, Deke," I decide to say.

He lets out another long breath, shaking his head. Then without another word, he turns and walks out.

"Let's go," I say to her.

She stands from the couch and walks out to my car. I follow her and close up the clubhouse. When I get in the car, she looks straight ahead. I turn the car on and take her home.

As I pull up to her driveway, she's already reaching for the door. "Wait," I say, grabbing her arm.

She finally looks over at me, and her green eyes are simmering with rage and her lips thinned.

"Trust me."

She says nothing. Doesn't even blink.

I hold in a sigh. I'm gonna fucking kill Kellan. I haven't worked this hard to get her where I want for him to come along and fuck it all up. "I know I haven't given you a reason to, but I need you to trust me on this." Deke was right; I could never come back from this. And if I want Austin Lowes to fall in love with me, fucking another woman isn't gonna do it.

"You're right. You haven't given me a reason to trust you, and I'm not gonna start now." Then she gets out, slamming the door behind her.

The next week went by quicker than I would have liked. And I hated it. This was the last free week I would have before I was gonna be spending all my time in a pool. My weekends full of swim meets. It was the last time before I graduated. And Kellan fucked it up by giving me that ridiculous dare.

I still picked up Austin and took her to and from school. She didn't say anything to me when we were alone. She spoke to me here and there in class and while at lunch, but I could still tell that she was mad. And I'm not sure what to do about it.

I have a little over three weeks left to complete my dare, and I'm gonna take up every single day of that. Because once I fulfill it, shit will hit the fan. And I'm not ready to clean up that mess yet.

Friday afternoon, we are all sitting at the lunch table with the exception of Kellan. He's been MIA since last Sunday. I see him in practice, but we ignore one another. So does Deke and Bennett. Shane seems to be the only one speaking to him at the moment.

"Austin, I need a favor," I say, turning to face her. She sits beside me eating Chick-fil-A nuggets.

"What is it?" she asks, not bothering to look at me.

"Can you take Lilly to school and pick her up for me next week?

Blanche is busy, and Bruce is going to be back in town ..." She drops her nugget in the barbecue sauce at the mention of her father. "So Celeste will be too busy—"

"Yeah," she says, interrupting me and digging it out.

Becky gives me a glare, and I ignore her. She's been cold since last Sunday, but that's to be expected. I'm sure Austin filled her in on my dare.

"Thank you," I say, but she's gone back to ignoring me.

"Hey, babe, I made our reservations for tomorrow," Deke tells Becky.

She looks at him but doesn't say anything. Their relationship is on the rocks as well. Not sure what happened there, but it's not good.

Deke throws me a glare.

"Okay, how about we go out to eat together?" I offer, trying to fix this since I'm the reason both girls are pissed.

"I'm busy," Austin states and then stands to throw her trash away.

I grip her arm and pull her back down into her seat. "Doing what?"

Her eyes narrow on me. And they look like she did that first night I met her in the cemetery. When she hated me. That seems so long ago. "None of your business," she snaps.

The bell rings, and she tries to get up again, but I don't release her. "Austin—" Becky starts, but Deke grabs her arm too and pulls her away from the table.

"Stop," I tell her.

"Stop what?"

She's playing my game. Where I act oblivious. I don't like it. "Stop acting like I've already fucked her." Her nostrils flare. "I was going to give you some time, but you've had enough."

"Enough time for what, Cole?" she demands.

"To get over this. To understand that Kellan is trying to play both of us. And you're letting him win."

"No." She leans in, her face inches from mine. I swallow the urge to kiss her. "What you don't understand, Cole, is that I don't fucking care."

She yanks her arm from my hold, gets up, and walks out of the cafeteria.

AUSTIN

I don't care!

I don't fucking care!

I've been repeating that in my head for the past five days. Five long fucking days. My mind has been a mess. And my chest tight. I don't love him. Hell, half the time I don't even like him. Then why am I so mad that he has to sleep with someone else? Especially someone he has slept with before?

I snort. Hell, for all I know, he's been sleeping with other women over the past month. I still swear he has a thing going on with Shelby, and I never gave much thought to that, but this is eating at me. Though I'm not sure what bothers me more. The fact he has to do it or the fact he wants to do it.

I saw the way he smiled at Kellan after he read the dare out loud. Like it was a fucking pass to screw around on me. For all I fucking know, Cole told Kellan to give him that dare. And I can't do a single thing about it.

I storm out of the cafeteria and down the quiet hallway. The second bell has already rang, and now I'm late. That's been my week. Turning the corner, I come to a quick stop when I collide with another body. "I'm sor …" My words cut off when I look up into a set of brown eyes.

Kellan! I straighten my shoulders and go to walk around him. He grabs my arm and yanks me back. "Don't touch me!" I snap.

Slamming my back into a locker, he places his hands on either side of my head and cages me in. Just like Cole used to do. I swear they are so much alike, it's scary. "I would ask how your week is going, but I can tell it's shitty."

I clamp my mouth shut, refusing to speak to him.

He smiles down at me. "He's gonna fuck her, Austin."

I say nothing but my hands fist, knowing he's right.

"He'll pick the group over anything. Even you."

I know. "I don't care what he does."

He chuckles. "Yes, you do. Or you wouldn't be walking around this school with a scowl on your face. Everyone is talking about it. They see the way you ignore him. How when he touches you, you pull away. And when the school finds out he fucked Kaitlin … because they will, Austin, I'll make sure of it. No one will feel sorry for you. They'll all say you sent him right into her arms."

I narrow my eyes on him. "I'm having a hard time putting two and two together. Why don't you help me out? Is it me you hate the most or Cole?" I come right out and ask. I've never backed down to Cole, so I'm sure as hell not going to with Kellan.

"I hate you both equally," he says as his eyes drop to my chest.

My breathing picks up as he pushes himself into me, pressing my back into the lockers. "Kellan," I warn.

"There is a way that can keep him from having to fuck her," he says as his hips press into mine. He's hard. My hands shoot out to his chest, and I try to push him away, but he doesn't budge. He presses his face into my neck, and I swallow the bile that wants to rise. "I'll retract my dare if you pull out of the group."

Could it be that easy? Could I just call a meeting and tell them that I'm done? That I won't tell a soul what I know, and they'll let me leave.

He chuckles, and I grind my teeth. *It's a trick.* "Then that will show that I actually care. Which I don't."

"But we all know that you do, Austin. End it with some dignity and pull out of the group. Or let him cheat on you and make you more of a joke than you already are." He kisses my neck, and I pull it away from him the best I can with his body pinning me to the lockers. "You've got until Sunday," he whispers and then he licks up my neck to my ear, before pulling away.

I suck in breath after breath while my heart races as I watch him walk down the hallway. He places his hands in the pockets of his jeans, whistling a merry tune.

I fist my hands down by my side, trying to calm my racing heart. This bastard is not gonna play me. I'm so tired of them thinking that they can push me around. Bully me. Fucking blackmail me.

I pull my cell out of my back pocket and send a quick text to Cole.

Me: Dinner tomorrow night @ 6. My house.

Then I put it away and storm off to class. I know exactly what I need to do. It's a simple answer. It just took Kellan in my face to realize it.

———

I'm just putting the dessert in the fridge when I hear the doorbell ring. I open it up to see Becky and Deke standing before me. She looks unhappy, and he looks pissed.

I feel bad for them. She's been mad at him since Sunday. After Cole dropped me off at my house, she had called me. To my surprise, Deke told her what was going on. She was mad at him for even doing these stupid dares. But when she spoke to me, she cried. She told me that she couldn't imagine her life without him and what if someone had dared him to sleep with someone else. She wasn't sure if he would pick her over the boys' stupid group. That was when I realized if Deke was questionable, then there was no doubt about what side Cole would choose.

He'll fuck Kaitlin!

I'm just some girl Cole blackmailed. Deke loves Becky.

"You look gorgeous," I say, pulling her in for a hug.

"So do you." She hugs me and then pulls away, giving me a fake smile.

"Deke." I greet him.

He nods.

I loop my arm in hers, and we make our way into the kitchen. "You cooked all of this?" Becky asks wide-eyed, looking over the table.

I cooked my favorite meal, Italian stuffed shells with garlic parmesan cheese bombs, along with tiramisu cupcakes for dessert. "Yep. I hope you're hungry. There's dessert in the fridge."

She goes to open her mouth, but the doorbell rings again. "Deke, will you get that?" I ask and turn my back to him.

239

CHAPTER TWENTY-NINE
COLE

I square my shoulders as the door opens, and I'm not surprised to see Deke opening it. His SUV is outside, after all. Yesterday while in fifth period, I read Austin's text out loud to him and Becky. She immediately told me to reply that they would come too. Deke wasn't happy, but he didn't argue.

I go to enter, but he steps outside, making me take a step back. "You better have a plan to fix this shit."

"Deke …"

"This is getting in my way now, Cole. And if you don't do something, I'm going to kill Kellan myself." Then he spins around and walks inside, slamming the door shut behind him.

I shove it open and storm inside. But I come to a stop when I enter the kitchen. Deke and Becky aren't present, but Austin stands over at the counter. Her back facing me. Her hair is down in big curls, and she has a black dress on that stops mid-thigh. It makes me instantly hard.

I walk over to her, and she stiffens when I pull her hair off her shoulder. I lean down, kissing her delicate neck. "Hello, sweetheart," I say softly.

I've got to kiss ass! There's no way around it.

She turns around in my arms and looks up at me. She's not smiling, but she doesn't look like she wants to tear my head off. So things are getting better already. Then she leans up and gently kisses my lips.

I can't stop myself; I slide my hands in her soft hair and demand more from her. And she gives it. Her arms wrap around my neck, and her mouth opens for me. I press her back into the counter and moan into her mouth. Fuck Kellan! He isn't gonna fuck up my plans with Austin. She is the one I want to destroy.

But she's already destroyed.

She pulls away and runs her hands down my button up. She licks her wet lips and then turns back around, giving me her back.

We all sit at the table, an awkward silence falling between everyone. It reminds me of dinner with her dad last month. And just like then, I haven't eaten much. I've just sat here and stared at her, ignoring all the glares Deke has thrown me.

"Do you guys have plans afterward?" Austin looks at Becky.

"No." Her answer is clipped.

Deke tightens his hold on his fork like he plans to stab me with it. "I thought you wanted to go see that movie—"

"Not anymore," she interrupts him.

He slams his fork onto the table. Deke never has had much patience. "Why am I being punished for something Cole is doing?" he demands. "I'm not fucking Kaitlin."

My teeth clench. *Here we go.*

"Because that could very easily be you," she snaps back. "You guys play this stupid game as if your life depends on it. And it's ridiculous."

He opens his mouth, but Austin stands from the table. The room falls silent when she looks at me. "I spoke with Kellan yesterday."

Deke jumps to his feet. "About what?" he demands.

She looks toward him. "He helped remind me what kind of game this is. And although I don't agree with it either, I'm not a quitter."

"What did he say to you?" I snap. I saw him at practice yesterday afternoon and not once did he tell me he spoke to her. He actually avoided me like he has all week.

"He said that he would retract the dare if I pulled out."

Deke frowns, and my jaw tightens. "That isn't allowed. He lied to you," I growl.

She nods to me. "I figured. That's why I don't plan on pulling out."

"So what are you gonna do?" Becky asks, looking up at her.

She tilts her head to the side. "Have you guys thought about Kellan?" She ignores answering Becky's question. "Like really thought about him? 'Cause I have this week. And after our talk yesterday, things started to make sense."

"Like what?" Deke asks.

"First—who is Kaitlin to Bryan?"

I frown, not understanding where she's going with this.

"She is his ex," Becky answers. "They had a bad breakup last year. But no one really knows why."

She brings her hand up to tap her finger on her chin in thought. "Don't you find it odd that just weeks ago, Kaitlin came up to you and said that I was a dare? That *Bryan* had told her Cole had a month to play with me. Then she literally becomes his dare?" She looks at me. Deke frowns confused. But I get what she's saying. "It could be a coincidence, but then she says the rumor came from Bryan. Who I now know is her ex. And he's also a guy who you already got in a fight with over me once before then. Where would Bryan hear that from? It came to me. Last Sunday after you drew your dare and Deke was questioning him about it, Kellan's words were *why not? We all know he's just playing with Austin.*" Deke shakes his head with disgust. "And you guys both jumped Bryan and his best friend Christopher at the beach party after he dared his friend to fuck me. Where Kellan wasn't at."

"I don't get it," Becky says.

She looks at Becky. "Kellan is trying to fuck them at their own game." Then her eyes meet mine. "I can't figure out where Deke fits in, but he's trying to set you both up. He wanted you guys in trouble for laying your hands on Chris and Bryan, but they didn't rat you guys out 'cause they're more afraid of you than him."

"Son of a bitch." Deke hisses.

"How long ago did you sleep with her?" She looks at me.

"Freshman year."

"See. And now he's daring Cole to fuck Bryan's ex." She shakes her head. "He's playing very dirty."

She walks out of the formal dining room, and my eyes fall to my plate. She's right.

What are you gonna do about it, Cole?

There's nothing I can do. My hands are tied. Literally.

She reenters with what looks like cupcakes on a tray. She sets them in the center of the table and turns to face me. "You told me to trust you. And I'm going to give you one chance, Cole." Her green eyes hold my stare without an ounce of fear. "And don't you dare try to fuck me over." With that, she pulls her seat back and sits down. Placing the cupcakes in the center of the table, she takes one.

She's trusting me.

A part of me hates to fail her. Like everyone else in her life. The other part reminds me this is what I've wanted. But I've learned a lot about Austin Lowes since I met her. Whatever you dish out, she can throw back in your face ten times over. She is karma wrapped in a gorgeous tan and an innocent smile.

Deke and I slowly sit back in our seats.

"What time was that movie, babe?" Becky asks him.

"Eight thirty," he answers her but smiles at me. They both reach in and devour the cupcakes, and I watch Austin smile as she talks to Becky like nothing ever fucking happened. It makes me wanna know what else Kellan said to her. She's obviously choosing my side, but why? Did he threaten her? Blackmail her? Does she think I'm the easier one of the two? I'm gonna find out.

"Yeah, I'd love to go." Her voice gets my attention.

"Go where?" I ask.

Becky answers. "To your guys' swim meet next weekend. It's only an hour away."

"If it's okay, we could bring Lilly," Austin adds. "I know she would love to watch you."

Deke smiles through his cupcake, and I can see the chocolate in his teeth. I refrain from throwing one at his face.

She's getting to you.

Yes. She is. And I'm not sure what to do about that anymore.

I close the door after telling Deke and Becky goodbye to find Austin in the kitchen washing dishes. I lean back against the wall, watching her rinse them off before placing them in the dishwasher. "You know your father pays people to do that, right?"

"When living with my mom, we didn't pay anyone. If something needed to be done, I did it."

"Stop," I say, coming up behind her. I spin her around and grip her hip with my right hand. My left hand pushes her hair from her face. "What did Kellan say to you to make you change your mind? Did he blackmail you?"

She laughs at that. "No, but he is a lot like you in other ways."

"How?" I ask, my hand pausing in her hair.

"He pinned me against the lockers."

"He what?" I bark.

"Told me to end it with you and drop out of the group before you make an even bigger joke out of me."

"Austin …"

"If you've learned anything about me, it's that I don't like being cornered. I don't like being told what I can and can't do."

I smile softly down at her. Glad to see that fight back in her gorgeous green eyes. "Yeah."

"He gave me until tomorrow to make my decision."

My teeth clench at that. "And what if you don't choose what he wants?'

She shrugs. "He didn't say. But I remember hearing you say that you like to perform." My brows rise. "So …" She wraps her arms around my neck. "We are going to give them all a show, baby."

I laugh at the way she calls me baby. It's the first time she's ever said it, and I hate how it makes chills run up my spine. "What do you have in mind?"

She reaches up and gently kisses my lips. "Right now, I want you to take me upstairs and rip this dress off my body. And fuck me like they're watching."

AUSTIN

Sunday evening, we pull up to the barn at nine o'clock. We were supposed to be here thirty minutes ago. We spent all day in my bed, then took our time getting ready. Cole walks around and opens the passenger door for me. I smile up at him, and he has a smirk on his face.

He takes my hand in his and opens the barn door for me to enter. We come in, and all chatter comes to a stop. Deke sits on the couch texting on his phone. Shane and Bennett lean up against the table to the right, and Kellan stands facing them.

"Hello, everyone." Cole says cheerfully.

I watch Kellan's brown eyes narrow on him.

"Finally." Deke jumps up. "Let's get this over with. We shouldn't even be meeting tonight. We don't have a dare to do."

"That's because Cole is taking his sweet ass time fucking Kaitlin," Kellan says, looking at me. "Not sure why. She's a guaranteed lay."

I tighten my hold on Cole's hand. He ignores Kellan.

"I called the meeting," Bennett says and turns around to dig into a black drawstring backpack. Identical to the one that lies under my bed. He opens it up and pulls out five white envelopes. "Here you guys go." He hands one to Shane and Kellan. Then he walks over and hands Cole two. He tosses Deke the last one, and he catches it midair.

"What is that?" I ask.

Cole hands me one of them. I take it and feel the thickness.

"This ..." Deke holds his up and smiles at me. "Is payday."

"Payday?" I ask confused. "I don't—"

"That laptop you stole from Jerrold's," Bennett interrupts me, "had several accounts on it. I'm draining them one at a time into an account I set up. This is the smallest one. And this is your cut. We each got ten thousand."

"What?" My mouth falls open in a gasp. I shove my envelope into

Cole's chest and let go of it. It falls to his feet. "I can't take that."

Kellan snorts. "Surprise, surprise. The princess doesn't want it."

"That's blood money," I snap.

"It's whatever you wanna call it."

"It's illegal," I argue with him.

Cole reaches down and picks up my envelope.

"What you did to get laptop was illegal too. Or did you forget that?" Kellan arches a brow in challenge.

I look away from him.

"That's what I thought," he adds.

"Find anything else on the laptop?" Cole asks Bennett.

He shrugs. "Nothing useful. The guy is in some pretty sick shit when it comes to sex. But besides bank accounts, there was nothing useful."

"What about cell phone records?" I ask.

"What about them?" Kellan snaps.

Everyone's eyes turn on me. "What about them?" Deke asks in a much nicer tone.

"A lot of people don't like to log in every time they go to a site they frequent often, so they keep their passwords remembered. If you knew his carrier and typed it in, maybe it will still have him logged in. You could go through his phone records. See who he has spoken to." They all just stare at me, and I shrug, feeling awkward. "It could be nothing …"

"No. It's a good idea. I'll check into it," Bennett says.

I nod once.

Cole takes my hand and turns us to face Kellan. I square my shoulders, knowing what is about to happen. "She's not pulling out of the group," he growls.

"Who said she was?" Bennett demands.

"Kellan." Deke crosses his arms over his chest.

"What?" He and Shane both speak at once.

Kellan's jaw sharpens, and he narrows his eyes on me. "Even if you could retract your dare, which I knew you couldn't, I still wouldn't pull out."

Cole surprises me and jerks me to face him. His hands go to my hair, and his lips crash down on mine. My lips part on a gasp of surprise when his tongue slides into my mouth. His hands tighten in my hair, and my eyes close on a moan. My hands grip his shirt as he kisses me like he's desperate for me. Needs me. He tilts my head to the side, and I allow him to take my breath away. The man could kill me if he wanted as long as his hands were on me at the time. My pussy tightens, and my legs threaten to buckle as he fucking takes what he wants.

Giving Kellan a show.

My eyes slowly open as he pulls away. His blue eyes look over my shoulder, and he smirks. "And she's mine. Stay away."

The room falls silent as I regain myself and pull out of Cole's hands. I turn around to face them. Kellan glares at me, but his brown eyes start to burn brighter as a sinister smile spreads across his face. He takes a step toward me, and Cole yanks me back by my shoulder, ready to jump between us.

His eyes go to Cole. "If this is how you guys wanna play it." Then he walks past us and out the door.

Monday morning, I walk into the Reynolds house and see Lilly already coming down the hallway toward me. She wears a pair of jeans and a pink shirt that has a kitty on it, and her blond hair is in pigtails. She opens her arms. "Austin," she squeals and jumps into mine.

"Hey, princess. You ready to go to school?"

She nods excitedly.

"Do I need to pack you a lunch? Or do I need to give you lunch money?" I know Blanche is away this week, and I'm not all sure what she eats for lunch. Cole didn't give me any instructions.

"Cole made my lunch this morning before he left. It's already in my backpack."

"Awesome," I say. "Let's get going then."

"Austin?"

I look up to see a man coming toward me, and my eyes widen at how much he resembles Cole. He has his blue eyes, a straight nose, and high cheekbones. His broad shoulders fill his expensive looking charcoal suit, and he's smiling at me. "It's been a long time." He looks me up and down, and it makes the hairs on the back of my neck stand at the way his eyes linger on my legs.

"I'm sorry. Do I know you?" I ask. Even though I know who the man is. I'm not sure what he means by a *long time*.

He reaches out his right hand. "Liam Reynolds. Cole's father."

I got that much. He looks just like him. I shake it. He tightens his grip to the point it's painful, but I don't flinch.

"Good to see you again."

"Again?" I ask, sliding Lilly to my left hip. She's heavier than she looks.

He nods, placing his hands in the pockets of his dress slacks. "Yes. I believe the last time I saw you, you and Cole were seven."

I frown.

"Your father and I have been best friends long before he … dated your mother."

I almost snort at how he chose *dated* to describe their weekend hookup in a hotel room in Reno.

"Last time you stayed with him, he had a cookout, and you and Cole swam together. You actually played together a couple of other times too."

My frown deepens because this guy must have me confused with someone else. I've never met Cole before.

"Anyway," he continues at my silence. "I must be going into the office. And you must be getting to school. Don't wanna get in trouble." His eyes rake over me again, and I take a step back toward the door, tightening my hold on Lilly.

"It was nice meeting you," I say, bending over to grab Lilly's bag and then heading out the door.

CHAPTER THIRTY
COLE

"Where the fuck is she?" I growl, looking down at the clock on my phone. Austin is late as usual.

"She'll be here soon. She got stuck in traffic," Becky answers, pulling her books out of her locker. She shuts her door and turns to face me. "Have you decided on what you're gonna do?"

"Do about what?" I ask.

She places her hand on her hip. "Don't play stupid, Cole. You know exactly what I'm talking about."

I look at Deke, who leans up against the lockers, hoping he will shut her up, but he just raises a brow. He's thinking the same thing she is.

I sigh. "There's no way around it."

She takes a step toward me, glaring. "You're gonna fuck her over for a dare?" She spits with disgust. "Fuck, Cole, I thought better of you than that."

I run a hand through my hair. "It's not about the dare anymore. It's about Kellan—"

"Bullshit!" she interrupts me. "Forget about him and think about Austin."

"What about her?" I demand, getting tired of this subject.

"She—"

"Whew," Austin interrupts her as she comes running up to us. Becky takes a step back from me, and Austin steps between us.

Placing her left hand on her locker, she bows her head, breathing heavily. "Made it." She breathes.

"Did you just have sex in the parking lot?" Becky asks.

"You better not have," I snap.

Becky throws me a fuck you smile as if the thought of Austin fucking someone else would piss me off. And I fist my hands. I might be about to fuck someone else, but she better fucking not.

Austin pushes off her locker and rolls her eyes. "I … wish …" She pants. "I couldn't find a parking spot." She swallows. "Had to park all the way in the back … and run."

Becky laughs, and I ignore her.

I spin Austin around and she looks up at me, a soft smile on her face as she continues to pant. Her eyes heavy and lips wet. I lean down and capture them with mine. She doesn't hesitate. I push my hips into hers, and she moans when she feels I'm already hard. Fuck, I always want her. Too fucking much. I've become a fifteen-year-old boy again who can't keep my dick in my pants. But I only want the same woman over and over instead of something new. Different.

My right hand grabs her thigh and pulls it up to wrap around my hip. Someone whistles as they walk by us, but I ignore them as my lips continue to devour hers.

Fuck me like they're watching.

That's what she had said to me and that thought has me being even more aggressive. I'll give them a show. I'll show them that she is fucking mine.

Her fingers dig into my shirt as she pulls me toward her. I slam her back into the locker. She whimpers into my mouth, and I swallow it.

When I pull away, I'm panting too. She leans her head back, resting against the locker. I smile down at her, loving that her eyes are closed and her chest heaving. I make her just as weak as she makes me.

I take a quick look around the silent hallway and find we are alone now. The bell rang long ago. "Come on," I say, pulling her away from her locker.

She straightens her hair and pulls her shoulders back. Pulling herself together.

"How was Lilly for you this morning?" I ask, walking her to her first period. I hate that I need her help, but right now, there is no one else. And she was right before. Lilly does like her.

"She was great," she says. "I promised to take her for ice cream after school again."

I chuckle. "That's why she likes you so much."

When I finally leave practice, it's late. While I was swimming, Austin messaged me that they were going to swim and then watch a movie at her place. I planned to join them but needed to run by my father's house on the way.

I put my car in park and leave it running in the driveway as I run into the house.

"Cole?" I hear his voice.

I sigh. "Yes?"

"My office."

I walk down the long hallway and make the last right and walk into his office. He sits behind his desk with his hands folded on the brown wood.

"What?" I ask, not entering.

"Sit," he says, gesturing to the chair in front of his desk.

"I'll stand," I say, resting my shoulder against his doorframe.

He sighs heavily, showing me his disappointment.

"I saw Austin Lowes today."

My brows rise at that. "She didn't mention it."

He leans back in his chair. "She's pretty. Very pretty." I fist my hands, knowing that he looked at her that way. And I hate that he used the same word her mother's boyfriend told her. "But of course, she is; her mother was too before she became a worthless druggie." He sighs. "Anyway, Bruce is back in town." I grunt. "He told me that you two are dating."

"Something like that," I say, not wanting him to know that she's getting to me. He'll use her against me. That's what he does.

He smirks. "He also told me that you denied fucking his wife."

"That's because I haven't. You just assumed."

"Well, he knows someone is."

"No offense, Liam, but I couldn't care less what his wife does behind his back. We all know he's not faithful."

His nostrils flare at that. "Are you wearing protection with Austin?" he demands.

I refrain from chuckling at that. *Now he wants to have the sex talk?* Doesn't he know I've been fucking girls since I was fourteen? I have always used protection before, but things are different with Austin. "That's none of your business."

He slams his hands down on his desk and stands. "It is when she tricks you into knocking her up like her mother did Bruce. I don't want another unwanted child running around this house."

My anger rises at those words, and I push away from the doorframe, straightening my back. "Don't worry, *Father,* if I knock her up, I'll take care of *my* child. I already take care of yours. What's one more?"

"Don't you fucking dare, Cole!" he snaps.

"No, Dad. You fucking don't," I shout.

His blue eyes narrow on me before he slowly lowers himself back down into his seat. "Go ahead. Knock her up and see where you're at in five years. Your swimming career long gone. And a child with a woman who can't keep her legs closed for other men."

"You know nothing about her." She's all mine.

"I know enough."

"What Bruce has told you?" I snort. "Like he's been there for her." He doesn't even know what her mother's boyfriend has done to her. Or he does and doesn't fucking care.

His eyes meet mine. "I know that you've become obsessed with the whore, and that you made a deal with Bruce." I grind my teeth at him calling her a whore. She doesn't spread her legs for anyone but me. And it's gonna stay that way. "And the moment you give her up, he's gonna nail you to the fucking cross for taking something from him that didn't belong to you."

I'm not surprised Bruce told my father that I stole his car. They tell each other everything.

"Why do you care? I'm out of here after graduation no matter where I go."

His lips thin. He hates that I have my own money and that he can't control me. "Don't start acting like a father now, Liam. You never have before." Then I turn around and walk out of his office.

When I walk into the Lowes house, the lights are off, and the grand foyer is covered in darkness. I know that Bruce and Celeste aren't here. Whenever he is home, they are either at the country club or out on his yacht. He likes to entertain people in this city, and they love to bow at his feet like he's a fucking saint.

I walk up the stairs and open the door to her room, but it's empty, so I continue down the hallway to the media room. *Beauty and the Beast* plays on the screen, and I walk around to face the couch. My chest tightens at what I see.

Austin lies on her left side with her back to the cushions, her arm hanging off the couch. Lilly is also on her side facing her, cuddled up to her. They're both passed out.

I go to the stack of blankets over in the corner and grab one, covering them up with it. I sit down, my elbows on my knees and my head in my hands.

She's in my head.

Fuck, even my cock is always hard for her. She's everywhere. And consuming me.

You gotta fuck Kaitlin.

I wasn't lying to Becky earlier today. This is no longer about Kaitlin or Austin. This is about the game. The feud between Kellan and me. I'm not willingly going to walk away from this dare and leave the group. I can't. I have more dignity than that.

So what are you going to do?

I sigh, not having a fucking clue.

"Cole?"

I look up to see Austin blinking. She slides her arm out from underneath Lilly's sleeping body and sits up, rubbing her eyes. "What time is it?" she whispers.

"Almost nine."

She covers up a yawn. "Man, I didn't realize I was so tired."

I stand. "I'm gonna take Lilly home."

"No." She throws off the covers and gets up, making sure not to wake Lilly. "Let her stay here."

"Austin …"

"She's fine, Cole. She's already asleep. And I'm taking her to school in the morning anyway. All her stuff is already here from when I picked her up earlier. I will just put her in my room. She can sleep with me."

I go to protest more, but she picks her up and carries her out. I turn off the movie and fold the blanket up before putting it back where I found it.

I shut the door and walk down the hall to her room. I enter and find them both already in her bed, cuddled up and the covers to their neck.

My stomach knots up. Shit is going to hit the fan soon, but it's not gonna be because I fucked Kaitlin. It's gonna be because more secrets are gonna catch up with me, and they are gonna blow up in my face.

AUSTIN

Becky and I are walking down the quiet hallway, late to class as usual. The bell rang over fifteen minutes ago. Lilly and I picked her up this morning, and the girls wanted donuts. I tried to tell them we didn't have time, but Becky turned on me and had Lilly chanting donuts along with her at the top of their lungs.

Becky crams the last part of hers in her mouth. "We're so dead," she mumbles.

My phone dings as we stop at our lockers.

Shark: Where are you?

I roll my eyes. "It's like he thinks I'm incapable of getting Lilly to school."

Becky laughs and pieces of her donut flies from her mouth. I chuckle. "Well, you do get her there late."

"But she makes it."

Me: At school. Was running late.

I open my locker and grab my book for first period.

"Shit!" Becky hisses.

"What?" I ask as my phone dings again. I ignore him this time. He'll see me second period.

"I think I left my chemistry book in the lab."

I slam my locker shut. "Let's get it. It's on the way."

She throws her backpack over her shoulder, and we take our time walking to the lab room to retrieve her book.

I open the door, and she walks in. I follow her but come to a stop when I run into her back. "Becky …"

"Oh, God." A woman squeals.

I look over to the far corner where the teacher's desk sits, and a girl is getting off it. A man stands, straightening his tie. "Girls." He clears his throat. "What can I do for you?"

The girl bows her head, allowing her hair to cover up her face, and she turns her back to us.

"I left my book in here yesterday," Becky says.

He nods at her but makes no move to come out from behind the desk. I look and can see his slacks are undone but pulled up. "There's one on the back shelf." He gestures with his chin.

Becky walks over there and grabs the book and then turns, shoving me out the door. "Thank you," she calls out and then bursts out laughing. The door shuts behind me.

"Who the hell was that?" I ask.

"That was Bryan's twin sister fooling around with the student teacher."

"What?" I ask with surprise. "I didn't know he had a twin sister."

She nods. "That's another reason Bryan hates Cole so much."

"He slept with her?" *Why am I not surprised?*

"Yep. Cole has fucked the love of his life and his twin sister."

"Is there anyone in this school Cole hasn't fucked?" I growl.

She comes to a stop at our first period. "Me."

I laugh, shaking my head, and open the door. The teacher throws us a glare, but I just give her a smile. I have a hard time getting myself to school on time, and this week, I gotta get a six-year-old too. And my best friend since Deke is also busy with swimming. Who likes to spend too much time deciding what to wear.

We sit down in our seats, and I look over at Becky.

"What?" she whispers when she sees me staring at her.

"Do you really think Cole will sleep with Kaitlin?" I ask the question that I haven't had the courage to ask. Because I know the answer.

Her eyes look down at my bag by my feet, avoiding eye contact with me.

"That's what I thought." I sit back in my seat.

I hate that I fucking care so much. That the thought of him with anyone else makes my stomach knot and my chest hurt.

"Maybe not," she says, surprising me. "I mean, something's keeping him from doing it."

"That's true ..." I trail off.

She leans over her desk toward me. "Deke told me that Cole always completes his dare the very next day." I frown. "I know he's not the greatest guy, Austin, but he feels something for you. I didn't need to watch him put off a dare to know that, though."

I tap my pencil on my desk. "So I have to stop it."

She shakes her head. "They will kick you out of the group if you mess with a dare."

I snort, and the girl who sits in front of me turns to glare at me. I give her a big smile, and she rolls her eyes before turning back to face the front of the classroom. "I don't wanna be in their boy group.

They would be doing me a favor."

She smiles. "So do you have a plan?"

I nod. "Yes, I do."

"Need my help?" she asks, wiggling her eyebrows.

"Absolutely."

The next three weeks flew by faster than I wanted them to. Cole and Deke were busy with practice, so I got to spend a lot of time with Becky. I even convinced Cole to let Blanche have her afternoons free, and I continued to pick Lilly up from school. Becky and I would take her to get ice cream or go to my house and swim. She loved having "girl time" as she called it. I don't think she gets much of it other than the time she spends with Celeste. And she has been up my father's ass. He's avoided me, and I've stayed out of his way, praying he leaves town soon.

But I couldn't help notice the way Cole's mood got worse as he neared the end of his deadline. He was agitated. His attitude dark. His hands were always fisted, and he didn't speak much. But that hasn't slowed down his affection toward me. He's been over the top ever since I told him we were gonna put on a show. And that's exactly what we have done.

It's officially Friday. And tomorrow is the big day. He hasn't said much to me today, but I haven't taken it personal.

"You guys don't have a meet this weekend?" Becky asks Deke.

He shakes his head and pops a chip in his mouth. He too is on edge. I caught him and Cole arguing earlier this morning, but they both shut up the moment they saw me walking toward them. I never did catch what they were saying, and I know Cole wouldn't tell me even if I asked.

I open my mouth to speak but close it when Kellan walks up to the table. "Afternoon, guys," he says with a sinister smile.

I glare up at him.

Cole ignores him as he looks down at his phone.

"Party at my house tomorrow night," he says, looking straight at Cole. "And of course, you're invited, Austin. Wouldn't want you to miss it."

Cole looks up at him through his lashes, showing indifference. But I can feel the heat rolling off him.

"Oh, she'll be there," Becky answers for me, and I refrain from laughing.

"See you then," he says cheerfully and then places his hands in his pockets and walks away, whistling like he did when he told me to walk away from Cole.

I smile at Becky, and she smiles back.

CHAPTER THIRTY-ONE
COLE

I walk out of the cafeteria and stop at my locker. I yank the door open, grab what I need, and then slam it shut.

"You can't go," Deke growls, coming up to me.

"I'm getting really fucking tired of arguing with you about this," I snap.

"Then do the right thing."

"Why do you fucking care?" I shout, making a kid jump who was walking by. "Huh, Deke? Why do you fucking care what I do?"

He lowers his eyes to the floor and runs his hand through his hair. "Becky was right."

"Fuck! Not this again …"

"I've seen a difference in you too, Cole." His eyes meet mine. "Haven't you felt the difference?" I snort, rolling my eyes. "Ever since Eli died …"

"Don't," I snap, stopping whatever he was about to say.

"No, you're gonna hear this." He steps to me, and I fist my hands, ready to punch his ass. "Austin was just someone you wanted to destroy. You wanted someone as fucked up as you, Cole. So bad that you couldn't stand it. Even I could see that."

"Deke," I warn.

"But no matter what you throw at her, she dishes it back. You like the fight better than if she was to lie down and cry. Beg you to stop." I hate how right he is. "If you fuck Kaitlin tomorrow night, are you prepared for what she's gonna do to retaliate?"

"What does that mean?" I demand, not liking where he's going. This thought had never crossed my mind.

He lowers his voice. "It means she's gonna run right to Bryan and fuck him. That's what she does. She fucks you back twice as hard. And he's gonna jump all over that. Finally getting his chance with her and be able to fuck you over at the same time."

I see red and punch him at the thought of Austin and Bryan together. He stumbles back into another kid, knocking him to his ass. Deke stays standing and chuckles like I softly slapped him. "When was the last time you hit someone, Cole?" I lower my hands. "When was the last time you needed to release that anger since she came into your life that night?"

"What …?" I trail off confused by his words.

"She has changed you. You may not see it, but we all have. You only hit someone when she is the reason. When you're protecting her. When someone threatens to take her from you. And that is exactly why Kellan is doing this to you."

"Deke," Becky calls out from down the hall with Austin, hearing the commotion. Austin spins around, her hair slapping her in the face, and her eyes land on mine. They start heading for us.

I fist my hand, and my shoulder throbs. I look at Deke. "You're wrong."

He shakes his head with a chuckle. "Go ahead. Fuck Kaitlin and see what happens. Austin will hate you, and you'll hate yourself more than you already do." I flinch at his words. "Because this is something you can't control, Cole. She will be your living nightmare. Not one you only see when you close your eyes. But every minute of every day."

"Are you okay, babe?" Becky asks him, coming up to us.

"I'm fine."

She spins around to face me. Her crystal blue eyes hard and she fists her hands like she plans on hitting me. "What the hell is wrong with you?" she demands.

"Stop," Austin says, coming to stand between us. Becky turns back around to face Deke, and Austin turns toward me. Her green eyes are void of any emotion. "Do what you need to do," she says.

Deke's head snaps up to look at the back of her head.

"What do you mean?" I ask, my heart pounding in my chest from Deke's words.

Let's give them a show.

He's right once again. She would go to Bryan and do just that. And it would drive me mad. More than I already am. "Austin …"

"Exactly what I said," she interrupts me. "Tomorrow night at the party. Do what you need to do, Cole." She leans up and softly kisses me on the lips. I don't move or kiss her back. Then she walks off with Becky right behind her. Deke and I turn to watch them walk down the hall.

He comes to stand beside me and sighs. "She's gonna eat you alive, man."

"FUCK!" I turn and punch my locker.

I stand in the kitchen of Kellan's parents' house with my back against the countertop. My arms crossed over my chest and a pissed-off look on my face.

Austin's words have continued to swim in my mind since yesterday.

Do what you have to do.

What kind of bullshit is that?

She's fucking with my mind. She does it so well.

Was that her way of telling me to fuck Kaitlin? If so, it's a trap. No woman willingly tells a man to fuck another woman. No matter what the circumstances. Or was that her way of telling me to choose her and withdraw from the group?

"Here. You're gonna need it," Deke says, handing me his Solo cup.

"No." I don't drink at parties unless it's at my house. That was a rule I made after I lost three friends. I'm not gonna let Kellan force me to go against that. He's already forcing me to do enough.

"Hello, boys," Kellan says, joining us.

Bennett ignores him as he drinks from a Solo cup.

Deke throws him a glare. I watch the entrance to the kitchen, waiting for either Kaitlin or Austin to walk in. At this point, I'm not sure who I want to see less.

"I'd choose Becky."

"What?" I snap, looking over at Deke.

He ignores my harsh tone. But no one can miss the cut on his bottom lip from my fist yesterday.

"Becky was so mad when I told her about your dare. She was afraid the same thing would happen to me. And I never made her think that I would choose her. But that's why I was so pissed at Kellan." He takes a quick sip of his drink. "Because the moment I heard you read the dare, I knew I'd pick her over the group." He looks me in the eyes. "It's okay to choose her, Cole. This group will come to an end soon. After graduation, they'll go their separate ways, but where will Austin go? Will you willingly leave her?" He shakes his head as if he already knows my answer.

"You make it sound like I love her," I growl.

"Don't you?"

"No," I snap. She's supposed to fall in love with me. I'm the one who is supposed to have all the control and ruin her. Not the other way around. I've seen what loving someone can do to another person. And it's pathetic.

He just smiles.

"Fuck you, Deke."

"Showtime," Kellan says, getting our attention. He rubs his hands together excitedly, and my eyes follow where his are. Kaitlin just walked into the kitchen. She has her red hair down. She's wearing a tight pair of blue jeans and a black top. A big smile on her face.

She does absolutely nothing for me.

She turns around and holds out her right hand, and my eyes widen when I see Bryan take it in his.

"What the fuck?" Kellan snaps.

They walk toward us, and he picks up a Solo cup and pours her a drink. He lifts his eyes to mine. "Boys." He nods and then pulls her out of the kitchen.

Deke tries to hide his chuckle but fails. "Well, that changes things," he says happily.

"Absolutely not," Kellan snaps. "He still has to fuck her."

"That's not gonna happen. She's obviously back with Bryan," Bennett says, shaking his head.

"That was his dare." Kellan growls. "He fucks her or he's out."

"What is he supposed to do?" Bennett asks. "Rape her?"

"If that's what he has to do," Kellan says with a nod.

"Absolutely not!" I snap.

"What the fuck, man?" Shane demands. "What is wrong with you?"

He lets out a growl of frustration. "Then you're out." He looks at me.

I raise my hands. "Then I'm out."

Deke smiles at me, and he knows why I just stepped away. It had nothing to do with Kaitlin. And everything to do with Austin.

Fuck! She's gotten to me.

"No," Bennett says, pushing off the opposite counter. "You're not going anywhere, Cole."

Kellan opens his mouth to argue, but something behind me gets his attention. I turn around to see Austin and Becky walking toward us. She looks like she just walked off a runway in Milan. Her hair curled and down. Her green eyes lined with black. Her lips painted red. And she wears a red fucking dress that makes me weak in the knees. It's low cut in the front, showcasing her perfect tits. She smiles at me, and everyone parts for them as if they're fucking royalty.

"Desire" by Meg Myers begins to play over the speakers of the house, and her smile widens like she knows a secret.

"Fuck this shit." I hear Kellan hiss, but I ignore him.

She comes up to me, and I reach out for her. My hand wraps around her thin waist and pull her to me.

"I didn't do it," I tell her, needing her to know. I wouldn't have done it anyway. I was just trying to buy time to get out of it, but I couldn't figure it out. I couldn't do it because I couldn't picture her being with anyone else. And I don't want anyone else.

This woman is as twisted as I am. She is as broken as me. Together, we are two fucked-up people living in a world where you're supposed to be perfect. She's not up to pretending, and I'm not up for faking.

"I know," she whispers against my lips.

I search her eyes, and they sparkle. Just like every other time she has gone toe to toe with me. I love that look on her.

"You're up to something," I say.

Her eyes drop to my chest as her hands run down it. "I don't know what you're talking about," she says, licking her red lips. I want them wrapped around my cock.

I grip her chin and lift it, so she has to look up at me. "You had something to do with Kaitlin and Bryan." I'm reaching, but what else can explain what just happened. And the look in her eyes. I've underestimated her too much. But I don't anymore.

She smiles. "I dare you to prove it."

AUSTIN

He stares down at me. Those gorgeous blue eyes searching mine. He pulls away, takes my hand, and drags me out of the kitchen. I bite my lip to keep from laughing at his urgency. He pulls me into a room and slams the door shut.

"What did you do?" he demands, spinning to face me.

I cross my arms over my chest.

"Austin," he growls, coming up to me. "Tell me."

I love when he's like this. When the roles are reversed, and he can't stand to not know what I did. What I'm capable of. "I wasn't gonna let you fuck her, Cole. If that's what you want, then fine, let me walk right now. No more you and me. No more game." He said he didn't do it, but was that because I stepped in?

He steps to me, his hand coming up to cup my face. "I couldn't do it because of you." I swallow nervously at his words. "I was never going to do it." He pushes his body into mine. "You're not going anywhere, Austin. I've been so dead set on making everyone see you as mine, but I didn't realize until tonight that all along I've been yours."

"Mine?" I question, and my heart starts to pound faster.

He nods once. His eyes searching mine. "I'm all yours."

"You're giving me a choice?" I can't help but ask.

He chuckles. "No, sweetheart. I'm not." Then his lips are on mine.

His hands go to the hem of my dress, and I lift mine above my head and pull away from his lips as he lifts my dress. "Fuck." He growls when he sees I'm not wearing a bra.

I smile as "A Little Wicked" by Valerie Broussard plays through the speakers.

He takes a step back from me, and I slowly push my red thong down my legs. He watches in complete fascination as I toss it to the side. "I'll leave my heels on for you."

His eyes meet mine as his hands go to the belt on his jeans. "You won't need them while on your knees."

I'm sliding my dress on as he pulls his jeans up. "What did you do?" he asks.

"I'd rather not tell you," I say truthfully.

He looks up and glares at me. He hates being in the dark. Sighing, I say, "I blackmailed Bryan."

His eyes widen. "You what? How?"

"I caught his sister fucking someone she shouldn't have been. I went to him and told him that if he didn't get back with Kaitlin I'd turn his sister in."

"And he bought it?"

"I wasn't joking," I say simply. "He had a few choice words and said I was bluffing. When I pulled out my phone to show him the pictures, he threw his hands up in defeat."

"You took pictures of her fucking someone?"

"No." I smile.

He stares at me. His jeans pulled up but still unbuttoned, showcasing his black boxers. He's still shirtless, allowing me to enjoy the gorgeous view of his body.

"I refused to let Kellan win." I shake my head. "If you wanted her, that was a different story—"

"I didn't want her," he interrupts me flatly, walking over to me, and I don't back down. The hard look on his face makes me think he's mad at me, but I don't care. I had more than this stupid game at stake. I wasn't gonna let this school see me as anything but strong. I'm not the girl who gets played. And I'm certainly not the girl who lets men like Kellan walk over me.

He cups my cheek. "You're such a fucking shark," he says, and a smile spreads across his face.

"Well, around here, if you're not one, you're dead."

"I'd never let anyone touch you, sweetheart."

"No one but you?" I ask, my arms coming up and wrapping around his neck.

"No one but me," he promises, and then my dress is on the floor again.

Monday morning, I walk into second period and sit down next to Cole. He's looking down at his phone like always. "Can you take Lilly to dance tonight? I have somewhere I have to be," he says without looking my way.

"Of course. What do you have to do? Practice?" I ask, but he doesn't respond. "Cole?" I snap, getting his attention.

"What?" he growls, looking up at me.

I arch a brow at his shitty attitude. I'm not sure what the hell is going on in his head now. It's been two weeks since the party at Kellan's house, and things have been extremely tense. No one has called a meeting at the clubhouse, and I'm not sure what we all do now that Cole didn't complete his dare. I heard Shane say something about doing a redraw, but Bennett quickly shut that down.

Once again, Kellan hasn't been around. But I know they see him at practice, and they had a meet over the weekend. It was here in Collins, so thankfully they didn't have to be on a bus with him. But it's bound to happen.

"I said what do you have to do?"

He looks away from me. "It's personal."

I open my mouth to argue further, but the teacher stands from her desk and starts the class.

I sit back as he puts his phone away. I watch him out of the corner of my eyes. His jaw is sharp like usual, and his eyes clouded. He's in his own little twisted world where blood and anger control him. I hate that I can't pull him out of it. He'll come over later and fuck me. Then afterward it's like all his power and anger just fade to nothing. And then he's smiling and laughing with me like nothing ever happened.

It's confusing and gives me whiplash.

I sent Cole a text that I had dropped Lilly off over an hour ago. He read it immediately but never responded. I didn't let it bother me. Even though we are officially a couple now, not much has changed.

I make my way into the kitchen and grab a bottle of water before I go up to my room. When a noise has me pausing.

"Cole!"

I frown. *Is Cole here?* I didn't see his car outside. I place my bottle of water on the countertop and make my way down the hall to the back terrace. I go outside and look in the pool. But no one's out here.

"Cole."

I hear it softly this time. "What the hell?" I whisper, making my way down the hall to my father and Celeste's bedroom.

I go to open the door, but my hand freezes on the door handle. "Oh, God, Cole!" I hear Celeste cry out.

My heart beats faster in my chest. "Fuck, yeah. Oh, that's it …

Cole!" She cries out his name again and again.

I go to twist the knob, to barge in on them, but it's locked. I hear a banging sound and realize that it's the bed hitting the wall.

She screams his name this time. The thought of running to the garage, grabbing a hammer and beating my way through this door crosses my mind. But what will that prove? The thought alone is too much to bear—I sure as hell don't want to see them in the act.

I take a step back and run up to my room. After shutting my door, I let the first tear fall. I could put up with a lot of shit, but this was the last straw.

Cole wasn't in class second period the following morning. I never sent him a text asking where he was, and he never text me to offer any information. I figured he was still at my father's house sleeping off his long night. I ignored everyone, even Becky. She noticed but didn't push me for an explanation.

It's not until after last period that I see him in the hallway, placing his keys in his locker. He was able to skip school but unable to miss practice. They have a meet this weekend after all. Deke walks right up to him. "How did it go, man?" he asks.

"Good," he says with a nod.

Kids fill the hallways, throwing books in their lockers and getting ready to leave for the day.

"Awesome. So you finished the deal?" he asks like they're talking about buying a car. Not screwing a woman.

"All done."

I snort as I walk by him.

"Hey, sweetheart," Cole says, reaching out and wrapping a hand around my waist. He pulls my back to his front and leans his head down to my ear. "Miss me?"

I spin around in his arms, reach up, and slap him across the face. The sound echoes off the walls. I stare up into his blue eyes as they harden. My heart starts to beat, festering at my rage. His betrayal. My stupidity. He may have not fucked Kaitlin, but he's been screwing my stepmom behind my back. I'm so stupid.

Deke takes a step back from us.

"What the hell was that for?" Cole demands, glaring down at me.

I throw Deke a look of disgust, and his brows rise. Then I look back at Cole. "I'm sure you can figure it out." I turn and walk toward the door, not bothering giving them another second of my time.

He grabs my arm and yanks me back. "Cole!" I snap.

"What the fuck was that for, Austin?" he demands. "Because I didn't tell you where I went? It was none of your fucking business!"

My anger rises and tears spring to my eyes. I try to yank my arm from his hold, but he won't let me go. "Just forget it." My voice cracks, and I hate myself for caring so much. For thinking he actually cared. His agenda from the get-go was to break me. And I willingly let him.

"No. I'm not going to forget it." He steps into me, his blue eyes softening. "What's wrong?" he asks, cupping my face.

My first tear falls, and I fist my hands. "I know where you went."

Deke's eyes widen, and Cole's jaw sharpens. "How do you …?"

"I heard it," I say, interrupting him.

He looks at Deke, and he throws his hands up, shaking his head. "I haven't said anything."

"What do you mean? You heard *it*? Who did you hear it from?"

"I'm not gonna spell it out for you, Cole."

CHAPTER THIRTY-TWO

COLE

My jaw tightens as I lose my patience. "I don't have time for this, Austin. Tell me what the fuck you're talking about!" I demand.

"I don't want to talk to you," she says.

"Too bad." She tries to take a step back. "Why are you so pissed at me?"

Another tear falls down her face. And I try to figure out why my quick trip to Texas could have hurt her so much.

"God, you have some nerve." I frown. "You think I'm an idiot. You think I'm stupid and wouldn't find out? Wouldn't hear her?"

"What are you …?"

"I know you're sleeping with Celeste!" she screams.

"What?" Deke whispers.

"Fuck!" I couldn't stop the word from leaving my mouth.

Her eyes narrow on me to little slits. "No, fuck you, Cole!"

She starts to turn, to run down the hallway to the exit, but I grab her arm again and yank to her to a stop. "I'm not sleeping with her."

"Yes, you are!" she yells. "Stop lying to me."

I release her and take a step back. "I'm not. I promise."

She huffs and crosses her arms over her chest. "Where did you have to go yesterday and today, Cole?"

My jaw tightens. "I can't tell you that."

"You can; you just choose not to."

"It's none of you Goddamn business, Austin!" I snap.

"It is when you're sleeping with my stepmother," she yells back.

I run a hand through my hair. "What makes you think I slept with her?" I ask trying to settle my rage. It's gonna get us nowhere.

"I told you. I heard her."

"Heard her what?"

She rolls her watery eyes but indulges me. "When I got home yesterday after taking Lilly to ballet, I walked into the kitchen to get a bottle of water, and I heard her yelling your name from my father's and her bedroom."

My eyes widen.

"Shit." Deke hisses.

"But you should know that since you were there with her."

I reach out for her. "Austin …" But she pulls away and starts to walk down the hallway once again.

"I've never slept with Celeste," I say, watching her come to a stop, and I swallow. "And I haven't slept with anyone else since …" I trail off.

She spins around. "Since you started sleeping with me? How original, Cole."

"No." My eyes meet hers. "Since the accident," I say, not caring that Deke is here. She deserves to know.

She's breathing heavy, and her eyes still narrow in suspicion. "That was almost nine months ago."

I nod. She doesn't take a step toward me, but she also doesn't make a move to turn and leave. I run my hand through my hair nervously. "After the accident, people steered clear of me. I had so much hate, so much rage, that the guys were the only ones not afraid to talk to me. Be around me. If I wasn't with them, I was at physical therapy or in a pool." Her eyes drop to her hands, inspecting her nails. "But when I showed up with you at school, everyone thought I was back to my old self. The old Cole who partied every night of the week and slept around …" I walk over to her, needing to close the distance. I place my finger under her chin and lift it to where she has to look up at me. "I know I've hurt you." My free hand runs over her scar on her forearm. "And I've forced you to do things that you didn't want to do."

"Blackmail," she corrects me.

I smile down at her. "But I've never cheated on you." Pushing her hair behind her ear, I say. "You're all I want."

She sighs. "Cole …"

"Please," I beg. "Believe me." She bites her bottom lip nervously. "I need you to believe me."

"It doesn't make sense."

"I know." My teeth clench. "But I'm gonna figure out what went on and why."

She finally nods her head once, and I lower my lips softly, kissing her forehead. "I'll come over after practice, okay?"

She looks over at Deke, who watches us like a nosy little bitch. "Okay," she says and turns around, walking out the door.

I turn around, get what I need out of my locker, slam it shut and head toward the guys' locker room. "Are you really fucking Celeste?" Deke asks.

I come to a stop and glare at him. "No. Kellan is."

His eyes widen. "How long have you known this?"

"Couple of months," I say truthfully.

"Why haven't you said anything?" he asks, his brows pulling together.

"Because it wasn't important."

"And now?" he asks.

"Now, it's become a problem I'm gonna fucking fix."

I get out from underneath Austin's arms—she passed out about an hour ago—and pull my jeans on and nothing else. I make my way out of her room and down the stairs. The rain pours on the house and lightning fills the dark halls. It's late. Has to be past midnight.

I walk into the formal dining room to find Celeste sitting at the table. Her back to me. She's on her phone. "Yeah," she whispers. "Okay, I'll see you tomorrow. I love you," she says and then hangs up. When she stands and turns around, she startles, placing her hands on her chest. "Cole!" she squeals. "What are you doing here?"

My eyes go to her phone in her hand and then back to hers. "I'm gonna take a guess and say that was Kellan." She glares at me. "Love already, huh?" I run my fingers along the wood of the china cabinet. "That was fast."

Her eyes narrow. "Like you're one to talk. Everyone can see how obsessed you are with Austin."

"Funny you should mention her." I take a step forward. "You're trying to fuck up what's mine."

"She told you?"

"No," I lie, and she snorts in disbelief. I close the small space and cup her cheek. She stiffens. "I have a way of making people talk, Celeste. Am I gonna have to make you talk?"

Her bottom lip trembles. "It was his idea ..."

"She heard your voice. Not his."

She lets out a long breath. "He said you're falling for her. That you won't let her go. That she needs to go, and since you won't step away, she needs to."

"She's not going anywhere," I say firmly.

"Cole ..." she whispers. "Please ... he made me ..."

I bring my hand and wrap it around her throat but don't take away her air. She inhales sharply. I can feel her pulse race, and I smile. "Am I the one you think of when he fucks you?"

She shudders.

I pull away. "'Cause if that's what you want ..." I run my fingers across her collarbone.

"Cole ... please ..." she begs, and her body shakes with nervousness.

She should be afraid of me. "I've got insurance, Celeste."

Her eyes widen in surprise. "Last week when you met him at the hotel. Last month when you met him outside of town at that log cabin. We had a deal. Are you going back on it?" She shakes her head quickly.

"Good. Now leave what's mine alone or ..." I lean down to

whisper in her ear. "You *will* be screaming my name. But it won't be from pleasure." I pull back. "Understand?"

She nods.

"Say I understand, Cole."

"I understand, Cole." She swallows.

"Good girl." Then I turn around and walk back up the stairs.

I enter Austin's room, shutting the door and locking it behind me. Removing my jeans, I crawl onto the bed and straddle her hips. She lies on her back with her head turned to the side. She's completely naked.

I lean down, kissing her neck. She still smells like sex. Like me. And I love it. "Sweetheart."

"Hmm?" She moans, turning her head more to allow me better access.

"Wake up, baby." I slide a hand between our bodies and run it over her shaved pussy.

"No …" She breathes. "I'm too sore."

I chuckle. "Want me to kiss it?"

"God." She sighs.

I trail kisses down her bare chest as I slide a finger into her. She whimpers.

Sitting up, I position myself between her legs. I lift her right leg and place it over my shoulder and then lean into it, softly kissing it. She lifts her hips up off the bed. Needing more. "Tell me you want me."

"I want you, Cole." Her hips buck again. "Please."

I smile and then bite her inner thigh. She screams out my name as my teeth sink into her flawless skin.

When I set her leg down, she's panting. I run my finger over the bruise that's already forming. "I'm gonna mark you from head to toe, sweetheart." And she's gonna be the only one screaming my name in this house from now on.

AUSTIN

The next week went by faster than ever. Things were going well between Cole and me. People still stared at us in the hall as if they were waiting for me to slap him or for him to shove me up against his locker and make out with me. He didn't disappoint them. There was talk around the school as to why I slapped him. The rumors were far from the truth, and I didn't have the heart to tell them that their imaginations were weak.

Friday after school, the guys had to stay later for practice 'cause they had a swim meet coming up. I helped Cole out and took Lilly to dance and then back to his house before returning home. I had just walked up the stairs to my room when I hear *his* voice.

"Files?"

I stop and turn to look over the banister but don't see anyone. But that was definitely my father. *What is he doing here?* I thought he was out of town for a few weeks?

"My laptop got stolen ..."

My stomach drops.

"Jesus!" my father hisses. "But what about the emails?"

"They've been deleted. They wouldn't be able to find them unless they searched the hard drive and knew what they were looking for."

"Are you sure?" he asks nervously. "No one steals a laptop for no reason," he snaps.

"I'm positive."

I make my way quietly back down the stairs and out the front door. I jump into my car and dial Cole's number. He doesn't answer. I call Deke's. Nothing.

"Shit! Come on guys," I say, my knees bouncing. *This is not good.*

CHAPTER THIRTY-THREE
COLE

I'm showering in the locker room, washing my hair when I hear Deke. "Cole?"

"What?"

"Get your ass out of the shower. We gotta go."

I take my time. "Where we going?"

"Austin has called me twenty times …"

"What?" I ask, spinning around, the water causing shampoo to run into my eyes.

"I checked your phone, and she's called you fifteen. Something's wrong, man."

I turn off the water, rip the towel from the wall, and quickly dry off, making my way to the lockers. Shoving guys out of my way. "She sent a text too."

Austin: Have everyone meet me at the clubhouse. Now!

"Shane! Bennett!" Deke calls out. "Let's go!"

"Why is her phone going straight to voicemail?" I snap, trying to call her for the twentieth time as Deke flies down the highway.

"We're almost there," he says.

He pulls up outside the clubhouse, and I'm out of his SUV before he can even bring it to a stop.

I barge in the door to find her pacing back and forth with her head down. "What the fuck is going on?" I demand. "I've been calling you."

She comes to a stop. "I've been calling you too."

Deke and the rest of the guys enter, and she runs a hand through her hair nervously. I look her over for any blood or bruises. I don't see anything, but I can tell that she's shaken.

"What's wrong, Austin?" I ask.

"I got home from dropping Lilly off at your dad's, and I heard my father talking in the kitchen." I frown. "I thought it was odd because he was supposed to be gone. I was just going to ignore him when I heard another voice. And he sounded familiar." Her eyes shoot to Shane, and he sits down on the couch. "But the other man started talking about emails."

"Why kind of emails?" Bennett asks.

"He swore he had deleted them. He said that the only way anyone would be able to find them was if someone looked on the hard drive. That they would have to know what they are looking for."

"Who was this guy?" Bennett asks.

Her eyes meet mine, and she swallows nervously. "It was Jerrold."

AUSTIN

Shane jumps to his feet. "Are you sure?"

I nod. "Positive. He told my dad that his laptop was stolen. And he got pissed. Said that you don't steal a laptop for nothing."

"Did he see you?" Cole demands. I shake my head. "Are you sure, Austin?" he snaps.

"Yes. I ran back down the stairs and came straight here."

"Fuck!" he growls, running a hand through his hair in frustration.

"Did you check the hard drive?" Deke asks Bennett.

"Yes. But I didn't see anything out of the ordinary."

"Then you obviously missed something," Cole snaps.

"I'll look again, but even now, I still don't know what I'm looking for exactly."

"Why the fuck would Jerrold be talking to Bruce in the first place?

Let alone about emails?" Deke wonders out loud. No one has an answer for him.

Cole looks at me. "You're staying here."

"I can't …"

"This isn't up for discussion, Austin!" he shouts.

"Cole—"

"No!" he interrupts me.

I glare at him. "You don't even know what I was going to say."

"I know you were going to argue, and that's enough."

I place my hands on my hips.

He turns his attention to Bennett. "I want that laptop here tomorrow. And I wanna go through it with you."

Bennett nods. "Of course."

"Everyone leave," he orders.

I turn around and walk up the stairs, making sure to step extra hard to let him know that I'm mad at him. Once I get up to the loft, I rip my shirt up and over my head and push my shorts down my legs. I yank back the covers and crawl into the bed. I hear the door open and close as everyone leaves. Then the lights turn off one by one.

I close my eyes as I hear him coming up the stairs—louder than I was.

He undresses and crawls in next to me. I can barely make out his outline through the light streaming in the small window. He lies on his back, his right hand under his head as he stares up at the ceiling.

I turn over, giving him my back. "Austin …"

"I'm really tired of you bossing me around, Cole," I growl.

He sighs heavily. Moments later, his hand grasps my shoulder. "You don't understand what he is capable of. Jerrold is a very dangerous man, and I don't want him anywhere near you." He kisses my bare shoulder.

I walk out of second period and storm over to Deke. "Where is Cole?" I ask.

He just stares at me. I stayed the night with Cole at the clubhouse two nights ago, but last night, I stayed at Becky's. As far as we know, my father is still in town, and Jerrold could pop over at any time. Last night after practice, Cole had sent me a text saying he was spending his evening with the guys going through the emails. Today, he didn't show up. And that's not like him to miss class.

"Deke …" Becky growls in warning.

His jaw tightens. "At the clubhouse."

I turn to leave, but he grabs my arm, stopping me. "Don't go."

I jerk my hand free and storm out of the exit. I squint, the sun actually out today, and run to my car.

I've been calling him since last night, and although he doesn't rush to call me back, he usually at least reads my messages. I've sent him ten. Not one has been read. *Something is wrong.* And Deke not wanting me to go confirms that.

I walk into the clubhouse and come to a stop. The punching bag that hangs from the rafter is on the ground, ripped open. The table knocked over. Papers scatter the floor. The couch up against the far wall. A couple of the chairs are knocked over onto their sides.

I take the stairs two at a time, and stop at the top. Liquor bottles and beer cans litter the floor and bed. He's lying on it, dressed in the same clothes from yesterday. Passed out on his stomach, he has his hands above his head. The pillows cover the floor along with the sheet and comforter.

"Cole?" I ask, placing my hand on his arm.

He doesn't budge.

"Cole?" I say a little louder.

He growls.

"Cole!" I snap, shoving his arm.

He rolls over onto his back and opens his eyes. They're bloodshot and land on mine. I tense. I've never seen them look so cold. So void. "Are you okay?" I ask softly.

He blinks a couple of times as if he's seeing two of me. Then he slowly sits up.

"Leave," he orders roughly.

"Cole what's going on?"

"Leave, Austin," he snaps.

"No, Cole! What the fuck are you doing here? Drunk of all things?"

He grabs my arm and yanks me down onto the bed. He buries his head into my neck. "Cole …"

I try to shove him off, but his hands grip my wrists and he pins them down effortlessly. I start panting.

"Fuck, sweetheart." He straddles my hips. "You smell so Goddamn good. Did you come to cheer me up?" he whispers.

"What's wrong?" I ask, ignoring him.

"Did you come for me to break you?" His nose traces my jawline. "Because that's what I need, Austin. I need to break. Destroy. God, I want to wrap my hand around your delicate throat and squeeze while I fuck you." His body pins me to the bed, and I feel how hard he is.

I take a calming breath, trying to slow my racing heart.

He kisses up my neck gently to my ear, and my skin breaks out in goosebumps. "I wanna see tears run down your gorgeous face with your mouth open in a silent scream. Begging me to stop. Begging me for air. So I'm gonna ask you again. Did you come to cheer me up?"

He pulls back and looks down at me, and I swallow at the look of nothingness in his eyes. I have no clue what happened or why he needs to break me once again, but I want to give it to him. I hate how much I want to give him what he wants. But I can't deny that it sounds like exactly what I need too. "Yeah, Cole," I say softly. "I came to cheer you up. Now, I dare you to do your worst."

CHAPTER THIRTY-FOUR
COLE

I sit up in bed while Austin lies passed out next to me. It's a little after eight at night, and she fell asleep hours ago. I used her. I fucking took and took from her like she was a lifeline.

I had reverted to my old self. How I was before I ran into her in that cemetery. Deke was right—she had changed me—but I found my way back to the real Cole.

The heartless bastard who feeds off violence. I choked her. I ripped hair out. I fucking marked her with my hands and my mouth. She cried big, beautiful tears as she stared up at me while my hand was wrapped around her throat. And her body shook from the orgasms I gave her. She never broke like I wanted her to. She didn't beg when I held her wrists above her head. Or when I flipped her over and buried her face into the bed. At one point, I had her bent over the railing with my hand fisting her hair. She let me use her however I wanted.

And I fucking loved that she was so strong. That she can take my demons.

I get out of bed and pull on my jeans before walking into the bathroom. I splash cold water on my face. Looking up at myself in the mirror, I watch as the water runs down my face and splashes on the countertop. Gripping the edge, I bow my head. I have a fucking migraine, but I know that's from the alcohol I've consumed over the past twenty-four hours.

I hear the door open to the clubhouse downstairs, and I grind my teeth. I'm in no mood to put up with bullshit. All I want to do is crawl back into bed with Austin and wake her up with my hand around her throat again.

"No, Deke." I hear Becky's voice.

I walk out of the bathroom and go to the stairs.

Becky stands downstairs, her hands out wide. "What the hell happened?" she demands.

He says nothing even though he knows. He was here along with the rest of the guys to witness my destruction last night.

I start to walk down to them. "Why are you here?" I demand.

Becky spins around to face me, and her eyes narrow on me as I come to the bottom step.

Deke sighs. "Sorry, man. She wanted …"

"I've been calling Austin. Where the hell is she?"

I say nothing. Her eyes take in my lack of shirt and look over the scratches that Austin gave me. She broke skin when she clawed at my chest while I choked her. It was the best sex I've ever had.

"If you hurt her—"

"She's asleep," I say, interrupting her.

She runs over to the stairs and shoves me out of the way before she charges up to the loft.

"I'm sorry, Cole," Deke says softly. "She was worried that …" He trails off.

"That what?" I snap.

He swallows and looks around the mess that I have made of the clubhouse. "That you killed her."

I snort. Why would I kill her? She's exactly what I've needed all along—something to use.

"You need to tell her," he says.

I shake my head. "The less she knows, the better."

"You're wrong, man. She needs to know what is going on."

"No."

"This involves her," he snaps. "Do you want her to get hurt?"

"I'm her biggest threat." We both know that's a lie. Jerrold could be looking for her right now, but I don't want to admit that. That would mean I'm the one who put her in harm's way by bringing her into this fucking mess.

He laughs darkly. "Are we back to that now?" My eyes narrow on him. "Jesus, Cole. You're not the same guy who found her in the cemetery."

"Yes, I am." I never went away. She just smothered him. She just made me think I was a better person. I was wrong.

He steps into me. "Her life is in jeopardy. If you don't step up and do something, then I will."

"What does that mean?" I snap.

"It means that her life is no longer in your hands," he growls. "I promised the woman I love twenty minutes ago while she was crying in my arms because her best friend wouldn't answer her phone that I would do whatever I needed to make sure Austin is okay."

"That wasn't your call to make," I snap.

"I'm making it my call because you refuse to tell the poor girl the fucking truth."

"What happened to her being whatever I tell you she is?" I demand.

"Things have changed," he says softly.

"No. You have changed," I growl, and he fists his hands down by his sides. "Becky has made you fucking soft."

"Cole?"

I spin around to see Austin standing at the bottom of the stairs. Her hair a knotted mess around her face. Her green eyes heavy, she has mascara lines down her cheeks from when she cried while I fucked her. She wears one of my t-shirts that falls off her shoulder and that's it. Thankfully, it's long enough to cover her pussy. She has bruises around her neck and on her arms. And teeth marks on her inner thighs. There's more, but the shirt hides them.

"Jesus," Deke mutters, looking over her.

"What's going on?" she asks, ignoring him.

"Nothing," I answer.

"Cole," Deke growls my name in warning.

"Shut up, Deke," I snap.

"Cole. Tell me what is going on," Austin demands.

"It doesn't concern you."

"Stop lying, Cole," Deke says.

"No ..."

"What is going on?" Austin shouts.

The room falls silent, and I rub my temples. That migraine getting to the point my vision is blurry.

"We went through the emails," Deke finally says. "The ones on the hard drive."

My teeth clench, and I fist my hands. I could punch him, but that would take too much energy. And I already feel too weak from the drinking binge and rough sex. If I hit him, he'd hit me back, and he'd probably knock my ass out.

"And?" she asks.

"And we found emails that indicated the car wreck was not an accident."

"What do you mean?"

"The emails proved that Jeff was paid to tamper with the brake lines that night ..." He stops, and I fall onto the couch.

Placing my elbows on my knees, I lean forward and cup my head. My heart races at hearing his words.

"I don't understand," she says softly.

"They prove that he had been talking to your dad. They had a set amount and a plan." He pauses, and I close my eyes. "Bennett checked the funds and confirmed that your father paid Jeff fifteen thousand dollars to ensure that the brakes would fail on Cole's car the night Eli, Maddox, and Landen died."

My muscles tense at his words, and my chest tightens. Bruce fucking tried to kill me, and he succeeded in killing my friends. He paid the scumbag Jeff to do it. When I was about to kill that fucker, he kept bringing up the fact that I killed my friends, but it had been him all along.

"I don't ..." She trails off. "Why would my dad want to hurt Cole?"

I look up at her but remain silent. She stands there next to Becky who silently cries because Deke has already filled her in. Austin has no fucking clue, and I wish he would just shut up. I don't want her to know. Not this. Not now.

"We don't know for sure, but we have a guess." Deke sighs.

"Which is?" she asks.

"Lilly," Deke answers.

Her frowns deepens, and my heart pounds at the mention of my little sister.

She looks at me. "Why would he want to hurt you because of Lilly?"

Deke runs a hand through his hair and answers. "Because Lilly is Bruce's daughter."

AUSTIN

I stare at Deke utterly confused. *Lilly is Bruce's daughter?* My father is Lilly's father? My eyes go to Cole. He sits there on the couch, blue eyes still bloodshot, skin pale. He looks like he's half dead.

I swallow the knot that forms in my throat. "Your mom and my dad had an affair?" Lilly is six. My dad and Celeste have been married for ten years now.

He fists his hands and his jaw sharpens. "No."

"Then how do you explain …?"

"Bruce fucking raped her," he interrupts me.

"What?" I breathe.

Becky sniffs beside me, but I can't look away from Cole. His eyes look at me with disgust. My father, being the bastard that he is, fucking raped his mother? She had a baby. A baby his dad didn't want. And Cole takes care of her. He's raising her.

Tears start to burn my eyes.

"Austin?" Deke gets my attention.

His blue eyes are the softest I've ever seen them. It makes me more nervous than I've ever been around Deke because he actually looks worried about something. "We now know that Bruce, Jeff, and Jerrold were working together. You need to get out of that house. It's not safe there."

"I have nowhere to go—"

"You'll stay with me," Becky interrupts me.

"I'm not eighteen yet. I can't just leave. They'll know something is up …"

"You don't have an option," Deke growls. "We can't chance Jerrold coming over and seeing you there. If he does, it will only take him seconds to put two and two together, and then once he tells Bruce …"

His voice trails off, and I understand completely. My father would kill me if he found out that I know he paid another man to try to kill Cole.

Becky reaches out and rubs my back gently. I avoid looking at Cole due to the shame. This whole time, he knew that Lilly was my half-sister, and he never once told me. But why would he? Why tell the girl who he only wanted to use?

"I'll get my stuff," I say and spin around, running up the stairs.

Tears run down my face as I change into my clothes from earlier and shove my shit back in my backpack. I cry for what happened to Cole's mom. For my half-sister's mom. Did my father have something to do with her death? The thought makes me sick to my stomach.

I pick up my bag, throwing it over my shoulder, and turn around. I come to a stop when I see Cole standing at the top of the stairs with his hands tucked in the pockets of his jeans. His face has that usual mask. God forbid the man show any emotion.

His eyes trace the marks around my neck, and I swallow the lump in my throat but say nothing. There's nothing to say to him.

Then without a word, I walk around him, down the steps, and out the front door.

CHAPTER THIRTY-FIVE
COLE

I wake hearing loud voices. I make my way down to the office and crack the door open. My father stands behind his desk.

My mom sits in one of his black leather chairs. Tears run down her cheeks.

"I'm pregnant," she whispers.

He runs a hand down his face. "Is it even mine?"

She sniffs. "I don't know ..."

"How long have you been fucking him?" he growls.

"I didn't ...."

He slams his fists down on the table. "You're fucking pregnant, Betty!"

"He raped me," she cries.

"Because you let him." He slaps her across the face.

I go running in. "Mom!"

"Get the fuck out of here, Cole!" my father growls.

"Go, Cole." She shoves me out of the room and shuts the door. I place my ear against it and listen.

"Fuck! How could you let this happen?" he demands. "Now, you're just another broken bitch. Like all the rest."

"I'm leaving, and I'm taking Cole with me," she says, ignoring his words.

"You're not going anywhere. And you sure as hell aren't taking my son with you."

"You're not gonna put your hands on me," she snaps.

"I'll do whatever I damn well please." I hear him slap her again, and I try to open the door, but it's locked. She cries out.

"Mom!" I say, pounding my fist on the door. "Mom, open the door."

"You think I'm gonna let you leave me? You think I'm gonna let this town think you fucked another man who didn't fucking want you or his child?" His voice rises. "You and Cole will stay where you belong. Under my roof. Under my fucking control."

"I don't need you," she shouts angrily. "We don't need you."

I hear books crashing to the floor and her strangled cry. "You're right," he growls. "You don't. But if you walk out that door, I will take Cole from you and this baby as well. I will dump you out in the mud with nothing but the clothes on your back. You may have come from money, but I hold all the power in this house."

I stand in the loft, facing the bed. The front door slamming pulls me out of my memory. The sound of Austin leaving me. She deserves better. Someone who isn't so fucked up. A man who treats her better than every other fucking bastard in her family.

I run a hand through my hair. My head pounding.

I hurt her. And the worst part is that I liked it. My body physically craved her to a point it was unhealthy. Her cries. Her tears. I fucking took and took. And she didn't stop me. Why would she? I told her what I wanted to do to her, and she willingly challenged me. She was testing me. And I failed her.

I've become my father. The man I despise.

He destroyed my mother. He quit loving her and gave up on her, but I never did. I loved her so much. It didn't matter that he thought she was broken. To me, that made her special. She was a fighter. Just like Austin is.

Reaching down, I grab the empty bottle of Jack and throw it at the far wall with a shout. It shatters into a million fucking pieces.

My heart pounds in my chest, and I'm gasping for air. That pounding in my head intensifies, making my ears ring. I charge into the bathroom and open the cabinet. Grabbing a couple of Advil, I turn the sink on, cup my hand, and swallow some water to take them. Hoping they will dull the pain enough for me to think straight. To figure out what to do.

Deke was right, once again. *Bastard!* She's not safe at her dad's house. She's not safe with me either. And she can't go back to her mom's.

What are you gonna do about it?

I should protect her. I can protect her. That's what a man does.

She looked at me as if I planned all of this. *My sick game.* That I had a vendetta against her from day one due to what her father did to my mother. It wasn't about that. It wasn't her fault. Just like it was never Lilly's fault.

My phone rings in the other room, and I make my way to it. **Deke** lights up my screen.

"What?" I bark. I'm pissed at him even if he was right. She deserved to know her life is in danger.

"She went home, Cole!" My jaw tightens. "I tried to stop her—"

"You should have fucking forced her," I snap, interrupting him.

He sighs. "The thought crossed my mind, but Becky was right there. I couldn't …"

"Couldn't what?" I question when he trails off.

"Hurt her."

AUSTIN

"I'm going home," I tell Deke as we stand outside the clubhouse.

"No, you can't …"

"I need answers." And we both know that Cole isn't going to give them.

"I won't let you." Deke comes to stand in front of me. He's crossed his arms over his broad chest and glares down at me.

At one time, I feared Deke, but that time has passed. "I'm not going to stay with Becky because I'm not going to risk her life. And you're not going to either." With that, I yank open my door and get

---

into my car. And take off.

I storm into my father's house. "Dad? Dad?" I shout.

"What the hell …?" Celeste comes running down the hall. "What happened to you?" she asks wide-eyed, looking over my neck at the bruises and hickeys Cole gave me.

"Where's my father?" I ask, ignoring her concern.

"He left for Florida earlier this morning. Why? Is something wrong?"

"I know." I cut to the chase. I'm not in the mood for small talk. I'm fucking pissed.

Her already big eyes grow bigger, and her face pales. "Austin …"

"I fucking know," I shout. "You think you could keep that from me?" I shake my head. Would they have ever told me that I had a sister? "That I wouldn't find out?" I dig into my pocket and rip my phone out.

"What are you doing?" she asks in a panic.

"Calling him …"

The phone is ripped from my hand.

"Give me my phone," I demand.

"You can't," she says as tears start to well in her brown eyes. "Please. It was supposed to be a one-time thing, but then it happened again. And again." Her first tear falls. "I'm so lonely," she admits, and I stand confused for the second time tonight. She sniffs. "Cole came to me and told me to get him off your back. And I've tried, Austin." She drops my phone and places her hands on my shoulders. "Please understand I'm trying. But Kellan won't let it go." She pulls me into her and buries her head into my chest and sobs. "I'm so sorry. I called out Cole's name while I was with Kellan. Please forgive me."

What. The. Fuck.

"I didn't mean to hurt you. Kellan wanted me to do it, so you would leave Cole. He wants to hurt him." She sobs.

I pry her hands from my shoulders and take a step back from her.

"Kellan wants you out of the group. He knows you had something to do with Cole not doing his dare," she rattles off, "but he can't prove it. He was so mad that you outsmarted him." She reaches up and wipes the tears from her face. "I told him you're smarter than they are."

Damn right I am.

But I've underestimated all of them, though. Even Cole.

"Austin, I …"

"I'm done with this conversation," I say, interrupting her.

She swallows nervously. "Please. Please don't tell Bruce."

I look her in the eyes and smile. The terror on her face makes me want to laugh. "Your secret is safe with me." Then I reach down, pick up my phone, and walk down the hallway and out the back door, wanting some fresh air.

I spent all day Saturday and Sunday relaxing in the pool. Celeste steered clear of me. If she wasn't in her room, she was out. Probably fucking Kellan somewhere. At this point, I don't care who she screws. My father raped a woman, got her pregnant, and then tried to kill her son. My father deserves to pay for that. And his trophy wife fucking a senior in high school isn't enough if you ask me.

Cole blew up my phone Saturday night like he finally had something to say to me. I ignored them all. But I made sure to read his messages just so he would see that I saw them. He was on the top of my shit list. And it seemed to be growing by the second.

I spoke to Becky and told her that my father was out of town. His calls stopped after that. I only did it 'cause I knew she would tell Deke, and he would pass the message on to Cole.

Monday finally rolled around, and I got up, got ready, and drove myself to school. I sat down in first period and spoke to Becky like nothing ever happened. She stared at me like I needed to be admitted to a psych ward. I just smiled. Because in a way she was right. I officially no longer care about anything but revenge. I'm gonna do what they all did. Turn off my emotions and play the fucking game. Like I should have done from the beginning.

CHAPTER THIRTY-SIX

COLE

She's avoided me completely this week. Five whole days of not a single word. Not even a glance my way. And it's not like I haven't tried. She just acts like I don't even exist. It's taken all I have not to pin her up against a locker and choke her until she's clawing at my arms and chest, silently begging me to let her breathe. But I know Austin Lowes. She would willingly pass out before she begged me for anything.

And I no longer want to hurt her.

"You okay, man?" Deke asks as we walk to our cars in the parking lot of the school after practice.

"Fine."

He sighs. "Becky's worried about Austin."

I come to a stop and turn to face him. "Why? Did Austin say something to her?"

He shakes his head. "Just that she isn't herself."

I snort. "Of course not. She's been blackmailed and lied to."

"Hey, guys. Wait up."

We look over at the door to see Shane and Bennett approaching. "What do you think it's about?" Shane asks.

"Think what is about?" Deke asks him.

"The text Austin just sent us," Bennett answers.

I dig in my pocket as Kellan joins us. Deke and I no longer speak to him either.

Austin: Clubhouse ten tonight.

Kellan smiles. "Maybe she's finally pulling out."

She wouldn't do that. Not now. I'm not sure what she's thinking but running isn't something she does. He's stupid to even think that.

"Guess we'll find out at ten," Bennett says.

I pull up to the clubhouse at ten on the dot. Her car is already parked outside along with Deke's Range Rover and Bennett's white Mercedes. I had every intention to be here early and try to talk to her, but I had a phone call that ran longer than planned.

I walk inside to see her sitting on the couch with her eyes looking down at her phone. She wears a pair of black shorts and a black top. Her hair is down and straight, and she looks absolutely amazing.

My chest tightens when I think about how I've hurt her. Lied to her.

Ever since she walked out of this door a week ago, she has consumed my thoughts. Fuck her dad for trying to kill me. He'll pay for that in time. Right now, I gotta do whatever I can to get her back.

"Why are we here?" Kellan demands, walking in and not wasting a second of his time.

She places her phone on her lap and then stretches her arms out on the back of the couch, looking up. She smiles. "As you all know, Cole and I are no longer"—she pauses, thinking of the right word—"anything. But I'm not dropping out." She looks at Kellan. "Thought I would get that out of the way since you were hoping for that." His mouth sets in a hard line. Her smile widens. "And I know you are fucking Celeste, so you can stop having her scream out Cole's name." Shane starts to choke, and Deke chuckles. Her eyes meet mine for the first time in a week. And they look as cold as ice. "Plus, I no longer care who Cole fucks," she says voice flat.

"Austin …"

"How did you find out?" Deke asks, interrupting me.

"I went home and demanded to speak to Bruce, but Celeste told me he had already left for Florida. I then told her that I *knew*. I was referring to Lilly being my sister, but she thought I meant her fucking Cole." Kellan's eyes narrow. He opens his mouth, but she continues. "But that is not why I called this meeting. There is something we need to take care of."

"What?" Deke asks her.

"Jerrold." Her eyes meet mine. "I think he's earned his death." Then she looks at all the guys.

Kellan walks over to the couch, and I take a step closer but both ignore me. He stops and looks down at her. "If we do this, you're involved. One hundred percent."

"Absolutely not—"

"I'm in," she says, interrupting me.

"Austin!" I snap.

She continues to stare up at Kellan with a look of indifference. But he could be setting her up. Now that she knows he's screwing Celeste, he could want her dead so she can't tell Bruce.

"She's not doing anything," I add when no one else objects.

"I have a say, Cole. I'm part of this group." She fucking smiles at me. "Isn't that what you wanted?'

"She's playing him." We all hear Shane whisper to Deke.

Austin directs her attention to Shane. "The only thing I'm *playing* is the game," she corrects him.

"It's too risky," I say, shaking my head.

"Since when do you care about my life?" she asks.

I run a hand through my hair. "Since I found out that your dad tried to kill me, and he is working with a guy who you stole that information from."

"That didn't stop you from putting your hands around my neck," she says, crossing her arms over her chest.

My teeth grind. I wanna say I would never hurt her, but that would be a lie. That's all I've done to her.

"Right!" She looks back up at Kellan at my silence. "So what's it gonna be?" she asks him.

He looks down at her. "Tonight."

She nods.

"Home invasion," he tells her.

I go to open my mouth, but she snorts. "No."

He raises a brow at her.

"The six of us are not doing a home invasion unless you want us to get caught. And I don't know about you, but I'd rather not go to jail."

He crosses his arms over his chest. "Then what do you suggest?"

She gives him a big smile. "You guys are sharks. Time to act like it."

I turn to Deke, and he's already staring at me with a look of concern in his features. I walk outside for some fresh air, and he gets the hint, following me.

"What do you want me to do?" he asks the moment he gets outside.

"Austin and I will ride with you." My jaw tightens. "But she never gets out of the car."

"She's gonna be pissed."

"I don't give a fuck," I snap. At this point, her safety means more to me than her being mad at me. I can deal with her anger. Kellan setting her up or her getting hurt is a different story.

He nods once. "She never gets out of the car," he agrees.

I spin around to see the door open to the clubhouse, and she walks out followed by Shane and Bennett. Kellan walks out with a smile on his face. And I fist my hands. There's no way he should be happy right now. Not after she called him out about sleeping with Celeste.

"Austin, we're riding with Deke."

"No. I'm driving. I don't wanna come back here …" I grab her upper arm. "Cole!" she snaps. "Stop!"

I ignore her and drag her over to Deke's SUV and toss her in the back seat. She cusses me as I slam the door shut.

"You don't know the plan," Kellan says.

I ignore him. I go over to my car and retrieve my black bag out of the trunk, grab what I need out of my console, and then jump in the passenger seat of Deke's Range Rover. I look in the back, and she sits by the door, looking out the window. Her eyes narrowed on nothing.

Deke gets in and looks at me.

"What's the plan, Austin?" I ask.

She says nothing.

"I'm not gonna ask you again," I growl.

Her head snaps over to look at me. Her green eyes burn with rage, and I smile at her. She's so gorgeous. "Bennett said he likes to take late-night swims, so I suggested we drown him in his own pool," she huffs.

I nod and turn back to face the front. "Head to his house."

Deke starts the car and "With Me Now" by Blacklite District blares through the speakers.

I smile. *Good plan, sweetheart.*

We pull up to the house a block away. I remove my seat belt and turn to face her. "You're staying in the car."

"Cole …"

"This is not up for discussion, Austin!" I pick up my bag at my feet and unzip it. I pull out my gun and place it in the back of my waistband of my jeans. Just in case. Then I place my rope and set of handcuffs on the center console.

"What do you need those for?" she growls. "You have to make this look like a freak accident. If he has marks around his wrists and ankles, then they will know he was murdered."

"Those are for you," Deke tells her as he eyes her in the rearview mirror.

"What?" she snaps. She's no longer scared of him, and that has me worried. A part of me knows that if he puts her in a situation that she needs to get out of, she would do anything to get free. That's why I'm glad Deke is stronger than she is.

He nods. "You try to leave, and I have permission to do whatever is necessary to keep you in the car." He gives her a big threatening smile.

She looks at me, her eyes narrowed. "He's bullshitting me, right?"

I shake my head. "No."

Her jaw tightens, and she looks over at the door. She lunges for it. "Fuck this …"

Deke reaches out and grabs her hair, yanking her back into the seat while he leans over into the back. She doesn't cry out. Instead, she lets out a growl of frustration.

"Your ass is staying in this car," I snap, grabbing my hoodie out of my bag. "And that is all there is to it." I get out, slamming the door shut.

I pull on my hoodie and zip it up, before putting the hood over my head.

"Where's Austin?" Kellan asks as we meet up.

"Not coming," I state without looking over at him.

He snorts. "Knew she'd back out."

I say nothing. Kellan underestimates her way too much. And that is what will get him in trouble with her.

We come up to Jerrold's back gate. "What are we gonna do?" Shane asks.

"I'm gonna kill the bastard," I state.

"We could just shoot him," Kellan offers.

"No!" I snap. Austin was right. This can't look like a murder. His wife is dead, and his brother is missing. If he is murdered, then this will look too suspicious. I turn to Bennett. "Are the cameras still in the house?"

He nods. "I never removed them."

"Where is his laptop?" I ask.

"At my house. Want me to go get it and plant it here?"

I shake my head. It will have Austin's fingerprints on it. And cameras from his work may place her there. Even if she wasn't the one who actually took it from his office. Too risky. "No. We stick with the plan. I'll drown him in his pool."

"What if he's not in it?" Kellan offers.

"He's there," Bennett says. "Or I wouldn't have mentioned it as an option."

"How do we plan on getting in?" Shane asks.

I used to spend a lot of time at this house. Eli and Aimee's parents died when he was young, so when Aimee got married, he moved in with them. "There's a side gate that Eli used to sneak out of to do his dares. It's on the north side," I say and start walking in that direction. They follow me.

I check my phone to see if I've got anything from Deke, and there's nothing. It worries me. I know he would never hurt her on purpose, but I told him to do whatever it takes to keep her in the car. And I'm not sure how much fight she has in her. At what point will she back down from him? At what point will he stop hurting her and just let her go? Guess I'll find out when I get back.

"Something wrong?" Kellan asks.

I don't answer him and put my phone away. Not like he cares anyway.

We get through the gate and into the backyard. We round the pool house and come to a stop when we see the bastard in his pool just like Bennett had predicted. Doing laps.

"How we doing this exactly?" Shane asks.

"I'm doing it." I turn to face them. "Alone."

They all nod. All but Kellan. He eyes me skeptically. "Why you?"

"Because I said so," I growl. He didn't want to be involved with Jeff, yet now he wants to be part of Jerrold's death? He isn't making sense.

He crosses his arms over his chest and nods once. "Fine. We'll stay back unless you need us."

I snort. "I won't need you."

Turning back around, I readjust my hood and make my way over to the rectangular swimming pool. I come to a stop, watching him swim away from me. I place my hands in my pockets and wait. He comes up for a breath and then goes under, pushing off the far wall, and shoots toward me.

As I watch him swim underwater, I think of every reason this fucker is going to die.

"Please, Cole," Eli cries as we sit in the ditch.

"You're gonna be okay," I reassure him, knowing that I'm lying. There's nothing I can do for him.

"No." He swallows "You have to save Aimee ..."

He won't let this go. "She'll be fine."

He shakes his head quickly and coughs. "He beats her."

"Who?"

"Jerrold." I tighten my hold on him. "I hear him ... her cries ... He won't stop."

"Eli ..."

"I have cameras in the house ..." His eyes plead with mine. "They go to my computer ... You have to help her ..."

I nod. "I will. Promise." My voice cracks as his fists loosen on my shirt.

"Thank you," he whispers.

"Eli?" I ask as panic bubbles up inside me.

His eyes meet mine, a calmness brushing over his face. "I love you, brother," he whispers.

"I love you ..." His eyes gloss over, and his body falls limp on the ground. "Eli?" I shout. "No ..." I grab his shirt and yank his lifeless body into my lap. "Eli?" I shout. "Please ... no.!"

I failed him. I broke into their house and stole his computer, but it wasn't enough. We didn't move fast enough. Eli's death had put Aimee into a deep depression. The cameras showed her crying, and I couldn't watch it anymore. I couldn't take the pain. The reminder. I shut those cameras out for four months. Then when I was ready, it was too late. She was already dead. The bastard had killed her. We sat and watched Jerrold tell Jeff what he did to Aimee and where he hid her body.

That's why it's time for this bastard to die. One, for killing Aimee. Two, for working with Bruce to try to kill me. Successfully killing my friends. And three, what he would do to Austin if he knew she was the one to take his laptop. I feel a calmness fall over me. Not my usual anger and need to break something. Instead, it's the need to protect something—Austin. She's my last chance at saving someone, and I won't fail this time. I'll die trying.

He's getting closer. I remove my hands from my pockets and kneel. I smile as he comes up for air. "Hello, Jerrold. It's been a while."

"What …?"

I grab his head and slam it down on the edge of the pool. Blood covers the concrete instantly, and his body goes limp. I pull him away from the ledge and see I've knocked him out. Blood pours from the side of his head into the pool. "You deserved far worse," I say before pushing him underwater.

AUSTIN

Deke starts the SUV, headlights off, and I cross my arms over my chest as I look out the back passenger window. I can make out a dark object coming toward the Range Rover.

It's Cole.

He jumps in the front passenger seat and immediately looks back at me. I refuse to acknowledge him or give him any sign that I care he made me stay in the car. That he allowed Deke to do whatever was *necessary* to stop me.

I didn't want to fight Deke because I understand that he is not my problem. Cole is.

And I'm not sure what to do about it at the moment. I went from something he can torture and lie to, to something he has to protect.

Fuck that! I don't need protecting.

"Is it done?" Deke ask him as he pulls away.

"Yes," he says simply.

"How did you do it?" he asks.

"I slammed his head down on the concrete …"

"It was supposed to be an accidental drowning," I snap.

He turns around in his seat. "I made it look like he slipped and fell into the pool," he states, eyes narrowed on mine. "Then I held him underwater." He turns back to face the front. "It's done. He's dead. The end."

We pull back up to the clubhouse, and the guys pull up behind us. I go to my car, but Kellan hollers that we need to have a meeting. So I turn and march my way inside. I stand by the door with my back against the wall. Ready to get the hell out of here and away from Cole.

"What is this about?" Deke asks, checking his phone. It's after midnight on a Friday. I'm sure he's going to go meet up with Becky if she's not already waiting for him at his house.

Kellan looks at me. "Cole's dare. I say we move on."

Deke raises a brow, and Cole stiffens as he stands by the table. "I can redraw—"

"No," Kellan interrupts him. "We can move on to the next person." He shrugs carelessly. "I don't mind. Does anyone else have a problem with that?"

No one says a thing. The room falls silent, and even I can tell Kellan is setting someone up for something. I get my answer a moment later.

He rubs his hands together. "Okay, so we'll move on, and come Sunday, Austin will draw."

Cole spins around to face me. "Absolutely not. She's out of the group."

"What?" I snap.

Kellan looks at me. "If you don't leave willingly, then we all have to vote you out. Do you choose to leave willingly?"

"No," I say without looking at Cole. He brought me into this; I'm not gonna let him throw me out. Not after all I've done. All he's put me through.

"Then we will vote you out." Cole growls. "Who says she's gone?"

Deke is the first one to say I'm out. I ignore him. He made it very clear tonight when he yanked hair out of my head that he will do whatever the fuck Cole says.

Shane comes next. Bennett sighs as if he doesn't want to but folds anyway.

Everyone looks at Kellan, and he smiles. "I say she stays."

The air in the room changes, and Cole takes a step toward him. "What the fuck?" he barks. "You've wanted her gone since day one, and now all of a sudden you want her to stay?"

I could argue that Kellan may think if he votes me out, that I'll tell my dad he's fucking my stepmom, but I'm not sure that is the reason.

He shrugs. "She wants to stay."

"I don't give a fuck what she wants," Cole shouts.

"That's obvious," I say.

Cole spins around to face me. His eyes narrowed in anger, and I square my shoulders. "Everyone, get the fuck out!" he barks.

Kellan smirks at me as he walks by. Shane and Bennett hang their heads as they walk to the exit. Deke is the last one, and his eyes shoot from me to Cole as if he's waiting for one of us to tell him to stay. We don't.

The moment the door closes, Cole turns on me. "You're not doing this."

"You no longer control me, Cole," I reply flatly.

"Cut the shit, Austin!" he snaps.

"No! You should have cut the shit, Cole!" I shout. "Long ago. You should have told me about Lilly. About Kellan and Celeste." His eyes narrow on me. "Fuck!" I shout frustrated. "I did so much. I let you take so much." I shake my head. "But not anymore. You brought me into this."

His jaw sharpens.

"I let you use me," I growl. "I let you fucking take and take because you needed something. Someone. But not again, Cole. Find someone else to fuck with. Because I'm done."

I turn and go to walk out the door, but he grabs my arm and yanks me back. "Don't touch me," I shout. Spinning around, I go to slap him, but he was ready for it. He grabs my hands and pushes me onto the couch, pinning my hands above my head.

"Cole," I say, my heart pounding.

"Guess not much has changed since that night in the cemetery, huh, sweetheart?" he asks with an arch of his brow and a cocky smirk on his face, referring to how easily he was able to pin me down.

"What? Gonna stab me this time?" I ask, fisting my hands. "Gonna let Deke just kill me?"

His cockiness fades, and he loosens his grip on my wrists but doesn't let go. "I don't want to hurt you, Austin."

I narrow me eyes. "Quit trying to mind fuck me. It's not gonna work."

"I'm not …"

"Bullshit!" I shout.

I want to break you. His agenda hasn't changed.

He lets go of my wrists, and I shove him off me. He falls onto the couch, and I scramble to get up. I straighten my top that rode up, grab my phone that fell onto the floor, and head to the door. This time, he doesn't stop me.

"You know he's setting her up, right?" Deke asks me as we both sit on the couch in the clubhouse.

It's Sunday, and we have all gathered back here for Austin to draw her dare. I've been in a pissy mood ever since she walked out of here on Friday night.

"Yes."

"What are we gonna do about it?"

I look over at him. "Be there when he does."

He nods and goes back to texting on his phone.

The door opens, and she walks in with a look of indifference. She's as good as I am at giving a blank expression. I fucking hate it.

I sit back and watch Kellan look over her tight skinny jeans and black high heels. She wears a black top to match that is low cut, showing off her tits. She looks like she's getting ready to go have drinks with her girlfriends at a bar, not draw a dare.

Shane passes out a piece of paper to each of us. I lean over and whisper into Deke's ear. "Leave it blank."

He nods and folds it up.

One at a time, we each get up and drop them into the bowl. When we're all done, she draws.

Her eyes instantly go to mine. I refrain from smiling.

"What does it say?" Kellan demands.

"Nothing," she replies and tosses it the ground. She draws again.

"You can't draw more than once," I say as I stand.

"What the hell?" she demands when she opens the folded piece of paper and looks at Deke. He says nothing.

"You guys can't do that," Kellan snaps at us.

"Actually, they can," Bennett says with a smile. And I wonder if he had the same idea as we did.

She reaches in and draws again. I go to rip it out of her hand, but she opens it up and reads it out loud. "As dark as night, as red as light. Let's take a match and make it shine bright. Consequence- you must show the world your darkest secret."

"What the fuck does that mean?" I snap.

"It's a riddle," Kellan says with a smile.

"I fucking know that!" I growl. "What the fuck does it mean?"

"I don't know. It's not my dare. Shane?" He looks at him.

My eyes narrow on Shane. "What does it mean?" I demand.

"I don't have to answer that." He crosses his arms over his chest. "She will find out soon enough."

Monday afternoon, we all sit at the lunch table. Becky and Austin talk about a test we had today while Deke speaks to me. I completely tune him out.

"So I spoke to Celeste when I got home last night, and she's throwing me a birthday party."

Becky frowns. "Is that what you want?"

She shrugs. "Not really but she is kissing my ass. And she feels a birthday party will help it."

"When is your birthday?" I ask her, wanting her to tell me. But I already know. Turns out that Facebook page I made came in handy.

She ignores me and takes a bite of her cheeseburger.

"When's your birthday?" Deke asks her.

Of course, she answers him. "March seventeenth."

His eyes widen. "St. Paddy's day?" She nods. "Holy shit! What a day to have a birthday. Plus, that's this Saturday." She nods. "And it's the start of spring break."

"It's not a big deal." She brushes it off.

"You're gonna be eighteen. Of course, it's a big deal," Becky says. "I'll come over and help you decorate."

"I'll post it on social media. It'll be fun," he says with a smile.

She sighs but takes another bite of her cheeseburger.

The bell rings, and everyone gets up. "Austin? Can I have a minute?" I ask.

She looks over at me. "No."

I grab her hand when she goes to pull away. "I need to talk to you …"

"Well, I have nothing to say," she says before turning and walking away from me.

I fist my hand and slam it on the table. I'm not sure how much longer I can take her ignoring me. It's eating at me. Driving me crazy. I don't like it. She can't avoid me forever. I'll get to her one way or another.

AUSTIN

"Wake up! Wake up!"

I groan at Becky's annoying, chipper voice. "What are you doing?"

"HAPPY BIRTHDAY!" she yells, jumping on my bed. Her blond hair going everywhere. "Now it's time for you to wake up. I made breakfast."

"You can cook?" I ask, pulling the covers up over my head.

"Of course, silly." She laughs. "Come on. It's downstairs."

"I think the birthday girl is supposed to get breakfast in bed," I say, yawning.

She just laughs and yanks the covers off me.

I groan as I sit up. I reach over to my nightstand and check my phone. "It's not even nine yet," I call out.

"We have a busy day," she yells from the stairs.

Becky stayed the night with me last night for us to ring in my birthday. We stayed up watching scary movies and talking about boys. Well, I'm still not talking to Cole, so I just listened to her talk about how much she loves Deke. It was exhausting, to say the least.

I make my way downstairs and into the formal dining room. Becky sits at the table with two plates. Both have pancakes on them, but the one in front of my seat is stacked six high with eighteen individual candles on them.

"You couldn't find a one and an eight?" I ask with a laugh.

"This way is more fun." She winks at me, then grabs the can of whipped cream that sits in the middle. She shakes it up before leaning over the table and spraying the top of the pancakes. Then she lights them. "Make a wish and get to blowing."

I laugh, lean over, and blow them out. It takes me two tries, and by the time I get them out, the wax has dripped onto the whipped cream.

I wipe it off and place it on the side of my plate. "What are the plans today?" she asks, digging into hers.

My fork pauses over my stack. "I wanna spend some time with Lilly," I say.

She stops chewing and looks up at me. "Okay," she says through a mouthful of pancakes. "Then let's do it."

"I haven't spoken to Cole …"

"So." She swallows her bite. "Who cares? You have every right to spend time with her."

I nod. "I hate that I haven't got to see her."

She gives me a soft smile. "You can spend the day with her alone if you want. I can go home—"

"No," I interrupt her. "We can have a girls' day. We can take her to a movie and then go for ice cream."

She nods. "Sounds good."

I pick up my phone and go to *Shark* and send a text.

Me: Is Lilly free for the afternoon? I would like to spend the day with her. Wanna take her to a movie and to get ice cream.

I set my phone down and take a bite of my pancakes. "Mmm," I mumble my approval.

I look up when Celeste walks in. "Happy Birthday," she says with a soft smile. We're still not talking much either.

"Thanks," I say with a head nod.

She sits down next to me, and I stuff another bite into my mouth. "I spoke to your dad this morning. He won't be able to make it for tonight."

Thank God. I don't wanna see that bastard.

"For your birthday, we decided to give you a trip."

I swallow my bite. "Trip?"

She nods. "For you and a friend to go anywhere you want for a week."

I look at Becky, and she smiles.

"Thanks," I say although I won't use it. I want nothing from my father or her. One is a rapist. The other a cheating, lying bitch.

My phone rings, and I look down to see **_Shark_** written across my screen. I let out a deep breath. I've avoided speaking to him, but since I messaged him wanting to see Lilly, I answer. "Hello?"

"Hey." Cole's raspy voice comes over the line. He's just waking up. And my legs tighten, knowing he's still in bed.

I hate how much my body still wants him. That's why I've avoided him. I can't afford to let him back in. To make me look like an idiot once again. "Hey," I reply.

"Happy Birthday, sweetheart."

My chest tightens at the softness in his voice. He is a lie. It's all a lie. "What do you want, Cole?"

He sighs heavily, and I imagine him running his hand through his disheveled morning hair. "I just wanted to call you and tell you happy birthday. Instead of texting." I remain silent. "And of course, you can spend the day with Lilly."

I smile at that. "Thanks. I'll be over to get her in about an hour?" I ask.

"I can bring her to you," he offers.

"No," I say, shaking my head at myself. I wanna pick her up so I can leave afterward. If he brings her over here, he may try to stay and visit.

"Okay," he says slowly. "I will get her ready."

I hate how much I've missed of her life, but I can't deny that Cole has been there for her. That he stepped up and did what neither my father nor Cole's would do.

"Thank you," I say.

"No need to thank me, Austin."

I say goodbye and hang up before he can say anything else. Placing my phone on the table, I go back to eating my pancakes and ignore the looks I can feel Celeste giving me. I still haven't told her that I know Lilly is my sister. Not like it would matter. Plus, I'm sure Kellan has already told her. At one point, I thought I could trust Celeste, but now I know I can't. Nor can I believe anything she says. Becky is my only true friend. I can trust her with anything.

Becky and I did exactly what we had planned to do. We picked Lilly up from Cole's, and he didn't mention anything due to her being present. He kissed and hugged her goodbye. She jumped into my arms, and we left. I took her to the newest Disney movie, and I couldn't even tell you the name of it. I spent the entire time looking over at her. I watched her laugh and smile. I cried, and when she asked what was wrong, I told her I thought the movie was sad. My chest hurt at what my little sister has been through. I still don't know how their mother died. Does Lilly remember her? She never talks about her.

The time with her went by too quickly, and afterward, we took her back and dropped her off. Once again, Cole didn't try to speak to me.

As soon as we got back home, we started decorating the house. I had finally accepted Deke's friend request weeks ago, and I saw his invite to my party. More people than I could count said they were coming. Deke loaded Becky's car with alcohol the day before, so we set up everything in the kitchen and then went upstairs to start getting ready.

Just as I was putting on my heels, my mother called me. I stared at it for a few rings and then sent her to voicemail. She immediately sent me a text.

Mom: Have your father call me.

That was all it said.

CHAPTER THIRTY-EIGHT
COLE

I pull up to Bruce's house. The party isn't supposed to start for another hour, but the driveway is already packed full of cars. I'm not surprised.

Kids litter the front yard and porch. They nod their head to me and call out my name. Like always, I ignore them.

The past couple of weeks have had me on edge. I've been in a pissy mood because Austin has been ignoring me. And because I've been too busy with swim meets to try to spend extra time with her. But yesterday was Friday, officially kicking off spring break. I have no obligations this weekend and no school next week. So tonight I plan to corner her and talk to her. Make her talk to me. She can cuss, she can yell, and hell, she can even slap me. We are getting to the bottom of this shit tonight.

I don't care if it's her birthday. I have waited long enough.

I enter the house and make my way down the hallway. People move out of my way. I enter the kitchen, expecting her to be in here, but she's not.

"You looking for Austin?"

I turn around at a male's voice and come face to face with Bryan. I fist my hands.

He takes a step back, raising his, not wanting me to beat his ass like I did at the beach. "I don't want trouble. It was just a question."

I unclench them. "Where is she?" I ask, cutting to the chase.

"Last I saw her, she was in the game room playing beer pong."

I shoulder past him and move farther down the hallway. I keep an eye out for Deke because I saw his SUV parked in the driveway.

I round the back corner and open the door that I know is their game room. "Bite Your Kiss" by Diamante blares through the speakers. I spot her immediately. She's standing at the end of the ping pong table. The guy opposite of her makes his shot, and everyone cheers as she throws back whatever was in the cup.

She smashes the now empty cup on the table, and her eyes meet mine. "Cole," she shouts excitedly, and my jaw tightens.

She's fucking trashed. Her party hasn't even started yet, which tells me that she's been drinking for a while.

Everyone turns to look at me, and the guy across from her steps back from the table. "Here you go, man," he says, offering up his spot.

She waves him off. "He doesn't drink, Myers." She hiccups and then laughs at herself.

"You obviously have had enough for the both of us," I state.

"It's my birthday." She holds her hands out wide before they fall to her sides, slapping her bare thighs. "I can do whatever the fuck I want."

I don't like the way she says it. As if she could kiss any guy in here. Fuck any guy in here. "Austin," I growl.

She narrows her eyes on me, then looks around at everyone in the room like she is sizing them up. I notice the way a girl by the name of Amanda looks me up and down before giving me a big smile. Austin sees it, and she rolls her eyes before they come back to me. "I'm curious … how many girls in here have fucked Cole Reynolds?" she asks as if reading my mind. Deke stands off to her right with Becky, and his brows rise. Everyone stares at her, wondering what the hell is going on. "Come on. This is just for fun," she says, encouraging them.

One by one, the girls slowly start to raise their hands. Including Amanda. All but a few, Becky included, keep their hands down. I never slept with her. I would have, but she was always Deke's. We all knew that.

Austin spins around, looking at all of them, and then smiles at me. "Pick someone else, Cole. Because I'm done being *yours*."

My hands fist down by my sides.

"Okay, I think we should—"

"Play strip beer pong," she interrupts Deke. "For every one you miss, I'll take something off." She tosses the ball to me. I catch it midair. "What do you say?"

"Don't," I growl in warning.

She tilts her head to the side. "Don't wanna play my game, Cole?"

"Austin!"

"How about ..." She leans over the table. "I dare you."

"Not gonna work, sweetheart." I give her a threatening smile.

She looks at the guy she called Myers and smiles at him. "You'll play with me, right?" she asks, placing her hands on her hips.

She looks like a fucking doll dressed in a short, black tulle skirt and black t-shirt that reads BIRTHDAY across her chest in gold letters with her favorite pair of black heels. She's worn them before while I fucked her. Her long hair is down and straight, and her eyes are lined with black. And red fucking lipstick.

I promise, there's not a guy in this house who doesn't want to *play* with her—my toy.

He takes a step back up to the table. I grip his shoulder and yank him back. "Everybody out!" I shout.

They all turn toward the door and run out. All but Deke and Becky.

Austin pushes her right hip out and picks up another red Solo cup. She drinks it.

"Just what the fuck do you think you're doing?" I snap.

"Why are you even here, Cole?" she asks, ignoring my question.

I step to her, and she tilts her head back to look up at me. "Was I not invited?" I ask, arching a brow.

Her green eyes hold mine for a long second before a drunken smile grows across her face. "I already told you once, Cole. I no longer care what you do."

The door opens, and I spin around to yell at them to leave, but

Bennett and Shane walk in. Then Kellan.

She picks up another Solo cup and begins to drink it as well.

"You've had enough," I snap and yank it from her hand.

Her green eyes narrow on me. "That's it," she snaps. "I've tried to be nice …"

Kellan's laughter cuts her off.

She glares at him and then returns her attention to me. "I'm done. Done letting you all boss me around like I don't have a say. Being told what to do and how things are going to be. And all these secrets. Well, guess what? I have secrets of my own." She smiles at me. It's not soft or inviting. "I've got insurance too, Cole."

"What are you talking about?" Kellan asks nervously.

"Every time we've been sitting at the clubhouse and you all thought I was playing around on my phone, I was really recording you."

"Shit." Deke chuckles impressed.

"So go ahead, push me a little more and see what I do with all that information." She shoves me out of the way and goes to storm out, but I grab her upper arm.

"You're bluffing," I say. She has to be.

"I am?" She tilts her head to the side. "Wanna take that chance, Cole?"

My eyes narrow on her as "Go to War" by Nothing More starts to play in the room.

She jerks her arm out of my hold. "I didn't think so." With that, she walks out.

Shane runs a hand through his hair. "She has to be joking."

"Doubtful," I say. She's a shark just like us, after all.

"What the fuck?" Kellan shouts. "This is all your fault." He points at me. "You wanted to bring her in. You wanted to fuck her. And you kept secrets from her."

"Me?" I demand. "You gave me a dare to fuck another girl when you knew we were together."

He snorts. "You were never together. You have forced her along this entire time." He reaches for the closed door. "And now she's gonna fuck us! Just like I told you she would!"

Bennett and Shane both turn and follow him out.

"What do you want me to do?" Deke asks as Becky runs out after her.

"Nothing you can do. I fucked up." I should have just come out and told her the truth in the beginning.

He sighs heavily. "You could tell her about—"

"She doesn't wanna hear about that right now," I interrupt him.

"Why *did* you come, man?"

I turn around and face him. "Why wouldn't I?" I snap.

He runs a hand through his hair. "Are you trying to piss her off?"

"No!"

"Then maybe just give her some time to cool off," he offers.

"It's been two weeks. How long does she fucking need?" I demand.

"I don't know what you want me to say." He throws his hands up in the air. "Or what you want me to do. Fuck! You two are going round and round in circles and not getting anywhere," he growls. "You hated her. Now she hates you …"

"I never hated her." *I wanted to destroy her.* There's a difference.

He sighs heavily. "I … don't know why you can't just tell her."

My heart starts to pound in my chest. "Tell her what?"

"Come on, Cole? Playing dumb with her may work, but it's not going to work with me. I've known you all my life."

I cross my arms over my chest. "And?"

He steps into me, eyes narrowed. "And I don't know why it's so fucking hard for you to be a man and tell the girl you love her."

"I don't!" I snap.

He throws his head back, laughing. "So you don't plan on her moving to Texas with you after graduation?"

"That is for her to be close to Lilly," I growl. I should have never told him my plans.

He stares at me, and I arch a brow. *Throw something else at me, Deke.* I'll block it.

"You know." He uncrosses his arms over his chest. "Everyone always talks about how fucked up you are." My hands clench. "But

I never believed them. Until now. You can kill someone without a second thought, but you can't admit you love someone?" He shakes his head. "Never thought I'd see the day when you actually surprise me." Then he turns and exits the room.

AUSTIN

I walk into the kitchen and grab the Fireball and take a sip from the bottle.

"What the hell was that?" Becky demands, running up to me.

"Me putting them in their place," I say and tip it back again.

She sighs. "What do you have on them?"

"Enough."

She rolls her eyes. "That's not what I asked, Austin."

I take another drink as Deke walks into the kitchen. I don't expect to be invited back to the clubhouse anytime soon. But too bad. Because my ass isn't walking away. Not this far into the game.

He comes over to us, his eyes on Becky. "We're leaving, babe," he says, and my eyes catch Cole storming past the kitchen and out the front door.

I take another drink.

"I'm staying again tonight," she tells him.

He nods, already knowing that. Then he looks at me. He opens his mouth to speak and then closes it.

"What?" I snap.

He just shakes his head. "Nothing." Then gives Becky a kiss before he turns and walks out.

"You can go with him if you want," I offer.

She shakes her head. "Absolutely not. I'm your only friend, remember?" She gives me a smile before taking the bottle from my hand. "Someone has to watch over you."

I roll my eyes but sigh in disappointment. I've never had a good birthday. I've never spent it with family or real friends. Since I left California, I've learned a lot. And one thing is that those friends were as fake as a blow-up doll. I hate that I'm fighting with Cole. I hate that he put me in this position. That he lied to me about something so important it could change my life.

Where do we go from here? Will I ever get to see Lilly after we graduate? My chest tightens with that thought.

Becky places her hand on mine and gives me a soft smile. "You should give him a chance."

"Some people don't deserve a chance," I say simply.

"Austin—"

"I don't wanna talk about it," I interrupt her. "Can we just get drunk?"

She chuckles, handing me back the bottle. "Drink up, birthday girl."

I open my eyes at the sound of thunder and groan.

My head pounds, and my mouth is dry. Lightning strikes, lighting up my room, and I run my hand along my bed, looking for my phone. I find it face down and press the button to light up the screen. I squint and it reads 4:25 a.m. I've only been asleep for an hour. The party ended hours ago, but Becky and I weren't ready to call it quits just yet.

My hand grips my cell, and I sit up slowly, letting my body adjust to being awake. Everything aches.

Becky is passed out in bed, her back toward me. Throwing the covers off, I make my way into the bathroom. I come to a stop in front of the sink and turn on the water. Lightning lights up the room through my large oval window and then thunder booms, rattling the walls.

I place my phone on the countertop and open the medicine cabinet. I pick up the Advil and shut the glass cabinet just as the lights go out.

"Shit." I sigh.

The lightning strikes, lighting up the bathroom once again, and I see a dark form in the mirror. "What the …?"

A hand fists my hair, and when my head is yanked back, I drop the pill bottle to grab at them. But before I can get a hold of anything, my head is slammed forward.

CHAPTER THIRTY-NINE
COLE

I wake up to my phone ringing.

"Hello?" I mumble, without looking to see who it is.

"Get your ass up!" Deke says in greeting.

I run a hand down my face. "What do you want? What time is it?"

"Eight. Get up and get your ass over to Shelby's."

"Why?" I yawn.

"Because Becky just called me, and the girls are there."

I sit up in a rush. "Why are they at Shelby's?"

"Don't know. She called me and said Austin is there needing medical attention. I'm on my way …"

"I'll meet you there."

I'm dressed and walking into Shelby's house in less than fifteen minutes. I've called Austin's phone over twenty times and all have gone straight to her voicemail.

"What's going on?" I demand, entering her kitchen.

Shelby jumps up from the chair, her hands out in front of her. Austin sits at the head of the table, her elbows on the dark surface and face in her hands, her hair is down and blocking my view of her.

"Get the hell out of here, Cole!" Shelby growls.

"What happened to her?" I demand, ignoring her order. She looks fine. Maybe she is just really hungover.

"Don't act stupid," Shelby snaps. "We all know you did this to her."

"He didn't do it," Austin replies in a tired voice.

"Me? I didn't do shit ..."

"You expect us to believe that?" Shelby snaps. "Last time she was here, she needed fifteen stitches because you took a knife to her arm."

"You what?" Becky demands from the other side of the table.

My teeth clench. "I've hurt her, yes, but I didn't do this. Hell, I don't even know what *this* is. Why the fuck is she here?"

"I'm calling the cops," Shelby says, turning to the kitchen counter where her cell phone lays.

Deke grabs her shoulder, pulling her back. "No, you're not."

"Why, Deke?" she snaps. "Did you help him? Will you go to jail too?"

"What is going on? What are you guys talking about?" Becky asks, her blue eyes going back and forth between us. "Deke, what have you done?"

"He didn't do it," Deke says, ignoring Becky's questions.

Shelby narrows her eyes on him. "You'd take his side ..."

"He didn't do it!" Austin snaps. She drops her hands from her face, and they slap down onto the table. She looks up at us. Becky closes her eyes and turns away.

"Fuck." Deke hisses.

My heart stops when I see her. She has three cuts on her face that Shelby has stitched up along her right eye. Her skin bruised and swollen. Her right eye purple.

"You don't know that," Shelby argues. "You said the guy was wearing a black hood. It was dark. And Becky was asleep. It could have been Cole—"

"No," she interrupts her. Then she looks me in the eyes. "Cole is a lot of things, but he's not a coward. If he wanted to hurt me, he would have done it with the lights on, and his eyes on mine. He wouldn't hide."

I hold her stare, but my stomach knots at her words.

"Who did this?" Becky asks as tears well in her eyes.

Austin looks at Deke, then back at me. "I don't know."

"Bullshit! You know. Who the fuck hurt you?" I demand. The shock wearing off. The anger seeping into my veins.

"Cole …"

"Who did this to you?" I snap.

She just stares at me. Her eyes are bloodshot, and they look glazed over, and I wonder if Shelby was able to give her anything for pain since she probably still has alcohol in her system.

I walk over to the table, kneel, and cup her cheek. "Who, sweetheart?"

She sighs. "It was Kellan."

My jaw tightens.

"Why would Kellan want to hurt you?" Shelby asks skeptically.

I stand and start to pace. *He's gonna fucking die.*

"It's not that I don't believe you, Austin," Deke begins. "But can you prove it?"

She nods. "My phone."

"What about it?" I snap, that need for blood growing stronger and stronger. The feel of it on my fingers. The smell of it in the air. It's been too long since I've beat a man with my bare hands.

"He took it."

"Why would he want your phone?" Shelby asks.

"Last night, I told the guys I had insurance in case they tried to fuck me over. Then this morning when I woke up, I took my phone with me to the bathroom. He grabbed my hair and slammed my head into the mirror. I passed out from the hit. When I woke up, my phone was missing."

"He's fucking dead …" I growl.

"Positive?" Deke demands, interrupting me.

She nods.

"That doesn't mean it wasn't Cole …" Shelby points at me.

"Deke and Cole are the only two who know that I have a retina scanner on my phone. They know that they can't get into it. Kellan does not."

I come to a stop and look down at her.

"Whatever he wanted he's not gonna get." She sits back in her chair. "Plus, I'm not dumb enough to keep that shit on my phone."

She stands from the table, and I walk over to help her out, but she pushes me away. "I'm going home to go back to bed."

"I don't think that's a good idea," Deke urges.

She closes her eyes and takes a deep breath. "I'm tired … hungover … and a bit bitchy." They open and narrow on his. "I wanna go …"

"Come with me," I offer.

She looks up at me. "No."

She's still mad at me.

I cup her face, and her eyes search mine, but I still see the hesitation in them. I'm not sure what I can do or say to get her back. If words are even good enough. But I have to try. Especially now. I don't want to hurt her. I have to protect her. I'm all she has.

"Please?" I ask.

She looks away from me, running her hand through her hair.

"Just a place to sleep. I will take you home afterward." *Lie.*

She finally nods. "Okay."

AUSTIN

"Austin?"

I hear my name through the pounding in my head.

"Austin? Oh God, Austin. Wake up."

Hands grab my shoulders, and I feel like I'm in an earthquake.

"Austin? Please …"

"I'm up," I say roughly, wanting the noise to stop. It's too loud.

"You need to go to the hospital."

I open my heavy eyes to see Becky kneeling by me on the bathroom floor. "What …?" The memories come back to me as I stood before the sink and my face being slammed into the mirror.

I lift my hand to my head and hiss in a breath.

"Be careful," she says, grabbing my hand to help me sit up. "There's glass on your face." Sitting up, I bow my head. "What the hell happened?" she demands.

"I'm fine," I say as my head pounds.

"No, you're not. God, Austin we need to get you to the hospital."
I shake my head. "No."

"Yes," she snaps. "I just found you passed out on the bathroom floor. And you need stitches. You probably have a concussion."

"Shelby," I say. She's the only one I wanna see right now. I go to the hospital, and they'll know I've been drinking and am underage. They get the police involved, and I refuse to tell them anything. That's what the fucker wants. He thinks he can play me. I refuse to let him win.

"Hand me my phone."

"Where is it?" she asks, standing.

"On the countertop." I lift my hand to my head again, and it comes back bloody. I rub it between my fingers.

She looks around then shakes her head. "No, it's not."

I release a long breath, closing my eyes and trying not to vomit. My head pounds like a drum, and I feel dizzy. "It's too early to just show up at her house. I'll give it a couple of hours."

I wake up to voices coming from downstairs in the clubhouse. When I sit up, my head still pounds, and my eye is swelling shut.

I should have kept my mouth shut. I thought telling them that I had proof on them would make them back off, but I should have known it wouldn't work with Kellan. The bastard.

I get out of Cole's bed and stand. A wave of dizziness hits me, but I manage to wait it out.

"Why are we here, man?" I hear Bennett ask.

"I'll let you know why when everyone has arrived," Cole tells him.

I pick up his black zip-up hoodie from the end of the bed and put it on because I'm cold. Then I make my way down the stairs, needing a drink.

I notice Cole sitting in one of the lounge chairs talking to Deke who sits in the one next to him.

Shane sits on the couch, and Bennett stands by the table. Cole looks up as I hit the last stair, and he stands when his eyes meet mine.

"Hey, sweetheart," he says softly.

I swallow nervously as he walks over to me. "How do you feel?" he asks, pushing hair behind my ear.

"Fine," I lie, taking a step back from him. I'm still mad at him. I'm still so confused about what I do now. There are so many questions I want to ask him, but I know I'll never get the answers.

He sighs. "You're lying."

"I'm thirsty," I admit.

He nods and pulls away from me to go over to the little bar area.

"What the fuck, Austin?" Bennett snaps. "What the hell happened to you?"

"I'm fine," I say, waving him off. Maybe I should have stayed upstairs.

"Here." Cole hands me a bottle of water.

He cups my face as he leans down to kiss my forehead gently, and my chest tightens. I've held in so much anger for the past two weeks that it's emotionally and physically exhausted me. My eyes start to fill with tears, making his figure blurry, and I hear him sigh.

I refuse to let them fall. To show him that I feel anything for what he has done to me. What he has kept from me.

"What's up, fuckers?" I hear Kellan's voice as the door opens, and my body stiffens, remembering what he did to me this morning. What he could have done to Becky. The commotion woke her up, but Kellan was able to escape before she noticed him. I'm thankful for that. I'd hate myself if he hurt her too.

Cole spins around. "I'm calling it off," he says.

"Calling what off?" Shane asks slowly.

"All of it," he says.

Kellan snorts. "So your ex plaything informs us that she has insurance on us, and you call it off? I say she's bluffing."

That's because the bastard thinks he has the proof. He doesn't. I made sure to delete that shit off my phone for good reasons. He'll never find where I backed it up at.

Cole steps to the right, and Kellan comes into view. His eyes meet mine, and a slow smile spreads across his face when he sees my eye.

"You know … there's a battered woman's shelter at the edge of town who will take you in." He smirks. "Unless you're into that kind of thing. Then by all means, let him beat you."

The room falls silent, and I swallow nervously as I see Cole's body tense and eyes narrow in anger. He glares at Kellan who sits down on the couch. Kellan lifts his chin to me. "I still call bullshit. But if you wanna turn us in, then go ahead." Kellan shrugs. "I dare you to."

I go to open my mouth to tell him that I know what he did, but Cole speaks.

"Fuck it." Then he storms out of the clubhouse.

Deke is the first one to jump up and follow him. I don't wanna be left alone with Kellan, even if Bennett and Shane are in here, so I follow them too.

I shove open the door and walk outside. The sun is starting to set. I must have slept the day away. I needed it.

The door opens behind me, and the guys walk out as well. Cole pops open his trunk and reaches in. I take a step back when he pulls out a black and white baseball bat.

"What are you doing, Cole?" Bennett asks him.

I look over at Deke as he comes to stand next to me. Normally, I would take a step back, but I feel like he's getting close to protect me from Kellan. Not harm me.

Cole doesn't answer. Instead, he walks over to Kellan's blue Corvette and lifts the bat over his shoulder, his grip tightening. Then he swings. It hits the driver's side window, and it shatters into a million pieces.

"What the fuck?" Kellan roars, running over to him.

Deke goes after him and pulls him back.

"What the fuck are you doing, Cole?" Bennett demands.

Cole reaches in through the now busted window and opens the car door. He leans inside it and starts opening and closing compartments. Seconds later, he stands and faces us with my cell phone in his right hand.

"This your cell phone, sweetheart?" he asks me, but he's staring at

Kellan. The bat hangs down by his side.

Kellan breathes heavily as he glares at Cole.

"Yes," I answer.

"Why is her cell in your car?" Shane asks in confusion. "And why is it busted?"

Cole places my crushed cell in the pocket of his jeans and walks over to Kellan and Deke. "You went into her home after the party this morning. Put your hands on her and stole her phone." He arches a brow. "You wanted to delete what she had on you. But you couldn't get the phone unlocked, could you? So you busted it."

"Is this true?" Bennett demands.

Kellan takes a step toward Cole. He raises his hand, stretching out his arm. Kellan comes to a stop when the end of the bat presses against his throat. Kellan fists his hands down by his side as his eyes shoot daggers at Cole. "Go ahead. Beat me with the bat."

Cole smiles, and it's not friendly. "I don't need a bat to hurt you, Kellan." He lowers it and takes a step toward him. "I'm gonna kill you with my bare hands."

Kellan swallows. "She is gonna turn on you."

"I deserve that," he says without hesitation. "And you, you will get what you deserve for touching what is mine."

"You did that to her, Kellan?" Shane asks, pointing at me as if there's another girl here with a black eye.

He smiles. "I did what you all were too afraid to do."

"Jesus!" Bennett hisses, grabbing his hair. "What the fuck were you thinking? You could have killed her."

Kellan laughs darkly. "All of a sudden we care who lives and who dies?" He shakes his head. "We knew going in that we all weren't going to make it out. We started with eight, and already, we're down to five."

"That wasn't Cole's fault." Deke snaps.

He smirks and looks over at me. "Right. It was Bruce's. The man who raped his mother."

Cole's body stiffens. His grip on the bat tightening. And I know he wants nothing more than to knock Kellan's head off right now.

"Kellan …"

"The guy who gave you the two most important women in your life." He pushes his chest into Cole's, cutting off Bennett. "But what you don't see is he has the power to take them both from you." Kellan smiles at him. "I'm not the enemy here, Cole. Bruce Lowes is. And he is going to fuck up your world more than you can ever imagine." He looks over at me and winks. "Enjoy it while you can." Then he walks around Cole and gets into his car before taking off.

Once again, we all stand in silence. Cole stares straight ahead, staring at nothing. Deke runs a hand through his hair. Shane's head falls back, and he closes his eyes as if he's praying to God for something. Bennett stares at me. I look away from him.

"I'm out." Cole finally speaks.

"What? Cole, you can't …" Bennett starts.

"It's over," he says, walking over toward me.

"Kellan's gone," Shane adds. "We'll vote him out."

Cole comes to a stop and turns to face them. "Are you guys not listening? I said I'm out. And that's final." He turns back around and comes up to me. I flinch when he lifts his hand, and his eyes cloud over. "Austin—"

"You can't just quit," Shane interrupts him.

"I can do whatever the fuck I want," he snaps. "Now drop it!" He grabs my right hand and pulls me back into the clubhouse.

I stand awkwardly by the table as he paces back and forth.

The door opens, and Deke walks in. He doesn't acknowledge me. "You know I'll back you a hundred percent."

Cole nods.

"But are you sure this is what you want to do?"

He comes to a stop and looks up at Deke, then at me. "It's over."

I swallow the lump in my throat at his words. As if he's talking about us. But that's crazy because we were never anything. It was all a lie.

I take a step toward them. "Don't do this for me." My voice is rough, and I clear my throat.

"This has nothing to do with you," he snaps.

Deke lets out growl. "Stop lying." He looks at me. "This has everything to do with you."

"Deke!" Cole growls.

He slaps Cole on the back. "It's about time, man." Then he turns and walks out, leaving us alone.

CHAPTER FORTY

COLE

Fuck!

She was right! Not like I doubted her. But finding her phone in Kellan's car made me want to knock his head off his shoulders with that fucking bat.

"Cole?"

I pulled out! That was the right thing to do. It's over. No more dares. No more group. And it means she is safe. Well, for now. Kellan was right that Bruce can take her from me. He can destroy me in a completely different way now. And I know that he wouldn't think twice.

Fuck, I'm so tired of people being right.

"Cole?"

"What?" I snap.

She takes a step back. "Will you take me home?"

I shake my head. "You can stay the night here."

"I can't …"

"We're on spring break." I walk over to her. "And you're safe here. Plus, we need to talk." It's time.

"About what?" She asks nervously.

"Everything," I say simply. "You've earned the truth." Her eyes search mine for any indication I'm lying, but she won't find it this time.

AUSTIN

At my silence, he pulls me over to the couch, and I sit down next to him. "I wanna know about Lilly." There's so much more I want to know, but she is the most important right now.

He nods and takes a deep breath. "I found out Bruce raped my mom when I heard her talking to my father in his office. He blamed my mom. Said that it was her fault. She should have been stronger." He fists his hands in his lap. "I didn't understand what they were talking about exactly because I was only eleven at the time. She tried to leave him, but he wouldn't let her go. He never loved her. He was just sick and twisted and loved the idea of making her stay.

"Anyway, fast forward nine months, and my mom was a week past her due date when Celeste came to my school and pulled me out of class. She told me that my father had called and told her my mother had fallen down at home and was rushed to the hospital. It sent her into labor, and although the baby was okay, there were complications. Blood loss …" He pauses, and my throat starts to tighten. "She didn't make it through surgery. My father didn't want a baby. But his wife had died, and no one knew what Bruce had done. To put the baby up for adoption would make him look bad, so he decided to keep her. I hated my father from then on. For not protecting my mother. For not loving Lilly. To me, she was his daughter. She was the baby of the woman he was supposed to love." He shakes his head. "And I hated Bruce." He looks up at me.

"Then why do you let Lilly go to my father's house so much?" This question has been on my mind. "Knowing what he is capable of," I grind out. I've always known my father to be a sick bastard.

"Celeste was around a lot and helped me more than anyone else was willing to."

"Did she know what Bruce did to your mom?" I ask softly.

He nods. "Yes. She never came out and said it, but she didn't have to." I look down at my hands. "I let Celeste keep her at times, but Bruce was never home when I allowed that. Except with you."

"What?" I frown, looking back up at him.

He cups my cheek. "I didn't tell you about her. And at first, I didn't want you to spend time with her. Afraid Lilly would get attached and it would hurt her when you left." I swallow at that. "But as time passed, I wanted you to spend as much time with Lilly as possible, so I let her go home with you even when Bruce was there because I knew without a doubt that you would protect her, Austin. You didn't need to know she was your sister to keep her safe."

"With my life," I say without thought. I may have not known Lilly was my sister, but I love that little girl. And even when my dad was home, and I had Lilly, he never came around us. Never even looked at her in passing. He acted as if she didn't exist.

He leans in and kisses my forehead. "I know."

Tears start to well in my eyes. "I'm so sorry, Cole. For what Bruce did to your mother." My chest tightens. "I'm so sorry that I didn't know about Lilly sooner. I could have helped ..." My voice cracks. "I could have come back here. I should have ..." I choke on the words.

He reaches out and pulls me to him. I bury my face into his shirt and inhale that scent that I've missed the past two weeks. "It's not your fault, Austin." He kisses my hair. "You didn't know." He sighs. "I was afraid of losing her. To you. To Bruce. Even Celeste held her over my head. She helped me raise her the first few years. I was twelve when she was born and knew nothing about babies. My dad didn't want her and neither did Bruce. But I wanted her. She was part of me." He smiles softly at me. "Part of my mom."

The first tear falls down my cheek. He wipes it away with a small smile. "But you're here now, Austin. And I don't plan on you going anywhere."

"I ..." I pause, not knowing what to say.

"What is it, sweetheart?" he asks softly.

I shake my head and pull away from him. "What is your end game?'

"What?" he asks, standing.

I wipe the tears from my face and look up at him. "What do you want from me?" My heart pounds at those words. That his answer isn't gonna be what I want to hear.

He frowns.

I stand. "No more games, Cole. Now more secrets. And no more lies. Just tell me …" I let out a long breath. "What is it that you want from me?" He's gonna break my heart, and I deserve it because I allowed it. You don't fall in love with a man like him and expect him to feel the same about you. It doesn't work that way.

He cups my face with both of his hands. "I want you, Austin. That is not a lie."

"You want to break me—"

"Not anymore," he interrupts me. "I did want that, yes. But it's no longer enough."

"What does that mean?" I whisper.

He pushes his body into me. He tilts my head back, and he lowers his lips to mine. A simple kiss that takes my breath away. This man has taken so much from me already. I'm not sure I have anything else to give.

"I want you to want me. I want you to need me." His eyes search mine. "Because that's how I feel about you. I'm not the same since I met you. You have bled for me, but I'm starving for you. People say when you meet the one you love, that person can calm you down. Make you better." He shakes his head. "You fucking fan my flames. You make me feel invincible." He sighs heavily. "You deserve better than me," he whispers, placing his head against mine, "but I'm too selfish to let you go."

I give him a soft smile. "I want you just the way you are." He pulls away. I cup his cheek. This man is the devil himself, but I've never been afraid of hell. "And I'm not going anywhere."

He gently kisses my lips. "What about Kellan?" I ask, knowing we have a long way to go. And that he is pissed at me.

"Everything is gonna be all right, Austin. Trust me."

As my eyes search his, I realize just how much I want him to be right. "I trust you, Cole," I say, licking my wet lips, tasting my tears.

He watches the motion and leans forward but comes to a stop with his lips inches from mine. I lean in, closing the distance and pressing mine to his. His fingers slide into my hair, and I moan into his mouth as his tongue meets mine. That familiar feeling that only he can give me starts to build, and I wrap my arms around his neck.

Two weeks of not even looking at him has me worked up.

He pulls away. "Austin, we shouldn't."

God, I've missed him. My body craves him in an unhealthy way.

"I want you," I say breathlessly.

His eyes search mine and then land on my stitches. He gives me a small smile and takes my hand, pulling me up to the loft.

Then his lips are on mine. The next thing I know, he is undressing me.

"Fuck! I've missed you," he growls before nibbling on my lip.

"Me too …" I trail off, sucking in a deep breath. "I want you." I pant as my hands go to his jeans.

CHAPTER FORTY-ONE
COLE

I lie next to her. My heart pounding, and her breathing is still ragged. I turn onto my side and push her hair from her damp face. Her eyes are closed and a soft smile on her lips.

She opens her eyes, and her smile widens. "Who owns this place?" she asks.

I frown.

"You guys spend a lot of time here. Does someone's dad own it?"

"I own it."

Her eyes widen in surprise. "You own it?"

I nod. "When my mother passed, she left Lilly and me each a trust fund. I got access to mine when I turned eighteen and bought this that day. It was abandoned and cheap. The guys and I wanted a place to get away, so it just made sense."

She nods. "When you told me what my dad tried to do to you, I thought that he had something to do with your mother passing."

"The thought crossed my mind for many years," I admit.

"But not anymore?"

I shake my head. "Although I miss her and wish she could have been here to see Lilly grow up, I think it was just something that happened. I was angry about it for a very long time, but it was no one's fault."

She lies down and runs her hand over my chest. "Why did you quit the group?"

"Because it wasn't safe for you, and I knew you wouldn't drop out unless there was no longer a group at all."

"So it's just over?" she asks.

"Yeah," I say with a smile. "It's just over."

"What do we do now?" she wonders.

"We enjoy what's left of our senior year as a real couple."

She gets up and straddles my hips. I place my hands on her bare thighs as she smiles down at me. Even with a bruised eye and stitches in her face, she is still the most beautiful woman I've ever seen.

"Does this mean you're gonna go to prom with me?" she asks.

I laugh. "Yes. That's exactly what it means."

"Guess I better start looking for a red dress then." She wiggles her eyebrows.

I groan. "I love when you wear red."

She gives me her wicked smile that makes my cock hard. "I know." She leans down, giving me a soft kiss.

I pull back. "What are your plans after graduation?"

"Haven't really thought about it. Why?"

I take a deep breath and let it out. "You know when I had you take Lilly to ballet and I was gone the following day? I told you I had something personal to do?"

"How can I forget? That's when Celeste pretended to be sleeping with you."

I ignore that. "I was in Texas."

Her eyes widen. "You flew to Texas?" I nod. "Why?"

"Deke and I have scholarships to the University of Texas. And I needed to see my counselor about housing because I'm taking Lilly with me, and kids can't live in the dorms."

Her eyes fall to my chest. "Oh. I didn't think about Lilly leaving with you."

I place my hand in her hair and force her to look back up at me. "While I was there, I bought a house for Lilly and me." Texas is where I'm going to call home for the rest of my life. I'm gonna go to college there and swim while I get my degree. Then Deke and I are gonna open our own business together. We've had it planned for years.

Her eyes widen once again, but she says nothing.

"And I want you to come with us. I want you to live with me and Lilly."

"Cole … that's …" She licks her lips. "Too much."

"No, it's not." I sit up. "Tell me you'll come with us. Tell me you'll live with us."

"If you want, I can help you with her …"

"No, Austin. You're not understanding me. I want you there to be part of Lilly's life, but I want you there for my life too." I run my hand through her hair. "Move in with me, Austin." I can't imagine my life without her. This amazing woman is everything I never knew I wanted. And in case I had any doubt, the past two weeks without her made me realize just how true that is.

Her dark green eyes start to well up with tears. "I don't know …"

"You dared me to show you a side of me that no one sees. And I have, Austin. Now I'm daring you to give me a chance to be more than the guy who hurt you." I give her a soft smile. "Move in with me and let me show you that I can be what you need."

AUSTIN

Cole and I walk into my father's house. "What do you wanna do today?" he asks me with a smile on his face. It's been two weeks since my birthday, and things have been going great. Too great if you ask me. I've never considered my life to be normal, but things have been just that. Cole and I spent all of spring break together hanging out with Becky and Deke or just chilling at my house with Lilly. My bruised face had healed some by the time we went back to school. Shelby removed the stitches, but the bruises are still visible without makeup. But no one questioned it. Shane and Bennett have been calling Cole, but he keeps their conversations short when he does answer. I think he's mad at them for not throwing Kellan out of the group when he and Deke first suggested it. And as for Kellan—he's been everywhere this last week. Over spring break, it was easy to avoid him, but now that school is back in session, not so much. He's everywhere I look and always smiling at me. It gives me the creeps and pisses Cole off. And I hate that I'm always looking over my shoulder. When I'm not in school, I always have the Taser on me, prepared to use it at any given second.

"Let's take Lilly to the zoo," I offer.

He nods. "Sounds good to me."

"Austin? Is that you?" I hear Celeste call out.

Instead of answering, I walk down the hall, Cole's hand in mine, and enter the living room. I come to a halt when I see she's not alone.

Cole's hand tightens on mine. "Mom?" I shriek. "What the hell are you doing here?"

I never did respond to her text she sent me on my birthday. And she never sent me another one.

She smiles brightly at me. Her green eyes go to my hand in Cole's, then she looks him up and down before her eyes return to me. They trace over my face, and I square my shoulders, knowing she can see the faint bruise. We just got back from spending the night at his clubhouse, and I didn't put any makeup on. She allowed Phillip to hit me, but he also hit her. I'm sure she thinks Cole did this to me.

Celeste clears her throat and pushes her blond hair behind her ear nervously. "Your mother wanted to come and give you the good news in person," she says.

"Good news?" I ask arching a brow.

My mother smiles brightly and holds out her left hand. "We got married."

My eyes go to Phillip for the first time as he sits on the couch next to my mother. He doesn't smile at me; instead, his eyes take in my face. My freshly fucked hair and lack of clothing. I'm wearing Cole's black zip-up hoodie and a pair of cotton shorts and tennis shoes. That's it. No shirt underneath and no bra, which is why it is zipped all the way up to my neck. Cole ripped both off me last night.

Cole takes a step forward, jerking on my hand, reminding me he is here. I pull him to a stop.

"When did this happen?" I ask, trying to figure out why she's here. Why she thought I would need to know this. I couldn't care less what they do. You would think she already knew that.

"Two weeks ago." She claps her hands. "On St. Paddy's day."

I'm not surprised.

"You married this piece of shit on your daughter's birthday?" Cole growls, finally speaking.

My mother narrows her eyes on him, and Phillip stands, bowing out his chest, thinking he's the superior man in this room. *He's not.* "I don't know who you are, son, but I'd suggest you not talk to her mother that way."

Cole snorts. "I'm not your son, and she's sure as hell not a mother to her."

My mother shoots to her feet. "Who the hell is this, Celeste?" she demands.

"His name is Cole, and he's my boyfriend," I snap.

Celeste runs a hand through her hair. "I think it's time you and Phillip go." She clears her throat. "You got what you were promised."

"Promised?" Cole questions.

I don't care what they are talking about. I just want them gone.

Phillip chuckles, throwing his arm over my mother's shoulders. "It's adult business, *son.* You wouldn't understand." Phillip looks at me. He stares at my eye again and smirks. "Guess I trained you right." Then he looks at Cole and winks.

"Out!" Celeste snaps.

I stand frozen to my spot as they walk past us and down the hall. Celeste follows them out and shuts the door behind them.

"What the fuck was that?" Cole demands, letting go of my hand.

Celeste joins us once again and sighs. "It's nothing—"

"Bullshit!" he interrupts her, making me jump. "Why the hell were they here and what were they promised?"

She looks at me and then down at the floor.

"I don't want to know," I say softly.

Cole looks at me, and his features soften. "Austin ..."

"I don't care, Cole. Don't you see? She got what she wanted. She got rid of me, and she got him to marry her." Then I turn, walk out of the room, and head up the stairs to my bedroom. I sit down on the end of the bed and pull my cell out of his pocket, going to my mom's number. I hover over it for a few seconds, trying to remember a time when she was actually a mother to me. When she hugged me. Kissed me. Tucked me in. Any time that she actually acted like she cared about my well-being. And I come up with nothing.

I delete her number as the door opens. Cole walks in and kneels in front of me. "I gotta go," he says, pushing some hair from my face.

"Where are you going?" I ask. "I thought we were gonna take Lilly to the zoo?"

He nods. "Later. I got something I have to go do." Standing up to his full height, he leans over and kisses me on the forehead. His phone starts to ring in the pocket of his jeans, and he pulls it out. I see *Deke* flash across it. He silences it. "Why don't you go and get Lilly and then meet me at the clubhouse," he offers, and I nod.

"Here." I stand and remove his hoodie. His eyes go to my naked chest, and his hands grab my hips.

"Are you trying to distract me?" he asks roughly.

"No," I say honestly. "Just thought you would want it back."

He leans down and kisses my cheek. Then his eyes meet mine. I wait for him to give me something—some indication of where he is going or why Deke is calling him—but he doesn't. Some things about Cole will never change.

He turns and walks out, and I sit back down, knowing that deleting my mother's phone number was pointless. She won't be calling me anymore anyway, but I'm okay with that. Like Cole said, she was never my mother.

I'm pulling a shirt over my head when there's a knock on the door. "Come in," I call out.

The door opens, and Celeste peeks her head in. "May I speak to you?" she asks.

"Do I have a choice?" I reply.

She sighs heavily. "I wanna explain myself," she says entering. "I haven't really had the chance …"

"You've been avoiding me," I argue.

She nods once. "I have, and I'm sorry." She swallows. "I wanna explain about Kellan too …"

"I don't care about Kellan," I growl, interrupting her.

"He's just worried!"

"Worried?" I snort. "About what?"

"About you and Cole."

I don't respond to that because she has no idea what is going on between us. And she doesn't need to know.

Running a hand through her hair, she takes a step farther into my room. "I'm sorry that Cole hurt you."

"He didn't do it."

"Austin, I know you think he loves you, but he doesn't." She shakes her head as she looks me up and down as if I'm not good enough for him.

"This has nothing to do with love," I grind out.

Her brown eyes soften, and her look turns to pity. "You were lucky this time. But next time …"

"Kellan did this to me," I say, pointing at my face, unable to listen to this anymore.

She shakes her head. "No. He wouldn't do that."

Unbelievable. "Cole found my phone in Kellan's car."

Her hands fist. "If Cole found your phone in his car, then it was because Cole planted it there."

"Jesus." I hiss. "He has you brainwashed."

"Kellan is trying to help you. Cole wants to hurt you," she shouts, finding her anger. "That's why Kellan wants you out of the group. He's mad at you, but he's trying to protect you in the long run."

I shake my head at her words. She says Kellan wants me out of the group. But when Cole tried to get me thrown out, Kellan was the only one who wanted me to stay. So either Kellan hasn't filled her in on what's going on or he's lying to her. "You have no clue what you are talking about," I say, not wanting to argue with her.

"You don't know what Cole is capable of."

Oh, I do! "Apparently, I don't know what any of you are capable of because I would have never thought you'd call out my boyfriend's name while you fucked his friend," I snap.

Her eyes darken, and her lips thin. She takes a step toward me. "Don't push me, Austin."

"What are you gonna do, Celeste? Ship me back to my mom's? I'm eighteen now. You can kick me out, but then you'd have to explain to my father why I no longer live in *his* house." I smile. "And I don't think you want him to know about Kellan, do you?"

"You little bitch!" she snaps.

"Why did you bring me here?" I ask, ignoring her anger. "You guys are all full of secrets and lies. So why bring in someone who has the power to expose you all?"

She gives a dark laugh. "You don't hold that kind of power."

I take a step toward her. "I've got more than you."

She lets out a growl and spins around. Storming out, she slams my door behind her, not giving me an answer.

"Lilly?" I call out, entering Cole's father's house an hour later. After he left and I had my not so productive talk with Celeste, I relaxed in a long shower and took my time getting ready.

"She's in her room," a woman with jet black hair and just as dark eyes says. Blanche is always smiling.

"How is Sophia doing?" I ask about her daughter.

Blanche and I have become close the past couple of weeks. I found out that she has been with the family since before Lilly was born. She used to help take care of Cole as well.

"She's doing well. She made the choir at church," she answers with pride.

"That's awesome. Tell her congratulations."

She nods, and I make my way upstairs. I open her door and step into her pink room. "Lilly?" I call out.

"In here." I hear her across the hall.

I walk into Cole's room. "Where at?" I ask with a chuckle, wondering if we are playing hide and seek.

"Here," her little voice calls out.

I find her in his large walk-in closet, sitting on the floor. "What are you doing in here?" I ask, sitting down next to her.

"I can't find Hippo."

Her favorite stuffed bunny. "Where did you have him last?" Doubt it was in Cole's closet.

"I gave it to Cole to wash." She pouts. "I spilled milk on him."

"Maybe he's down in the laundry room," I offer.

"Maybe," she says as tears spring to her brown eyes.

I get up on my hands and knees. "Here, I'll help you look in here first. Okay? Then we will go downstairs and look." I pat her knee as a tear runs down her face. "We'll find him."

I look around the closet, not really knowing where it could be. It's pretty clean. Not like a lot of things are lying on the floor that it could be hiding under.

My eyes catch sight of a brown box sitting back in the corner. It doesn't have anything written on it, but it looks out of place. I reach out for it and then pull my hand back, biting my lip. *Shouldn't snoop.* As far as I know, there's some little black book in there with all the girls he's ever slept with. That's one thing I don't want to find.

"I tried calling him," she says her voice still soft.

"How about I try?" Leaving the box alone, I pull out my new phone and press call on **Shark**.

It begins to ring, and after the fifth time, it goes to voicemail. "You've reached Cole …" I hang up and look at her. "He'll call us back."

She hangs her head and stands up. "I'm gonna check my room again."

I stand too and go to follow her, but the box gets my attention again. Looking back over my shoulder, I make sure Lilly is gone and bend down, removing the lid.

It's full of pictures. I pull a stack out and look through them. They're of Cole when he was younger. He looks around Lilly's age. He's swimming in an indoor pool. There are some of him sitting at a kitchen table with boys his age all around him. I linger on the other kids to see if I recognize them as the guys in the group. I'm not sure how long they have all been friends. In the next one, he is leaning over blowing out a number seven candle. I shuffle through a few more but stop when I come to one with him and an older blond. She's pretty. Dark blue eyes and a kind smile. She stands next to him with a proud smile on her face, and he holds a gold medal around his neck. A swimming pool in the background. This must be his mother. And for some reason, she looks familiar. I go through a couple of more and come to a stop at a picture of Cole, along with three other boys and one girl. The boys are smiling, one mid laugh, but the girl is not happy. She has her arms crossed over her chest and a scowl on her face. Her right hip is pushed out, and her green eyes are narrowed as she glares at the camera.

"Don't let her play," the boy says to the other one.

"I don't wanna play with you anyway," I say, reaching out and shoving the boy with the blue eyes.

He growls and shoves me back, pushing me down onto my butt. They laugh at me before they turn around and walk off.

It's me! The girl in the picture is me! I remember now. My father had a get-together with his friends, and I was the only girl there, and the boys wouldn't let me play their stupid game.

"I don't wanna play with her," the little boy says with his lips pulled back.

"Cole, that's not very nice," the pretty blonde says, bending down to our level.

"So. She poured my juice out, Momma," he whines.

"That's because you threw dirt at me," I say.

"Cole Ethan Reynolds," she scolds. "You tell her you're sorry right now."

He crosses his arms over his chest. "Sorry," he growls.

She pats his back and nods her head at him. "Now you play nice."

He watches her walk off, and then he turns back to face me. "I'm not sorry."

"You will be," I tell him.

His blue eyes narrow on me. "No, I won't." He yanks the Barbie out of my hand and rips her head off and then throws her head down into the dirt, stepping on it. Then he tosses her body out to the grass. "Have fun playing with that now."

I place the picture in my back pocket with a smile on my face. Even back then, Cole Reynolds was a pain in my ass.

"I found Hippo!" Lilly says excitedly, bouncing back into the closet. She hugs him tightly to her chest wearing a big smile on her face.

"Ready to go?" I ask.

She nods happily and reaches out for me. I pick her up in my arms and kiss her soft cheek. "Let's get going then, princess."

I pull up to the clubhouse and see Cole's car is parked outside. Lilly and I walk in hand in hand, and he stands from the couch. "Hello, girls," he says, holding his arms out. Lilly runs to him, and he picks her up, giving him a hug.

"I thought I lost Hippo," she tells him.

"What? I had put him on your bed," he tells her with a frown.

She nods. "I found him on the floor."

"He must have fallen off."

Lilly hugs him as I look him over. Earlier, he was dressed in blue jeans and a white long-sleeve t-shirt. Now he's dressed in a short sleeve black t-shirt and his black jeans. His hair is damp as if he just got out of the shower.

He sets her down, and his eyes meet mine. "Ready to go?" he asks, stepping into me.

My eyes search him for a hint of where he went or what he did. But his stare gives nothing away. He never does. "If you are," I answer.

He nods. "I am."

Then he takes my hand, and I look down at them to see his knuckles busted and dried blood. "Cole …"

"Shh," he whispers against my lips. His eyes go back and forth between mine. "What did I tell you, sweetheart?"

I frown. *What did he tell me?* "When?"

He smiles softly at me. "That time I came and saw you and you were swimming in the pool."

"That no one would ever touch me again," I say, remembering it.

He nods, sliding a hand in my hair. "That was a promise I'll never break, Austin." Then he kisses me gently.

When he pulls away, I pull the picture out of my back pocket. I hold it against my chest so he can't see it just yet. "I went through the box in your closet."

His eyes meet mine, and he tilts his head in confusion. "Box ...?"

"The one hiding in the corner. And I found something."

"What is it?"

CHAPTER FORTY-TWO
COLE

She turns the picture around, and I look down at it to see Deke, Eli, Bennett, and me. We were young. No older than seven. Maybe eight. There's a girl in the picture. We're all smiling, and Deke is laughing. The little girl looks pissed. She has her brown hair up in a ponytail, and her green eyes are narrowed in anger at the camera.

I look up at her and then back down at the picture. "Who …?" My eyes shoot back to hers, and she smiles at me.

I turn around, walking away from the girl that my mommy is making me play with.

We don't want her here.

I had to play with her yesterday too without my friends, and we swam. She wouldn't stop talking about dolls.

I fist my hands. My mommy made me apologize. But I'm not sorry. She wasted my juice. And she ripped Deke's shirt when she yanked on it earlier while we played tag. Celeste made us let her play with us.

"Cole?" Deke calls out to me from the swing set.

I go to walk over to him, but I'm shoved to the ground. "Hey!" I turn over onto my back to look up at the girl.

She points her finger down at me. "You ruined my doll!" she screams.

"Austin?" my daddy's best friend, Bruce, hollers at her as he comes over to us. "Did you just shove him?"

She crosses her arms over her chest. "He ruined my Barbie." She huffs.

He lets out a growl and then grabs her by her arm. She cries out, and he lowers his face down to hers. He says something to her and then yanks her away. She softly cries as he drags her back into the house.

"That was you." I say, looking at her wide-eyed.

She nods once, smiling. "That was me. You owe me a Barbie, by the way."

I step into her and cup her cheek. The smile drops off her face. She was there in my closet all those years. I never looked at those pictures. My mother had them in her and my father's closet. After she died, he threw all her stuff out so his whores wouldn't see it, but I kept that box. I never got into it because it was too painful to see them. There are some of my mom and me, and I hated that I would never have any to show to Lilly of them together. I almost burned them so many times. "I owe you a lot of things." I say honestly, and she frowns. Bruce had yanked her into the house that day, and I never saw her again. He had shipped her back to her mom's. Back then, I was thankful. We hated her. She was a girl. We thought they had cooties and couldn't play with us. But what if I hadn't have got her in trouble? Would she have stayed with Bruce and Celeste? If so, her mother's sick boyfriend would have never touched her. Hit her. She would have found out about Lilly eventually, and I would have had her all along.

"Cole?" She gets my attention. I blink. "I'm sorry if you're mad I went through your box …"

"I'm not mad." Far from it. I lean in and kiss her.

Things were different after I quit the group. Austin and I seemed to be in our own little world all the time. We spent every moment we could together and with Lilly. She and Becky brought Lilly to our meets. Blanche cut back, and Austin took her to school and picked her up.

We hung all over each other at school, but that was nothing new. It was just no longer for show. It was because we just wanted to touch one another. Kiss one another. She spent nights at my father's house. He never said a word about it and neither did Celeste. I think she's going through some midlife crisis. Even at her young age. Kellan's drinking a lot and fucking his way through the high school. So my guess is that whatever they had is on the rocks.

"So you girls ready for tomorrow night?" Deke asks them as we sit at our table in the cafeteria.

Austin nods, and Becky smiles. "What are we gonna do afterward?" she asks.

I place my arm over Austin's shoulders. "I don't know about you guys, but we are going back to the clubhouse." We've spent a lot of time there lately, and I have never been happier that I bought that run-down barn.

Becky frowns. "You can't not party on prom night."

"Oh, we're gonna party," I say, leaning over and burying my face into Austin's neck.

Austin chuckles and pushes me away. "I agree with Becky. There are a ton of parties going on. We should go to one."

"Why would I go to a party with people I don't even like when I can spend the evening alone with you?" I am completely obsessed with Austin Lowes. Pathetic, right? But I wasn't all that surprised when I was finally able to admit it to myself. The whole damn school knows it too. Good thing I don't give a fuck what anyone thinks.

"Because it's our senior prom, and that's what we do," Becky answers.

I look at Deke. "Help me out."

"I already told Becky we can do whatever she wants to do," he says, leaning back in his chair.

I sigh. "Pathetic."

Austin hits me in the ribs, and I cough like it hurt. "I think it's sweet that he puts her wants first."

I smile. "We both know that I always give you what you want first."

"Cole!" she snaps, making us all laugh.

"Fine," I say, throwing up my hands. "We can go to a party." Becky claps excitedly. "But you're staying the night with me."

She leans over, kissing my lips softly. "I guess. Since you asked nicely and all."

I grip the back of her neck. "You love that I don't ask." Then I kiss her how I want. Possessively.

"Cole?"

I pull away and look up to see Bennett and Shane sitting down at the table. I guess you can say we made up, but we're still not how we were. "What's up?" I ask.

"I was just doing some research, and it seems that Bruce has bought out Jerrold and Jeff's company."

"How is that possible?" Austin asks. "They're dead."

He nods. "Yes, but it seems that Jerrold had sold Bruce Jeff's shares after he went missing."

"How are we just finding this out?" Deke asks. "Jeff has been dead for three months. Jerrold a little over a month."

"I'm not sure why it took him so long to take over but …" He pauses.

"But what?" I ask.

"I liquidated all of his accounts. Bruce has to know that the money is gone. When I was done with it, there was nothing left."

"Can he trace it back to you?" Austin asks worried.

He shakes his head. "I covered my tracks, but that doesn't mean he won't be suspicious. Especially given how Jerrold died."

Jerrold's death was ruled a tragic accident. *Tragic, my ass!* But Austin's father was still suspicious. Too many things were happening to people who he was doing business with. I have no doubt that he will eventually start to connect the dots. But we will be long gone by then.

"So what do we do?" she asks him.

"I'm still doing my homework. At the moment, there is nothing we can do. I just wanted to let you all know." He nods. I look over at Austin and open my mouth when he speaks again. "Can I talk to you, Cole?" He gets up, not even waiting for my reply.

"I'll be right back." I sigh and get up, following him out of the cafeteria and into the empty hall. "What is it?" I ask when I see him leaning against a locker.

"The final dare."

"What about it?"

"We need to do it."

"No—"

"Just hear me out," he interrupts me.

"Austin is no longer a pawn in this game," I growl. "I won't use her to get back at Bruce." Then I turn my back to him and start to walk back into the cafeteria.

"He's gonna kill her."

I come to a stop and spin back around to face him. "Bennett …"

"We both know what he is capable of. And how much he hates you." He runs a hand through his hair. "Everyone in this city knows that you love Austin."

I swallow at that. I no longer deny it, but we still haven't said it. We've only got less than a month of school left, and then she is moving with me to Texas. Her agreeing to that was better than hearing the words *I love you*. After all, they're just words. Her actions say more than they could ever mean.

"What are you getting at, Bennett?" I snap.

"I'm trying to tell you that even he knows you're not faking it anymore. He already tried to kill you once and failed. This time, he won't go for you. He'll go for her. And he'll succeed."

"What do you suggest I do?" I growl.

"Let her go."

I shake my head. "That risks putting her in danger."

"She's already a target, Cole."

"I said no, Bennett."

He sighs as if disappointed in me.

"But we can do the final dare," I say, taking in a deep breath.

"We'll just change it up."

"And Kellan?"

"What about him?" I snap at the sound of his name.

"Do we bring him back in, or do we leave him out?"

The final dare was decided before Austin ever entered my life, but even now, having her doesn't change the plan. Bruce must die. Especially since he tried to kill me. He can't get away with that, and I can't let him touch Austin. I'd die protecting her.

This dare was the one dare that was the exception. Just like I told her Jeff was. We didn't need to draw this one. We knew what we were gonna do before senior year even started.

"I don't trust him," I decide to say.

He nods. "It's your call."

I walk back into the cafeteria and sit down next to Austin. She looks over at me. "Everything okay?" she asks.

I nod and lie. "Yeah."

AUSTIN

"Your dress is gorgeous," I say, looking over at Becky as we stand in my bedroom. She chose a strapless champagne mermaid dress. It shows off her thin size and flares out at the bottom. She loves to watch it flare out when she twirls.

"Thank you." She smiles. "When are you gonna get dressed?" she asks looking at Cole's zip-up hoodie that I still wear and yoga pants.

"As soon as I finish my makeup." I lean over and line my lips with the deep red liner and then fill them in to match.

A hard knock sounds on my door, and I look over at it frowning. Cole never knocks, and Celeste stays clear of me. "Come in," I say.

My father enters, and I straighten to my full height. His dark brown eyes have their usual look of impatience in them. "Becky, I need to speak to Austin," he tells her.

"Sure, sir." She nods once and then ushers out of the room.

I turn to face him, giving him my full attention. We don't speak much, and I prefer it that way. I still haven't told Celeste that the thing I had been told was that Lilly was my half-sister. And after the secret she told me, I decided to keep my mouth shout about it. My father already tried to hurt Cole once. But no one knows the exact reason. We could guess all day long, but that's not enough. There was a time I wouldn't have cared what happened to Cole, but things change. People change. He and Lilly have become the most important people in to me, and I refuse to give him any more power than the bastard already has over people in my life.

"I wanna talk to you about your future," he states.

"Can't it wait until another time?" I ask, turning my back to him and toward the mirror.

"No," he growls. "I leave tomorrow for New York and will be gone for a few weeks. I would like to get this out of the way before I leave. It will almost be graduation when I return."

I refrain from smiling, knowing how close we are to graduation. How close I am to getting the hell out of here.

He doesn't wait for me to give him the green light. "What are your plans after graduation?"

"I'm not sure," I lie.

He sighs. "College?"

"Most likely." Honestly, I have no clue what I want to do with my life besides be with Cole and Lilly. I've never been one to plan because plans never seem to work out. Life happens, and things get in the way.

"Well … where would you like to go?" he asks.

I slowly spin back around to face him. My eyes narrowed in suspicion. "I haven't decided." Another lie.

He nods as if he believes me, but his dark eyes say otherwise. "What about the University of Texas?" he asks.

My heart starts to pound in my chest, and I swallow nervously.

"It's a great school," he continues at my silence. "They're ranked very high in swimming."

How does he know? Cole and I haven't told anyone except for Deke and Becky, and that's only because we trust them. They would never tell another soul.

"Anyway." He reaches into the pocket of his suit jacket and pulls out a folded-up piece of paper. It's a check. "I decided since I didn't get you anything for your birthday that I would help you out with college."

I thought Celeste had said they got me a trip for my birthday? Doesn't matter, I won't be using it.

He reaches out his right hand. I just stare at the check in it. He shakes it a little. "Go ahead."

I don't move because I don't know what he's up to. The guys aren't the only sharks in this town. They grew up in an ocean full of them.

"I'll just leave it here." He lays it on my bed and straightens his tie, then turns around and walks out.

It's been two hours since my father gave me the check in my bedroom. I shoved it in a drawer without even looking at it. Afraid to see what he wrote on it. As far as I know, it could say anything from ten dollars to a hundred thousand dollars. Reading it would make him think I am actually considering his offer. I'm not.

"You okay?" Becky asks for the fifth time.

"Yes." I continue to lie, running my hands down my dress.

"Red is your color," she says, and I smile, knowing that's how Cole feels.

"Thank you," I say.

The doorbell rings, and Becky smiles. "I'll go and get it." She runs out of my room.

Closing my eyes, I take a deep breath. I need to clear my head. Forget about my father and this game he is suddenly playing with me. He hasn't said more than ten words to me in three months, and now he is giving me money to go to college? The same college my boyfriend just happens to be going to? He knows. He has to. But how? Does he know that Lilly is going too? Would Liam try to stop her from going with Cole? I don't see why he would.

I open my eyes to see Cole standing in my room. Those blue eyes running up and down my dress. Like before, they are still clouded, but I know what's inside him. His heart. His soul. Cole and I may not have a traditional relationship, but I wouldn't trade him for anything. He's mine. And I'm his. It's the only thing I've ever been sure of in my life.

"Hey, sweetheart," he says, coming up to me. His hand cups my cheek.

"Hey, baby," I say, and he smiles.

"You look gorgeous." He lowers his lips to mine. "Just like I knew you would."

"You too," I say, running my hands up his black tux with a red tie to match my dress. The man could wear anything and bring me to my knees.

His eyes search mine, and he frowns. "What's wrong?"

"Nothing," I answer.

He lets out a long breath. "You know I hate it when you lie to me."

I roll my eyes. "It's nothing …"

"Austin."

"I spoke to my father earlier," I say, giving up.

"And?"

"And it was weird."

"How?" he urges.

"He asked me about my future. If I was planning to go to college. I lied, but he seemed to know that."

He chuckles. "Well, you are an awful liar."

My eyes narrow. "He then went on to tell me that the University of Texas was a good school. Had high rankings for swimming." His laughter dies. "Then he tried to hand me this check." I storm over to my dresser and yank the drawer open. I hold it up.

He walks over to me and snatches it out of my hand. Opening it, he glares down at it. "He gave you this?" I nod. "Tonight?"

"About two hours ago." He pulls his cell out of his tux and places it to his ear. "Who are you calling?" I ask.

"Bennett."

"Why?"

He hands me the check, and I read over it. It's made out to me for fifty thousand dollars. But it's Celeste's handwriting.

"Hey, man, I need a favor," he says turning his back to me. "Those accounts for JJ's Properties. I need you to check them again," he orders.

"What is that?"

He doesn't answer me.

"You sure?" he questions and then nods to himself. "Okay. Thanks." He hangs up his phone just as my bedroom door swings open.

Deke and Becky walk in. "What's taking so long?" he asks.

Cole holds up the check. "Bruce gave this check to Austin. Fifty grand to go to college."

"That was nice of the bastard." Deke snorts.

"To the University of Texas," Cole adds, and Deke's eyes narrow. "And the best part. It is a check from JJ's Properties."

Deke's eyes widen. "Are you serious?"

"Why does that matter?" I ask, my eyes going back and forth between them.

"Because …" Cole turns to face me. "JJ's Properties is the company that Jerrold and Jeff owned. And Bennett just checked and informed me that only twenty-three cents remain in the accounts. Combined."

CHAPTER FORTY-THREE

COLE

Why would he give her a check that isn't good? Why give her a check at all? He's fucking with her, but why? She's lived here for four months now, and he's ignored her ninety percent of the time. What's changed?

I know the answer to that question—me. Just like Bennett said, the whole city knows how I feel about her. And the whole city knows that Bruce hates me.

I take the check back from her and fold it up before placing it in my pocket of my tux.

"Let's go." I take her hand.

"What does that mean?" she asks, worry in her voice. "Why would he give me a check that wouldn't clear?"

"I don't know," I answer.

"Because he's a fucking bastard," Deke growls.

We start down the stairs. "Cole …"

I stop and turn to face her. "Don't worry about it, sweetheart. I'm gonna find out."

She nods, but I see the hesitation in her green eyes. She doesn't believe me, but what Austin Lowes doesn't know is that I'm not going to give up.

Austin was quiet during dinner. The girls chose a seafood restaurant that recently opened. I thought it would help cheer her up, but it didn't. I can see her mind working by the way she stares off into space. And I hate not knowing what the hell Bruce is up to.

By the time we get to the school, she's a little better. Her smiles seem to be real, and she is actually making eye contact with me.

"Wow," Becky says as we walk into the gymnasium. "They went all out." She tilts her head back and looks up at the decorations.

"Yeah. Pretty," Austin agrees.

They usher us into a line, and one by one, each couple goes and stands in front of a backdrop to have their picture taken.

Once done, I look up to see Bennett and Shane walking over toward us. Both solo. "Where are your dates?" I ask.

"In the bathroom," Shane answers.

Deke and Becky join us just finishing up with their pic. "Can we speak to you guys for a second?" Bennett asks.

My jaw tightens. I know why he wants me alone. He wants to talk about the check Bruce gave to Austin. I'm not in the mood. "No," I say.

I grab Austin's hand in mine and take a step away from them, but it's Deke's hand that lands on my chest. "It'll just be for a second."

My eyes narrow on his. He planned this. He was texting away on his phone while in the limo to the restaurant, and Becky asked him several times who he was talking to, but he never answered her. Now, I know why. "Deke—"

"Go ahead, babe," Austin interrupts me. "Becky and I will wait right here." She pulls away from me and turns, talking to Becky.

The guys all walk back toward the door we all just came through, and I follow them with fisted hands.

"What?" I demand as we enter the silent hallway. "This better not be about Austin and me."

"It is." Bennett starts. "You need to step back."

"I've already told you no."

"Cole," Deke starts, "trust me, out the four of us, I know the most how hard it would be to step away from someone you love, but this is the only thing left to do at this point."

"It's not!" I snap.

"It is," he argues. "Bruce is playing a game with her that we don't know. Kellan has gone off the deep end. He's drinking all the time, missing school, and he no longer gives a fuck about swimming. He never comes to practice. If he doesn't wake the fuck up, he's gonna end up losing his scholarship."

"I don't give a fuck what he loses."

"He has to be working with Bruce." Shane finally speaks. "No one else would tell Bruce that you guys plan on going to University of Texas together."

"How do you fucking know what we're gonna do?" I demand, turning to him. "We only told Deke and Becky." I spin back around to face Deke. "You been telling everyone?" I shout.

"Cole!" Bennett raises his voice, and I look at him. "I put two and two together when you called me about the check her father wrote her."

"Well …"

"Everyone knows where you got your scholarship from. I'm sure everyone just assumes she would be going with you."

"I didn't think of that," I admit with a grunt.

"That's because you're too close. Take a step back," Bennett goes on.

"And what if he hurts her?" I shake my head. "I can't take that chance."

"Bruce is about to leave for New York for a few weeks. He can't do anything to her while he's gone. But Kellan … we think that's when he'll make his move."

"Cole …" Shane swallows nervously.

"What?" I snap.

"That dare that she drew … It wasn't mine." I open my mouth to ask what the fuck he's talking about, but he continues. "Kellan had me write that dare down. That's how he knew it belonged to me when you asked him what it meant."

I step into him, but Deke yanks me back. "You fucking …"

"I wasn't gonna let him hurt her," he says quickly.

I shrug Deke off me and run a hand through my hair. The dare doesn't matter. She isn't doing it. She's out of the group. "So what do you expect him to do?" I ask at a loss.

Deke shrugs. "It's hard to tell. At this point, I think he still wants to hurt you, and he will go through Austin to accomplish that. We all know he's not gonna harm Celeste. But …"

"But what?" I demand.

He looks at me. "But if you step back, he might not touch Austin at all."

"That's a big gamble," I snap.

"I agree, but what other choice do we have?" Deke places his hand on my shoulder. "You need to decide right now, Cole. What's more important? Spending the next month with her or the rest of your life. Because we all have the same feeling that you won't get both."

AUSTIN

"Well, that didn't last long," Becky says as she stares over at Bryan and his prom date. It's not Kaitlin.

"I told him he only had to date her for a couple of weeks. I figured by then the dare would have blown over."

She shakes her head with a laugh. "Those two weeks were a fake relationship, and she still managed to cheat on the guy. No wonder he dumped her before."

Yep. I blackmailed him to go back out with her, and she still managed to fuck him over. I think they're made for one another.

"Hey, babe," Becky says as the guys come back to join us.

I give Cole a smile, but he doesn't return it.

"You okay?" I ask, rubbing his upper arm.

He doesn't respond.

"Who wants to have a little fun?" Deke asks, pulling a silver flask out of his pocket.

Becky laughs. "What is in there?"

"Fireball." He winks at me. "I know how much you two like this shit." He nods over at the table. "Go get a glass of punch."

I pull away from Cole and walk over to the table with the white tablecloth over it. "What's going on with Cole?" Becky asks, filling a cup three-quarters full of punch.

"Who knows?" I sigh. I didn't think he was all that upset about what my father did, but maybe I was wrong.

I fill myself a cup, and we make our way back over to them. Deke takes a quick look around to see if any teachers are around before he unscrews the lid and pours some into my cup. Prom started over an hour ago, but we were in no hurry to be the first ones here. We don't plan on staying long anyway. We all decided last night just to make an appearance and then bail. The best thing about prom are the after parties anyway. If we wanted to dance, we could all use our fake IDs and hit the clubs in surrounding towns.

I twirl my cup around to mix up the drink and take a sip. I hiss in a breath at the taste. Fruit punch and cinnamon isn't the best combination, but it's all we got at the moment. "Want a drink?" I offer Cole. Not like he is driving tonight. The guys got us a limo.

He doesn't even look at me, just shakes his head.

I turn to fully face him. "Are you mad at me?"

He looks down at me. "No." His reply comes out flat.

"I haven't said anything," I say just in case he thinks I have.

He sighs heavily. "I didn't say that you did."

"Then why are you giving me the cold shoulder?" I take another drink.

His eyes narrow on me. "I'm not."

"You are," I argue, taking another drink.

He reaches out and takes the cup from my hand. I protest as he hands it off to Bennett. He looks at it for a long second before he takes a drink of it. The look he makes afterward lets me know he won't be drinking any more of it.

"Here with You" by Sick Puppies starts to play, and Cole grabs my now free hand and starts dragging me toward the dance floor.

"Cole?" I whisper harshly, trying to dig my heels into the gym floor. They just slide. "Cole." He comes to a stop and spins me around to face him. "No one else is dancing, babe." I look around nervously as everyone starts to stare at us. The gym is packed full of students, but most of them huddle against the walls or are in line for their picture to be taken.

"I don't give a fuck what they are doing," he says flatly. Then he cups my cheek. "I wanna dance with you."

A soft smile spreads across my face. "I'm surprised you know how to dance," I say truthfully.

His wraps his right arm around my side, pulling me closer to him with his hand on my back. His left hand takes my right. "My mother taught me," he says, making the smile fall off my face.

"I'm sorry," I whisper.

"Don't be." He lowers his head to nuzzle my neck. "You're the only woman I've ever danced with besides her."

I smile as I pull my hand away from his and wrap them both around his neck. Other couples join us on the dance floor, and I catch sight of Deke and Becky coming to dance next to us. She laughs at something he says before he pulls her into him.

Cole pulls his face away from my neck and looks down at me. I give him a soft smile. He brings us to a stop and cups my cheek. My smile slowly drops off my face and turns into a frown. "Tell me what's wrong." I look over at Deke quickly, but he has his tongue down Becky's throat. "What did the guys want to talk about?"

"Nothing important."

"Cole …"

"Don't, Austin." He slides his hand into my hair. I wore it down for this reason—so he can run his fingers through it. He tips my head back. "Let's just enjoy this night. Okay?"

My eyes search his, and I don't like what I see, but I say, "Okay." He lowers his face to mine and kisses me.

I wake up with a pounding headache and sore body. I moan, rolling over and digging my head into the pillow.

"You okay?" I hear Cole ask, and then I feel his hand on my bare back.

"I drank too much last night," I mumble.

He laughs, then I feel him get out of bed.

After prom, we ended up hitting two different parties before we came to the clubhouse. Cole didn't have a sip, but Deke got as drunk as Becky and I did.

"Here."

I roll over and look up to see him standing by the bed, dressed in a pair of his black boxers. And that's it. A cup of water in one hand and two Advil in the other. Sitting up, I take them both from his hands.

I watch him turn his back to me, running his hand through his hair. He's been on edge ever since his talk with the guys last night when we arrived at the prom. Even the parties didn't cheer him up like I thought they would. He stayed by my side the entire time and quiet. He even ignored Deke's drunk ass when he got loud.

Swallowing the pills, I lower the glass to my lap. "What's wrong, Cole?"

"Nothing," he answers. His back still toward me, he walks to the bathroom.

"You're just as bad of a liar as I am." I know him now. "Please?" I beg. "Just tell me. Whatever it is. I want to know."

He comes to a stop and sighs heavily. "The guys want me to pull back."

"Pull back from what?" I ask confused.

He turns back to face me. "You."

I narrow my eyes. "They want you to dump me?" I clarify.

He runs a hand through his hair. "They think that's the only way that you will be safe."

"From who?" I demand.

"Kellan. Your dad."

"I'm not afraid of them." I snort.

He comes over to the bed and sits down beside me. He runs his hand through my hair. Well, the best he can. It's tangled from his hands being in it last night. "I'm not afraid of them either, but I want to keep you safe."

"And you think breaking up with me is the only way?" I ask, crossing my arms over my chest.

"I think they have a point."

"What about my point?" I snap.

"Austin … don't."

"No. You don't, Cole." He opens his mouth, but I continue. "When am I gonna get a say? When am I gonna get to decide what happens in my life?"

"When it makes sense," he growls, his eyes narrowing on me.

I snort. "You cutting my arm didn't make sense. You stealing a car didn't make sense."

He stands. "I stole that car for insurance. It made perfect fucking sense."

"Insurance on what?" I demand, picking up the water and standing. The room sways, but I manage not to fall over like a hungover idiot.

"It doesn't matter anymore." He brushes it off.

"It does!" I shout, getting pissy. "Everything fucking matters now. There are so many lies and secrets that I can't seem to keep up with them. Deke was the only one on our side, and all of a sudden, he wants you to walk away from me?" I shake my head. "He has to have a reason. And you're gonna tell me why. I've put up with enough shit to know what I'm up against."

His eyes narrow on mine, and I arch a brow, not backing down. He looks away from me, and I know I've won when his jaw sharpens. "That car belongs to Bruce."

"What?" I gasp. "Why would you steal my father's car?" I demand.

His eyes come back to mine. "He keeps it at a warehouse that my father owns. I stole it to guarantee he wouldn't send you back."

"You're not making any sense, Cole," I growl.

He takes a step toward me. "That night at dinner while you and Celeste were washing dishes, he had told me that he was shipping you back to your mother's with twenty thousand dollars. I asked him to give you to me. That if he gave you to me, I would keep you out of trouble."

"I'm not some fucking toy," I snap.

"You were at the time," he growls back.

I fist my hands.

"He told me no. That's when I informed him I had something he wanted. I pulled out the key to his car and told him he could have it back after graduation if he let you stay here." He smiles at me. "And he accepted it."

"That's why he wouldn't send me back after I got suspended," I whisper. He nods. "You dick."

"You don't understand …"

"No. I guess I don't!" I snap, walking over to the railing that looks over and down to the first floor. I grab my black bag and unzip it.

"It's not like you didn't know my intentions," he says from behind me. "I never once pretended to care about you."

I flinch at his words and yank my shirt out of my bag. "That was obvious when you cut my arm."

"Austin …"

"Or when you had your best friend video tape me crawling all over you." I pull the shirt up over my head not even bothering with a bra. "Let's not forget the recording of you fucking me in the bathroom."

"Things have changed."

I spin around to face him. "What the hell has changed, Cole?" I demand. "Because it sounds to me like it's still the same." His eyes are narrowed on me. "We're still playing a game. Just a different level. And you're gonna do whatever your friends suggest."

"I don't take orders from them," he growls.

I laugh as I grab my shorts out of my bag. Pulling them up my legs, I say, "They tell you to walk away from me, and you actually want to do it. Sounds like they're giving you orders."

"It makes sense," he argues. "They made a point. Your dad is onto us."

"I don't care!" I shout, throwing my hands out to my side. "What is he gonna do? Give me a fake check? So what? It didn't matter if it was real, I still wasn't gonna take it. I don't need it." Between the three accounts that Jerrold and Jeff had, we've each made enough to live comfortably. Well, I have. I don't take much to survive. "You've been feeding me these lines of bullshit of how you want me to go to Texas with you, and all of a sudden, you want to get rid of me."

"I still want you to go to Texas with me." He runs his hand through his hair nervously. "We've got one final dare to do. I don't want you anywhere near me when we do it. It's too risky."

I push my right hip out and cross my arms over my chest. "You drew without me present? Because the last memory I have was of you all breaking up the group."

He shakes his head softly. "We didn't draw for this one. It was decided long before you ever came along."

I don't like the sound of that. "And what is it?'

"I can't tell you …"

"Cole!" I snap.

He stares at me. His eyes clouded and jaw tight.

"What is it?" I demand, taking a step toward him.

He lets out along breath. "To kill your dad."

I just stare up at him.

"He deserves to die for what he did to my mother. For taking advantage of her. For trying to kill me and successfully killing three of my best friends. But he also deserves to die because of what he did to you." I swallow. "For making you stay with your mother." He shakes his head. "You deserved better than that, Austin. Better than me. And I can't have you anywhere near me when I complete it. I don't want you getting involved. Or getting hurt. That would defeat the purpose." His eyes search mine. Still I say nothing. "This is just temporary. Give them a different kind of show."

I take a deep breath, turn around, grab my bag, and walk down the stairs. This time, he doesn't follow me, and I have a feeling he doesn't plan on it either.

It's officially over.

The game ending.

I hate that tears sting my eyes. That Cole Reynolds made me feel something for him that I never thought I'd feel. He took from me, but I also willingly gave him things I can never get back. One of those is my heart. He just shattered it.

And it has nothing to do with the dare he plans on doing to my father. He was right—that bastard deserves to die for what he's done.

CHAPTER FORTY-FOUR
COLE

It's been two weeks since she walked out of the clubhouse for the last time. I see her in the halls and in class, but she doesn't look my way. And I try not to look at her. It's harder than I thought it would be. She doesn't sit with me at lunch anymore, and I know she has completely shut me out. And I hate that things will never be the same with her.

I've lost her.

I knew it the moment I saw her talking to that guy from her birthday party. I can't remember his name, but I recognized him by her locker. He had been playing beer pong with her that night I walked into Bruce's game room. He had looked at her like he was dreaming of her naked. That look hasn't changed.

"I don't know how you do it, man," Deke says as he sits down at the table in the cafeteria across from me.

"Do what?" I ask, not bothering to look at him. Instead, I scan the door waiting for her to enter.

"Not talk to her."

I say nothing.

"I mean, I would go crazy if I knew Becky was dating someone else."

"What?" My head snaps to his.

"Myers," he says, looking down at his phone. "They're dating."

"No, they're not."

He looks up at me. "Yes, they are. He took her to a movie last night. And they're going to some play this weekend."

"How the fuck do you know that?"

"Becky told me."

I fist my hands on the table. "I'll break his neck …"

"You can't do that. You broke up with her."

"Because you guys convinced me that was my only option," I growl.

He nods. "And I still stand by that."

"Maybe I should call the whole thing off—"

"No!" he interrupts me. "Kellan sees you two are no longer together. We need him for the final dare. And if he thinks you two are together, he won't do it."

At this point, I don't care what happens to Bruce. "We don't need him."

"We don't, but he knows the plan. We can't have him turning on us."

I look up to see Austin walking into the cafeteria with that fucking idiot by her side. He laughs, and she smiles. I wanna knock him the fuck out.

"You said Becky was worth the group," I say to him. He nods once. "You said you would pick her over us."

"Yes. And I still would, but she is not in danger."

"I can protect Austin." I slam my fist down on the table.

He sighs. "You've only got two weeks left, Cole. And then she's all yours."

I want to believe what he says, but what if he's wrong? What if she never comes back to me? What if she realizes that I wasn't enough for her? She was always out of my league. I'm just the guy with anger issues and an obsession for blood. She is more than that. She deserves more than that. What will she do when she realizes that?

AUSTIN

Graduation is four days away, and I hate that it's so close. For as long as I can remember, all I thought about was freedom. Now, I dread it.

I've got no mother. I never did hear from her after she and Phillip left my father's that night. But I never expected to. Cole is good at one thing. And that's making things disappear.

I've got no Cole. I catch sight of him at school in the halls and classroom, and he looks angrier than ever. Mad at the world. Mad at me. Like I did something wrong.

I still have Becky, so that is a plus. But I don't see her very much. She spends all her time with Deke, and he is always with Cole, which leaves me alone.

Celeste is always crying. I found her last night in the kitchen sobbing over a bowl of ice cream. I ignored her because I don't care what is wrong with her. My father hasn't said anything else to me since he gave me the check almost a month ago. But I think he got the hint that I wasn't going to take his money when he found it ripped to pieces on the kitchen island.

I don't want anything from anyone. I just want out of this town. Out of this nightmare and out of everyone's life.

A fresh start. A new beginning.

I wanna go where no one knows me. Where I can be someone different.

I pull up to my father's house and put my car in park. It's late. The clock on my dash reads a little after ten. I went to another movie with Myers tonight. He wanted to come over afterward, but I shut that down. I'm not ready to jump in bed with anyone just yet. I hate to burst his bubble, but I'm not looking for what he is interested in. I'm using him to get to Cole. I hope all that anger I see means it's working.

The worst part is that once again, I haven't got to see Lilly. We talk on the phone, but that's it. And the conversations don't last long. I think another thing that sucks is that I know Cole is gonna be a part of my life forever. Because I'm not gonna push Lilly out of my life. I'm gonna talk to her. See her. Watch her grow up.

I get out of my car and make my way up the stairs to the front door. The wind blows my hair around, making it stick to my lip-gloss. Opening the door, I come to a stop when I hear Celeste crying down the hall. I sigh. *What the hell is wrong with her?*

"Please?" she begs. "Don't do this."

I head for the stairs but stop when I hear a male's voice.

"It's over," Kellan growls. "It's been over. But you refuse to believe it." Just then, Kellan walks into the foyer. He comes to a stop noticing me.

Celeste follows behind him. "You can't do this …" Her voice trails off when she sees me. "Austin," she says in surprise, reaching up to wipe her wet cheeks. "I didn't expect you to be home so soon."

I look at her. "I'm going to bed."

"Have you told her?" he demands.

She shakes her head quickly.

"Tell me what?" I ask. He narrows his eyes on me, and I roll mine. "I'm tired, and it's too late to play games with you, Kellan. What has she not told me?" Is she divorcing my father? Is that why he has been gone so much? Maybe he's got some ass on the side as well? I wouldn't be surprised if she's ten years younger than Celeste.

"All her secrets," he says simply.

"Kellan, don't—"

"I don't have time for this," I say, running a hand through my hair, interrupting her. I'm exhausted.

I take the first step on the stairs when he speaks. "Why do you think you're here?"

I pause. My eyes meet his. "Excuse me?"

He smiles, proud of himself. All of a sudden, I'm interested. "It's 'cause I wanted you here."

"What?" I ask confused.

"I was with Celeste when your mother called her and said that you were too much for her. That it would make Celeste look like a saint in this city to take in Bruce's troubled teen. But she didn't want you. She wanted Lilly."

I look at her, and her eyes are narrowed on him. "What?" I ask because that's all I can say.

"So you still haven't figured it out yet." He smirks. "What she did. What she is capable of?"

"Don't," she growls at him.

His smirk just grows. "She can keep a secret, babe," he tells her.

My brows rise. What could she have possibly done? It can't be worse than what the guys have done.

"Celeste here"—he looks at her over his shoulder—"killed Betty, Cole and Lilly's mother."

My heart starts to pound at his words.

"It was an accident," she says defensively.

"Don't lie," he growls.

"You what?" I ask wide-eyed. "Why would you …"

"At first, everyone suspected Liam or Bruce, but no one could figure out why they would kill her at nine months along. If they were going to do it, they would have done it the moment they found out she was pregnant. But when Celeste found out she was pregnant, she was pissed. She wanted a baby. She wanted to have Bruce's child." He looks me up and down with disgust. "But Bruce didn't want kids. So Celeste went over to her house and confronted her. Said that she wanted joint custody of Lilly, and when Betty said no, she pushed her down the stairs."

All this time, Cole thought it was an accident.

"I told you all of this in confidence," she barks at him.

He ignores her, staring right at me. "Then she called 911 and said she heard her fall down the stairs. As if she cared about her pathetic life." He shakes his head.

"No!" I say slowly. "Cole said she fell and died in surgery due to complications."

He laughs. "Cole only knows what Celeste told him."

She had gone to his school and pulled him out of class. Told Cole that his father had called her and said his mother passed …

She grabs his sleeve and starts to yank on it. He doesn't budge, and his brown eyes don't leave mine. "She waited thirty minutes before she called for help. Lilly was delivered in the ambulance on the way to the hospital. Betty was dead by the time they arrived at the hospital."

I look at her with wide eyes, hoping for her to give me some sign that he is lying. That he's being the Kellan I know and trying to mind fuck me. But she starts pounding her fists into his arm. "You son of a bitch!" she shouts at him.

He reaches out and grabs her arm. "And now you're gonna see history repeat itself." He pulls her across the grand foyer, and I stay planted where I'm at, trying to wrap my head around all of this. He starts dragging her up the stairs, and when she cries out, it pulls me out of my trance.

I run up after them and grab her free arm. Kellan spins around at the top of the stairs and pulls a gun out of the back of his jeans and points it at me. My stomach drops as I stare into the barrel. I throw my hands up in the air, my breathing picking up.

"Back up!" he orders.

I take one step at a time, slowly descending the stairs backward and swallow. *What the hell is he doing?* I feel my phone in my back pocket and go to grab it, planning to call 911.

"Keep them up!" he snaps, and I flinch at his tone.

"Okay, okay, okay," I say, and my voice shakes.

"See …" He goes on. "Celeste is pregnant." She starts to sob. "With my child." He rolls his eyes. "After getting Betty pregnant, Bruce had that situation fixed so it would never happen again. That rules him out. And I'm the only other guy you've fucked, right, baby?" he asks, pressing the gun to her temple.

She sobs but nods her head.

He goes on, satisfied with her answer. "And just like Bruce and Liam, I don't want a child. But unlike them, I plan on doing something about it."

"Please, Kellan," she begs. "I love you." She sobs.

He smiles. "You were nothing to me." Then he shoves her forward. And she falls down the long staircase like a ragdoll. I run over to her as she hits the marble floor and slide on my knees to her side. Her head is tilted to the side and blood pours from her nose and mouth. I feel for a pulse, but there's nothing.

"You killed her." I begin chest compressions. I've never done it before, but I've seen enough medical shows to have an idea.

He comes down the stairs slowly, looking at me strangely.

"You killed her," I cry out, stopping to pull my cell out to call the police.

"You are trying to save her? She killed the love of your life's mother. Who just happened to be your half-sister's mother as well."

"She's pregnant," I say frantically. My hands shake uncontrollably. "The baby didn't do anything to you."

"Oh, but it will. That's why it's got to go." He grabs my hair and yanks me back from her. My cell falls to the floor. I twist and turn in his grip as he drags me across the marble floor in the grand foyer.

He yanks me to my feet, and I'm gasping for a breath when he slams my back into the wall. He wraps his hands around my throat and leans in. "You've been playing a game all along, Austin, but it's been my game. My rules. And now it's over." He shoves me away, and I slide on my knees, hitting the floor once again. When I turn around, he has a knife in his hand. He twirls it around. "Cole has always been fascinated with blood. And I gotta say, I didn't understand it until I watched him smear it with his hands all over your skin."

What? Smear it over my skin? The night in the cemetery. "How did you …?" I trail off at his laugh.

"Celeste called me when you arrived. I had Shane and Bennett take me back to my car. By the time I got back up there, Cole and Deke were already playing with you. I stood back and watched you all night. I knew you were perfect for me the moment I saw you light Jeff on fire."

Someone had been watching me after all.

He takes a step toward me, and I crawl back until I hit the side of the staircase. Celeste's body lying only feet from me. Her eyes still open as more blood covers the floor. "Then when you stole the car with Cole, I tipped the cops off. I have them all in my pocket, after all. My uncle is the chief. I wanted you to get caught."

"Why?" I demand.

"Because if you were locked up, he couldn't have you."

"But you hated me … you tried to kick me out of the group …"

"All part of my plan. Every time I pushed you away, Cole pulled you closer." He smiles. "And Celeste played along so well. See, I told her the final dare. Killing Bruce. She wanted the guys and me to kill him, and then she wanted me to kill you and Cole and run off into the sunset with her and Lilly." He snorts. "All the lies she told Cole." He chuckles. "You. It was so fucking perfect."

"You sick bastard," I spit out.

He chuckles. "He and I are the same, Austin. We both used you however we wanted."

I shake my head. "Cole would never hurt me. Not now." Lie. He's hurting me right now. He left me. All because he thought my father was a threat. But he wasn't. Kellan was the one all along.

"You're right," he agrees with a sigh. "He wouldn't harm a hair on your head. But I'm gonna paint these walls with your blood." He gives me a sinister smile. "After all, his favorite color is red." He lunges for me, and I crawl away before jumping to my feet. But he's faster. "Little bitch!" he snaps, reaching out and grabbing my ankle, causing me to trip. I cry out when my face hits the marble floor. Pain explodes behind my eyes. I'm flipped over onto my back, and he straddles me. He drops his knife, and it hits the floor with a clank and then his hands go around my neck. He cuts off my air.

"I wanted Bruce to take care of you," he growls. "Just like I wanted him to kill Cole when I drove his car to fuck his wife." He laughs at that. "But I'll just have to do it myself. In case you just recorded me killing Celeste."

I try to push him off, tear his hands free, but he's too strong. I try arching my neck to get in a breath, but it gives him better access to tighten his grip.

"My only regret is that I won't get to fuck you." He sighs as I try to buck him off. "Because I listened to the recording of Cole fucking you inside that bathroom, Austin." I try to claw at his face, but his reach is longer. Making my hands only touch air. "I got off on it so many times, imagining it was you and me."

Dots form in my vision as my body grows heavy. My arms fall to my side, and something cold touches my fingers.

It's the knife.

I wrap my hand around the rough handle and shove it into his side. He immediately releases my throat as he screams out.

I suck in a ragged breath, my throat burning. He falls back onto his ass as he looks at the knife sticking out of his side in horror. I begin to cough.

"FUCK!" he screams, throwing his head back.

I get up to my feet and run to the kitchen where there is a landline. I pick it up with bloody, shaking hands and dial Cole's number.

He answers on the first ring. "Hello?"

"Cole!" I choke out his name. My voice now rough and entire body is shaking uncontrollably.

"Austin! What's wrong?" he demands. I hear Deke's voice in the background.

I burst into tears and begin to tell him Kellan is here. Any other girl would call the cops. But since I know Kellan has them in his pocket, they're out.

"Slow down, sweetheart. I can't understand a thing you're saying."

"He's here!" I scream out. "Kellan's at my father's house. He killed Celeste!"

"I'm on my way …" The line goes dead.

I turn to see Kellan leaning up against the countertop, the cord from the wall in his hand. The knife still in his side.

I should have yanked it out.

Made him bleed out faster. Even now, his face is pale, and he's hunched over. Blood covers his clothes and there's a puddle where he stands.

He gives me a bloody smile. "He's not gonna make it." Lifting the gun, he fires.

EPILOGUE

COLE

Twelve years later . . .

It's the usual cloudy day in Collins, Oregon. Any second, the clouds are going to open and pour down rain. I miss it here. This town had a lot of demons, but it was quiet at times. You never get that in Dallas. There are always people no matter where you go. And the traffic—it drives me mad sometimes.

I kneel and place the bouquet of yellow flowers on the grave. They're the only ones at this cemetery. Not much has changed. The dead are still forgotten at the top of this hill. I come back to visit it twice a year. Every Christmas and on her birthday. I wish I could come more, but work isn't slow by any means. Running a law firm isn't an easy feat. Even if you have Deke Biggs as your partner. But I make sure to come and tell her that I miss her. How much I loved her. How I wish she could see Lilly grow up. She's gonna turn eighteen this year, and I just can't wrap my head around it.

I turn around, giving the grave my back and look down the hill at the house that was torn down years ago. The Lowes estate was demolished after Bruce was arrested on three counts of manslaughter. We were supposed to kill him, but like I once told Austin—plans change. And that's exactly what happened when Deke and I showed up to the house after she called me that night.

My phone rings, and I look down to see it's the Lowes residence. I answer, expecting it to be Celeste. "Hello?"

"Cole!" Austin strangled voice calls out my name.

I jump up from the couch in the clubhouse. "Austin! What's wrong?" I demand.

"What's going on?" Deke asks also standing.

She starts to cry uncontrollably, and I can't understand a thing she is trying to say. "Slow down, sweetheart. I can't understand a thing you're saying."

"He's here!" she screams. "Kellan's at my father's house. He killed Celeste!"

"I'm on my way ..." The line goes dead.

Deke and I pull into the drive in record time and jump out of my car. He's already called 911 on our way. I burst through the front door and don't even bother giving Celeste's lifeless body a second of attention, knowing she's already dead.

"Austin?" I yell out, pulling my gun out of the back of my jeans. "Austin?" I shout, running down the hallway.

I follow a blood trail into the kitchen and come to a stop when I see Kellan leaning against the countertop. He chuckles when he sees me, but it causes him to cough. A knife sticks out of his side.

My eyes look at the wall ahead of me, and it's also covered in blood. Austin's blood. She lies on the floor on her side. I run to her.

"Austin?" I choke on her name, brushing her hair from her face. The smell of the blood so strong it causes bile to rise, but I swallow it down.

"What the fuck?" Deke gasps, entering the kitchen.

"Take him!" I call out.

"She needs help," he says, looking down at her body with narrowed eyes. There's so much blood I don't know where it's coming from.

"Take him!" I bark. "Help is on their way." I turn my attention back to her, and I hear Kellan grunt as Deke drags him out to the car. Taking him where the cops will never find him. He's not dead yet, but once I'm done with him, he'll wish he was.

Austin's eyes are closed, and her body lies limp. "Please, baby," I beg. "I can't lose you." My throat tightens. I feel her neck for a pulse, and I feel nothing.

My heart stops, and I drag her away from the wall to the center of the kitchen floor. I begin CPR.

The guys and I called off the last dare. Bruce didn't need to die. We had enough evidence on the laptop that Austin had Shane steal to prove Bruce had three people killed. I never did find out why he tried to kill me. Deke thinks he wanted me dead so Celeste could have Lilly. I always knew she wished Lilly was hers, but that didn't make sense to me. Bruce never wanted kids. Why would he want Lilly then? I reminded Deke that some people are just evil. They do things just because of the simple fact that they can. I should know. Look at what I put Austin through.

Bruce was arrested three days after I found Austin dead on his kitchen floor, and his conviction gives him no chance of parole. He'll spend the rest of his miserable life in a cell wondering how in the hell he got caught. Trying to figure out how four teenage boys and his teenage daughter managed to fuck him. It wasn't the original plan, but it was good enough for me.

Kellan, on the other hand, begged for his life. I told him outside the clubhouse that night that I found Austin's cell in his car that I was going to kill him with my bare hands, and I did just that. I hated that he was already almost dead when we found him, but a part of me, a very big part, was proud of what Austin did. She fought. She did what I knew she was capable of.

And as for her mom and stepdad? Austin never came out and asked me, but I didn't have to tell her—I took care of them. Deke helped me. We made it quick for her mother, but her stepdad suffered. He also cried like the little bitch he was. Their bodies will never be found. Or missed.

After I found Austin lying there in her own blood with no pulse, I just wanted to move on. Put all the dares and deaths behind me. After I killed Kellan, I no longer had a need for blood. To kill. Once again, she had changed me.

I twirl the wedding ring on my left hand as I turn back to face the grave. I look over it with a sad smile and let out a long breath. "I'll be back to visit soon. I love and miss you," I say and then give it my back.

I walk down the hill, passing the spot where it all began. Where I found the gorgeous brunette spying on my friends and me, and I smile. That was so long ago, but I remember it like it was yesterday.

I come to the bottom of the hill and see the black lifted Chevy come into view. The passenger door opens, and a little boy jumps out—my five-year-old son. "Daddy!" he says, running to me.

I open my arms and pick him up. "Hey, buddy. Ready to go home?" I ask him.

He nods. "Mommy is hungry."

I laugh at that. "Mommy is always hungry." Setting him back down on his feet, I look up to see my wife slowly getting out of the truck.

"We should have driven my car," she whines, rubbing her growing belly and aching back. "You can't expect me to get up and out of this monster at six months pregnant. She's really active today."

I chuckle, stepping to her. My hand sliding into her hair. "Have I told you that you look gorgeous today and that I love you?"

"I'm a whale," she whines.

I kiss her red painted lips. "You're a shark, sweetheart."

She pulls away, and her green eyes search mine. "Are you okay?" she asks, and her eyes go to the top of the hill.

I nod. "I said what I needed to."

"I wish Lilly could have made it," she says, and tears start to form in her eyes. I still find her beautiful when she cries. And she does that a lot with this pregnancy.

"Me too. Maybe next time."

She nods and looks over at our son who is digging in the dirt. "Come on, Eli," she calls out, and he dusts off his hands and runs over to her.

I turn and look back over the hill where my mother was buried long ago. I used to ask myself why I survived that car crash. And then one night, I found a girl in a cemetery and all my questions were answered.

I've never been a religious man, but I prayed that night I found her on the kitchen floor, and for some reason, God answered them and gave her back to me. Gave me another chance at living. Because without her, I wouldn't have survived.

It's been two months since she was released from the hospital, and we've officially moved into the place we call home in Texas. She sits with Becky at our kitchen table. Her morning hair a mess and no makeup on her face. I've never seen her more beautiful.

Becky looks up at me, and her words trail off.

Austin looks over her shoulder at me, and a smile spreads across her face when her eyes meet mine. But it drops when I don't return it. "You're up to something."

"Aren't I always?" I ask with a straight face.

Her eyes narrow on me. "Cole …"

When I kneel on one knee, her words cut off and those dark green eyes widen in surprise. "Cole," she whispers my name.

"Austin Anne Lowes," I begin and tears well up in her eyes. I open the box, and she gasps when she sees the princess cut red ruby sitting on a platinum band. I take it from the black velvet box and hold it up to her. There's nothing for me to say. The ring says it all.

She takes it from my hand and reads the three words I had engraved on the inside of the band—I dare you.

I used to think that I was going to go to hell. And that thought hasn't changed. One day, I'll have to pay for my sins, but as I watch my pregnant wife hug and kiss our son, I realize I'm okay with that. Because my life right now is heaven on earth.

THE END

ACKNOWLEDGMENTS

First I would like to thank my assistant, Kelly Tucker. The most organized person I have ever met. I drive her nuts, but she loves it and I love her too. She's the best assistant a girl could have and without her I would go insane.

I would like to thank Jenny Sims, my wonderful editor. I've been working with her for four years now and she's awesome!

To my cover designer, Tracie Douglas with Dark Water Covers. Thank you for making me another gorgeous cover!

A big thank you to my formatter and friend, CP Smith. Thanks so much for your help!

I want to thank Give Me Books and all the blogs that shared and reviewed I Dare You. You guys are amazing.

I want to thank my lovely betas, Andrea Wilkovich, Rita Rees, Mari Reads, Jackie Ashmead, Amy Cortez Rangel and Stephanie Anderson-Cochran. Thank you so much for taking the time to read I Dare You. And for all of our suggestions. I truly appreciate it.

I want to thank The Sinful Side for pimping and I love these bitches! This lovely group of ladies are awesome at pimping and making me laugh. It's amazing how you can become so close with someone when they live halfway around the world. These girls are my sisters, and I love them very much.

And last but not least, my readers. Thank you for taking a chance and wanting to read my books. I hope that you all love them as much as I do.

OTHER TITLES BY SHANTEL TESSIER